R. E. (Robert Edward) Francillon

Romances of the Law

R. E. (Robert Edward) Francillon

Romances of the Law

ISBN/EAN: 9783337049416

Printed in Europe, USA, Canada, Australia, Japan

Cover: Foto ©Andreas Hilbeck / pixelio.de

More available books at **www.hansebooks.com**

ROMANCES OF THE LAW

BY

R. E. FRANCILLON

AUTHOR OF "QUEEN COPHETUA," "OLYMPIA," ETC.

WITH A FRONTISPIECE BY D. H. FRISTON

PHILADELPHIA
GEBBIE & CO., Publishers
1889

CONTENTS.

ROMANCES OF THE LAW.

TOUCH-AND-GO WITH A
GREAT ESTATE.

I.

WHEN a lawyer consents to tell the story of the most remarkable case in which he was ever engaged, he does so on the express understanding that the confidences of his clients shall be observed, however long ago they were made. After full consideration I can see no possible objection to telling the story of the most singular piece of business that I ever knew in the course of a very long experience indeed. But my chief reason for finding no objection is that I can do so without naming real names. That being fully understood, I shall be able to keep to the literal truth without having recourse to fictitious incidents in order to lead my readers away from the real quarter. For nothing but the real names, both of places and people, could possibly tell more than I am amply justified in telling. Perhaps, after all, I am a little over-scrupulous; but I don't think that will be regarded as a fault on the wrong side. No doubt some of my readers will gather that the period of my professional adventure was previous to the passing of the

B

Municipal Reform Act of 1835, a date far back enough, at any rate, to give me the right to amuse myself, if not my readers, with a—let me say elderly—solicitor's first contribution to literature. Apart from real names, the facts of the case are true, word for word.

My father and I were in partnership as solicitors in the good old town of Burgham. which you may place in any county you please. I was born there, and so was my father before me, and my grandfather before him; and the name of Key (to take my first *alias*) was as well known as the spire of St. Michael's. Our office, in the very shadow of the spire, consisted of an outer office for the clerks, of one private room for my father, of another for myself, and of a third, in which an articled clerk sat among the office-lumber, and amused himself as well as want of opportunity allowed. His name, I remember, was what I will call—more for the sake of appropriateness than of anything else—Richard Musty; and a queer young fellow he was—the queerest, I used to think, within six thousand miles of Burgham. He was a country parson's son, and of about my own age; so that I was ready and even eager when he first came to us to make a friend and companion of him out of office-hours, so far as my greater professional dignity allowed; but it was impossible. What good or return he expected to get out of the premium he had paid us was a mystery; he had found the money hard to raise, and he might just as well have thrown it into the river. He was steady, too steady by half; he was older then, young as he was, than I am now. But he was as fit to be a lawyer as I am to be a poet; and I can't say more. Sometimes I used to think him a born hopeless fool, and I don't believe he ever came to know the difference between a *cestui que trust* and a *surrebutter*. He had never left his father and mother till he went to Cambridge with a view of taking orders; but family misfortunes had obliged him to leave college without a degree, and so—I believe to his intense misery—he had made up his mind to be a failure in another direction. He was always shabby, never too clean, never did anything wrong—morally, never anything right—intellectually, and seemed to have no friends. What he did with his time, in or out of the office, neither myself nor my father was able for weeks to discover.

" What, in the name of goodness, are you doing there, Musty ? " I remember saying to him at last, when, impelled by a fit of curiosity, I went one day suddenly into his room, and caught him with a camel's hair paint-brush instead of a pen in his hand, with which he seemed to be busily engaged in washing a skin of parchment with pure water. " Have you forgotten that that lease is to be ready in an hour ? " Not that I expected to get the lease from him in a month, but I wanted an excuse for my sudden intrusion.

He turned as red as fire.

" Nothing, nothing at all, Mr. Key," said he.

" ' Nothing ' is the worst thing you can do here," said I sternly. I was idle enough myself in those days, but it was in a very different sort of way. " I *must* know what you are doing with that old deed."

" It—it isn't a deed, indeed," stammered he, as if his occupation were criminal instead of merely imbecile. " Look here, Mr. Key. I found it up there on that shelf, and I don't imagine it can be of any use to *you*," he went on with a curious emphasis on the " you : " if the fellow hadn't been so simply scared, and so incapable of such a thing at any time, I should have suspected a sneer. I looked at it, and I was yet more puzzled, for it was not a deed : it was not a legal document at all.

" It is a mediæval Latin manuscript," said he. " But it is of no value. So far as I have read, it appears to be a treatise by some monkish writer concerning the Praises of St. Willibrord, who was, I believe, a saint and bishop of the Benedictines. What horrible hideous jargon those miserable monks used to call Latin, to be sure! Just listen here. *Nictelaminibus ita depauperatus —* "

It might have been Hebrew to me; for, though I had been pretty good in Latin at the Grammar School, the yellow document in question was written in such a close, cramped, ancient, and illegible hand, and was so full of abbreviations and contractions to boot, that Musty's skill in deciphering a single word a little surprised me.

" Have you got any more of these? " asked he.

" If there's one," said I, "there may be fifty. I suppose they came here with old Parson Evans's papers, when he died—the old rector of St. Michael's, you know —and, being parchment, I suppose they looked legal. Yes, Musty, I think you had better devote your time to reading them and cleaning them all. It seems to me that's about all you're likely to be fit for here. Never mind the lease," I said, with what I took for fine sarcasm. " Get on with St. Willibrord, as you seem so fond of that style."

" Style! " cried he, forgetting all his shyness, and bringing his fist down upon the table with an angry bang. " Call *that* style! And to think that those inestimable lost books of Livy may be hidden from the light by trash and rubbish about some wretched St. Willibrord—that they may even be here, under my very hand! Ah, if such a triumph as that were for me—if, like Cardinal Mai, who gave Cicero's ' Republic ' to the world—But I believe such things are not much in *your* line, Mr. Key."

So that was Dick Musty's craze. Well, if he liked to waste his time in grubbing under old Latin sermons in the hope of discovering the lost books of Livy, the craze did nobody any harm but himself, but decidedly he was not fit for a lawyer. I told my father the story, thinking it a good joke; but the old gentleman, though the most good-natured man alive, took the matter very differently from what I had expected. He started up and went straight into Dick's room.

"Mr. Thomas"—he always called me Mr. Thomas in the office—"Mr. Thomas tells me, young gentleman," he broke out, "that you are reading Latin sermons instead of studying your profession—you, a poor man, who will have to earn your own daily bread with brains of which you haven't an ounce to spare. You're not wasting *my* time; but you gave me a premium to see that you didn't waste your own. And as duty's duty, young gentleman, I'll see that you don't. Old Latin sermons—they're no use here. Give that rubbish to me. I'll lock it up in my own desk, and if I find out that it's nothing but what you say, I'll get rid of it for waste parchment; I won't have such stuff and rubbish lumbering about here. Here, give it to me, without another word. It sha'n't be *my* fault if you choose to waste your time."

Dick Musty sighed—he even turned pale. But there was no arguing with my father. The old sermon—for such it was, and nothing more—was duly locked up in my father's desk, and there that matter ended. And I think it proves pretty clearly that Richard Musty was a very odd sort of an articled clerk indeed. However, it seemed to show that his brain, if addled and muddled by useless studies, was not quite so hopelessly absent as I had hitherto believed.

I had not been back at my work half an hour, when my father came into my room looking pale and unwell.

"Tom," he said, "I had a bad headache when I got up this morning; and instead of getting better, it's been getting worse and worse all day. I'm afraid it made me over-irritable just now when you told me about that young nincompoop of a Musty, and I don't feel like myself at all. I shall go home and lie down, for my head's just splitting. There'll be nothing to-day you can't attend to; I shall be all right to-morrow, I dare say."

Now my father was a man who had never known what it means to be ill. Still, though a mere headache in his case was a ground for a little anxiety, I was not in the least prepared, when, at the usual hour, I left the office and went home to dinner, to find that my mother had sent for the doctor, who had made my father go to bed at once; and who next morning declared him to be in the first stage of typhoid fever, of which there were several cases about just then. Burgham was not drained so well then as it is now.

I felt the good of having one's head a few years older than one's shoulders when I went to business that morning, and, full of anxiety for my father, sat down at his table and in his chair, with the whole of the office upon my own hands, and with an unusual amount of heavy and responsible work to be done. My father had been so much in the habit of attending to everything himself, down to the minutest details, while I, on the contrary, had always taken everything so easily, not to say idly, that I was almost painfully nervous about that first day, which was nearly as new a feeling to me as a headache to my father. I hoped that nobody would call. And therefore—need I say it?—I had scarcely opened the last of the office letters before somebody did call—a Mr. Horace Jones. And the name meant nothing to me; for though Miss Jones of the Brambles was a good client of ours, still she had no relation named Horace, and the surname was, in reality, an exceedingly common one.

Enter Mr. Horace Jones, however; and I did not like the looks of him. Not being a professional story-teller, whatever may be said of us lawyers to the contrary and notwithstanding, I will not try to describe him otherwise than by saying that I knew him to be a cad and a blackguard as soon as I set eyes on him. There are men—I have known many of them—who have the art of drinking, gambling, and worse, without turning a hair of their outward respectability; but Mr. Horace Jones was not among them. Drunkard, gambler, and worse was written from the crown of his hat to the ends of his toes. And in such a case a man finds it hard to be taken for a gentleman.

"Who are you, sir?" he asked roughly. "I called to see *old* Mr. Key."

"If you mean my father," said I, in as dignified a manner as I could, "I am sorry to say he is very unwell, and may not be able to leave his house for some time. If it is anything to which I can attend, I am his partner, and—"

"O! Well, you'll do, I dare say. For that matter, you *must* do; for mine's business that won't keep, I can tell you. Got a cocktail handy? No? Precious lot you English lawyers. So the old un's kicked the bucket at last, I hear. Wish to—Hades I'd known it before. Well, never too late for that sort of thing. So the sooner you get things fixed, young man, the better for you."

"It seems to me, Mr. Jones, that you have made some mistake," said I.

"Mistake! Do you mean to say you don't know *me?* Well, I suppose when a man has been away from his native home twenty-seven years about the world, he does get changed, more or less, and can't, when I come to think of it, expect to be recognized all at once by them that weren't born when he went away. But—mistake! Don't *you* be mistaken, young man. So old Jones of the Brambles has gone under the daisies—that's what I mean."

"Mr. Jones of the Brambles? Why, he died three years ago. You can't possibly have any claim on the estate now."

"*Three* years ago? Three times three times three—twenty-seven years ago. More fool I not to have found it out ages ago! I broke the old cove's heart, I believe. Rum things some hearts must be, to be sure. And as for having no claim—Oho! Old Jones of the Brambles, that died twenty-seven years back, was my father; and I'm young Jones, old Jones's son. Twig now?"

Was the fellow mad or drunk? thought I. Certainly he was right in saying that a Mr. Jones of the Brambles had died twenty-seven years ago. But that was long ago, according to something more important than years. That was when the Brambles, near Burgham, was nothing better than an old farmhouse on the edge of a large rough piece of moorland which was collectively known by that appropriate name. But Mr. Jones the first's son was dead too, as I had said, three years ago; and Mr. Jones the second had died when the Brambles—

But, as this is a legal story, I shall make no apology for entering into the history of a title, not only because it is absolutely essential, but because it is exceptionally simple and easy to follow. Indeed, the whole point of the story depends upon its absolute freedom from complications and questions of every sort and kind.

The Brambles, then, otherwise called Easton Field, was a farm just beyond the last dwelling-house in the High Street of Burgham; that is to say, the continuity of the High Street ends abruptly at its eastern end, and the open country begins at once, without any shading off of villas and cottages as is usual even in smaller towns, and as is the case at the street's western extremity. I am now, of course, speaking of the Brambles—as Easton Field was always commonly called—as it was when I was quite a child, and when its clumps and patches of heather and thorny bottoms were the playground of the town. Indeed, it must have been a sort of town playground in quite ancient times, for there was a broad flat meadow still called the "Butts" from days long before those of the rifle volunteers. This rather nondescript tract had belonged to Welwood Priory, and, that being dissolved, had gone to one of the colleges—I forget which—in the University of Oxford. It was valueless as land; for building space was then practically worthless at a place like Burgham, though the case would be very different now; and to turn it to agricultural purposes would have required an exceedingly large capital, with very little prospect of a speedy return. I should say its net annual value to the Oxford college might have been as much as five or six pounds a year.

But there happened to be in Burgham, about fifty years before the time of my story, an uncommonly sharp fellow, a land surveyor, of the name of John Jones. I think he must have been the cleverest fellow that was ever born in Burgham. Anyhow, he bought the whole interest of the Oxford college in the land for a mere song, let a part of it to a neighbouring farmer for some trifle or other, and left his son, Wilfred Jones, a—coal-field.

Wilfred Jones was not sharp in the sense that his father had been. He was a splendid fellow; not grasping, not pushing, but a man of tremendous perseverance and energy. He was the king of Burgham when I was young, and he deserved to be. Instead of the Brambles being a fringe of Burgham, Burgham became a suburb of the Brambles. I must describe no farther, lest I should point too distinctly to real names. The Brambles became a great estate in next to no time; and it brought the railway to Burgham, and the railway helped it on at its own speed. The old farmhouse in the corner grew into a park and mansion. I can remember, better than yesterday, how the whole town was thrown into a kind of collapse when Wilfred Jones of the Brambles—he would stick to the old local name—died at the early age of seven-and-forty—no more. Every man, woman, and child in the place had lost a private as well as a public friend. My father drew his will, which left everything he had (except certain large legacies which the estate could well afford) to his only child, Miss Margaret Jones, now—at the time of which I write—a charmingly pretty and amiable girl of three-and-twenty. She was the greatest heiress in the county, bar none; and the county people thought as much of her as if she had come in with King William the Conqueror, instead of, as my father used to say, with old King Coal.

Somehow, I never now seem to see girls as pretty or as nice as Miss Margaret. Every man in the town was —at a humble and respectful distance—in love with her; and, what is really the strangest thing in my whole story, so were all the women too. She was wonderfully like her father (her mother had died at her birth) in a feminine way. There was a sort of public anxiety as to if, when, and whom, she would marry—not that there was so much question about the " if " as the " whom." It would be a misfortune for all Burgham if, as clever and charming girls who are their own mistresses have a particular knack of doing, she married wrong. Well, for a wonder she had taken it into her head and her heart to choose as wisely as her own mother had chosen before her. Mr. Evelyn Viner was only a younger son of one of the best—but not the best-off—families in the county; and no doubt Miss Margaret's hand would be an excellent thing for him. But nobody, somehow, ever looked upon him in the light of a fortune-hunter; and you may be sure there were plenty of people who would be ready enough to do it if he were. In fact, he was the most popular man in the county, and the most deservedly so;

and that he and she should make a match of it was as
natural as that he should represent Burgham in Parlia-
ment on the first opportunity.

I should have mentioned—the matter is of some
importance for critical readers, though the general reader
may skip over this paragraph without any risk to the
thread of the story—that until the time of Mr. Wilfred
Jones, nobody had lived on the Brambles but two or
three cottagers, who were tenants from year to year at a
rent of about forty shillings per annum, and that it was
rated and so forth to the parish of St. Botolph's in Turn
—the very singular name of a parish which, like some
others in England, had no parish church, the people
mostly making use of that at the village of Welwood,
where the priory had been in old times. Miss Margaret
herself used to go to Welwood church, like her father
before her. Don't let anybody, however, who has no
special local knowledge try to make use of "St. Botolph's
in Turn" for a key; for I have taken infinite pains to
manufacture a name which will suit my purpose just as
well as the real one, while it does not resemble it in a
single leading letter. What it meant, nobody in Burgham
knew—or, for that matter, cared to know.

So, striking out all my digressions, Miss Margaret's
title to that great mine of wealth called the Brambles
was this, and it was as clear as day. She took it both
under her father's will and as his heir-at-law; her father
had taken it from *his* father as heir-at-law; he, John
Jones, had bought it from an Oxford college that had
held it for more than two hundred years.

What could my visitor mean—unless drunk, or mad,
or both in one?

"No," said I, "I do *not* twig now."

"And that's Fame!" said he. "Well. I'm not going
to be long-winded; for I'm dry. I've come to you
because, in the first place, your firm's got a good name

about here, and a good name's the thing I want more than anything; and because, as our family lawyers, you'll see things without bother. Here you are, then. I'm the son of old John Jones—"

"I see. You died three years ago, and now, you've come to life again with a new Christian name; and I can't say you're much the better for the company you've been keeping in the other world. Well?"

"You mean my travels have made me rough and ready, eh? So they have—ready for everything I can get, too. Pocket as dry as my throat; and no wonder. But, hang it, young man, I'm not used to being told so; and I wouldn't risk losing a good job, if I were you. I'm Horace Jones, eldest son of old John Jones of the Brambles. Well, you see, the old boy and I didn't hit it off together very well. He was a slow old coach, and I wasn't a slow young un. He was a skinflint, too; and, you wouldn't believe it, but the unnatural old villain put me to such shifts that I actually had to take the king's shilling; and I took means to let him think I'd died of yellow fever in Barbadoes, just to prevent him making a new will and cutting me off with another. I've knocked about since then, here and there; but I've been a confounded unlucky sort of a devil, I must say. I'm a married man, too, and a family man; four of 'em, Mr. Key, with a mother I wouldn't live another hour with if it wasn't that she keeps things going while I'm waiting for things to mend. Now the question is, what do I come in for, eh? I'm thinking of taking a public down Deptford way. Mrs. Jones was in that line when I first knew her; and I want capital, and the more the merrier. What's the figure? Three figures? Maybe four?

What was I to say? If this fellow were telling the truth, it was not a capital of three figures or four figures, but an estate bringing in an annual income of five figures, to which he, a broken-down shameless drunkard, with a barmaid for a wife, was heir-at-law. For John Jones, having only his son Wilfred to follow him, and little but the then undeveloped Brambles to leave, had *not* made a will. Yes, and if there were a grain of truth at the bottom of the man's story, if he were not an impostor from first to last, the great estate would be no longer Miss Margaret's; it would no more be a blessing to the country; it would no longer give a fit career to a man like Evelyn Viner; it would no longer be a fountain of charity and honour; it would no longer be—— But why say what it would *not* be? It would, it must, in this man's hands, become a curse and a ruin.

The worst of it was, that the story was only too likely to be true. If Wilfred Jones had ever had an elder brother—of whom it was likely enough that I myself should never have heard—it would be notorious in an elder generation, and nobody would dare to invent the existence of a non-existent man. Again, this Mr. Horace Jones had evidently no idea of the extent and value of the property to which he was laying claim. He would not, unless preternaturally cunning, talk so simply about it, as if at most it could only be a few thousand pounds. I did what I still think was the most prudent thing. I sent out for a bottle of whisky, and told him to wait until I returned from some business that had to be attended to immediately. Ill as my father was, this was a matter that I must consult him upon, and that instantly. I did not venture to mention the matter even to our old managing clerk, for fear lest even our office-walls should have ears, or a little bird should be sitting on the window-sill to carry the matter.

"Good God!" exclaimed my father, starting up in bed; "you don't tell me that Horace Jones is alive, after all? Yes, Tom, there *was* such a man. And he *did* break his father's heart when he enlisted—though going for a soldier was the most decent thing I ever heard of his doing.

And he *did* die—at least, so the poor old gentleman believed; and old John Jones did *not* make a will. And —and, Tom—if this is the man, the Brambles is his, as sure as it's law that when a man dies intestate his real property goes to his heir. Poor girl! But it can't, Tom; I say it *sha'n't* be true! I'll get up this minute—I'll—"

"I must go back to him. What shall I say to him?"

"Yes, Tom; I *am* too ill. I don't know. He must prove his identity up to the hilt, that's clear. If he does, perhaps he'll accept a compromise. But then he says he's married. Tom, this case must be fought, tooth and nail. I hate tricks; but, hang it, Tom, there's nothing I wouldn't do to keep the Brambles for little Peggy, Mrs. Viuer that is to be. Well, you go to him, say nothing about the value of the estate, and tell him to prove every word he has said to you. And get his address, and put the detectives on him up in town. Don't let him think you're nervous, Tom. Be cool, and don't admit that two and two are four."

When I went back to the office, I found half the whisky gone; but the man still there. I hope I acted coolly; at any rate, I committed myself to nothing, gave no information, and told Mr. Horace Jones that I should require clear proof of his identity before taking any further steps in the matter. I lent him a guinea, for the sake of keeping my eye on him till I saw him off by the next train.

The story worried my father dreadfully; though I don't know how I, in my own ignorance of all the circumstances, could possibly have kept it from him. As for myself, I instantly wrote up to a friend of my own in London—a young solicitor with nothing to do, but as sharp as a needle, and with a passion for investigation— to go to work in a private capacity, and to let me know all he could find out about the man who called himself

Horace Jones, and who said he lived at—let me say, 36, Belvidere Gardens, Clerkenwell. I had not heard again from the man himself. But I had best give my friend's report of him in his own words.

" Dear Key,—Belvidere Gardens is a back slum, a sort of mews. No. 36 is a small barber's. I have been shaved there; and Mr. Potts is not only very small but a clumsy barber. I should say a good deal of drink went on at 36 Belvidere Gardens. Mr. Horace Jones lodges there. I had some conversation with him. He says he is a gentleman kept out of an immense property by an ungrateful niece and some swindling pettifoggers; but he is in right hands, and means to have the law of them all. I "lent" him half-a-crown, for new acquaintance's sake. I judge him to be a man who is always half drunk, and could never, under any circumstance, be otherwise. His wife—if he be more than half married as well as less than half sober—is a lady of colour, who, I believe, has followed a regiment in her time. I believe that sometimes she beats him, and sometimes he her. She has been the bread-winner hitherto in some capacity—in what I can't precisely learn—he doing little but lounge about at bars. But for the last week or so they have been flush of money, and done nothing but quarrel. They have paid Mr. Potts some arrears of board and lodging. The less I say of their four children—two boys and two girls—the better. It is bad to think of them. They are Horace John, aged twelve; Margaret, eleven; Amelia, nine; and Adolphus, seven. Your friend goes by the name, in the Gardens, of ' Gentleman' Jones; I am absolutely unable to imagine why. I hope you are satisfied. I am so much so that I don't want to go to Belvidere Gardens again. The man is *not* mad, unless you spell ' Mad' with a B. But he is, I am convinced, as incapable of anything bad on a *large* scale as he is of anything good on any scale at all.   He is the very type of a half-crown rogue."

The time went by, until at last I began to flatter myself that nothing more was going to happen, and that Mr. Horace Jones had been nothing but a scarecrow, whose only object had been to bewilder a lawyer out of a guinea.   But after a calm comes—what we know.

It was Mr. Evelyn Viner himself who came one day into my office with a letter.

"What, in the name of impudence, is the meaning of this?" asked he.

The storm had broken at last.   It was a letter from a highly respectable legal firm in London to Miss Jones herself, asking her to name an attorney who would receive for her notice of a declaration in ejectment, according to the old procedure.   What did it mean? Simply that Mr. Horace Jones had persuaded a respectable firm of his identity and of his right—no doubt backed by counsel's opinion—of his right to the Brambles as heir-at-law to John Jones; that he had found out for himself the value of the estate; and that he meant to take no compromise and give no quarter.   Indeed there was no earthly reason why he should, if his story were true.

And this is what I had to explain to Mr. Evelyn Viner, and to Miss Margaret through him.

II.

I could scarcely summon up courage to face my father, though I had no reason for feeling that I had committed any blunder.   Everything was perfectly straightforward and fair.   So busy was I with reviewing the whole situation—surely the most important, short of life and death, that ever fell into a lawyer's hands—that I took no heed of the usual hour for closing.   It was a terrible responsiblity, this case of the Brambles; and, unless we could carry it into court, and cross-examine Horace Jones into his grave in Barbadoes, the Brambles must pass out of the worthiest hands into those of these vermin.   I believe that law and justice almost invariably agree, or at least that they used to before law became the chaos of bungled statutes that it is now; but I could not feel so then.   If only old John Jones had not, out of some imbecile faith in the return of a prodigal, I suppose, been such a confounded ass as to have made no will!

It was dark when I remembered that I had not dined. And that made me notice, as I went out into the passage, that there was a light shining from under the room where we kept our articled clerk and other lumber.   I went in; and Dick Musty must have been as surprised to see me there at that hour as I was to see him, for he started and flushed up just as he had done once before.

"What on earth are you doing here?" I asked.   "I'm going to lock up—of course you can sleep here if you please;" which, of course, I did not mean.

"I—I had been getting interested in Blackstone," said he.   "I didn't notice the time."

I noticed that he was certainly reading, and was pleased to think that the young fellow was at any rate trying not to waste his time.   Indeed, to be interested in Blackstone was more than I had ever been in the days of *my* articles.   I felt sure that, if it had not been for this terrible affair of the Brambles, it would have pleased my father also, who wished the young man well.   It may seem odd that I should bring so slight an incident as this into my story; but it struck me at the time that the fact of Dick Musty's keeping away from his lodgings and his

Greek and his Latin to read law in our lumber-room was stranger even than Horace Jones's return from the grave.

My father, though better, was still very weak; but he could never rest at night until I had told him everything about the day's work, so that I could not put the last piece of bad news off till to-morrow.

"We must have counsel to plead to the declaration and advise," said he, without one word of courage. "Go to the Brambles to-morrow and see poor Miss Peggy, and tell her not to be down-hearted, poor girl. Try and look cheerful, Tom. If we are to lose, we'll lose hard. Of course you'll see that she instructs you. Let me see—if it comes to the assizes, we'll have Markham—send him a retainer at once, before the other side can get him. And I'll tell you what—you shall go to London and see Winter himself about the pleadings. There's no living man better. Hang the costs! If we can't get them from the other side, we'll do without 'em, Tom. Miss Peggy sha'n't be a penny the poorer for me. Tom, this isn't a private case. It's a public cause."

My poor father, though as good a man of business as ever stepped, had, I always used to think, a good deal of the knight-errant about him for a sober attorney. I could see he knew it was a losing fight from the very beginning; but—well, I suppose, like every other man in Burgham, myself included, he was in love with Miss Peggy Jones. At any rate, I sympathised with his reckless scorn of costs in such a cause, and half wished I had the moral courage to forge a long-lost will to checkmate the long-lost heir.

I went over to the Brambles next day and found Miss Margaret very grave and quiet and calm. I had expected to find her in so very different a mood, that I knew not what to say.

"I hear you told Mr. Viner yesterday that I ought to

defend this case," said she. "On what ground? Do you really suppose it is an impostor, and not my Uncle Horace, who has put forward this claim? On your honour, Mr. Key, do you believe that my uncle is dead, and that some person has falsely assumed his name?"

I could not play with the truth before such straight true eyes as hers.

"I cannot tell you what I think," said I. "But I know, as my father says too, that he must prove himself up to the hilt, that's all."

"No. If he makes me believe it, that must be enough for me. I must not leave it to judges and juries to tell me what I ought to do. And I do believe him to be my uncle, my own father's brother, Horace Jones."

"Good Heaven!" I exclaimed, "you *cannot* mean that you will, without the strictest proof, let your father's land go to such a man, to such a woman; that you will throw away all your own happiness, all the good and welfare of your native town—"

"My *own* happiness will not suffer, thank God!" said she, with a grave smile that told me how well she had learned that her future husband's love did not hang one jot upon house or land; and I wished that Evelyn Viner were by, that I might take his hand and tell him, in the name of the whole town, that he was worthy to be the husband of even Margaret Jones, rich or poor. I suppose they had talked it over yesterday, and had decided what was right for them to do, like a couple of fools. "Of course, I am sorry if my uncle is not likely to prove so good a neighbour as we—I—should have tried to be. But justice is justice, Mr. Key, and I cannot try to keep what is not my own."

"It is *not* justice," said I, and I am of the same opinion still. "Your grandfather believed his eldest son dead. He meant your father to have the Brambles. Why should he have made a will?"

" How do we *know* that he believed my uncle dead ? " asked she.

" Because he made no will."   But that was bad logic, and I knew it when I said so.   " Madame, you *must* compel this man to prove himself your uncle to the satisfaction of all England.   It is your duty as your father's daughter; your duty to all Burgham," said I.

She sighed.

" I want to do my duty," said she.   " And you, and your father, want to help me to do it, I know.   Please do not stand in my way."

" At least, Miss Jones, allow my father to be satisfied that he is the man he claims to be.   We have no evidence at all— "

" Moral evidence," said she, " and to spare."

" Moral rubbish ! " I am afraid I exclaimed.   " Let us be convinced a little more than morally; we will not work against justice, you may be sure.   That is due to us, because we are your friends."

" I know that," said she.

" We must plead to this declaration within a certain time.   Authorize me to do that for you—that will commit you to nothing ; and meanwhile we will satisfy ourselves whether it is necessary that the Brambles should be the property of an—Uncle.   Only give us time, in order that *we* may be clear."

" I think there can be no harm in that," said she, though I could see the impulse was upon her to leave the Brambles that very hour.   " Of course it is right for our friends to know that we are not doing wrong in what we do.   And no doubt our uncle's title, for his children's sake, ought to be made clear."

She was using Queen's grammar; but I knew what she meant by her " We " and " Our " very well.

To fight a lost battle is bad enough ; but to fight it for a client who is determined to lose is harder still.   However,

I had to be content with the very limited power I was allowed, only taking care to strain it as far as possible. I at once sent a retainer to Serjeant Markham, who then led our circuit, though pretty certain that the fee was thrown away. Then I set hard to work upon instructions for Mr. Winter to plead and advise, more particularly upon the evidence that would be required. Mr. Winter was the great pleader of the day. As we had no intention of getting our costs, we might indulge in any expense we pleased, and lose with a flourish and with all the honours of war.

It was of course exceedingly inconvenient that I, in my father's state of health, should be up in town and away from the office for even a day or two. But there was no help for it. Such a case demanded our most extreme personal attention, and my father would not be satisfied without a conference with Mr. Winter. Happily, we had no other business on hand that was immediately pressing. So I left our managing clerk in charge; arranged that all letters and clients who could not be put off should be brought or sent to my father at his house; gave Musty, for form's sake, a lot of work that would keep for many months, with strict injunctions to let me find it finished by my return; and travelled up to London.

I must own that Messrs. Heath & Crane, who were the claimant's attorneys, met me in the most open and straightforward manner. They concealed nothing, and showed no symptom of wishing to take us by surprise. They were not even anxious that Miss Jones should give up the Brambles without fighting; on the contrary, they seemed to wish for a verdict, so as to establish their client's title beyond any possibility of future cavil.

"If you are holding out in order that we may make Miss Jones an offer to induce her to spare us the expense of a trial, I may as well tell you at once that you are mistaken," said Mr. Crane. " We are as sure of a verdict as I stand here. I may assume, between ourselves, that you are not going to put in a will; and I know that my client's identity is beyond question. We shall most assuredly make no sort of offer whatever; we shall not advise our client to make one; and, even if we did advise it, it would not be made. Our client, rightly or wrongly, considers himself to have been grossly ill-used; and, rightly or wrongly, sees no reason why Miss Margaret Jones deserves one penny from him. If he chooses to do anything for her afterwards, that is his own affair. But he certainly will not buy her out. The proofs of identity are freely at your service, and you are welcome to make the most of them. If you think it worth while to put us to strict proof, you will find us fully prepared."

I smiled at the idea of Miss Margaret's taking a penny for giving up even what was her own, much less anything that was not her own. I knew too well that, with her, it must be all or nothing; and that she would, as a matter of course, refuse any imaginable compromise. However, I committed myself to nothing, and completed my instructions for counsel to advise on evidence after examining the claimant's case of identity at my leisure. Alas, his case was only too clear! For any good I could do in London, I might just as well take the next train to Burgham.

However, my father would never forgive me if I came back without having done my best—I believe the dear old gentleman would have dissolved partnership with any man who was clever enough to know when he was beaten. The worst of it was, that a conference with Mr. Winter was almost as difficult to obtain as an interview with Royalty. After a world of importunate patience, till I expect his clerk nearly hated the sight of me, I obtained an appointment for a quarter-past eleven o'clock at night at his private house in Russell Square. I was punctual to the minute, you may be sure; and I found the great junior busily engaged in reading a—novel. It seemed as incongruous as finding Dick Musty over Blackstone. But I have become more used to incongruities since those days.

"Wait a moment—I must know whether that poor girl really did die of a broken heart," said he, turning rapidly over the pages. "Ah, yes. Well, never mind. Better luck next time, Mr.—ah, yes—Key. Well, Mr. Key, there is no doubt but that the intestate's eldest son is entitled to recover on the strength of his own title as heir-at-law. And there's no question, it seems, of his title's being barred by length of adverse possession; and if there were, it would not apply to a claimant who has been beyond the seas till so short a time ago. Unless you can set up a will—"

"No. There was no will."

"Or deny that the intestate was seized—"

"We should not think of doing that, even if we could, Mr. Winter."

"Or that he was not married to the claimant's mother when the claimant was born—"

"Out of the question. His marriage will be amply proved."

"Then, why, in the name of common sense, Mr. Key, do you come to me?"

"For this reason. To be advised whether they have evidence enough that the claimant is really Horace Jones, and not some other man."

"Ah, that's another pair of shoes! Put them to the proof of that, if you can. What do they say?"

"I'm afraid their case is—well, rather strong. They can show, and we can't deny, that Horace Jones enlisted in a certain regiment of the line. They have evidence, military and medical, that he was ill with yellow fever at Barbadoes, and did *not* die. They will call the former chaplain and the surgeons and some officers of the regiment, to carry the case so far. That he married a woman of colour—a sutler woman—will be shown in the same way; as well as that the Horace Jones they knew belonged to Burgham; and to that they have witnesses from Burgham too. And every witness concerned will swear to the identity of Horace Jones the claimant with either Horace Jones of Burgham, or with Horace Jones in Barbadoes; and to the identity of Mrs. Horace Jones here with the woman who married Horace Jones out there."

Have you any evidence that all these witnesses— excellent witnesses, as I gather from what you say—are in unanimous error, and that the claimant is *not* Horace Jones? What do his alleged relations say?"

"I am sorry to say that we have no evidence at all. And his only relation is my client, who—well, Mr. Winter, she is a lady with a most remarkable sense of justice, and—"

"On what, then, *do* you rely?"

"On the chance that the claimant, when he comes to be cross-examined, might break down. We have retained Serjeant Markham—"

"Who knows how to puzzle the devil himself about his own identity. True. I daresay he could puzzle even me about mine. But jurors, let me tell you, are not quite the puzzle-headed fools that it is the fashion to call them. They will most assuredly believe the chaplain, and the surgeons, and the officers, and the good witnesses from Burgham. They will believe your client's silence, and your own inability to show who the man is, if he be not Horace Jones. And in this belief the judge will direct them to remain. And Serjeant Markham is the last man at the Bar to make a fool of himself, as you, Mr. Key, seem bent upon instructing him to do. If he does cross-examine the claimant, he will practically throw up his brief as soon as he sits down. Your client has no case, Mr. Key, absolutely none. Good-night, Mr. Key."

In my own mind, I had foreseen what Mr. Winter's advice would be; and I even felt conscious that it was a case in which his want of courtesy had been exceedingly excusable. He, unlike us, was not a Burgham man, and had had no opportunity of falling in love with Miss Margaret Jones. He had taken the view of a man of sense; and his view was final. We simply had not a leg, not even a toe, to stand on. Poor Miss Margaret must lose every penny she had, her husband must work for his bread, and the Brambles must go to Mr. and Mrs. Horace Jones and their gutter-children after them; to a drunken scamp and a Mulatto camp follower. I need not dwell upon what that would mean.

With a heavy heart next morning I called at Mr. Winter's chambers in the Temple, and paid his clerk his easily earned fee for answering what he must have thought a fool's question. Then I looked up my friend who had sent me the report on the manners and customs of Mr. Horace Jones, and then took the train to Burgham. It is not a short journey, though I need not specify the number of miles or hours; and, for that matter, railways were neither so fast nor so dangerous as they are now. So it was late in the afternoon when I reached Burgham, and I went to the office before I went home, in order to put off for a few minutes telling my father all the bad news.

"I want to speak to you, Mr. Thomas," said the managing clerk, as soon as I arrived.

"Well, Merrit? I hope it's nothing wrong?"

"No, sir, it can't be anything wrong. But it's queer. Every day you've been gone, I've shut up the office at the usual hour. You know, sir, we always lock all our own doors; so the housekeeper herself, if she wanted to, couldn't get in without asking for the key. And she never has asked me, and I've never parted with our keys for a single minute from the breeches-pocket where I keep them, and where I've got them now. Well, Mr. Thomas, I was out late one evening, having tea at my sister's, and my way home lay past the office-door. Naturally, I looked up, and there was a light shining through the window of your father's room as clear as I see you now."

" Well?"

" At first I thought it must be fire or thieves. So I rang up the housekeeper, and we looked into all the rooms, and there we found— "

" What?"

" Nothing, sir. Everything was dark and quiet, just as if there'd been no light at all."

" Your sister makes her tea strong, I suppose. That's all?"

" It's all very well to have your joke, Mr. Thomas, and of course the steadiest of men may see wrong once in a way; but that's *not* all. I was so sure I'd seen that light in that window, that I made a point of going to my sister's next night too, so that I might see if it happened again."

" Well? Did it happen again?"

" Yes, Mr. Thomas. It *did* happen again. And I woke up the housekeeper again. And we found nothing again. And when I went back into the street there wasn't the ghost of a light to be seen. So it couldn't have been the reflection of anything, you see."

" And you found, in the morning, not a sign of anybody's having been in the room?"

" Not the shadow of a sign. And, sir, that isn't all. Every night I've passed by—I've made a point of it before turning in—and every time I've seen that light, except the last one or two. I can't make it out at all. And the odd thing is, there's nothing wrong."

" Have you told my father ? "

" No, sir. He's seemed so worried and nervous that I didn't like to trouble him. I thought best to wait till you came home."

" Quite right. My father must not be worried any more just now. Well, Merrit, I've been thinking some time you ought to have a holiday. Go to the sea for a week. We can manage that, now I'm back again." The man worked hard, and it was as likely as not that his brain might want resting. " Has anybody seen the light besides you ? "

" I haven't asked, sir. I've been afraid, Mr. Thomas —in fact— "

" In fact, you suspect something you don't like to tell. What is it, please ? "

" Your father is unquestionably in a nervous condition, Mr. Thomas. I've noticed that ever since you've been gone. And sometimes people in that state do very curious things. So I thought it best to wait till you were back again."

" You mean that my father—impossible ! My mother would know. Put that out of your head at once, Merrit, if you please. All the same, you've done quite right to wait for me. Yes; you ought to take a holiday, I'm sure. Anyhow, there's nothing wrong, it seems. Nothing but a common ghost, I suppose; I don't mind *them*. And how has Mr. Musty been getting on all this while, eh ? Not much use to you, I suppose ? "

" I'm altering my opinion of Mr. Musty, Mr. Thomas, I am indeed. He's been working like a pavior. He's here before I am in the morning, and stays as long as I'll let him. I believe there's stuff in that young man, though it's been long enough coming out, I must say."

" I must see my father now. We'll talk to-morrow about your holiday."

My mother's account of my father was by no means a

good one. He had been going backward instead of forward, and was, the doctors suspected, kept down by some mental trouble. He was morbidly anxious about letters, and altogether as different from his old easy-going self as a man could be. She did not wish me to see him that night; but he had heard my voice—he had gone to bed early—and sent for me. When I had told him all my news, he said sadly,

"For the first time in my life I see we're beat, my boy. Winter's right. We're only a couple of obstinate fools. Poor girl! Well, God will temper the wind. But it's bad to feel beat, very bad indeed."

"Has father been at all strange?" I asked my mother.

"Only in the way you have seen," said she. "He is not like himself; but that is all."

So unlike himself that I began anxiously to wonder whether there might not be something in Merrit's suspicions, and that my father, in some mysterious way and without my mother's knowledge, might not be paying some nightly visit to the office, of which he had another set of keys. People with minds out of gear manage to do things sometimes that healthy persons would find impossible.

III.

After supper I strolled out with a cigar to settle in my own mind about what ought to be done, and how I should let Miss Margaret know that she was henceforth without a penny in the world of her own, unless she chose to beg for charity from Mr. and Mrs. Horace Jones. My only comfort was that she would bear to hear the news a great deal better than I could bear to tell it to her. In our last interview she had shown me the sort of stuff of which she and Evelyn Viner were composed; and that made it all the worse to exchange such neighbours for Mr. and Mrs. Horace Jones. I loved my father dearly, and was terribly anxious about him; but the immediate trouble of the hour, on which the fortune of a whole town seemed to hang, was all-absorbing. And besides, it was the first serious matter in which I had ever been engaged; and I could not help asking myself a hundred times a minute, if I had neglected any loophole of escape which greater knowledge and experience might have been able to find. But there was none, absolutely none. My Lord Chief Justice would have been as hopeless as I. Mr. Winter had as good as told me I was a fool for clutching at what was not even so much as a straw.

Poets are not the only people who, when they are in a professional difficulty, stare up at the stars. I did. I was in the lane which led from the High Street, past our office door, into St. Michael's Yard, when I looked up towards the Great Bear, and saw—a light in the window of my father's room.

My first impulse was to go home and see if my father was safe in his room. But on second thoughts I felt it better to wait a little, and then to effect an entrance with more effect than Mr. Merrit had done. Putting the idea of thieves out of the question, the occupant of the room must either be the housekeeper or my father. If the house-keeper, she certainly had no business there, and must be taken by surprise. If my father, he must be dealt with very carefully indeed. So I waited for five minutes, to see if the light was likely to vanish of its own accord, and then, instead of ringing the housekeeper's bell, I bethought me of an old trick which, I am sorry to say, I had not unfrequently put in practice when a younger man, in order to get in and out of the office when I wanted my temporary absence to be unknown. Without much, though with some, risk of feeling the hand of a passing constable on my shoulder, I climbed over the old coped wall that divided St. Michael's Yard from our back premises, then pulled myself on to another wall, and thence, very easily, to the cover of a closed cistern which was under my own window. I did not make much noise, and there was enough wind about to cover any that I could not help making. Then I took out my pocket-knife, and, by a trick not unknown to schoolboys and house-breakers, and in which former practice had made me expert in relation to this particular window, passed it between the upper and lower window-frames, pressed back the very inefficient fastening, and had the window open in less time than it has taken me to write the words. Then I took off my boots, dropped them quietly into the room, and followed them. I had no light; but I knew every inch of the ground. My door was locked, but Merrit had given me up the keys. I went out into the passage, in the dark and in my stockings, and listened at my father's door. I did not hear a sound.

I made up my mind that the best thing I could do was to open it quietly, enter in a matter-of-course way, and if, as impossibility itself could not keep me from fearing, I found my father, make believe that there was nothing out of the way in the situation. I would simply ask him if he did not think it time to shut up the office and come home. So I pulled back the outer door of green baize, and opened the inner, and at first, coming so suddenly out of the pitch darkness, was too dazzled by the candle-light to understand clearly what I saw. The candle had not gone out when *I* came in.

It was not, thank God, my father, haunting his office at midnight in a state of over-strung nerves. It was not the housekeeper, who ought to be in bed and asleep, and was no doubt doing her duty. It was Richard Musty—

Richard Musty, sitting at midnight at my father's table, in my father's chair, with a candle before him, and half his face buried in his hands.

Had *he* gone crazed? But I did not think of that then. The possibility of crime was more in my mind. I went up to him and brought my hand down heavily between his shoulders.

"What the devil," I cried out, "are you doing here?"

Most decidedly I meant to startle him. But I could not possibly startle him more than he had startled me, when I found out who it was that had been, night after night, engaged alone in an office which he could not possibly have been able to enter without false keys, or with any honest cause. He could not even have practised my mode of entry without false keys, because I had had to unlock my own room-door, and had not had to unlock my father's. And he of all men—too much of a blockhead even to be a rogue, as I had imagined until now. But though it was natural for him to be less startled than I, he did not seem to be startled at all.

On the contrary, he merely turned round and faced me with the saddest, most hopeless look I had ever seen.

"I did not expect you," was all he said. "But it doesn't matter now."

"Not matter?" said I. "Not matter, that I find my father's office broken into, night after night, by one of his own clerks; not matter, that I find you out in what amounts to burglary? If you have anything to say for yourself, say it; if not, I shall know what to believe, and make a proper search for an explanation, both here and elsewhere."

"I have nothing to say, Mr. Key," said he. "Of course I shall not appear in your office again."

"I could have told you that myself," said I. "Then you have nothing to say? Well, my father must decide what to do with you. I know what *I* should do." I was not keeping my temper, I own. "I suppose I oughtn't to cross-examine you, but I must either do that or send for the police, it seems to me. And for your mother's sake I should like to avoid that, if I can."

"Then—then I will tell you," said he. "Perhaps, perhaps I have done what a lawyer, a mere lawyer like yourself, would call wrong, technically wrong. I am not a mere lawyer, Mr. Key."

"A *mere* lawyer? I never knew you were a lawyer at all," said I. "But unluckily it is mere lawyers who have to define burglary, and—"

"I am not a burglar!" said Musty, showing a little spirit for the first time. "I have been here every night, that is true. It was the only time at which I could have sufficient access to your father's room. But my means of access were not what you suppose. I never used to leave the premises,—that is all. Before the hour for closing I used to hide in that closet, which your father's absence from the office made it perfectly easy for me to do. Mr. Merrit and the clerks of course used to think I had gone away for the day. Your father's room-door was never really locked, for I suppose it was forgotten either when he was taken ill or else when you went away, and nobody ever thought of it afterwards, not even Mr. Merrit, though he used to find the door unlocked whenever he came at night. It's curious what stupid people some lawyers are. Just because it was supposed not to want locking at the right time, nobody seemed to think it odd that it was found unlocked at the wrong one. No *mere* meta-physician would have made such a blunder as that, Mr. Key. I used to think it lucky. It enabled me to be found at my own desk when the clerks came in the morning. I used to keep food in the coal-scuttle. You'll find some there still. You're welcome to it. It's no use to me any more. And now I've told you the whole story."

"You have told me nothing, sir!" said I. "What possessed you—" I really did not know what to ask. He had spoken in such a forlorn, dreary, strangely cynical way that I began to suspect, not a crime, but—at last—sheer lunacy. Idiotcy would be perfectly natural in the young man.

"Very well, Mr. Key. There was a document which it was necessary—at least I thought so—that I should examine. To your eyes it was only an old Latin sermon, or essay, about the virtues of some miserable saint or other of the Middle Ages. But I had reason to think—reason which I should vainly try to make you understand—that it might, nay, must, be a palimpsest: perhaps even the word is strange to you. And yet even you, Mr. Key, must have heard that some of our most precious classics have been lost by being erased and over-written with worthless monkish chronicles; but that many have been recovered, in our own times, by chemically removing the monkish stuff, and, by a re-agent, restoring the old writing so as to be legible again. I had reason to think, from certain partial experiments I had already tried, that this absurd puff of St. Willibrord covered—well, nothing less than some portions of the lost books of Livy. I need not go through the course of reasoning that led me to that conclusion. Enough that the reasons were sound; and, after all, in such matters instinct and insight are the best of all reasons. Certainty must always depend upon something higher than mere evidence, Mr. Key, which can never amount to proof, however strong it may be. It is only faith which can ever be sure. And so—"

"And so you believed, because you wished to believe, that you would find Livy in a lawyer's office in Burgham. Why didn't you say so before?"

"Because I didn't choose to be called mad by mere people of common sense, like you and your father, until

I could come to you and say, 'See here!' And now I say, 'See here; see the result of my disappointed faith, and of labour in vain.' You are right. I am good for nothing. I am an ass and a fool."

I began to see at last with what sort of man I had to deal. "So you found nothing?" said I.

"Worse than nothing. Look here," he said, uncovering the parchment that lay before him, and which was, indeed, the old Latin manuscript which my father had thrown into a drawer to keep this queer sort of a clerk from wasting his time; as if a fanatic of any sort, and not only a lover, will not find out the way. "Yes, that monk, whoever it was, was not so bad as some of them. *He* only used an old deed to scrawl over; if a man must write rubbish, he can't do better than use rubbish to write it on."

"An old deed of the times of the monks? But that must be a curiosity in its way, after all. What is it? That old writing beats me."

"I don't know. I didn't care to recover more than enough to show me that I had thrown all my labour away. If *you* care to know, it seems like the record of a conveyance, by the corporation of Burgham to the priory of Welwood, of the Campus de Easton, in the parish of St. Botolph *intra muros et terminos de Burgham;* which means 'within the walls and bounds.' I have read no more. And enough, too."

"Quite enough," said I. "Go home and go to bed: of course I must speak to my father about you, though the affair, I am glad to say, doesn't look as bad as I feared."

I locked up carefully enough this time, let myself and Dick Musty out by the same way I had entered, so as not to disturb the housekeeper, and carried the old parchment home with me to show my father. It was of no practical use; but it certainly was, or might be, of interest to local antiquarians. It was remarkable, any way, that the document should have remained in the custody of the parsons of St. Michael's, as it must have done, ever since the days before the Reformation; but certain old documents have a wonderful way of escaping the doom of waste paper, to which things of more value are so perilously liable. An old invitation to a long-eaten dinner will survive under circumstances in which an important receipt will prove mysteriously and hopelessly missing.

But nothing of all this could possibly affect the miserable case of which my mind was full. I forgot, or rather did not even trouble to remember, to mention the matter to my father, after all. He had too much on his mind to be troubled about Dick Musty, for whom I now felt rather pity than anger, inexcusable as his conduct had been.

I remember, as well as any in my life, the day when my father at last decided, finally, that fighting would be worse than folly, and that the Brambles must go to Mr. Horace Jones. Mr. Evelyn Viner had been talking everything over with us—not that there was much left to talk about—and had stayed to dine. He took things well, I must say. Instead of losing his appetite, he talked about what chances he would have if he went to the Bar, and would not even go back to the great question now that it had been settled for good and all. He made all sorts of talk for everybody; and presently, in an incidental way, we got upon local matters, and one of us mentioned the singularity of the name of that churchless parish, " St. Botolph in Turn." We all made guesses at its origin, and at last I said,

" I think it must mean St. Botolph in-Ternus, or in-Terminibus, or within the walls or boundaries of the town."

"By Jove," said my father, "it might be! But I didn't know you were such a scholar as that, Tom. How did you get hold of that idea? St. Botolph in Turn *is* within the town boundaries; so much is true."

"I'm afraid I can't claim the guess as quite original," said I. "Oddly enough, I got it from an old deed that was among old Parson Evans's papers, which I've got upstairs, and will show you if you like, as it seems curious in its way. I'll tell you the whole story; but not now."

I brought the half-deciphered document out of my bedroom, which my father recognized at once as the parchment he had taken from the hands of Dick Musty. We looked at it in the manner of the very unskilled archæologists that we were.

"How odd!" said Mr. Evelyn Viner. "Campus de Easton means Easton Field, the other name for the Brambles. A curious accident, indeed."

"And the Brambles is still rated to St. Botolph," said I.

I wished I had not brought down the document, after all. But Mr. Evelyn Viner spoke as if it mattered nothing to him. I believe in his heart he was fool enough to be half glad that Miss Margaret was to come to him poor, so that he might work for her.

"Tom," said my father, " this document is really a curiosity. I must show it to the mayor, and we'll have the rest of it made out when we've got nothing else to do. It's odd I never noticed there was anything of the sort about this deed. But I remember, it was the day I was taken ill. It shows how careful a town ought to be about preserving the evidence of its boundaries. The nature of the ownership of the Brambles has always happened, you see, to make it perfectly immaterial whether that part of St. Botolph lay within or without he town; and Mr. Wilfred Jones voted as a freeman.

This old document may prove important evidence of town rights in time to come. Why—but—great Heaven!" he suddenly cried out, starting from his chair.

I thought he had been seized with a sudden fit, and was about to fall. Mr. Viner also started towards him; and, in truth, there looked reason for alarm, considering his recent illness and his chronic worry about the Brambles, and his apoplectic flush, and his vain efforts to speak a word. But at last he waved us away from him, and fell back again into his chair.

Then he raised his fist and brought it down upon the old Latin sermon with a bang that made the glasses ring.

"Hurrah!" he shouted. "Three cheers for Miss Peggy, and a fig for Mr. Horace Jones!"

Had he gone mad after all?

"Tom! Has there been a single case of the Brambles passing to the heir-at-law of an intestate within the memory of the law?"

"No," said I. "How could there be—till now—when it belonged to a college till it was bought by Mr. John Jones? But—don't you feel well?"

"Well? Tom, don't *you* be a fool! Then there's been continuous custom —continuous custom, because there hasn't been the possibility of a breach—"

"What breach? What custom?" I could only look at Mr. Viner in despair, and think what I could do, with my father going out of his senses before my eyes.

"Is the Brambles in Burgham or no?"

"Surely, sir, if that document is to be believed."

"It *is* to be believed. It is legal proof, and proof in good custody, sir; and uncontradicted and uncontradict-able by all the Horace Joneses in the habitable globe! The Brambles *is* in Burgham. And what is the tenure of lands in Burgham? You—a Burgham lawyer—don't know?"

" I— "

" Then I'll tell you, and I'm ashamed of you !   It's
Borough English, sir !   And, by the custom of Borough
English, all lands and tenements within the Bounds of
Burgham go to the *youngest* son, instead of the eldest,
when there's no will ! "

I need not carry the history of the case farther than
by saying that the strange old custom of Borough English,
which still prevails in other places than Burgham, and
the origin of which has defied theory to discover, effectually disinherited Mr. Horace Jones simply because he
was his father's eldest son, and gave the Brambles to
Miss Margaret because she was the heiress of the
youngest son of old John Jones.   I have told my story ;
but only because I think it is strange enough to be worth
the telling.   It has a moral for " mere lawyers " like
myself, and it is this.   Don't think Practice everything,
and Learning nothing.   England is a curious country,
and the Middle Ages take a long time to kill.

As for poor Dick Musty, through whom—by no means
through any merit of his own—it had come out that the
Brambles had never ceased to be a part of the ancient
Borough of Burgham, Mr. and Mrs. Viner could not see
that he was undeserving of a most unreasonable and
disproportionate reward.   Learning from my father and
myself his complete unfitness for the law, they sent him
back to Cambridge, where he got his degree and a fellowship and settled down at last into a happily useless
member of society, not without some reputation as an
authority on palimpsests and doubtful readings.   I
suppose he is as dead as Livy by this time, seeing how
long ago all this happened.   Everything ended rightly ;
but even now I almost tremble when I think how that
Great Estate hung upon such a mere " Touch-and-Go."

A MOST REMARKABLE WILL.

I.

PROFANE laymen believe that, when the cloth is removed
at a lawyers' dinner, the oldest member of the profession
present rises, and solemnly proposes, amid enthusiasm
too deep for applause, this solemn toast—" The man who
makes his own Will."   The story has, at any rate, the
merit of being well invented ; for most assuredly that
man has a fool for his client in a double and treble
meaning of the famous saying about men who are their
own lawyers : and it is true enough, and I, an old lawyer,
say it, with all respect for that science of common sense
popularly called " the law," that the people who find
their way into court, and learn what Costs mean, have
mostly got into the predicament through having too
strong an antipathy to lawyers and their bills.   But I
think it is even worse than common folly when a testator,
mostly out of self-conceit, leaves a Chancery suit instead
of an inheritance to his heirs.   Women are not, in this
respect, quite so criminally imbecile as men are, because
they are mostly free from the little knowledge which is
at the root of most bad wills.   But then they are apt to
make a more thorough hash of things when they make
any at all.   On the whole, I should place makers of their
own wills in the following order of badness, taking the
extreme type in each degree of comparison : *Positive—*

Bad, Elderly Gentlemen. *Comparative*—Worse, Elderly Ladies. *Superlative*—Worst, Lord Chancellors. But not even a Lord Chancellor ever managed to draw up so extraordinarily bewildering a will as Miss Bridgita Molloy. She could have taught something even to the late Lord W——y. As the case never actually came into court, the details will probably be new to most of my readers ; but I heard them all at the time, and have the clearest recollection of them—and no wonder. On this occasion there is no harm in giving real names. And that is fortunate ; for the story could not possibly be told without them. It simply defies invention.

Miss Bridgita Molloy was a maiden lady of royal descent, who lived at an English watering-place—I really forget whether at Bath, or Clifton, or Cheltenham, or Malvern, or Leamington, or Buxton; but it was at some such place, and luckily the name of the town is the one detail which does *not* matter. For the sake of avoiding blanks and dashes, I will call it Chatterbury, as more or less applicable to them all—at least, in Miss Molloy's time. She was a little eccentric in trifles ; but, in all essential things, as notoriously whole-minded, and strong-minded too, as any lady of sixty in the whole kingdom. I must enter a little into her family history ; but only so far as is needful. She had been the second of three beautiful sisters, the daughters and coheiresses of a gentleman of large estate in Ireland. They were much run after in their girlhood, and had once been known as the three pocket-beauties—less in allusion to their size than to their reputation—then somewhat uncommon in Dublin—of being worth marrying for something more lasting than beauty. Well, to cut a long story short before it is well begun, the eldest, Miss Lucis Molloy (a quaint first name ; but it always struck me as a singularly pretty one for a pretty girl), eloped with a gentleman, also descended from royalty—so far descended, indeed, that there was scarcely a further social depth left him to descend to—named Fitzgerald O'Birn; and the youngest, Miss Judith, went off with a foreign refugee, a sort of Hungarian-German-Polish dancing-master Count, named Ferentz Steldl. Ferentz is the Hungarian for Francis, I believe; Steldl, I fancy, is Bavarian or Tyrolese. Both marriages turned out miserably—so miserably, that Miss Bridgita forswore romance, and even matrimony, and actually kept her vow.

She also kept more than her vow—she kept her fortune. When the creditors got hold of Mr. Molloy's great estates, he left the very handsome surplus left him in cash and Consols absolutely to his one wise daughter. Not a penny went into the pockets of Count Steldl or Mr. O'Birn. It was a bitter disappointment to both gentlemen; and I believe they avenged their wrongs upon their wives after the manner of their kind.

So while poor Madame Steldl suffered and starved all over Europe, and poor Mrs. O'Birn starved and suffered in the larger and darker continent of London, Miss Molloy lived alone and in dignified opulence at Chatterbury. She was a first-rate economist, and her patrimony had prospered. She used to amuse herself by speculating in stock—always shrewdly and cautiously. By the time she was sixty, it was reckoned that her income could not amount to less than a safe twelve hundred a year, of which she saved at least five.

Now what in the world was to become of all this money if Miss Bridgita Molloy ever happened to die? I have been thinking of the best form in which I can tell the story of what did happen shortly; and I think it best, on the whole, to undergo a transformation, and multiply the result by two. That is to say, I will henceforth speak as if I were myself Miss Molloy's solicitor, my old friend, the late Charles Lake of Chatterbury; and I will, in addition, use the privilege accorded to authors and to counsel of speaking after the facts, and so of putting them into clearer and more readable form than if I followed them in order of detail.   So, for the present, instead of being your correspondent, Mr. Editor, Mr. Thomas Key, formerly of Burgham, I will, for the nonce, write to you in the person of Mr. Charles Lake of Chatterbury, a very dry matter-of-fact man of business indeed, who told the tale as it was told to me.

II.

One afternoon the mail-coach from London set down two gentlemen at the Old Swan, Chatterbury.   Both had remarkably little luggage for those days, when men could not run from York to London and back again in a few hours.   Both ordered a bed, both walked into the coffee-room, and one of them rang the bell.   When the waiter answered it, one of the gentlemen ordered cold brandy, the other hot whisky.   And the waiter's report at the bar was not favourable to either.   But with that opinion lack of luggage may have had something to do.

There were other resemblances between the two men. Both were well past middle age ; neither looked like one of the hunting men, or officers on half-pay, or rheumatic patients, who formed the bulk of the male visitors to Chatterbury.   But there all likeness came to an end. He of the whisky was a long lean man, with fierce untrimmed whiskers, a shiny bald head, bloodshot blue eyes, and a tell-tale nose, dressed in the height of the fashion, with a tendency of overstepping it into loudness. He had ordered his grog in a thick rich brogue.   He of the brandy, on the other hand, was short and squat, with a dirty sallow complexion, thick grizzled hair, and twinkling black eyes. He wore the then usual ornament, if ornament it be, of a moustache; and, for the rest, was clean, or rather half, shaved, and there was something Frenchified about his costume.

" Waitther !" said the Irishman. " If anybody calls here to-dee or to-morrow for Mejor O'Birn,—*I'm* Mejor O'Birn !"

The other started for a moment, and laid his glass down.

" Shall I comprehend, Monsieur," he asked, " that you give your name ? "

" Me name ? And why wouldn't I give me name ? " said O'Birn, with a little leap in his chair. " 'Tis none to be ashamed of, anyhow. I'd like to see the man with a name to his back as good as O'Birn."

" One hundred thousand pardons, Monsieur. I am glad that I know—that is all. Eh, but one thousand thousand pardons, Monsieur Fitzgerald O'Birn.''

The Major's jaw fell, and all his face, save his nose, grew suddenly pale.

" Sure, now, ye're not goin' to tell me ye're one of thim blagyard Jews !" cried he. " Sure 'twould be too crool an' all, when I've come down to see me own wife's sisther, that's rollin' over and over in jools an' gold. An' ye've followed me all the wee down here; an' this is a free country ! An' bad luck to the country where an officer an' gentleman mustn't pee a visit to his wife's relations without being hunted by all Jerusalem in full cry ! Come, Moses, ye'll give me another dee."

" Aha ! So you think no one shall know your name but the people which shall hold your bills, Monsieur O'Birn? I hold not your bills; I am not fool. You come down to see Mdlle. Bridgita, then, I shall comprehend ? "

' Sure, then, 'tis the divvle ye are ! But that's better, anyhow, than bein' what I thought ye— "

" You shall not be so sure, Monsieur. I shall know your Christian name, and I shall know the Christian name of the sister of your wife, because I am Ferentz Steldl, Monsieur O'Birn !   Aha! you shall have the tremblement perceptible, Monsieur O'Birn !"

" Hwhat!" cried the Major, leaping to his feet, with a shout and a glare. "Ye sit there in cold blood, and ye tell me, Mejor Fitzgerald O'Birn, ye're that—miscreant —that blagyard—that snake in the grass—that drinkin', swindlin', mane-spirited, undher-handed, slanderin', murderin', onrespectable thief of the whole world, Ferentz Steldl? And ye think to escape from the fist of a gentleman this dee?"

" Patience, patience, *mon beau-frère*," said Steldl, without the slightest change of tone. "Fine words shall not butter what you call the *panais*. It is you who shall escape from me. You shall leave this town. I shall guard Mdlle. Molloy, sister of my wife, aunt of my son, from you. For that I am here."

Something in the significant calmness of his foreign brother-in-law calmed the Major down. He returned to his chair, shifted his glass on the table, and said,

" An' 'tis for that I'm here too," said he. "I'm here to defend me own sisther, an' me wife's sister, an' me gurl's aunt, from all the Counts out of Hungary an' the Siven Dyles. An' ye'll move from your sate if ye dare."

" I shall not desire," said Steldl. "I am well where I am. I desire to have the eye on you, my *beau-frère*. While you shall sit there, I shall sit here, if it shall be to the death, Monsieur O'Birn. It shall be the duel *à la mort*, Monsieur, and we shall fight with the bottoms of the chairs."

" Then, faith, I'll sit like the hen of Banagher—an' she sat till the sod undher her began to crow. So ye think Miss Biddy 'll open the crack of her door to the likes of *you?*

" Why not ?   She is sister of my wife, and aunt of my
son."

" Aunt of my daughter, ye mane.   Poh ! what'd she
know of a son of yours ? "

" You mock of yourself, my *beau-frère*.   Have she not
buy my son Ferentz the commission of the Foot, and
keep him, so long he see not me ? "

" Then ye lie in your throat, Ferentz Steldl !   'Tis me
own daughter, an' her own goddaughter an' niece, Lucis
Bridgita, that she's kept at school at her own charge, an'
keeps in pocket-money as long as I don't see her more
than woonst a year."

" *She* do that for *your* daughter?   Impossible, Monsieur ! "

" *She* do that for *your* son ?   Mr. Steldl, ye lie ! "

The way in which these two gentlemen quarrelled,
without showing the least sign of coming to blows, gave
the waiter, who was not far off, an altogether fresh view
of the possibilities of human nature.   Obviously there
was a world in which gentlemen cared more for their
physical than their moral skins.

" Take yourself off, my *beau-frère*.   In effect, she adopt
Ferentz, my son.   She leave all to him."

"Ye're a fool, Steldl—that's what she's been makin' of
ye, the old screw o' the world !   As if she'd lave a penny
to any but her own niece Lucis, afther doin' all she has
for the darlin' child ! "

Steldl was the sort of man who would be given to
shrugging his shoulders, like a Frenchman in a play : so
he no doubt did so now.   " She cannot have done so
much for Miss Lucis, or I shall have hear.   I know not
till now she have done so much for the daughter of the
black sheep ; but what shall a school-bill be, after all ?
Bah !—a bagatelle.   But a commission in the Foot—ah,
that is another shoe !   And you consent not to see your
own flesh and blood for the sake of a bill of a school ! "

" I'm a betther sort of a father than to sthand in me own child's wee of a fortune. And ye sit there an' tell me she's spent the price of a commission on *your* son—unless 'tis in the Marines, where they'll believe the tale."

" *Parole de gentilhomme*, Monsieur O'Birn, I am father of Ferentz Steldl, lieutenant of King George—"

" And I of Lucis Bridgita O'Birn, that'll be in the shoes of Miss Molloy."

The two fathers emptied their tumblers, and the Major rang for more. Neither meant to lose this sitting match if he could help it, that was clear.

" If I didn't know," said Steldl slowly and impressively, " there is no school in the land who shall teach for no pay, I shall not believe. But she shall but toss one bone to one hungry dog—that shall be all."

Now Major O'Birn, though he had never met his brother-in-law in the flesh before, was a citizen of that world which knew that the refugee had taught fencing in his time, and had won several bets that he would make a bullet mark out a pack of cards. So, instead of retorting with a charge of hot whisky into his brother-in-law's yellow face, he contented himself by saying, with an angry grin,

" An' what'll ye say when I tell ye *my* wife is with her own sisther this very dee, as thick as bees in a hive ? "

The Irishman, though he had kept his temper the worst, won the match after all. Steldl leapt from his chair with a volley of language that proved his own temper to be no deeper than the thinnest part of his skin.

" *Your* wife, you fortune-hunting Irish beggar ? *Your* wife with Miss Molloy ? So that's why you've been keeping me here ? " He threw the rest of his liquor into the fire, and sent a blaze up the chimney. Then he buttoned his coat defiantly, saying, " *I* will see Miss Molloy."

" An' that's what I call mighty waste of good drink," said Major O'Birn, gulping down the remainder of his own. " Yes, ye may go, Steldl. I won't bother even to see her door shut in your face—though, faith, it would be fun."

" And I tell you, Monsieur," cried Steldl, raising his voice into a sort of scream, " that it is *my* wife which is now with Miss Molloy ! "

The two husbands glared at one another fiercely. And, short of running the risk of being knocked down by the other, that was all left them to do. Words had done their worst ; and they were evidently not men of deeds.

No ; Miss Bridgita Molloy had not turned out a bad sister after all. She would never even acknowledge so much as the existence of the Major and the Count, and had an odd way of speaking of the married Miss Molloys as if they were widows; but she did not visit the sins of the fathers upon the children. At a very early age, too early for them to make a deliberate choice between their father and their fortunes, she had sent both the little Ferentz and the little Lucis Bridgita to good schools, and, as they grew bigger, sometimes had them to Chatterbury for the holidays to meet their mothers, who accepted the arrangement more reasonably than mothers always will. For that matter, neither Count nor Major cared to be bothered with a baby, nor always with a wife, so that the two young children were removed from evil influence as much as lay in Miss Molloy's power. She was a very strict aunt and a terribly exacting patroness; but she meant to be kind, and was really kind in her own way. I never saw much of the children, but I liked what I did see. Ferentz was a fine, frank, high-spirited young fellow, without any of his father's vices, as is often the way with the sons of prodigal fathers, and Lucis was almost as pretty as her mother had been when she eloped with the Major. Rather a quiet girl, I used to think, but

amiable, and with a dash of her aunt Biddy's good sense
about her way of speaking. But it was one of Miss
Molloy's caprices that the left hand which she held out
to one sister should know nothing of how the right hand
was held out to the other. Neither mother, neither child
was ever her guest at the same time as the other mother
and the other child. I doubt if Ferentz knew that he
had a cousin Lucis, or she that she had a cousin Ferentz.
Most assuredly each of the mothers believed that she
alone was favoured with her sister's bounty. That reserve
was one of Miss Molloy's very strongest foibles, if one
may properly call a foible strong. She would never tell
even me, her lawyer, more than she thought absolutely
necessary about anything; and so of course even she,
with all her good business qualities, would sometimes
make little mistakes out of which I found it difficult to
help her.

And the same course that she pursued with her lawyer
she followed with her doctor too—that is to say, with a
certain doctor who happened to be a personal friend;
for she used to boast that she had never had a medicine-
bottle in the house but once, and that she had thrown
out of window. She often said that she had nothing of
a coffin about her but the strength of its nails; and yet
the very first time she was compelled to send for her
medical friend in a professional capacity, he found that
she must have been suffering for years from a most pain-
ful internal and organic disease, and a fatal one. How
do hungry relations always hear such news? Had she
made her will? If not, would she recognize the fact
that the nature of her disease admitted of no delay?
And so, for the first time, Mrs. O'Birn and Mrs. Steldl,
at the expense of their husbands' creditors, flew on the
wings of sisterly affection, and met together at Miss
Molloy's bedside. And, with the instinct of vultures, the
Count and the Major had been unable to keep from

hovering, as near as they dared, within the shadow of a death that meant so much to them. Neither, I firmly believe, had until that meeting the faintest suspicion that, if only a proper will were made, he would not become the father of Miss Molloy's sole heir. That discovery that her generosity had not been monopolized by either must have been a deservedly bitter moment for both the greedy blackguards. And, for all their brag, each knew that he dared no more knock at Miss Molloy's door than he dared commit assault and battery; while, for aught each could tell, the other might be high in the favour of the poor lady who was dying a few streets away.

It was—for it must have been—a strange meeting between the two forlorn, faded, worse than widowed, half-childless women by the death-bed of one who to them had for many years represented strength, health, comfort—all that they had wanted since they were girls together long and long ago. There they had to sit, one on each side of the bed, conscious of a question she had been commanded by her tyrant to ask, conscious that the other was similarly burdened, unable to ask it in the other's presence, not daring nor knowing how to ask it had she been alone by the bedside. For I declare that even I myself would sooner have led a forlorn hope than have asked Miss Molloy what she meant to do with her money. I like to think of the dismay of the two husbands, but I don't in pity like to think of what the two poor wives must have suffered in silence that afternoon.

I had already—I need not tell anybody who knows places like Chatterbury—been put in the position of being able to report the conversation between the two gentlemen in the coffee-room. They had not spoken in whispers, and the Old Swan had key-holes and its waiter had ears. So I was not very much surprised when, in the course of the evening, I received a summons to attend Miss Molloy.

" Ah ! " said her doctor, who was dining with me when the summons came.   I report the exclamation, because it was meant to mean a great deal.

" I hope and trust I find you better, Miss Molloy," said I, when I was shown into her bedroom, which she had not left for some weeks now.

" No, Mr. Lake, I don't," said she.   " I didn't believe I was a dying woman three hours ago, but I do now. Don't say anything stupid.   I've not lived such a bad life that I'm afraid ; and I've never been afraid to face anything in my life, except marriage, and I'm not going to begin now."   She was right; with all her little oddities she had been really a good, if somewhat hard-mannered, woman, and always a singularly brave one.   " I know I'm dying, because the hawks and kites are abroad.   We used to keep a banshee in the old times, and it's something between a Count and a Major.   Those poor silly sisters of mine have been here bothering me to make my will.   And if you don't know what that means, Mr. Lake, I do.   It means death, as sure as I'm lying here."

" You mean to say that your sisters have mentioned such a thing ? "

It was really not a case for common phrases.   Miss Molloy was—Miss Molloy.

" Not in words—no, poor things.   But there they sat and cried, and there was nothing but Will—Will—Will, in every tear.   'Tisn't them I blame, though 'tis not nice to be cried over that way.   'Twas as much as I could do not to say Won't—Won't—Won't; but I've always had the wit to hold my tongue.   Ah, Mr. Lake, since then I've been thinking how maybe 'tis better to have somebody to drop a real tear over your own self, if 'tis half brandy, and from a Count or a Major, than to have lived in peace only to die all alone.   But that's fool's talk ; and I didn't ask ye not to talk like a stupid that ye might listen the better to a fool."

"Surely," said I, "*you* are not alone. Lieutenant Steldl—Miss O'Birn—"

"Pooh! who remembers a dead aunt for a whole day, I'd like to know? Would I want to make a boy and a girl cry before their own troubles come? 'Tis business I sent ye for. There's pens and paper. I *am* going to make my will."

"I am sure you are right in that. I am entirely at your service, Miss Molloy."

"Then," said she, "I want you to draw my will *now*. No instructions, mind, to be drafted to-morrow. I might be dead by then—who knows? My pain's almost left me; and that's a bad sign, if death's a bad thing. It will be very short and very simple. Take a sheet of the big foolscap—that'll be plenty. Now write, *This is the last Will and Testament of Bridgita*—mind ye spell it with a *ta*, not a *da;* and with only one *t*, mind; for I'm particular about that way, for 'tis the way my mother spelt it, right or wrong—*of Bridgita Molloy, of Chatterbury, in the county of*—whatever it was—*spinster :* praise glory for that, anyhow! But ye needn't put that in—the glory, I mean—*Spinster : I give and bequeath to Rachel Andrews, my housekeeper, the sum of three hundred pounds, free of legacy duty, and I request her to take charge of my dog Dash, knowing that she will fulfil my request according to the intention wherewith I make the same. I give and bequeath to every person who shall have been in my service for one month preceding my decease the amount of one year's wages. I give and bequeath to my friend John Kirwan, of Chatterbury, Doctor of Medicine, the sum of five hundred pounds, free of legacy duty. I give and bequeath to my brother-in-law, Ferentz Steldl the elder*—is it all right, so far?"

"Quite. But how do you spell Ferentz?" asked I.

"*F,e,r,e,n,t,z*—Ferentz Steldl. The boy's name is Firentz, with an *i*. I won't have him bear his father's name.—*My brother-in law, Ferentz Steldl the elder, the sum of one shilling, free of legacy duty, to buy a mourning-ring. I give and bequeath to my brother-in-law, Fitzgerald O'Birn, the sum of one shilling, free of legacy duty, to buy a mourning-ring. I give and bequeath to my dear nephew, Firentz—with an i—Steldl, Lieutenant in the Army, the sum of one thousand pounds. I give and bequeath to Lucis Bridgita O'Birn, my niece, the sum of one thousand pounds. And all the residue of my property, whether real or personal, I give, bequeath, and devise to—"*

She paused. Up to this point she had not needed my help, so expert she seemed in the art of the testator.

"*Devise to,*" echoed I. "Well, Miss Molloy?" The residuary legatee was to be the important personage; for he or she would come in for at least twenty-five thousand pounds, and perhaps a good deal more, after all debts and legacies were paid.

But still she paused. All the rest had been mere child's play.

"Mr. Lake," she said at last, "I may be dying, but I'm not an old woman, and I might live for years. Now my sisters are gone, I feel less like dying than I did when I sent for ye to make my will. I've done all the justice I need do; and I don't want a handsome property to be split up—that would be a sort of a shame. Neither Firentz nor Lucis has any expectation of getting what I have to leave, whatever others may. It's for the sake of the property that it must go into one hand. And, Mr. Lake, I daren't trust the very walls of my bedroom with the name I choose. If I was to ask you to write the name in my will, I should have to speak it to you, and for aught I know the Count or the Major may have bribed the nurse to listen at that very door."

"Write it down for me, then; here is the pen."

"No. The paper might get dropped about, and—no; I'd rather *you* wouldn't know the name. It isn't that I

don't trust ye, but ye might say it out in a dream, and
your wife might hear it, and she might let it out by some
chance to somebody who might talk about it in a place
like Chatterbury, and then the Count or the Major would
get at the secret as sure as ye're alive. And then there's
no counting the villanies that wouldn't be done; they'd
be trying to get me shut up in a madhouse, and forging
and murdering some one maybe; anyhow, there'd be no
comfort in living, if I am to live any more. I've thought
of a way to keep off all danger, and to make it everybody's interest to support the will, and to save every bit
of bother. I'll write the name myself in the will with
my own hand, and then cover it over while ye write the
rest, and ye'll give me your word of honour ye won't try
to see what I've written till I'm dead and gone."

The whim was a stupid one, I thought, for a testator
who was in other respects proving herself so clear-headed;
but there was certainly no apparent harm in indulging
her. "But," said I, "as you wish to take such extreme
precautions, does it not strike you that it is easier for an
expectant heir to overhaul a will than for a solicitor to
break confidence in a dream?"

"I've thought of all that," said she. "Of course
they'll try to overhaul, and where there's a will there's a
way—but there's more ways of killing a dog than hanging him. I'll manage so that if every servant in the
house is in the Count's pay or the Major's, they shall
earn their money for nothing at all. So I'll take the
pen, if ye please, and the will; give me a dip of ink, and
any scrap of paper ye find handy."

I gave her all she asked for. She first of all, very
slowly, wrote down upon the scrap of paper what was
presumably a rough draft of what she was going to enter
in the will. Then she copied it into the document even
yet more slowly, dwelling, as it seemed, upon every
letter. Her hand must have grown feeble before her

brain, or else, like all testators of the fussy sort who look on will-making as a solemn function, she could not bring herself to let a paltry minute settle the destination of five-and-twenty thousand pounds. I have known men and women who would have made the labour of writing the two or three needful words last the better part of a day.

She thrust the scrap of paper on which she had made her first memorandum under her pillow, and then carefully folded the will itself so that I could see nothing without deliberately breaking my word. Dr. Kirwan and myself were appointed executors; and the execution of the will was witnessed by the nurse and a neighbour. There was certainly nothing remarkable about Miss Molloy's will so far but the excessive care she had taken that its principal provision should not even be guessed at until she died.

Nor did Miss Molloy die quite so soon as everybody had expected. The Count and the Major, finding a protracted stay at the Old Swan beyond their means, had parted, deadly enemies—all the more deadly because each inspired the other with a feeling of mortal terror. I am very much afraid that both Mrs. Steldl and Mrs. O'Birn had to bear, at her husband's hands, the burden of punishment for the sins of her brother-in-law. But, however that may be, the day came at last when I heard from Dr. Kirwan the long-expected news that my client, Miss Bridgita Molloy, was alive no more.

"She couldn't have lasted another week," said he. "But, all the same, I might have kept her going for another day or two, with care. Would you believe it, but the obstinate old lady, only the night before last, gave her nurse the slip, and, weak as she was, went all over the house to see if everything was in order! Death was a relief to her, and she was a queer old lady in some

ways—and the worst patient in all the town—but I'm
sorry she's gone."

And that, I am afraid, was the only note of honest
mourning which Miss Molloy, with all her many virtues
and her singularly few weaknesses, was privileged to
receive. She had always hidden her good qualities out
of public sight; and hardness of manner, like charity,
covers a great deal.

To the last she had stuck to her will. It was found
under her pillow when she died, sealed up in a large blue
envelope, and indorsed "*My Will—B.M.*" I own it was
with some curiosity that I opened it; for she had made
such a mystery of what should have been a very simple
piece of business, that I had some misgivings lest she
should have disinherited niece and nephew alike, and
made her dog Dash or some Anti-Matrimonial Society
her residuary legatee. My own sympathies were with
Miss Lucis; my wife's with Lieutenant Firentz Steldl.
That was a little matter of human nature; as a matter
of reason, we felt that they had equal claims, and that
twenty-five thousand pounds would have borne equal
partition very well.

So I broke open the envelope, unfolded the will, and
read:

". . . . . And all the residue of my property, whether
real or personal, I give, bequeath, and devise to G F X D
N W M D Y B D O V J W D M I H T I D Z X Z."

III.

That was the bequest—as clear to the sight as it was
dark to the mind. Had I been mistaken, and had Miss
Molloy been insane after all? If that were so, every

penny of the five-and-twenty thousand pounds would
have to be divided between the Count and the Major as
the husbands of her next of kin. No, surely *that* insanity
was impossible.

I twisted the document up and down, and round and
round. Those letters still obstinately remained as they
were; the alphabet, at any rate, had gone mad, unless it
was I who had gone insane. I needed some evidence of my
own senses, and carried the will straight to my co-
executor, Dr. Kirwan.

"She *was* an odd old lady!" said he at last. "But
I'll bear witness in any court you like that she was as
sane as anybody that ever made a will."

"But what's to be done?"

"Ah, what indeed?   What's the effect of this will, as
it stands?"

"I'm just hanged if I know. The will's otherwise
without a flaw. And in all my practice, and all my
reading too, I never heard of the alphabet's being made a
residuary legatee. I don't like to say, without consideration, that there's no principle a court of equity
would go upon; but I don't know of one. I don't see
even how it would come within the doctrine of *Cy Près*."

"What's that?"

"Why, that when the conditions of a gift can't be
literally carried out, the Court of Chancery will decree
some method conformable to the general object, and
following the intentions of the donor as nearly as
possible."

"Then," said Dr. Kirwan, "I should say the Court
would apply the estate to the foundation of a college for
the study of conundrums. But holloa, Lake, here's
something else dropped out of the envelope; perhaps it's
the answer. It's a letter addressed to you."

That, also, was sealed. When I opened it, I found
only these words:

"*If you are puzzled, lift up the carpet in the drawing-room in the corner between the fireplace and window, under the cheffonier.—B.M.*"

"Aha!" said the doctor. "A cipher, and the key. Let's go at once, and see. But—how would that affect the will?"

"It is a most ridiculous thing to have done," I said, really angry and annoyed. "I wish to Heaven I had known that *that* was what she was up to. I'm afraid there may be trouble."

"Won't a will in cipher be allowed?"

"I hope so. The court of Chancery will rectify a clear mistake or omission in a will, if it is apparent on the face of the will. And even parol evidence will be admitted in case of mistake in the name or description of a legatee. We shall have better than parol evidence in a written key; and the mistake in naming and describing the legatee, whoever he or she may be, by G P X, and so forth, is as apparent on the face of the will as a misdescription can possibly be. The key will, I hope, be evidence enough to show what Miss Molloy intended. But I'm sadly afraid that into Chancery it will have to go, and our friends the Count and the Major will have a few words to say to it if it once gets there. Of anything really wrong I'm not afraid; but of trouble I am. I'll have a good read in Jarman when I get home. But now for the drawing-room corner."

We went together straight to the house of the late Miss Molloy, and, according to our instructions, turned up the carpet in the corner of the drawing-room. Sure enough we found another sealed note addressed to me.

"*Look,*" we read, "*at page* 173 *in the second volume of Gibbon's* "*Decline and Fall.*" *It is on a shelf in the breakfast-room.—B.M.*"

I was too vexed at all this folly and mystification to smile.

"By Jupiter!" exclaimed the doctor, "this accounts for that midnight ramble over her house just before she died. She was writing these notes and hiding them. Poor old lady—it's not an uncommon thing, though, for people on their deathbeds to fancy themselves surrounded by spies and enemies. It isn't lunacy, though, eh?"

"But it's the cause of lunacy in others," grumbled I. "Well, now for Gibbon."

And there, exactly on page 173 of volume ii., was yet a third sealed note for me. And this ran:

"*Key behind wainscoat three inches towards cupboard from dressing-room window.—B. M.*"

"At last!" said I. "I was afraid we were going to be sent up all the chimneys before we'd done."

"By Jupiter, Lake, just think what would have happened if there'd been one link missing; if one of these pillar-to-post notes had been lost or gone out of the way!"

"It's too terrible a chance to talk of. It would have cost one of those young people near twelve hundred a year. Come, here's the dressing-room; let's be quick and have done with the whole thing."

"All right; here's a loose board, just where we were told to go. Come, out with you! Hold a match down, this is rather a dark hole. There—and here's— holloa!"

Dr. Kirwan pulled out a fragment of an envelope to which the red sealing-wax still clung, and on which I could read a part of my own name. There were also some odds and ends of *blank* paper scattered round. We pulled out all that was there. Alas, the fate of the key was only too plainly to be learned from the torn and half-eaten scraps of envelope and note-paper we found.

A scuttering and scrambling behind the wainscoat mocked us with the certainty that the mice had swallowed the Key!

IV.

What was to be done now?   The mice alone knew to whom Miss Bridgita Molloy's money belonged.   Try to realize the circumstances now, as I had to realize them then.   There was a will—a good will—and yet a will of which all the Equity lawyers on earth would be unable to make head or tail.   And not one breath or sign of her intentions had Miss Molloy let fall even to Dr. Kirwan or to me.   And there were the Count and the Major waiting for their prey.

The letters of the alphabet took to waltzing with the multiplication table in my dreams.   I did not know what to do.   I got a box of ivory letters and tried all sorts of anagrams, but could make nothing out of five-and-twenty letters, with only four vowels among them, and with so many z's and x's.   I proved the will in fear and trembling, fully expecting that the question of the soundness of the mind of the testatrix would be immediately raised by one or both of her brothers-in-law, who had of course been made aware of the contents, and were in possession of those letters without meaning.   But, strange to say, no steps were taken whatever.   It was not for a week, at least, after the will had been proved that I received a visit from Steldl the elder, accompanied by a dapper and smartly dressed young man, whom he introduced to me as Mr. Withers, from the office of Withers & King.   I supposed he was the legal adviser of the Steldl claim.

"You shall wonder, Mr. Lake," said the Count, "why I not think Miss Molloy what you call mad woman.   Not at all.   I think of that once; but then that give half the money to that vermin, Fitzgerald O'Birn, who shall lose it in every vile way.   I say it shall be a good will.   I take advice, I; and I demand you pay all what shall be left to my son, Firentz Steldl—"

"Wait a bit," said I. "He has already received his legacy of a thousand pounds."

"Bah! what shall be one thousand pound? He is what you call Residuary Legatee of Miss Molloy."

"I wish he were, with all my heart! But we must go to Chancery. There's nothing else to be done."

"No. He shall not go in Chancery. He shall have his right and his due. I am his father, Monsieur."

"When you can read those confounded letters into Firentz Steldl, I'll pay him every penny with all my heart, and take the consequences; but not a minute before."

"Very good, Mr. Lake. Then I shall read them into Firentz Steldl, and without magic; and then you shall pay. Now, Mr. Withers, if you please."

"Mr. Withers is your solicitor, I presume?"

"I have not the honour," said Mr. Withers glibly, "to be in the profession—in *your* profession, sir, that is to say. We are a firm of professional experts, sir. We practise the science of autography, and we collect and deal in the autograph letters of celebrated historical persons. Naturally our business has occasionally included the branch of cryptography—of the construction and solution of ciphers, which, though requiring a certain special aptitude as well as experience, is not so difficult as laymen might suppose, and is as certain in its results as arithmetic itself—beautifully certain, sir. Our friend Mr. Steldl has applied to me for the missing key of this little puzzle, and it took me barely half an hour's study to find."

"You mean you can read this jumble into sense?" asked I. "You must be a clever fellow, Mr. Withers. How am I to know it isn't guess-work? The correctness of your reading will have to be proved, you see."

"Up to the hilt, sir. The beauty of a cipher, or cryptograph, is that, if you once hit on the right key, it can only mean just that one thing—no doubt, no ambiguity. And as the discovery of the key is a logical process, and as no cipher can possibly have more than one key, why, sir, *solvitur ambulando*—the result is proved by the process, sir; or rather, result and process prove one another."

"Then I must have your process, if you please."

"To be sure. No patent. Anybody can do it. This cipher, sir, is even absurdly simple. Did you ever read the *Gold Bug* of Edgar Allan Poe? No? That's a pity, because I shall have to explain from the beginning. I have rather a contempt for that story—the cipher he makes his hero discover would have been found out by a child in half the time. And this cipher before us is of precisely the same kind—the very simplest form of cipher known."

"Well?"

"A person like Miss Molloy, presumably ignorant of the beautiful science of cryptography, would be almost certain to adopt the plan of making one letter do duty for another. Of course she has left no spaces between her words. Now, you know that the commonest English letter is *e ;* so that, ten to one, the commonest letter in the cipher will represent *e*. That letter is *d*. It comes no fewer than five times in the twenty-five. So, ten to one, *d* stands for *e*. You perceive?"

"At any rate, I follow, so far."

"Very good, sir. Now look at the cipher well, and keep it before your eyes. We'll assume for the moment that *d may* mean *e ;* and if *d* means *e*, it's likely enough *a* would be *b*, *b* would be *c*, and so on, and so on, taking the letter following. Let's try that dodge with *m*, because there's more than one *m*, and because *n* (which it ought to stand for) is a commonish sort of letter. Very well.

Putting *e* for *d* and *n* for *m* and dots for the other letters, we get, . . . *e* . . *ne* . . *e* . . . . *en* . . . . *e* . . . Now, Mr. Lake, the question, as I understand it, is—Did Miss Molloy leave her money to Lucis Bridgita O'Birn, or to Firentz Steldl? Assuming that one of those *e*'s must fall into where the name of the legatee must come, it will strike you at once that there isn't one single *e* in the *lady's* name. It will also strike you that the young gentleman is a *nephew*, and that we've got already *ne*—coming together. Let's chance it. Let's write *nephew* right out, and see if we get sense that way. It'll come like this, putting *p* for *y*, *h* for *b*, *w* for *o :* . . . *e* . . *nephew* . . . *en* . . . . *e* . . . Now, what strikes you next, sir?"

"Nothing whatever, Mr. Withers. Nothing at all."

"No? I'm surprised. Doesn't it strike you that *en* comes in Ferentz ; that the cipher and the name of Steldl both end in a letter between a pair of letters—*zxz : ldl ?* A most remarkable hint, indeed ; for it interferes with no former assumption—*z* would mean *l : x* would mean *d*. Now look how it reads :

. . . *e* . *r nephew f* . *rentz steldl*

Only one thing bothers me. Where the dot comes now in *f* . *rentz* there ought to be a *d* to represent an *e*. In reality there's a *j*. But that's a trifle; doubtless a clerical error. The whole thing's as plain as a pikestaff. Substituting letter for letter, and never mixing them, here you are :

my dear nephew Ferentz Steldl,

and *there* you are !"

I was certainly surprised at the fellow's ingenuity. Except for that missing *e*, the process was without a flaw ; and when we see a logical and faultless process arriving at a probable conclusion, what are we to say? And, by Jove ! Miss Molloy *had made a particular point of spelling Ferentz, Firentz* —with an *i*. Look back at the draft of the will, and see. That was downright proof, if any was needed; the *j* in the cipher, hitherto unaccounted for, would be *i*. The very simple little process had all the air of a miracle to me. I knew nothing then of the far greater marvels wrought by antiquarians in rougher and larger fields, or I should, perhaps, have been less surprised.

"It is read, Monsieur," said Steldl *père*, with a bow.

I was a little sorry for Miss Lucis; but I didn't grudge her cousin his good luck, and I was intensely relieved. I was thinking of the effect of all this as evidence, Steldl was looking at me in dignified triumph, Mr. Withers was regarding his success with artistic pride, when my clerk brought in a card—*Major Fitzgerald O'Birn.*

I thought best to have everything out and over then and there; so, without considering the presence of his brother-in-law and enemy, I had him ushered in.

"Good-dee to ye, Mr. Lake," said he, without deigning to notice, or even to see, Mr. Steldl, who, for his part, threw a double dose of benignity into his smile. "I suppose ye've been wondherin' why I didn't go in for provin' poor Miss Biddy *non compos*—wake in the top, ye know. As if I'd consent to go halves with a dirthy, mane, intriguing baste of a fellow that she'd cut off with a shilling with her own hand! All or none—that's the war-cry of the O'Birns! So I've just dropped in, on my wee, to ask ye for that twenty-five thousand that's due to Lucis, my daughther; and I'll take it hot with—I mane short, if ye plase. Or, if ye haven't it all in your pocket, a thrifle on account'll do for to-dee."

"I'm sorry for Miss O'Birn," said I. "But—she's had her thousand pounds—"

"——Her thousand pounds! I wouldn't give sixpence for a beggarly thousand pounds. 'Tis an insult to spake to a gentleman of such a sum."

"Her thousand pounds, and—I'm afraid—this gentle-

man, Mr. Withers, will explain—there is no longer any
doubt of Miss Molloy's intentions.   Lieutenant Steldl is
residuary legatee."

" An' who's Mr. Withers?   Is it in a conspiracy ye'll
be, with your heads as thick together as pays in one
shell?   Why, 'tis plainer than blazes that *gpx* sthands
for Lucis O'Birn.   What do ye see to that, sir, eh ? "

" I'm afraid it doesn't," said I.

" You're a pretty fellow for a lawyer !   But I suppose
ye'll have to believe what's proved.   Higgins, ye're
wanted ! " shouted he.

He too, it seemed, had brought a friend with him—a
little, pinched, shabby, elderly man, with red squinting
eyes.

" I'll inthrojuce you to me friend Higgins—a gentleman
and a scholar, that'll rade ye off Hebrew into Chinese
for a glass of punch, an' back into Hebrew for two.
Faith, I'd like ye to find a question that Higgins wouldn't
answer ye off-hand.   Says I to him, ' Higgins, what does
gpx spell?'   An' says he, ' Just Lucis O'Birn.' "

A smile of amused contempt came into the face of
smart Mr. Withers.

" An expert? " asked he.

" An' pray who may *you* be, sir ? " asked Major O'Birn.
" D'ye mane to tell me ye haven't heard of Higgins—
that ought to be a docthor of divinity and a member of
Parlimint, and could see ye undher the teeble whenever
ye plase?"   Having thus annihilated Mr. Withers,
" Higgins, do your duty," said he.

" There's nothing in it—nothing in it at all," said Mr.
Higgins, in a queer squeak, and in a shuffling sort of tone.
" What's the difficulty in reading that cipher I am at a
loss to conceive.   Do you mean to tell me that there is
anybody on earth, except Major O'Birn, who has found
the slightest difficulty in reading what couldn't puzzle,
for more than half a second, anybody but a born fool ? "

"You are pleased to be complimentary, Mr. Higgins," said I. "Mr. Withers, as an expert, assures us that a cipher can only be read in one way."

"It didn't want an expert to tell you that," said Mr. Higgins testily. "Of course you can only read a cipher in one way. How can one set of symbols stand for two different sets of words?"

"Then you will agree with Mr. Withers?"

"No doubt. If Mr. Withers has read the cipher he will agree with me. A cipher is made to a particular key, and it can't be fitted with two. When old women make ciphers, they mostly change the letters by counting forwards or backwards. So first I counted one forwards, and made *g* mean *h;* that came to nothing. Then two forwards, and made *g* mean *i;* nothing again. *J*—no. *K*—no. Then I tried the fifth letter forwards—*l*. According to that rule, *g* would be *l: p* would be *u: x* (making *a* follow *z*) would be *c*. Next comes *d*, which would be *i:* then *n*, which would be *s*—the true letter being always the fifth letter from the cipher forwards. Follow it out, gentlemen, and see for yourselves."

I did as he bade me. And the cipher read, letter by letter, as follows, with the peculiar spelling of the name of the testatrix and all:

GPXDN   WMDYBDOV   JWDMI   HT   IDZXZ.
LUCIS   BRIDGITA   OBIRN   MY   NIECE.

There was no more doubt that the cipher was this than it was *My dear nephew, Ferentz Steldl.* It meant both equally, and both at the same time!

I put it to every cryptologist in the world, is it within the bounds of credibility that a cipher of twenty-five letters should be readable in two exactly opposite and inconsistent ways, and that its two irreconcilable solutions should be gained by following two simple principles, both equally obvious and equally sound?   Incredible—nay, impossible! will be the unanimous answer. And yet the impossible, by a marvellous change of coincidences, was effected in that will of Miss Molloy. She could not intentionally have brought about such a result, even if she had tried. The *i* for the *e* in Ferentz, or rather Firentz, left no room for doubt that Withers's solution was true. On the other hand, the peculiar spelling of Bridgita was an unanswerable argument in favour of Mr. Higgins. Withers had started on the principle which has amused so many readers of Edgar Poe, and is in itself a perfectly true and sound one. Higgins had started on the principle favoured by simpletons who correspond in cipher in the agony columns, and imagine that their silly secrets are not open to anybody who takes five minutes' trouble to read them.

What was to be done—now?

Clearly the situation was not realized by either of the fathers of the rival legatees. But a gloom came over the face of Mr. Withers. He took up the paper on which Mr. Higgins had written his solution, and examined it intently.

"No sane woman would have used such a simple cipher as that," said he. "It is just the solution that would satisfy an amateur."

"True," said Mr. Higgins, with a slight sneer. "Jurymen are in the position of amateurs, I believe, and judges too."

"A cipher can't have two solutions," said Mr. Withers, throwing the paper down.

"True again," said Mr. Higgins. "Happily for Miss O'Birn."

"Have you studied cryptology as a science, Mr. Higgins?" asked Mr. Withers, with a wild effort at elaborate courtesy.

"I'm not such an ass," said Mr. Higgins, with no pretence of courtesy at all. "I'd as soon set up a science of handwriting as a science of whims."

"You are insulting, sir! There *is* a science of handwriting—ay, and of character in handwriting; and I shouldn't like to write like you, judging from what it's like to be."

"I always make it a point of insulting quacks and humbugs," said Mr. Higgins. "It's the first duty of man. I've read that cipher in the way that would satisfy anybody but an expert, and there's an end."

"Whom do you call quack, sir? Let me tell you that when a man deliberately insults my science, I—I—feel it my duty to knock him down."

"Gentlemen—gentlemen!" I cried out, "you have both been very clever—a great deal too clever for me. I would gladly have accepted either of your readings, Heaven knows. But I can't accept both; and both your reasons are so admirable that I can't accept either. And what's worse, it's your arguments, not your assertions, that will have to go into Chancery; and into Chancery we must all go. Yes, there's no help for it now; and, once in, Heaven alone knows when we shall get out again."

"I object to the law on principle; I shall have nothing to do with law," said Steldl; and I have no doubt but he had excellent reasons for the only principle I ever heard of his having. "I bring my expert; you are satisfied. I demand twenty-five thousand pounds for my son."

"I despise the law," shouted the Major. "An Irish gentleman doesn't mix up with pettifogging rascals. I wouldn't touch the dirthy thing with the end of an old boot. 'Tis as clear as day—Lucis Bridgita O'Birn."

"It must be compromise, or—Chancery," said I. "Have it as you will."

"Compromise—with *him?*" said Steldl, pointing to

the Major with his thumb. "Not one penny shall he rob my son."

"Compromise—with a Steldl?" said the Major, in his turn. "Maybe with old Nick I would; for old Nick's a gentleman," added he.

And there was the deadest lock I ever heard of since I was born! No Lord Chancellor ever drew up a will that more clearly meant two opposite and irreconcilable things.

And here, alas, is the end of this story, so far as I am concerned. I say alas in the conventional spirit of a lawyer (as he is supposed to be); for students of knotty points of Equity may search the Chancery reports in vain for any case bearing the name of Molloy, Lake, Steldl, or O'Birn. The effect of a will written in a cipher which can be read in two ways remains undecided to the present hour; and will, unless things repeat themselves in the most incredible way, remain undecided for evermore. The united wisdom of the House of Lords—for it must have got even there at last—was never occupied with investigating the secret thoughts of Miss Molloy.

I really regret, sometimes—quite independently of the advantage that would have accrued to my own banking account—that I did not, in the interests of the profession, apply to the Court instantly on behalf of myself and my co-executor. A certainly utterly ridiculous unwillingness to throw Miss Molloy's property into the very Maelstrom of litigation led me to put off the evil day as long as possible. For I could not help remembering that if, by any chance, the will should at last be set aside altogether for want of anybody's having brains enough to make head or tail of it, or for want of inherent perspicuity, or for any other sufficient reason, the Count and the Major must divide as next of kin, in right of their wives. And that would be worse for the property than a hundred

Chanceries of the good old Eldon days. They, in their determination to have all or nothing, were no more eager to push matters to an extremity than I. And so, I verily believe, should we have been standing at this triangular deadlock at the present hour, had not the delay itself brought about a most natural solution in the most natural way in the world. "When in doubt, do nothing," I constantly find to be the wisest maxim that ever was made.

My relief, at the time, hardly equalled my surprise. But, considering that Mrs. Steldl and Mrs. O'Birn had never quarrelled—considering that they had met again—considering what sort of young people their son and their daughter were—I must own that I was an ass to feel surprised on learning of the marriage of Lieutenant Steldl to Lucis Bridgita O'Birn. The history of the Montagues and the Capulets does not stand alone in the effect of the feuds of the old upon the hearts of the young. But this is no part of my story. Enough that *her* claims became *his*, while *his* remained his own—and therefore *her* own, too. And if two elderly rascals were kept in somewhat disreputable clover for the rest of their days, and if two executors were content to run a little safe risk in making things comfortable all round for everybody, themselves included, and if two cryptologists remained irreconcilable foes, and if two young people became happy in their own peculiar way, and if the Court was deprived of a big cause, and the profession of the bulk of the property of Miss Molloy—well, the fault is mainly my own. I profess only to tell the story, not to solve the mystery, of Miss Molloy's most Remarkable Will.

A CIRCUMSTANTIAL PUZZLE.

I.

THE almost insuperable difficulty of telling a story with
even a grain of truth in it is this—or, I should rather
say, the two insuperable difficulties are these : firstly,
there is never the faintest dramatic point about really
true stories ; secondly, if they are worth telling at all,
they are almost always incredible.   And the truer they
are, the more pointless and the more incredible they are.
The story I am going to tell is neither dramatic nor
probable.   And yet it seems to me worth telling—
independently of its inherent curiosity—as an instance
of those extraordinary freaks of psychology which now
and again throw out of gear altogether the every-day
experience of practical men, among whom I have some
claim to be reckoned.   It has also a yet more important
bearing upon the manner of making delicate investigations
which, if I remember to do so, I may perhaps take
occasion to point out before I have done.   As when I
sent you my last contribution to your museum of professional curiosities, I will merge my own proper
personality in that of my informant, the solicitor who
played so leading and, for a time, so uncomfortable a
part in the affair.   For all purposes it is more convenient
to translate " he " into " I," when one is telling another
man's story.   Indeed, it is almost essential to the process
of telling the tale as it was told to me.

I, then, early one forenoon, received a visit from my very best client, Mr. John Buller.

Mr. John Buller was a gentleman who, still hardly past the prime of life, had made a considerable fortune as a builder and contractor. Altogether there must have been something out of the common about him, for he had become the wealthy man he certainly was seemingly in defiance of all established precedents and rules. He was not what is commonly—and often very mistakenly— called a "good man of business;" he always had more irons in the fire than he could possibly attend to person- ally, or even superintend generally, and he placed such implicit trust in all who served him or dealt with him as to amount to credulity. Nevertheless, I am by no means sure myself of its being really singular that his many irons should have taken excellent care of themselves, and that he very rarely indeed, at least to my knowledge, found himself seriously deceived. I need hardly say that, like all men of such a temper, to be found out in deceiving him in the smallest trifle was to lose his confidence irrevocably and for ever; so that not only were moderately honour- able men put upon their honour to an unusual degree in their relations towards one who trusted them so com- pletely, but the dishonourable were by experience taught to fear injuring one from whom everything was to be gained but pardon. He certainly was not one of those who hold that in business a man should have no enemies and no friends. All men were his friends until, as some- times would happen, they became his enemies. And yet one might know him for years without suspecting that he had any sort of temper at all. Doubtless it was the consciousness on his own part of having one, and the suspicion that it might be a weakness or a failing, that made him seem needlessly hard and reserved. On the whole, I incline to ascribe his success in life less to courage and over-confidence than to a yet more un-business-like habit of always doing his work a little better than his contract required. I would pay ten per cent. higher rent, any day, to live in a house that I knew to have been built by John Buller. I should know that everything about that house was better than it seemed. And that is the chief reason why I set out by speaking of him as a gentleman. For he had risen from the lower rounds of the ladder, and, so far as he might be called a diamond, was decidedly an unpolished one. He was, I believe, a seriously religious man; he was an unquestionably generous and charitable one; not highly educated, but with plenty of intelligence and openness of mind. I should add that he had never been married; was without known relations; and lived alone in thoroughly respectable comfort, without pretence of any kind. The nature of his business, by no means confined to the limits of the northern town where we both lived, took him about a great deal, and no doubt largely helped him to do without much society at home. For that matter, he was, socially speaking, above one-half the place and below the other; so, though universally respected, he must, on the whole, have lived almost too much alone. But in this matter, as in all things, habit is everything; and so busy a man had little time to feel dull.

"Mr. Standish," he began, in the broad north-country speech, which I shall make no pretence of reproducing, "something mortal queer has happened, that I can't make head or tail o'. It's not the money's-worth, though fifty pound is fifty pound; but—Look here!"

"Your cheque for fifty pounds, cashed by the Redport branch of the County Bank, and returned to you in the regular course. Well, what's wrong?"

"Do you see anything queer about that cheque, Mr. Standish—anything out of the way?"

"No. It's drawn to yourself or order by yourself;

endorsed by you; and nothing wrong about date or anything else that I can see."

"And if you'd been a clerk at Redport, you'd have
cashed that over the counter without any bones?"

"Of course I should; as I suppose from this you have
an account there."

"And that's just what was done, then. And all the
same, that cheque was no more filled up, nor signed, nor
backed by me than it was by you."

"You mean to say it's forged? By Jove, that's a
serious thing! Do you mean to say that some rascal has
been clever enough to fill up and sign a whole cheque in
your handwriting, even down to the least turn of the
smallest stroke of the pen? I'd have sworn to this being
your own handwriting before a jury."

"Ay, Mr. Standish; and so would I, if I didn't know.
But I do know; and that's no more my cheque than it's
yours. And I'm hanged if I know what to do."

"You've seen the bank manager here? What does he
say?"

"No, I haven't. I haven't seen a soul; and what's
more, I don't mean to, unless I'm driven. And it's to
get out of being driven I'm come to you. This cheque
isn't the first of 'em, Mr. Standish—no, nor the second,
nor yet the third. There's four cheques of fifty pounds
apiece; and I've not drawn one!"

"And you haven't found it out till now?"

"I've found out nothing, Mr. Standish, mark that—
not one word. Nothing's found out till it's proved. I
want to know what I can do."

That premature question was the only sign of precipi-
tancy or impatience I had ever seen in John Buller. I
began to see that he was disturbed by something beyond
the loss, to himself or the bank, of two hundred pounds,
or by the always detestable necessity of being mixed up
in what looked like a criminal matter. So I made no

answer, which is always the best way of getting quickly at the bottom of a story.

" I'm putting up the new row of villas on the esplanade at Redport," said he. " It's a biggish job in a small way, and it's very much on my own account ; and what with the hands, and one thing and another, there's a goodish lot of cash floating about from week to week—going out, anyhow, though of course none to speak of coming in. So, to save a lot of bother, I've had for some time an account with the branch at Redport. You don't know the place, I believe?"

" I've never been over there yet; but I must run over some day, when I can get a holiday. Well?"

" It's been main through me that the place has got on well enough to make it worth the Bank's while to have a branch there; and if I was to draw for five times what's to my credit, I don't suppose they'd make any bother, looking to my credit at the main branch here. So this game might go on any time before I heard I'd overdrawn. As far as I'm concerned, a cheque on the branch at Redport's much the same as one on the bank here."

" Well?"

" You see, though that job's middling big, I've got too many bigger on hand to bother in person with Redport. It's two months since I've been near the place, and may, be it'll be another month before I can get over there again. So I've got a clerk of the works in an office in one of the villas, and he comes over to me here every Friday to report and take any new orders, and I give him cheques on the Redport branch for what's wanted— he brings me his accounts and vouchers, of course, and I settle that way whatever has to be paid running. And some of the cheques I receive I send over by him to be paid in there."

" Excuse me," said I, " but doesn't this seem rather a loose and rough way of doing things? In the first place,

I don't see why you should make any payments through the Redport branch at all; and certainly I don't see how all this concerns these forgeries."

" I'll tell you why I do it, and how it concerns these—Forgeries, too.   I want to keep as much cash knocking about in Redport as I can, and to keep as little from going out; that's the way to push a new place on.   And, for the same reason, I don't want those branch clerks to find they've got too little to do.   My clerk comes to me at four o'clock every Friday afternoon.   First of all, I give him a cheque for the men's week's wages.   Then we go through the accounts, and for any that I want to settle off-hand I either draw separate cheques in favour of the different parties, or else I give him another lump cheque for him to cash and pay out in gold.   In fact, there's all sorts of things to be paid in all sorts of ways.   If the account seems running low, it's easier for me to pay in a few cheques than to bother the bank here.   Anyhow, it saves me a bushel of bother, and don't oblige me to give more than an hour a week to Redport—and even an hour's too much at times."

" Just tell me precisely everything that happens, please. We're rather vague, where we are.   He comes to you at four every Friday, and you give him all these cheques—whatever he asks for—and then he goes back at once to Redport by rail ? "

John Buller glanced at me sharply.   By those words " whatever he asks for " I had trodden upon what is always the most sensitive of an over-trustful man's corns: I had hinted at the want of worldly prudence which such a man, far more than any other, hates to be suspected of lacking.

" I'm not quite a born fool," said he.   " We go through the accounts, and he stays for supper and a bed.   By breakfast-time next morning I've found a half hour to examine the accounts and to write the cheques.   I give him the whole lot in a leather case, and he goes back to Redport; and it's his duty, before he goes to the office, to go to the Redport Bank and pay in and draw out whatever's required."

I did not see how this made matters any better from a prudential point of view; but I did not venture again upon what I felt to be rather dangerous ground.

"Then all your transactions with the branch bank at Redport," I asked, "are confined to ten o'clock on Saturday morning? *This* cheque is stamped as cashed on the 15th, which *would* be a Saturday. Of course we shall learn from your pass-book, or from the cheques themselves, if that was so with the others. If so, the false cheques must either have been presented together with the others, or by somebody who knew your system. Also, it is clear they were drawn, judging from this, by somebody who had exceptional means of knowing your handwriting, and of practising it at leisure—and, if I may say so, how little likely you were, with such a system of business as yours, to detect fraud very soon. Also, by somebody to whom your cheque-book was accessible, in one way or another. Are these cheques taken from your cheque-book, or can the thief have got hold of some other?"

I could see that John Buller began to look strangely troubled.

"From mine!" said he, in a curiously defiant tone.

"And the counterfoils? Cut out, I suppose? That's the usual way."

"No; every man Jack filled up in a way that would take the very devil in. And yet, Mr. Standish, those cheques are no more my drawing than they're yours. I keep a private account of every cheque I draw; and it stands to reason that when four cheques that you know you didn't draw are alone missing out of an account of fifty that you know you *did* draw, then you can't be mistaken. That's as clear as day."

"All right, Mr. Buller; it *is* as clear as day. And though criminal business is very much out of my line, we'll have that forger beyond the seas in, comparatively speaking, the twinkling of an eye. What's the fellow's name?"

"His name? And how the deuce, sir, should *I* know his name?"

"Not know the name of your own clerk of the works at Redport? By Jove, Mr. Buller, I *shall* begin to think you a queer sort of a business man!"

"We're at crooked answers, Mr. Standish, it seems to me," he said, wiping his forehead hard, though the weather was unusually cold. "My clerk at Redport is Adam Brown."

"Then it's lucky Mr. Adam Brown didn't live when forgers were hanged," said I. "You won't be able to recover from the bank, I'm afraid; such forgeries as those defy even extraordinary care to detect them. A bank-clerk is expected to be a great deal; but nobody expects him to be a conjurer. But"—

To my amazement, John Buller sprang up in a towering rage.

"And you—you dare to hint that—that—that poor lad, who's as honest as the day, would steal one farthing from me—a young man I'd trust with untold gold—the orphan of the best woman that ever touched God's earth! I won't hear it, sir! I didn't come to *you* to hear slander against *her* son, that I've looked after for *her* sake, and who'd no more touch a farthing rushlight that belonged to me than you would yourself, sir! If there's one man who's as guiltless as the babe unborn, it's Adam Brown!"

"I honour your confidence in your *employés*, sir," said I. "Trust makes Trustworthy nine times out of ten. But look here. Here is a man whom you trust implicitly on your own showing. There is your cheque-book for one night every week under the same roof with him, the place where you keep it probably known to him. That man knows your writing, and how you fill up your cheques and your counterfoils. That man transacts *all* your business with the bank at Redport. That man, it seems, may account to you or not account to you just in what form he will. Nobody else in your employ seems open to suspicion; no stranger could act in such a way without instant detection. Think what any jury would say to such a state of things. We've as yet got no direct proof; but, with such circumstantial evidence to start with, direct proof is absolutely sure to come. Why, he might hope to carry on such a game as that safely for many years; at any rate, till he had restored what he had taken, as all those young rascals always 'mean' to do some day when some impossible horse wins some impossible Derby. And I'm afraid, previous good character in such cases always goes against a man. It doubles the guilt of his downfall, and is, indeed, the very means and cause of his being able to fall. Adam Brown is the man."

John Buller's anger passed suddenly, as if ashamed of itself; and there was no mistaking the profound grief and distress of the tone in which he answered me.

"You'll excuse me," said he. "It was because I saw all this just as well as you do that I came here, hoping you, as a practical and unprejudiced man, would help me to see t'other side of things. And I was disappointed you didn't, and that was what made me fly. Don't you go to mistake me for being any softer than my neighbours. If you can prove to me the man who's been tampering with my cheque-book is Adam Brown, I'll treat him like a viper, Mr. Standish—that I will! I'd sooner cut my own throat than throw a crust to my own son, if I had one, if I couldn't trust him as my own right hand. And, if you'll believe it, sir, Adam Brown has been more to me than if he was my own son. For he's the orphan boy of the only woman I ever wanted to marry, or ever shall. I don't suspect him for one moment—not I. But for that very reason I want you to show me how to put him above the suspicion of any outside man, such as you. Take my word for it, it's not Adam Brown. If it was, I'd have done his business for him pretty quick, without bothering myself to come to you. But make as if I thought it was : you prove the innocence of an innocent lad, and, by Jingo, you'll take off my mind the biggest load of bricks that ever was on."

The speech was inconsistent enough. But one thing was plain from it—John Buller was determined to disbelieve the clear evidence of his own reason. He had not come to me to find out a thief, but to get me to prove to his own satisfaction that the thief was an innocent man ; and, at the same time, to acquit him in his own eyes of intentional self-deception. He knew how he would have to act if he found his trust deceived, and the severity which he thought his duty in such cases frightened him, lest he should feel compelled to exercise it towards Adam Brown. I could not help smiling at the openness of the workings of his mind, or being touched by them, too. I had never suspected my substantial client of having been the victim of a romance since I had first gone down from London to Carcester.

"Then," I asked again, a little hypocritically, "you are convinced in your own mind, from your previous knowledge of his character, that Adam Brown is *not* the man?"

"I'm just as certain he's not as that I stand here. And, more for his sake than my own, I mean to know who *is* the man."

"Have you spoken about it to Adam Brown?"

"Not I. I'd as soon speak to you, Mr. Standish, on the supposition that it might have been *you*."

"Very good. If Adam Brown—"

"*If*, sir?"

"Since Adam Brown is innocent, we can very soon put him beyond the reach of any sort of suspicion, and without bringing the people at the bank into the affair—at least, not in any way that would make them think anything was seriously wrong in any particular direction. In the first place, arrange with them, both here and at Redport, not to cash any cheque of yours not bearing a certain private mark (which you will keep secret from all your *employés*) without forthwith advertising you of the person by whom it was presented. This will have the effect of narrowing matters very considerably. What had better be done farther I think we will wait and see."

"You quite understand, Mr. Standish, that whatever you do will find out who was the real man—not young Adam Brown? I—I doubt if I quite like to do that about the private mark after all. It seems a bit mean-like to my mind."

"It's the best way of clearing Adam Brown if—since he's innocent, it seems to me," said I.

"You think that? Well, you're right, I suppose. And, by Jingo, as he is innocent why should I be afraid? If he wasn't—if I wasn't as sure of it as I'm alive—but it can't be! I'd sooner doubt my own right hand! I will. I'll settle about the private mark this very day."

Of course I had not the faintest doubt in my own mind about the identity of this ingenious and systematic forger with Mr. Adam Brown. I had already given my reasons to John Buller; and they are so perfectly obvious, under all the circumstances, that I need not repeat them here. I could quite understand why John Buller, since he had a more than common interest in his clerk of the works at Redport, should be very anxious to be convinced that his belief in the latter's innocence was not inconsistent with the common sense proper to a shrewd man of the world, whose pride in never being " done " in always the greater in proportion as it is unjustified. Men who are really sharp and shrewd know too well that they are always and inevitably being " done " to bother their heads about their share in a universal doom.

I knew Adam Brown pretty well by sight, and a little by reputation. He was a good-looking, pleasant young fellow, certainly too young for his over-responsible place in John Buller's service, but well up to his work, and very popular with the young men of his own class in Carcester. His father had been an unsuccessful commission agent, and, as I had to-day learned for the first time, the successful rival in love of John Buller. I must leave it to others wholly to understand why the beaten suitor, whom nobody suspected of having a grain of sentiment in his composition, should have made himself a second father to this young man—in a reserved and wholly undemonstrative way, that is; for I feel certain now that Adam Brown looked upon himself simply as an ordinary *employé*, and did not fancy that the place he held in John Buller's business was due to the place in John Buller's heart of his dead mother. I daresay that little romance might prove worth writing for its own sake in the hands of a sentimental author. But this story is *not* a sentimental one.

So I was really rather sorry that circumstances pointed so clearly to Adam Brown as the guilty man, though of course I felt also that John Buller's eyes ought to be opened, and that such ungrateful crime ought to be punished as openly and as richly as it deserved. I had not the least intention of helping my client to persuade himself of the innocence of a guilty man. On the contrary, I fully meant to expose the young rascal before he could do worse harm; and for that purpose the plan of privately-marked cheques seemed the best that, upon the spur of the moment, I could hit on. It would satisfy John Buller by avoiding immediate scandal, and no doubt convict the forger just as well as any more open way.

But the explosion was to come more sharply and swiftly than I had planned.

On the following Saturday morning the spirit moved me to take John Buller's house on my way to my own office, for I was not particularly busy at the moment. I thought it advisable to see with my own eyes something of that curious weekly despatch of cheques and bills to Redport, and I wanted also to make more particular acquaintance with the physiognomy of Mr. Adam Brown. I believed in physiognomy in those days. I need hardly say that I no longer now do anything of the kind, beyond knowing when a man eats too much and drinks too often. I have seen such saintly faces in the dock, and men on whom Nature has stamped blackguard, or even murderer, have been among the best whom she has made. Adam Brown, who had finished his breakfast and was just on the eve of starting for Redport, fell into neither of these extreme classes, and might easily have belonged to either side of the broad band between them where good is inextricably and undecipherably mixed up and often confused with harm. As I have said, he was young and good-looking; and he had a good face too, like a lad's who comes of good people and has been brought up well. And, what was better, it was not a weak one, nor a stupid one. But, at the same time, it wasn't a happy one, and gloomy rather than merely grave. His eyes, instead of looking bright or open, as a young man's should always be in the morning, were dull and red, as if he had either slept but little or were in the habit of taking something stronger than tea or coffee for breakfast when at home in his Redport lodgings. In such cases, the eye and the hand are one; and his hand was not quite so steady as he held out his hand for the leather cheque-case, so I thought at least, as it ought to have been.

"I've only dropped in to see if you've made your arrangements about marking to-day's cheques," said I, as soon as Adam Brown had closed the street-door. "You've found nothing new, I suppose?"

"No. I wish to Heaven the thing was out and over; it worries me more than I try to say. There's nothing so horrible as having somebody about that you can't trust and you don't know who. And you're a married man, Standish; you don't know what it means to swallow all your own worries yourself, with nobody to give the least bit of 'em to. But—holloa! Hi, Adam!" he called out, throwing up the window and calling down the street. "Just to show you how things bother me," he said to me, "I've left out of the case just the very cheque from Archer & Company that I wanted to have paid in at Redport this very day. Hi, Adam! Ah, here you are! I was afraid you were out of earshot; but you're in lots of time for the train. There's something I wanted to say to you, and Mr. Standish coming in just now—"

There was nothing in the sudden recall, however unusual, to frighten an honest man. But I could not mistake my eyes—there are some cases in which we can't help reading faces, ay, and in believing what we read. If ever fright turned a man's face red and pale, it turned Adam Brown's now.

"Here's a cheque of Archer's," said John Buller, noticing nothing, "that I want paid in at Redport this morning, and I forgot it when Mr. Standish came in. Put it in the case with the others. Here it is. Three hundred and eighty-eight pounds nine."

Adam Brown held out his hand for the cheque; but a sudden inspiration, prompted by the young man's unmistakable confusion, made me say,

"Yes; there's plenty of time for the train, but not for me. There's something I must say to you, Mr. Buller, before I go on to the office, and I've only allowed myself a minute to spare. Would you mind leaving us alone for one minute, Mr. Brown? You can leave the case here; Mr. Buller can put in the cheque while he's listening to me to save time."

I watched the young man while I spoke, and what I saw made me feel more sure than ever. I held out my hand for the case, to pass it to John Buller, and felt Adam's fingers tremble as they touched mine. And yet not a word had been said that could alarm a perfectly innocent man, who has no secrets from his employer or even from his employer's attorney.

"Wait a bit," I said to John Buller, as soon as Adam had left the room. "Before putting in that cheque, just see if the others are as they ought to be."

"The others? Of course they are. What do you mean?"

"Why, as you made one mistake, you might by chance have made another, you know. Well, while you're over-hauling, I only just wanted to say—"

There was nothing I wanted to say, but I had no need to think of a pretext. I had my eye on John Buller, and before "say" was off my lips—

"Good God!" cried he. "Look here! Brown!" he shouted, "Adam Brown—"

"Don't frighten him," said I, rising and opening the door, knowing what John Buller had found in the case as well as if I had seen it with my very eyes. "Mr. Brown, you may come in now."

He came in, as a detected criminal comes before a judge, trembling and pale. I wondered he had been able to remain in the hall all alone for that terrible moment, during which, as he must have known, he was being tried, found guilty, and condemned.

To my surprise, John Buller, whom I had thought in the first stage of a passion, sat still, in front of his detected clerk, without a word. But I should not like to have been in Adam Brown's shoes during that silent pause. There was no sign or thought of anger in the long look of mingled sorrow and scorn—more of sorrow than of scorn—with which John Buller regarded the young man to whom he had tried to be a second father. I had done my duty, I suppose; but I could not help pitying both, and I know whom I pitied the most of the two. It was not the younger man.

I looked steadfastly at the fifth forged cheque for fifty pounds which John Buller had found, just as I had expected, in the leather case, and the preparation of which was quite enough to account for the sleepless look of the young man's eyes. It seemed to me that the imitation was even better than before.

"Adam Brown," said John Buller at last, in a voice full of sadness, and yet of the double pathos which comes alone from more dignified firmness than I should have expected from such a man,—"Adam Brown, I know well enough that you see your deceit discovered, and I won't add to your wrong-doing by tempting you to tell a lie. I knew your mother—long ago—and for her sake I first gave you work, and bread to work for. But it was for your own sake I trusted you, even as she might have trusted me; and the end is that I shall never be able to trust man, woman, or child again. That is the injury *you* have done to *me*; and there's none greater that man can do man. I fought hard against the belief of my own eyes—for weeks I've fought against it; but I know now. Don't be afraid. I'm not going to have you—your mother's son—put in the dock as a felon. But there's nothing I can do *for* a man—a boy—that—that—Go; and never cross my path again."

The culprit tried to lift his eyes, but failed.

"Sir," he began, "I do not defend—I do not excuse—I never intended—"

"I am sorry for myself. Do not make me despise *you*.

A man does as he intends. I'm wrong not to prosecute you; it's what I should do to any other man who did as —as you have done. Go. I give you the chance to redeem yourself, if you can; but not with me. Go."

Without one attempt to defend or excuse his guilt, far less to deny it, the young man was gone.

"I do *not* thank you for this, Mr. Standish," said John Buller. The tears came into his voice as he turned away.

II.

The more I thought things over, the less displeased I was with myself for the way in which they had gone. The more anybody thinks about it, the more finished a rogue, in spite of his years, will Adam Brown appear to be. His plan was as clear as daylight now. Obviously, he had easily found where his employer kept his cheque-book for the bank at Redport, and spent the better part of Friday night in filling up one of its forms, and manipulating the counterfoil so as to produce an exact facsimile of a cheque drawn and signed by John Buller. On my life, I believe he might, so perfect was his process, have got a jury to acquit him on the ground that some strange accident must have been his enemy, and that the cheque was really John Buller's after all; for the best men of business may be guilty of mistake or error now and then. Yes, but then you see that defence would not have done after all, seeing that here was the sixth cheque forged in six weeks; and that John Buller not only had never had occasion to draw these, and knew he never had drawn them, but had kept a perfectly complete and accurate account, inaccurate in no slightest particular, of all he had had occasion to draw and remembered drawing.

Mistake—if the reader will think for one instant—was thus rendered absolutely impossible. And not only was the matter clenched now by conduct on Adam Brown's part amounting to confession, without so much as an appeal for mercy, but *every cheque in the case bore the private mark except this alone.* And the packet had been in no hands but those of Adam Brown.

Of course it was natural that John Buller, like all men of his temper when they met with such every-day things as ingratitude and breach of trust, should feel misan-thropical, and as if confidence in his fellow-creatures was henceforth dead in him. But very few men indeed are Timons. We mostly return to our original nature: instinctive trust is happily a fine hardy growth that requires a great deal of killing. In a little while, no doubt, John Buller would trust the next stranger rather more implicitly than if he had been his own brother, and be all the better for being rid of such an exceptionally clever rogue, a man with a positive genius for forgery, as his ex-clerk of the works at Redport. Perhaps, even, his experience would have a wholesome effect upon him by teaching him that the son of a woman we have loved in our youth is not, solely for that rather sentimental reason, bound to be better than all other sons of Eve in general. Young men who have had mothers have also had fathers; and Mr. Brown, the commission agent, had not borne altogether the highest of characters while alive.

I did not see, or hear from, John Buller for the next few days; which was rather singular, as he nearly always had a good deal of business on hand which required the help of a solicitor, and as two or three important agreements to which he was party were just then passing through my hands. But I heard in various incidental ways of young Brown. A clerk of mine was an acquaintance of his; and he told me—without knowing any of the circumstances—that Brown had suddenly left John Buller and had gone up to London to find another situation; which, without any sort of character (for John Buller was incapable of giving a false or even a misleading one to anybody), I imagined he would find it hard to do, except as active partner in a firm of forgers. From another source I heard he had had a fortune left him, and was going to live on a fine estate in the country. Anyhow, he left both Redport and Carcester without leaving behind him a guess as to the true reason of his departure.

It was not, indeed, till the following Friday afternoon that I next received a visit from John Buller. I thought him looking fagged and harassed, and I told him so.

"I'm afraid you keep too many irons in the fire," said I.

"Not a bit of it. One keeps the other warm. If you was as much by yourself as I am, you'd want a bit more work than you could manage, just to keep you and yourself from quarrelling."

"Have you heard anything more of young Brown?"

"Young Who?"

"Young Brown."

"I've forgotten his name. And you won't remind me of it, if you and me's to keep friends. There's no such name. Talking of not looking well—it's you that don't look yourself, it seems to me. You want a day's holiday, and I've looked in to ask you to be so kind as to take one."

"You're very kind, I'm sure; but—"

"'But' be hanged! Look here, Mr. Standish. To-day's Friday; and there's the usual business of paying in and drawing out to be done over at Redport to-morrow. I can't do it myself, as I've got to be in three other places at once by the first train; and I'm not such an ass as to trust any of my people here with the value of sevenpence-halfpenny. Once bit, twice shy. I've done with trusting for the rest of *my* days. At the rate of fifty pound a week, it don't pay. You've never been over at Redport; and, though I say it that shouldn't, the place is worth seeing, as a specimen of what places can be made to grow. You take a day's run over there to-morrow—you and Mrs. Standish too. I'll give you a pass on the line, and telegraph to the Star to treat you like princes and princesses. All you'll have to do will be to hand my cheque-case over the bank-counter, which won't take you two minutes, or fifty yards out of your way to the new pier; and then you can make a Saturday-to-Monday of it, if you please. I want you to see Redport before it grows out of all knowing. Say yes, and I'll have the cheques and things ready for you to pick up at my house on your way to the train."

I was not particularly anxious for a holiday; and certainly no wish to spend one *en prince* at the Star. But, at the same time, I had no sort of objection to an idle day, and it was almost necessary, as a matter of business, to see the neighbouring town which was becoming every day more and more an office word. So, though more to please my best client than for any other reason, I agreed, only bargaining that I should be left free from the special attentions of the Star. John Buller thanked me for my promise to go as if I had done him some extraordinary favour.

. "Well, if you won't let me telegraph, when you do ask for lunch at the Star, mention my name. You won't see much going on in the building line just now; one of the things I've got to be away for to-morrow is to get another scoundrel—till *he's* found out, like the rest of 'em—in the place of poor young—of that young blackguard whose name I'll never remember again, if I live for a thousand years."

Now I don't want to have it supposed for a moment

that my going over to Redport alone—that is to say, without my wife—was due to any fault or neglect of mine. If I could have foreseen that my day of idleness was to be one of solitude also, I should probably not quite so readily have consented to take a holiday. As it happened, however, I found, when I got home from the office, that Mrs. Standish had almost that very moment received an urgent summons to the sick-bed of her sister, who lived at the other end of England, which obliged her to take the very next train from Carcester and to travel all night through. Naturally, until I had seen her off, I did not think again of my promised visit to Redport. So, as it was too late to back out of going, I decided to run over in the morning, do my business at the bank, and get back as early in the afternoon as the then infrequent trains between Redport and Carcester allowed.

So next morning, having told my clerks to close the office at the usual hour, which on Saturday was always an early one, I went to John Buller's house, and from his hands received the cheque-case which he had ready for me. Knowing his feelings about the matter, I refrained from making any sort of allusion to it, and even made a point, while receiving the case, of speaking carelessly about indifferent things. I put the case, otherwise untouched, in my breast-pocket, and there it remained till I reached the counter of the bank at Redport.

"Where's Mr. Brown?" asked the clerk, as he took the leather case. "It doesn't seem like Saturday morning without seeing Brown."

"He's away just at present," said I. "Mr. Buller asked me to give you this. All right, I suppose?"

There was no need to lessen my dignity in Redport as Mr. Buller's legal adviser, or to give Adam Brown the reputation he deserved, by explaining why I was doing the work of a builder's clerk and messenger on this occasion.

"All right," said the clerk, turning over the cheques and duly noticing whether they were properly endorsed, and so on. "Quite right. By the way, there's a message or something the manager wants to send to Mr. Buller, I believe. I was to tell Brown so when he called. I suppose you'll do just the same?"

"I can take any message for Mr. Buller," said I. "Anyhow, I shall be seeing him on Monday if that will do."

"I daresay it will. Would you mind stepping this way?"

I followed the clerk into an inner room, where I for the first time met the manager of the Redport branch of the County Bank, hitherto known to me as Mr. George Richards by name only. We bowed, and he offered me a seat politely.

"You are my friend Mr. Buller's new clerk of the works, I presume?" asked he.

"No," said I. "I have no business in Redport, except to cash and pay in these papers for Mr. Buller, while passing by. But if there is any message I can give him—"

"I don't know. You are not leaving Redport immediately, I suppose?"

"Well, as to that, I am. In fact, by the very next train."

"By the next train? H'm!" Mr. Richards was a very young man for his place, and I began to fancy there was something I did not like in his manner. "Going back to Carcester anyhow, I suppose?" he asked again.

"Yes," I answered shortly. "And I believe the train starts in half an hour. So if you can tell me what you want said to Mr. Buller I shall be glad, as I haven't much time to lose."

"Yes—of course—certainly. But there is a little

matter: would you mind telling me if you received these cheques straight from Mr. Buller?"

"Certainly I did. Is there anything wrong?"

"You received them just as they are now?"

"Exactly as they are now. What is it, Mr. Richards? I am really in a hurry—"

"I'm very sorry. But you see, I am in a responsible position, and one can't be too careful in these days. I have already sent a messenger to telegraph to Mr. Buller; would you mind waiting here till he comes?"

"The messenger?"

"No, till Mr. Buller can come over. I daresay it is all right, but—"

"But I can't wait, Mr. Richards. May I ask you what you mean? I can tell you that Mr. Buller is not in Carcester, and will not get your telegram till Monday, if then."

"That's awkward, by Jove, if it *is* so. But that we shall see."

"But meanwhile I must wish you good-day. If there's anything wrong you must settle it with Mr. Buller. I can't wait now."

"No? Well, then, Mr.—Mr.—I must frankly tell you that I must ask you to wait, even if it's till Monday, till Mr. Buller can come over here. It's an awkward situation I'm placed in, but—and I daresay Mr. Buller is *not* at Carcester, as you say; but—well: whether you're— it's all right or all wrong, you see, it's in you own interest that I must ask you to remain. You see here's a cheque here that I daren't cash without special instructions from Mr. Buller."

"Don't cash it, then. Good-day—"

"Quite so. But I'd advise you not to be in quite such a hurry to be off, all the same. In fact, it's my unpleasant duty to ask you to stay here at the bank until the fact of *this* cheque being in your hands can be more fully explained."

"I have explained it," I began rather angrily. "I received it from Mr. Buller, if it came out with the rest from that case lying before you. Why should you venture to speak, even to a stranger, as if you had any reason to doubt his word? I don't understand this at all."

"For this reason : I have the best reason for believing that this cheque was never drawn by Mr. Buller. And now you see how it becomes my unpleasant duty—"

"Nonsense! As if I hadn't received every one of those cheques straight from his hands! You talk as if you took me for a forger. Well, I suppose I must excuse you, on the ground of over-zeal."

"It is most improbable that this cheque was drawn by —well, never mind why. I'm bound to tell you that if you refuse to wait here for Mr. Buller's arrival of your own free will, and in your own interest, I shall have to call upon the police to assist me in the execution of my duty towards the bank and its customers and the public at large."

"Why," I began, my anger half losing itself in amusement, "this is something too absurd. You can't call in a constable unless you can give him good reason to suspect me of felony. I have half a mind to let you try, for the fun of the thing. Only it would be wasting my own time. So I'll put an end to your scruples about the public at large by telling you at once that my name is Standish, and that I am solicitor to Mr. Buller, and live at Carcester. And the next time I advise you, as a lawyer, to be more careful how you treat people who come to your bank."

"You are Mr. Buller's solicitor? Indeed? Of course that *is* important—very important; and no doubt you can send for somebody in Redport who knows you? No —we can't be too careful in these days."

" I don't know a soul in Redport."

" No? H'm ! Well, Mr. Buller will know you—when he comes."

" But I tell you he won't get your telegram for at least two days. This is monstrous!" I broke out, my amusement turning back into anger again.

" Monstrous or not—Well then, perhaps, as you feel safe from being brought face to face with—I should say, as you are convinced Mr. Buller is not at home, I suppose you have friends or clerks in Carcester who could give evidence as to who you say you are—are, I ought no doubt to say? The telegraph's as open to you as to me."

" You positively are so insane as to say you will forcibly detain me—*me*—in Redport unless I can convince you that I am myself? And for no reason—"

" You must make up your mind to it. I know what law is," said Mr. Richards ; "and—well, not to mince matters, I've already got our police-sergeant waiting in the next room. A messenger from the bank can despatch any summons to any of your friends, if you'll write it down. Yes—it *is* in my power to give you into custody on suspicion of having forged a cheque which you yourself admit has passed through the hands of no third parties—a cheque for £50, signed John Buller. And as to why I have particular reasons for my belief, I don't mind telling you it's because the bank here has had special notice from the chief branch at Carcester to cash no cheques signed "John Buller" till we've communicated with the drawer, and to detain the person presenting them, whoever he may be—unless the cheques bear a certain private sign. There's reason for that, you may be sure. And there is the sign on every one of these cheques—except the one for £50."

" You mean to say that this cheque for £50 is the only one unmarked?"

" The only one."

"Let me see it, if you please."

He held it so that I might see it, taking care tnat I should have no chance of wresting it from his hands. I certainly could not blame him any longer for over-zeal, seeing it was on my own advice he was acting. But what room could I find for a single thought, save that an unmarked cheque, as like those presented by Adam Brown as a cheque could be, *had been received straight from John Buller's very own hands by my very own?* Surely it looked more like witchcraft than forgery.

And yet Adam's effective confession of guilt, and the regularity with which the undoubtedly forged cheques had been presented—I could not make head or tail of it at all. I must have been bewildered; I must have seemed confused, as if with guilt or fright, for I was confused in reality. I could not even affect the indignation of injured honesty; I was not indignant with Mr. Richards for being suspicious of what might be witch-craft, but certainly had all the air of a forgery—I, Charles Standish, being the forger!

"It is utterly unintelligible," said I, using the common phrase of people who won't, rather than can't, explain things that seem going against them. "But I am sure of one thing—Charles Standish of Carcester I am. And I don't want to stay in Redport till Monday. I will tele-graph, as you say. I'll send word to my wife to—but no; *she's* not in Carcester either just now. I must send for one of the clerks at the office, I'm afraid, and make everybody wonder at what I can have been doing at Redport to need proof of my identity. Give me a form, and I'll write a message for my clerk—"

For my own credit's sake, and out of justice to Mr. Richards's zeal, I chose to wait in an inner office of the bank till somebody whom I knew should come. I need hardly say that Mr. Buller, being away from getting telegrams, never came. But it was not till hours had passed that I began to realise that it was Saturday afternoon—and that my idle dogs of clerks had of course taken advantage of my absence to close the office and go off to play at an exceptionally early hour. Closing time for the bank itself (also earlier than usual on Saturdays) had come when I saw in my mind, as clearly and truly as with my eyes, my telegram lying unopened on my clerk's desk at Carcester—and to-morrow was Sunday.

All I could do was to send off six telegrams to six different people, in the bare hope that one of them might bring over to Redport some respectable citizen of Carcester before the very last train. Not one brought a soul. And I could see what Mr. Richards thought of the result of my telegrams when I had, perforce, to put up with the accommodation of the police-station instead of the hotel, there to remain until John Buller himself should come and set me free.

In effect, I was a prisoner on suspicion of Forgery— and I had in truth presented an unquestionably forged cheque that had been through no hands but my own ! It was the most unaccountable mystery I had ever known ; and it kept me from sleeping, even more than the discomfort of my cell, as much as if I were really a conscious sharer in the villanies of Adam Brown. This could not be his doing—and what then of the rest, and of his admitted guilt concerning them ? Not even sleep, when it came in an uncomfortable shape at last, let me dream of a possible way through such a mystery.

It was not till Monday afternoon that I received the welcome news that John Buller was on his way to see me at the police-station in company with Mr. Richards. I must say that I had become more anxious now about getting home as fast as I could than about anything else in the world. It is not an amusing thing to be treated in a strange place as a suspected felon; and I have held very strong views about the treatment of unconvicted prisoners ever since that Redport Sunday.

"Here he is, sir," said Mr. Richards. "This is the —the gentleman who presented that cheque on Saturday morning. I hope and trust it's all right; but in these times, you see, one can't be too—"

"Thank Heaven, at last!" said I, springing from my seat, and holding out my hand. "I've never passed so long a day since I was born; but I certainly don't complain of Mr. Richards—he's been zealous enough, anyhow; and I only wish *my* clerks would simply do what they're bid, and give up that confounded habit of thinking for themselves. If you ever have to leave the Company's service, Mr. Richards, for want of thinking-power, never mind; I'll take you into mine. Well, Mr. Buller, you must have slipped into drawing *one* unmarked cheque, after all?"

"No, sir!" said John Buller, with strange vehemence, for him. "No—I did *not* draw that cheque—with or without a sign. I drew no cheque for fifty pounds at all. And if you're the rascal that has been up to these games, and got it all on poor young Adam's shoulders, I'm glad I see you here; I'm glad of it, with all my heart and soul. I'm hanged if I didn't know I was right, all along. Adam Brown, if a letter can find him, poor lad, goes back to my works at Redport this very hour!"

Could I believe my ears?

"You—John Buller—*you* believe *me* guilty of having forged cheques, and tried to throw the guilt of it upon Adam Brown? Think for one least moment of what you are saying—"

"Think? Thinking's plain enough, it seems to me—a mile too plain by the longest chalks you can draw. It's likelier anybody would be a rogue than the orphan lad I'd brought up as my own son. I daresay, like enough,

he was too taken aback by such a charge to say a word.
I wonder he didu't double his fist, and knock me down.
But I hope I'm a just man if I'm a bit of a hasty one.
I'm not going to be hasty with *you*. If you can
explain what's at best au ugly business, say it out like
a man."

"If I didn't respect an old client, and an old friend—
But I can't forget how you've been worrying about this
business. Explain? I will, though I don't see how you
and I can ever be friends again. You know as well as
I do that I never cashed a cheque for you in my life
before, or ever was at Redport till the day before
yesterday—"

"Ay; so you say."

"So I *do* say. And you know that I received that case
of cheques and bills—whatever they were, for I never
looked at them—from your own hands on Saturday
morning."

"Did you? That's my cheque-case, sure enough. But
suppose you did, what then? Because something comes
out of it, it doesn't follow it was I who put it in. No,
no. I never drew that cheque. You present it to be
cashed, and it purports to be drawn, signed, and endorsed
by me. You say you received it from me. I say you
didn't. And I ought to know; for you couldn't have
received a cheque that never was drawn. Justice is
justice. Adam Brown goes back to my works; and
you'll go to the country's, whoever you are. I don't
know what's the right way to start a prosecution,
but that's easy known. I'll see Standish this very
day."

"You'll see Standish?"

"Ay, Standish of Oarcester, my lawyer. Criminal
business isn't his line, he says; but he'll do it for
me."

"You mean I'm to prosecute myself? Well, it all

seems queer enough. Perhaps I don't know who I am. Do you?"

"No, sir, I don't, I'm happy to say. Forgers aren't in *my* line."

"Good Heaven! Do you mean to deny that *I* am Mr. Standish of Carcester?"

I saw a very decided smile come over the face of Mr. Richards. And it was not pleasant to see. For if John Buller, as he was quite capable of doing, chose to prosecute me for forgery—well, I should be acquitted, of course, but my character would be gone for ever and a day. The names of ladies are not more delicate than those of professional men.

"Come, none of that nonsense," said John Buller, "you're no more Standish than I am the Duke of Wellington. It does aggravate me to hear a man talk in that way. If you choose to deny that you're the Duke of Wellington, when I say you are, we'll have a wager upon that, and toss up for the winner. You come and dine with me at the Star, both of you, and I'll treat you like princes. We'll eat cheques for fifty pound apiece between slices of brown bread-and-butter cut thin, with lemon and cayenne. Its very odd, but I took a fancy to you the first minute I saw you. There's something about you puts me in mind of somebody or other—I never could remember names. But it's all one whoever we are. We're the sparks that fly upwards; and by Jingo, we'll have a jolly good fly . . . . . Who are *you*?" he called out at the top of his voice to Richards. "You're a murderer, sir, and a forger, and a fool. Come and dine with me at the Star. . . ."

I need not continue the talk of poor John Buller, whom over-work, and loss of faith in the one human being who was dear to him, had driven out of his mind. It was an overwhelming relief when my managing-clerk arrived, and when sufficient explanations were obtained to allow of my return home in company with my poor friend. Even to the zealous Mr. Richards the state of things was as clear as day, so far as he knew.

III.

It was not hard for me, now, to see how John Buller, once assured against his will of Adam's treachery in the first instance, had brooded over the shock, with an already over-lonely and over-burdened mind, till, as sure as Friday night came round, he, possessed by the demon of monomania—which simply means the abnormal growth of a natural and normal idea—drew the cheque which haunted and fascinated him. If my readers cannot follow the chain of mental association, with its manifold links of time, place, person, and occasion, in which his disturbed brain became tangled and coiled, I fear I cannot hope to make it very clear. But there are very few who have not met with the most extraordinary cases of mono-mania in some form, and noticed how consistent they are with all outward appearance of sanity. Are there very many of us who have not felt some form of it our-selves in some slight degree? But, fortunately, few of us live altogether alone; few of us are over-trustful or, therefore, half maddened when deceived; most of us have more, if not much more, self-control than was evidently possessed by John Buller. And yet he must have had a great deal. Only the insane can tell the very torture of self-suppression they have to undergo when they feel monomania slowly broadening into a wider, if not deeper, mode of lunacy. For, conscious of its own state every diseased brain must be when that state first begins.

And yet—*could* this be all? The madness of John Buller did not account for the more than apparent guilt of Adam Brown.

It was not till years afterwards—not till my poor old friend had left all his troubles behind him ; not till I had long ago given up puzzling my head about the matter—that I one day received a letter bearing an Australian post-mark, and addressed to myself in a strange hand. There was nothing curious in that ; but, as I read, the story I have been trying to tell came back to me as freshly as if it had all happened yesterday. For thus the letter ran :

" Sir,—It will doubtless surprise you to receive this from me ; for I cannot suppose that you will remember so much as my name. But you will remember—I fear only too well—a clerk in the service of Mr. John Buller, who was dismissed from his service for embezzlement. I am that man ; and my reason for calling myself to your remembrance is, that I have at last found myself able to repay the sums that I abstracted wrongfully, and for which only Mr. Buller's kindness saved me from being sent to gaol. I do not, moreover, want him to think me always such a hopelessly ungrateful and treacherous scoundrel as he must be thinking me. I got into bad ways, knowing them bad all the time. I wanted more money than I could get honestly, and I had to pay it. I needn't tell *that* story ; it's over now, and no harm done to anybody but me.

" I was tempted, by what I called to myself need and weakness, to ' borrow,' I called it then—to steal, that is to say—some of the money I drew from Redport bank. I had complete control of the accounts at Redport, and I suppose it was all so easy that at first it didn't so much feel like stealing, and so I went on and on. I used to

take sometimes more than fifty pounds together. I've
sent you a statement of all I took; and I hope it's
correct, for of course I had to muddle up all the accounts.
You see, sir, Mr. Buller always used to give me a fifty-
pound cheque over and above what I asked for, meaning,
I suppose, to keep plenty of ready-money in the works
for the week; and I never told him it was more than was
wanted, for the reasons I've written. The only excuse I
had is this—I never knew how much I owed to Mr.
Buller. I thought I was nothing more to him, and
rather less, than any other man. That's no reason I
should rob him, but it makes me a bit less of a thorough
blackguard. He ought to have had me sent to gaol. And
when he didn't, but just as much as told me to go and
do no more wrong, as if I had been his own son—well,
sir, it did go to the bottom of all the heart I've got, and
I'd like him just to know that he wasn't foolish in being
kind. If I ever did another wrong, or mean, or dishonest
thing, I should have been the biggest cur on earth. I got
a chance in New Zealand, and I should like him to know
that his words made a man of me. This is a poor sort
of a letter, but I can't say what I feel, and I won't
try.—Trusting to hear from you per return, yours
respectfully,

" ADAM BROWN."

And that is the not wholly unsatisfactory end of a sad
story. I suppose that the *first* cheque must have been
some sort of a blunder; and that an obstinate man's
supposition that forgery on somebody else's part was
more probable than a blunder on his own, resulted in
—what we have seen. I intended, when I set out, to
point a good number of morals, legal and otherwise.
But I will content myself with two. One is, that justice
has even queerer ways of going to work than law—as
when it punishes a man for a fault that hasn't been found

out by finding him guilty of one that he has never committed. The other is, that trust, even if carried to the pitch of insanity, is not by any means so mad a thing as it seems. John Buller's over-trust sent him out of his own mind, but it saved another man.

ONLY TEN MINUTES;

OR, WHAT MY DREAM TOLD ME.

I.

THE Kenricks were always a large family.   When I was
a lad, I drew up a genealogical table, whence it appeared
that I, Arthur George Ford Kenrick, was at that period
the possessor of eleven uncles and aunts on my father's
side, of twenty-eight first cousins in the persons of their
children, and of eight brothers and sisters of my own.   I
was the eldest son of a second brother.   My eldest uncle
—my uncle George, to wit, who was also my godfather,
as my second name testifies—was the great man of our
tribe, and the head of the firm of Kenrick & Company,
merchants, of Shanghai.   My father had also made a
very respectable fortune as a colonial broker : my other
uncles were all prosperous fathers of families, and my
aunts were all flourishing mothers.   As my branch of the
family tree developed from the budding stage of the
nursery and schoolroom, my sisters bade fair to follow
the good example of their aunts, and my brothers to take
after their uncles.   I must ask my reader to get it well
into his head that I am distinctly a member of a *very*
large and exceedingly marrying family on my father's
side.   That seemingly immaterial accident is the very
root of my whole story.

The only exception to the law of likeness which governed the Kenricks in general was, at least until my own birth, my uncle George. He alone had never married: indeed, he both professed and practised such misogynic principles as to have earned for himself the name of "the old bachelor" at nineteen years old. He had never stumbled over so much as the merest threshold of flirtation. He was friendly with his sisters-in-law and fond of his nieces; but a strange petticoat was a terror to him. A more easy-going genial man among men was not to be found in the world than George Kenrick; but the appearance of a woman acted on him like a sudden frost in summer. Nor did he by any means conceal his objection to the sex at large, but was a public and open railer at women and their ways. So that, in spite of his good looks, good heart, good temper, and good fortune, his enemies gave him up as a hopeless case and left him alone.

It is easy to imagine how such a brother and uncle was prized and honoured—for I can assure all whom it concerns that it is not only the needy who make much of a rich relation who has notoriously forsworn matrimony. But it so happened that Uncle George took it into his head that he would like to have a son and heir, so long as he could manage it without the help of anything in the shape of womankind. Naturally, as soon as I came into the world, Uncle George was asked to be my godfather; and I had the advantage, it will be remembered, of being the firstborn of the brother who came next to him. And, curiously enough, it so happened that, as I grew up, I became even less like a typical Kenrick than he. I was idle at my books; I was a dunce at arithmetic; I was mortally afraid of little girls. But I had a consuming passion for paints and pencils, and one lucky or unlucky day I made a shameless caricature of Uncle George himself, which happened to fall into his own hands.

I can see him now, turning it upside down, and downside up, and round and round; and I can see his frown trying to keep itself from turning into a smile. It was really a very good bit of art in its way, I believe.

"If a herring and a half cost threehalfpence, how many can you buy for twopence?" asked he.

I am sometimes uncertain of the correct answer to this day; but I said then, at a venture, "One and a quarter."

"You'll do, my lad!" said Uncle George cordially. "I'd give my eyes to be a painter instead of a China merchant; but I never could draw a straight line, and I never could manage to get less than value for my money. Never mind—we'll have an artist in the family yet, and I'll be he—by deputy. And if ever you get as far as 'rule of three,' I'll—"

What he would do, I know not. But he had a long talk with my father that same day. And it became an understood thing in the family (which could well afford the disappointment) that I was to study art at Uncle George's expense, and was to be his sole heir: in effect, that I was to be given over to him. So said, so done. It is not his fault that I am not a better painter than I am. Or rather it is his fault; for I should surely have studied harder had I not known myself to be sole heir, under his will, to all the results of the business at Shanghai. My father also altered his will; and, as I was more than amply provided for, divided among my eight brothers and sisters what would have been my share of his fortune. It was just, for I should eventually be richer than all my brothers and sisters put together; but I fancy that my father may have thought it politic to insure my uncle's mind against changing by making him feel that my career was altogether dependent upon him. My history thenceforth, up to the age of about eight-and-twenty, is soon told. I was taken from school and put to painting, which

I followed with much more pleasure than industry, and without exceeding my very handsome allowance by more than was natural in one who never could understand the price of herrings. My uncle returned to Shanghai; and very soon afterwards my father died, leaving behind him the will I have described.

It was in the autumn of a never-to-be-forgotten year that I started, alone, on a sketching-tour in North Wales, and arrived, on foot, at the little inn of Llanpwll. That little inn is an hotel now, and Llanpwll has been caught and tamed; but it was a pleasant place then, and full of wild charm. I used to like rambling about myself in those days, though less, I am afraid, for the sake of art than for that of the litttle adventures one picks up by the way; and very little adventures will serve the turn of one who is by nature a bit of a vagabond. At home in London I liked comfort and pleasure as well as any man, and was much too well off to be a free citizen of artistic Bohemia. So it was all the more pleasant to become, at times, a sharer with my fellows in all those luxuries of freedom, hunger, solitude, and fatigue which money cannot buy, and which, in great cities, are the privilege of none but the poor. I never rode, I frequented the humblest inns, I carried no baggage, and I outdid my brother painters in the roughness and shabbiness of my clothes; for painters were not then the well-trimmed race that they have since become.

I was just as well off in mind, body, and estate as a young man can be. I could work as much as I liked, and I could idle as much as I liked, and both in the way that best pleased me. I had perfect health, no restraints, and no cares either for the day or for the morrow: I had only to hold out my hand to life, and to draw it back well filled. I was not even in love; for though I did not altogether take after my uncle George in the matter of flirtations, and though my original fear of little girls had not been carried on into my intercourse with great ones, still my heart was just as free as my godfather's own. I looked forward to passing just as many or just as few pleasant days at Llanpwll as might please my humour, and then tramping on to find yet pleasanter days elsewhere. Fortune was my hostess everywhere, and always a kind one.

The next day I rambled about in search of a subject all day long, dined luxuriously on trout, and then slept a single sleep for ten hours without a single dream. For I must tell you that I never dream by night, whatever I may do by day. My habit is to go off when my head touches the pillow, and to wake up all over at once, as soon as sleep has done its duty. I doubt if, in those days at least, I really knew what dreaming meant. And I never felt so refreshed and so vigorous as I did at break-fast-time on that special next morning.

I had found a subject that satisfied me with its promise, and I was eager to begin. I need not describe it; there were water, wood, and mountain, and all the other stock in art of rambling painters in North Wales. I would really paint a picture this time.

But for once I had reckoned without my hostess—Fortune. On the very spot I had chosen for myself yesterday there sat an earlier bird intent upon my worm; a rival wooer of Nature, painting as if she had not an instant of her life to lose. *Her* life—for my rival was a she.

Owing to the nature of the path, I had come upon her almost before I saw her; and she was far too absorbed to have heard my coming. I hardly knew what to do. I never felt more eager for work; I had lived a life of mood-humouring, and I felt as if I must needs paint that picture or none, and to-day or never. And yet there was no possible way of saying to her, " Pardon me: but this

bit of Nature is retained." Meanwhile I took a good
long look at her; for one does not—or rather in those
days did not—meet a wandering sketcher in petticoats
every day at out-of-the-way places like Llanpwll. And
less often still used one to meet sketchers in petticoats
like her; and not more often now than then. Uncle
George, no doubt, would have run away. I kept my
ground.

She was beyond all question a remarkably pretty girl
—really pretty, and not merely from a painter's point of
view. She was very pretty, and very little, and very
young. She was a lady, every inch of her—not that this
necessarily amounts to much, seeing how few her inches
were; and she was tastefully as well as sensibly dressed
in—I am a bad hand at describing clothes—some very
plain dark stuff made in a very plain and homely fashion,
with some sort of hat as unpretending as the rest of her
costume. And now, having got rid of the clothes, for
her who wore them. Plain and homely as these were,
they did not altogether hide a most exquisite and most
perfect figure, charmingly slender and lithe, but in no
respect less full than is formed by health and Nature.
She was the sort of girl who would fly up a mountain,
and be fresher at the top than she was before she began
to climb. Her face, even at first sight, was indescribably
winning. When I call her pretty I hardly know, after all,
whether the word be the right one; or, if it be, whether
it was not her expression, and not her features, that make
it so. I suppose the truth is that her features were pretty,
and their expression a great deal more. She was brightly
and healthily fair, not wholly unburned by the sun and wind,
which is by no means always so unbecoming as women
believe. Her eyes were gray, her nose neither long nor
short, and her mouth neither large nor small. That is
not much of a description for a painter. But it must
pass. For it was a good face, at once pure and wise, and

lighted up with kind and gentle humour. I am not sure, after all, that she was so much absorbed in her work as not to have thoughts apart from, though they must needs be in harmony with, the picture she was trying to make her own. Though she had not heard my coming steps, I could see that the bright September air and the deep inaudible song that only belongs to mountain silence had as much to do with the light in her face as what was seen by her eyes. There was something unspeakably true, and simple, and natural, and wise in the best and sweetest way, as surely about her as there was in the light and the air. She seemed to make the day itself feel the better for her being there.

But, nevertheless, she had picked up my own particular worm. So I did the only thing that seemed to be left me. Here was an adventure, anyhow. There was a convenient bit of rock in which I could sit very comfortably and unseen—unless she happened to look up, which did not seem at all likely. I climbed to the top without making any noise, put a block on my knees, and began to sketch—*Her.*

So she sketched the scene, and I, till I could get my innings, sketched the sketcher. As the minutes went by I began to think that I had by no means the worse of the bargain. There is plenty of Nature in North Wales, but there are not many girls like this in Nature. Presently I began to hope that she would not leave her work too soon; at least, not until I had done enough to make a picture of at leisure. She worked hard and fast, and I harder and faster; and twenty times at least I caught some new light or shade of expression that obliged me to begin in spirit all over again. Never had I found a subject that had interested me, nay, fascinated me more —never since I had caricatured uncle George.

At last she laid down her work and rose. And, to my dismay, she *did* look up, and she saw me as plainly as I saw her. I laid my block face downwards, as guiltily as if I had been caught red-handed in the middle of a crime.

"Sir," she said, very quietly and calmly, but in a voice—a very sweet one, by the way—that seemed somehow to hide a smile, "would you mind being so kind as to hand me down a small basket that you will find behind that bit of rock on your left hand? Thank you; I am very much obliged."

As all the world knows, there are exactly eleven thousand three hundred and forty-five ways in which a girl can speak to a strange young man whom she meets alone by chance, and for the first time. The way in which this girl spoke to me was in the very best of them. It was most clearly not meant either to attract or to encourage or to serve for ice-breaking, or, on the other hand, to impress or repel; she wanted something, and she was not afraid to ask for it simply and that was all. It implied at once the courage that comes from trust, and the trust that comes from courage. I suppose she had never had cause to fear or mistrust any fellow human soul.

She opened the basket I had handed her, took out some sandwiches and a bottle of milk, and began to eat as unconcernedly as if no male creature were by to see. But if she felt no cause for fear, why—not being Uncle George—should I?

"We seem both to have been caught by the same bit," said I. "This is what I was hunting for all yesterday. But I suppose you know this country well?"

"Pretty well," said she. "But—may I not offer you some of my dinner, as you don't seem to have brought any of your own?"

"I don't know how to say No; but I must say it, if I may. I should like to see your morning's work, though —if—"

"Certainly," said she, handing me up a sketch which, combined with her entire freedom from all shyness about the matter, settled at once for me the question of whether she was artist or amateur. Beyond question she was fully as much an artist as I, and probably a great deal more. "I'm afraid it is a sad libel, though. Will you, please, let me see yours?"

"Of course—" I was beginning, when I suddenly remembered what my morning's work had been. I suspected myself of colouring, and the suspicion fulfilled itself, I am sure, in the usual way. "O, mine—I'm afraid," I said, leaping at whatever lie was nearest to hand, "I'm afraid I must plead guilty to hideous laziness in the face of your industry. I've been all this while going to begin. I wanted the afternoon light, you see—"

"How lucky! it is afternoon now. I wish you would let me watch you work, if I may? It will be a grand chance for me."

"But you are yourself a painter, are not you? And a fine one. I can't pretend. But our common choice of a subject should be a sort of introduction between us, any way. I've no doubt I am arguing myself unknown not to know you, and shall feel ashamed of my ignorance when I find out who you are. For I was certain by this time that I had fallen in with somebody who was somebody in the world of art, and whose name and works at least I ought to know."

"I don't think it likely that you ever heard of me," said she, a little stiffly. "I suppose you come from London. I don't. You are not likely to have heard of —of—of—Mildred Ashton. And as to being a painter, I only know I am a very poor one indeed."

"Then all I can say is, you will not remain unknown or poor for long. You have genius, Miss Ashton; that is a big word, but a true one."

Her whole face lighted up with pleasure.

"Do you really mean what you say?" asked she.

"I hope I always mean what I say," said I stupidly enough. It did not even strike me as strange that such chance companions as we were should be beginning to talk as if we were friends. I only noticed her childlike pleasure at my speech, and that it was far too simple and natural to be called vain.

"And you are a real painter?" she asked.

"It is my calling. Isn't it yours?"

"I have no other. But I want teaching very badly indeed. I have told you my name. What is yours?"

"Arthur Kenrick."

"No doubt I ought to know it, only I don't," said she, nearly echoing my own words. "The only Kenrick I ever heard of is a friend of a cousin of mine, who lives in China, at a place called Shanghai—"

"What! you know my uncle, Miss Ashton? That is strange indeed! I am the nephew of Mr. George Kenrick of Shanghai."

"No, *I* don't know him," said Miss Ashton. "But why is it strange that your uncle should know my cousin, when they both live in the same town? However, I am glad that I know it is so, and therefore a little about who you are. Are you not going to begin?"

It is only a great deal too easy to write down empty words. But until some man of science finds out how to reproduce their tone and colour, the pen must be content to be to the tongue what a mere photograph is to a picture. I am obliged to be vain enough to suppose that Miss Ashton took me for some sort of a gentleman, which means a man to whom any woman may speak freely under any circumstances and at any time. But she must have been exceptionally a lady to accept her freedom as so much a matter of course, and without the least shadow of a thought that her making a stranger's

acquaintance in this fashion might be thought a little
strange by others. I only wish I had the least power of
saying exactly what I mean. I can only wish that we
all lived in a world where introductions and credentials
could be ignored as foolish forms. As it is, those who
ignore them must either be worse and more foolish than
their neighbours, or else as wise as the serpent and as
harmless as the dove. And nobody who had eyes and
ears could doubt for a moment as to which order Mildred
Ashton belonged to. I worked and she watched, for the
greater part of the afternoon, without any talk worth
mentioning. I learned no more about her than her name,
and gathered no more otherwise than that she was poor,
lived outside the gates of the world, and loved her art in
a very different fashion from mine. I felt as if, until
to-day, I had been living—no, not living—existing—without a soul.

In a word, I was not the same Arthur Kenrick who
had come down to Llanpwll. That evening's trout, it is
true, had rather gained in flavour, and that night's sleep
in depth and sweetness; but I knew, when I rose next
morning, that I was a new man, wofully dissatisfied with
the old one. I had been drinking the cold dull water of
selfishness for eight-and-twenty years; yesterday I had
taken my first taste of life's nectar. But such tastes do
not quench the thirst for many hours. I went as straight
to the place where I had met Mildred Ashton as if I
could have fairly hoped to drink there a second time. I
had no right to hope; but, nevertheless, in the same spot
I found her again, working harder than before; nor,
when she saw me, did she show the faintest affectation
of surprise. Strangers as we were, and short-lived as
my new self had been—not a whole day old—I felt half
angry that she should treat me as if I were so utterly a
nobody. I fancied I should have been better pleased had
she stayed away that day. But then that would have

shown self-consciousness; and it was the absence of every hint of possible self-consciousness that was her greatest charm — perhaps the whole source of her charm.

There was no reason why I should not work within sight and speech of her; and so I did, with no barrier but my own increasing shyness between her and me. We talked a little but not much, between whiles, and then mostly about my own experiences of art and travel, in which she took the interest of one who has had no such experiences of her own. But even in such somewhat one-sided talk I could not help learning more about her than I knew yesterday. She lived in a far-away part of England—a flat uninteresting country of which I knew nothing. She was staying with some relations at a farm with an unpronounceable name some few miles away, and spent the whole of her time in sketching out of doors. She had some other relations in Shanghai, with whom she corresponded sometimes, and through whom she had heard of my uncle George in a slight and casual way. She had neither father nor mother, brother nor sister, and no doubt depended on the relations with whom she was staying until she could support herself by her pencil. When I left her that day all the pleasure of my new life had gone, and the beginning of its pain had come. And whether such pleasure or such pain be the better, is more than I can tell.

How our meetings grew into a habit, very matter of course on her part, full of excitement on mine, would be far too long to say. There was certainly nothing unnatural, however unconventional, in the growth of a friendship between two would-be artists of whom one wanted help and the other wanted—everything. We had found one another in a world to which conventions did not belong, and in which people soon learn to know each other apart from the accidents of fortune. There was certainly no very great harm for her to find out in me, and there was nothing but good in her. Let me leap to the end at once—I knew that I had found her who must be my wife, whatever else she might be; and sometimes I hoped, and sometimes despaired.

But why, you will ask, should I despair—I, a favourite of Fortune, who would be very rich some day, and was rich enough already—of winning a poor girl without friends or means? Ah, but that was just the thing that troubled me! With all my faith in her, I dreaded the thought of buying her hand to an almost morbid degree. Had she been rich I should have had a hundred times less fear. I must win her as the poor painter I seemed, or not at all; she must not be exposed for a moment to the temptation of taking me because I was rich; and if she took me with that knowledge I should never be able to rid myself of the doubt that she might never have taken me had I been poor. From the moment that my heart made itself up to win her I took every chance I could of acting out the part of the struggling artist without a penny, whose whole fortune is in the air. It would be time enough for her to learn the truth when she was won—if that was ever to be; if she was not altogether beyond and above my winning, as I very largely feared. Her manner was the same towards me as on the very first day. And yet I had not reached that point when a man would rather have a "No" than no answer at all. It was first love with me, remember, in which only the most hopeless fools can possibly be altogether wise.

I have said that I never dreamed. But one night, after a long afternoon spent in Mildred's company, a new and strange experience happened to me. I *did* dream. Regular and experienced dreamers may not think my dream a particularly strange or remarkable one. But it was remarkably strange to me, just because it was a Dream.

It was not of Mildred. Professed dreamers tell me that dreams very seldom relate to the days which they follow : that the fulness of the heart may be often the moving cause, but very rarely fashions the form. It seemed to me, with extraordinary vividness, that some genii of an Arabian midnight had transported me from Llanpwll to Shanghai. At least I suppose it must have been Shanghai, though the place was more like what, in my waking fancies, I imagine Pekin, or any typically Chinese city, to be. I can remember noticing, without any surprise, that all the houses, and even many of the people who crowded the streets, were made of porcelain, mostly blue and white, and all exceedingly small : the buildings did not reach above my shoulders, nor the people much above my knees. Nobody, however, noticed me, and this did surprise me a little, though I have been told that incapacity for feeling surprise at anything is the grand test of a dream. So, if this theory be correct, I was not dreaming at all, but was really in Shanghai, or Pekin, or wherever it may be. I walked about the streets, in search of some unknown something, careful not to crack any of the porcelain with the large stick I carried. Presently I had a curious feeling of laborious oppression, especially about the knees, which seemed to have become suddenly loaded with lead, so heavy to lift were they. I still laboured on ; and the oppression I felt took an external form, as if my own personality extended itself outwardly from me to everything about me. The air became a thick yellow cloud, very hot, and almost stifling, with a disagreeable flavour, like what I suppose a London fog in the dog-days would be. How I managed to enter one of the porcelain dolls' houses, I know not ; but I must have done so, for I presently found myself in a large room, papered all over with playing cards. And there I saw uncle George.

It did not surprise me that he was standing upright in a brass candlestick—that seemed quite as natural as that he was burning in some indescribable manner with a wick and a flame. If I shut my eyes I can see it all now as clearly as then, for never was any waking impression more vivid; and yet for the life of me I cannot describe the exact manner in which he was identified with a lighted candle. The really extraordinary part of the matter was that the flat dish of the candlestick had two stems, and that in the second, and in like manner, burned the figure of a woman, whose face did not seem wholly strange to me, though I could not connect it with any face I had ever seen. I could not tell whether uncle George saw me or no. He and the woman became more and more distinctly candlelike without losing their original natures; in a way, they were being transformed into candles without in the least ceasing to be entirely themselves. I did not in any way confuse myself with what I saw—another unusual feature, I am told, in a dream. Presently the melted grease began to run down, and to encircle the human candles with broad spiral folds. I counted the folds as they formed themselves with singular regularity—One: two: three: four: five: six: seven: eight: nine: a tenth was half formed, when suddenly the two flames began to splutter, and then to leap and flicker. I saw that they were on the point of going out, and wondered which of the two would be the first to go. It was the woman—out she went, and I saw her no more. My uncle still burned on, but always in the same unwholesome way. Sometimes his flame started up, yellow and clear; sometimes it spluttered down to a blue point, like the light of a glow-worm. I was about to speak to him, when out he went also; and, after a rush through leagues of air, I found myself transported back from China to my bed at Llanpwll, as unrefreshed as if my journey had been real.

"So that's dreaming, is it?" thought I. "I suppose it's all right to experience everything just once, but if it depends upon me, I'll never try *that* again. It seems to me uncommonly like a spasm of lunacy; and where the pleasure of it lies I can't see. And yet I'm as certain that I saw Uncle George turned into a candle, with my own eyes, as I am that I see the wall before me. And in the same candlestick with a woman—that's too utterly absurd." I leaped out of bed, and in ten minutes was in full swim across the little lake below the inn. By the time I had reached the other side the dream had left me—like a dream.

But the lake did not prove Lethe, for long. While I was going to the place where I now knew I should find Mildred, the grotesque scene of the human candles burning out in a room made of playing cards came back to me in all its vividness, and made me feel most absurdly uncomfortable. I suppose people who often dream get used to such night adventures; as for me, I could not convince my unreason that what I had seen was absolutely unreal. It was a relief to me when I saw Mildred again; for need I say that my heart had been filled with heavy forebodings about *her* by this idiotic dream?

"Do you ever have dreams, Miss Ashton?"

"Very often. Why?"

"Then perhaps you can read me mine." I told her my story; and telling it in the fresh air under the light of the sun proved a better way of putting it into the light of nonsense than even my plunge into the lake had been.

"It is certainly a very odd sort of nightmare," said she. "But I fancy you are wrong in thinking that it had nothing to do with the day. I daresay we had mentioned your uncle; no doubt you had been thinking about him, and a dream of China of course would suggest a great deal of china-ware. The fog and the weight of the knees are signs of unpleasant dreams that everybody knows. Of course, since you tell me that your uncle is a woman-hater you would naturally see a woman with him in a dream; and as to the candles and the flat brass candle-stick—what was the last thing you saw or did before sleeping? You put out your candle, I suppose; and—"

"And it was in a flat brass candlestick? That it certainly was. Well, I suppose you are right as usual, and that there was really nothing out of the common in recognizing one's uncle in a candle. I certainly don't see what it could portend: most decidedly it can never come true. You say you dream; have you ever known a dream come true?"

"Never, strange to say."

"Strange? I should have thought all the strangeness would be the other way, if all dreams were like mine."

"But they are not all like yours," said Mildred. "And surely it is almost a miracle, out of the millions and millions of dreams that are dreamed every night all over the world, so few thousands should happen by chance to be fulfilled. The fewness of their fulfilments is the most wonderful thing about dreams."

"Well, my uncle is not likely to turn into a candle, anyhow. However, I'm glad to think that my brain had some foundation of fact to build upon—"

"If you were used to dreaming, you would think nothing of it, indeed. I have much stranger dreams than that, often and often; but I take them as a matter of course, and never think of them after waking."

I wished with all my heart that she would take things less as a matter of course. Would she take it as a matter of course that I should ask her to be my wife, and that she should say No? But there was not much chance of let-ting one's own thoughts take the bit between their teeth in her company. She had an insatiable appetite for what I looked upon as hard work, but which never wearied her. I believe I had done twice as much work in these few weeks as in a whole year before—not that this is to say a great deal. Before long my dream was absolutely forgotten once more—no doubt, had it not been a new experience, it would, as she had said, have been absolutely forgotten long ago.

But presently it came back, in quite a new way. Had it not led the way to the interpretation of another dream? It needed some courage to risk putting an end to the idyl of Llanpwll. But it had to be done; I felt as if something would keep the end from ever coming unless it came to-day.

"I have not told you the whole of my dream yet," said I at last, laying down my brush. "Shall I tell you the rest? Though it seems impossible you should need to be told. There; I will and I *must* tell you. All day long I am dreaming that I love you—no, *that* is no dream—but that I have told you so, and that you have said— But why am I talking about dreams? If you haven't guessed that I loved you the first day I saw you, once for all, you know it now. Don't say we know nothing of one another yet, for we do—"

So much I know I said; I am not such an impostor as to pretend that I can repeat the rest of the words in which I asked Mildred to marry me. Were the sentences quite coherent, grammatical, and full of meaning for strange ears, in which you asked your wife (if you have one) to marry you—always supposing that you loved her below the depth of your tongue, and had more fear than hope of her answer? I spoke on with my whole heart; I looked in her face, not knowing what to read. It was full of what might mean a thousand things. I did not dare to hold out my hand; only while I spoke I was listening for the faintest shadow of a coming word. At last, as we stood face to face, her lips parted, and began to move.

"Mildred!" cried a sharp elderly voice from behind the corner of the rock. "Mildred! where in the name of mercy have you been?"

Could anything have been more horribly unlucky than the sudden appearance of this old lady just then and there? She had made no sign for weeks; it was as if she had been watching for the precise moment when she would be most in the way. I may wrong her; but I thought her the most evil-looking monster that had ever been seen—and had she been as young and as beautiful as Mildred herself, I should have thought the same. In point of fact she was very elderly and very plain; and I multiplied her in both directions by ten.

Mildred herself, for the first time, seemed to lose her self-possession, and to turn pale.

"My aunt, Miss Reynolds—Mr. Kenrick," she said falteringly.

Miss Reynolds scarcely deigned to curtsy; I just managed to bow.

"So!" said Miss Reynolds, turning her shoulder towards me contemptuously, and speaking to Mildred. "So this is the meaning of your painting mania, is it; your scarlet and yellow fever, eh? Coming out to meet young men, alone. Perhaps you think I haven't known it all along, and that I didn't think there was more Art about it all than you'd have me believe—and Nature; stuff! Human nature, you mean. I guessed as much, and now I know. You'll please to come home with me. Come."

"Miss Reynolds," said I, recovering my presence of mind, "I am not going to leave this spot till I know whether your niece will be my wife or no. And as to her, she no more knew until to-day that I love her—"

"Not leave this spot? You'll have to take root in it, then, young man; or rather you may leave it as soon as you like, for I say to you, No!"

"It is from herself that I must—" I began, trying to be as courteous to Mildred's aunt as she would allow me.

"Stuff and nonsense!" said Miss Reynolds. "And who, pray, are you? What have you to do with the matter, I should like to know?"

"Everything in the world. My name is Kenrick—Arthur Kenrick; I am an artist—"

"So I perceive, sir, from your clothes. May I ask, since you presume to my niece's hand, if you are an R.A.?"

"Not yet, Miss Reynolds; nor an Associate, even. But—"

"An exhibitor, no doubt. Can you give me the name of one of your works that has been hung on the line?"

"I have never as yet exhibited a picture. But—"

"I am aware," said Miss Reynolds, throwing a studiously veiled note of sarcasm into her tone, "that many famous painters keep aloof from the Academy on principle. It is only right I should know the circumstances as well as the name of the—the—person who tries to entrap my niece into a secret engagement without my leave. No doubt, though you do not exhibit, you sell your works for large sums?"

"I have not yet sold a picture, Miss Reynolds. But—"

"You mean to tell me you are a common drawing-master?" she said, with scorn unveiled.

"I am not even that," said I. "But if I were—"

"You have been saying 'But' five hundred times. 'But' what, if you please? I can't stay here all day."

"I was going to tell you, Miss Reynolds, that though I am not yet a famous painter, I am of, I hope, sufficient respectability and means. My father was a well-known and wealthy colonial broker in London; I am his eldest son—"

"Ah!" said Miss Reynolds, with genuine interest in her voice. "You only paint for amusement, then—though I don't see why a gentleman should go about in a

coat as shabby as yours.   Your father, I am to understand, died a wealthy man, and you are his heir?"

"I was speaking then of my respectability only—not of
my means.   I have not inherited anything from my
father.   My brothers and sisters are his heirs.   But—"

"'But' number five hundred and one!   I see.   You
offended your father by turning vagabond artist, and he
very properly cut you off with a shilling, though you are
his eldest son.   I thought a gentleman would have made
love in more decent clothes, smelling less like a pot-
house.   Good morning, Mr.Kenrick, and better luck next
time."

What was I to say to the old virago?   I could not
bring myself to speak of my real means and settled
expectations until Mildred herself had answered me; and
this treatment of me because I seemed poor, and her
insults towards my brothers in art, made any course but
silence on this score impossible.   To Mildred I would of
course tell everything so soon as she had answered me;
but to Miss Reynolds, not a word.

"Very well, then," said I.   "In the character of a
poor unknown landscape painter, disinherited—if you
will have it so—for preferring art to trade, but too honest
to cheat his tailor, I demand to know from Miss Ashton's
own lips whether she will give me any hope that she will
ever be my wife or no—if *she* knows me well enough to
trust her happiness in my hands.   I do not think she
will refuse me that hope because I am poor."

"O, if it comes to that," said Miss Reynolds, "I'll go
and pick a gooseberry or two with pleasure.   I'm not
afraid of what Mildred will say to you now—*she knows
my will.*"

I did not notice her last words just then.   They seemed
to signify merely that, whatever she willed, others must
obey.   And besides, Mildred, who had been standing by
in silence, spoke at last, and she said:

"Aunt Jane, you need not go. I would rather say before you, just now, everything that I have to say. I know you have meant to be kind to me, and I have tried to be grateful; but I must live my own life, after all. I had found that out before I knew—before I knew Mr. Kenrick; everybody has to find it out at first or at last, I suppose. I should have become a very bad companion for you. Yes, I do know Mr. Kenrick, I hope and I believe. I hope he knows me as well! I am glad that he is poor, and that he—"

She said no more, but she gave me her hand.

II.

So my dream had proved an omen after all, in so far as so exceptional a thing (for me) as a dream of any sort had immediately preceded, and been bound up with, the gain of my Mildred's hand. It may be that, in the elementary sort of dream philosophy which makes dreaming of one thing prognosticate an event of an entirely remote and different kind, to dream that one's uncle is turned into a candle may foreshadow one's own marriage —whether that be so or otherwise, experts will be able to tell. However that may be, in a new life the dream had very soon become an old and forgotten story.

Mildred's history turned out to be a very simple one, after all, as she told it to me, though it was by no means what I had imagined. She and the cousin of whom she had spoken were the nieces of Miss Reynolds, a rich, somewhat eccentric, exceedingly capricious, and extravagantly obstinate old lady, who had adopted Mildred in a very much less generous fashion than uncle George had adopted me. Mildred had tried her best to be grateful, but had found it absolutely impossible. She had a very strong nature and decided character, which Miss Reynolds, out of some uncomfortable mixture of duty, whim, and delight in tyranny for its own sake, had set herself to thwart and distort in every imaginable way. From what I could gather, Miss Reynolds was one of those people who cannot exist without a dependent on whom to exercise their passion for power, and who believe that power consists wholly in making other people conscious slaves. There are such men in thousands; such women in tens of thousands. No wonder that Mildred, having a spirit of her own, had been driven to rebel. Her idea was to make herself independent by learning how to paint pictures that would sell, and then to take her own life, so far as she could, into her own hands. I congratulated myself, more than I can say, on having let her believe that I was as poor as I seemed; and I resolved, in the same spirit, to keep up the part I had assumed until, on our wedding-day, I could give my wife the pleasant surprise of finding that, in following her heart, she had not condemned herself to a life of poverty and toil. Meanwhile the romance of our engagement would be doubled for me, and she would have the zest of feeling that she was sacrificing the world for love and liberty.

I would, for my own pleasure in its memory, linger upon the days of my courtship among the hills round Llanpwll. It had all the charms of romance for us both, without there being any real reason to fear that all would not end well. I hardly know whether to call it the best or the worst of our engagement that it was so short and flying. I was impatient for its close; but I lingered then upon every hour of it, just as in remembrance I do now. But it was impossible that it should be long. Mildred was ready to face the poorest, hardest, and most laborious life with me, and was proud to show how content she was to become the wife of one who would have no wealth but her. But there were pressing reasons why there should be no delays in our marriage, save such as the law compelled. Mildred, having rebelled against her aunt, was without either a home or means to find one, for Miss Reynolds simply cast her off without a word. I took lodgings for her at a farm, and within a month of our troth-plight married her in the little church of Llanpwll.

It was certainly a marriage in haste, and possibly many may think that I ought to have waited till I had written to uncle George and had received an answer from him. Very likely I ought to have done so; but, at the same time, I do not feel very much conscience-stricken by my omission. I knew him to be so generous, kind, full of sympathy with every right impulse, and regardless of anything like self-interest, that not even his own anti-matrimonial principles would stand in my way. He liked people to act for themselves, and hated nothing, not even strange women, more than the idea of being thought tyrannical. I was so anxious that he should take Mildred to his heart as a daughter, that I could not bring myself to prejudice him against her by letting him know of her existence before it was too late for him to do anything but make the best of an exceedingly good bargain; for if he could only be surprised into seeing Mildred without warning, he would receive her even into his misogynistic heart, I was sure. Besides, it would take much too long for letters to pass and repass between Wales and China when I was going to marry Mildred, whatever their tenor might be. I was my own master, and he wished me to be so; for Miss Reynolds did not detest free women more than uncle George hated slaves.

So I wrote to Shanghai the day after my wedding-day, and we remained at Llanpwll for our honeymoon. I could not even yet bring myself to tell Mildred that she was not the wife of a poor and struggling painter. I almost wished myself one in reality, for she made the illusion as sweet to me as it was dear to her. But she must know it at last; and though I was sorry to leave our first married home, I looked forward to the morrow when I should take her back with me to London and to the real life that was to be ours till the end of our days, so that London should become better and dearer even than Llanpwll.

It was the morning of our return. I had taken my last plunge into the lake, and was on my way back to breakfast, fresh and hungry, when Mildred met me half-way with a letter in her hand.

"There's a letter for you, too," said she. "But I couldn't wait for you to show you this. See what I have brought on myself," she said, with the brightest and happiest of smiles, "by marrying you!"

"Mildred," the letter began, "I waited to see if you were really so lost to all sense of shame as to marry that man in rags in opposition to my irrevocable commands. You have done so; and, as you make your bed, so you must lie. Understand that henceforth you are to have no expectations from me. If you had been commonly grateful, and had married to please me or had remained with me, you may be gratified to know that I had intended to make you my sole heir. As it is, I, on the day after your disgrace, made my will. Whom I have put in your place is no concern of yours. Enough that Scripture bids us give much to those who have much, and that I am your aunt who is ashamed of you,

"JANE REYNOLDS.

"P.S. If the man in rags is disappointed to find he has married a beggar, you can't say I didn't tell you so."

"*Are* you disappointed?" asked she.

"You have lost a fortune for my sake? Mildred, did you know this when—"

"When I married you? Of course I knew it, very well; only if I hadn't married you, I should have done something else to lose it soon enough all the same. If I couldn't serve aunt Jane for love, it isn't likely I should for anything less, I suppose."

"Dear, if I tell you that I have been keeping a secret from you ever since we were married, shall you be very angry indeed?"

I could see a half-frightened look come into her face.

"A secret? what do you mean?"

You see that, after all, she had no reasonable reason for knowing that I was not an adventurer who had somehow found out that she had expectations from a rich aunt, and *was* disappointed with my bargain on finding that her expectations had gone off to the other side of the moon, where all the lost things are; or that I had not two or three other wives elsewhere; or that I was not a professional burglar, or anything else she would not like to be married to. I know she did not suspect anything of the sort, for Mildred was always the most unreasonable of women where I happen to be concerned; but still a secret a whole honeymoon long has an unpleasant sound, whatever it may be, and I felt a little sorry that I had done anything to make her ever so little afraid. Happily, though, it was a secret that would very well bear telling.

We had reached the house, and were entering our breakfast-room.

"Should you be very angry," I asked, "if I tell you that I have been deceiving you from the beginning, and that instead of being what I told you—there, darling, it's out now—I *am* a painter; but the reason I've done nothing as yet is because I've always been too well off to be anything but lazy. You can't expect much from a

man with an Uncle George like mine. We're rich enough
already to do without your aunt's legacy; and my own
father left me nothing because it was a family arrangement that Uncle George will leave me everything. He's a
splendid fellow, and you'll be as fond of him as I am when
he comes home again. I couldn't find the heart to prevent your doing the brave thing you did in taking a man
without a penny, all for love and liberty—and now I find
out that you've lost a fortune by it, I'm gladder still.
Why didn't you tell me you had something to lose?"

"Are you the only one to have secrets? Well, then, *I*
wanted *you* to be sure that you married me for myself;
and I was afraid—"

"No, you weren't; you were no more afraid I should
marry you for anything but yourself than that you—"

"I was afraid you would rather not marry me at all
than let me lose anything for you. There!"

"We're quits, then; and we'll have no secrets any
more. . . But here's my letter lying here unopened all
this while, and taking up the room where a trout or two
ought to be. Hullo! From Uncle George's lawyer?
What can he have to say? 'Dear Sir,—I regret—'"

The first words silenced me. And I read, no further
aloud:

"Dear Sir,—I regret to have to inform you that I am
by this post advised of the death, at Shanghai, of Mr.
George Kenrick, your uncle, on the 21st ultimo. An
epidemic of cholera is raging there, to which he fell one
of the first victims. You will be exceedingly surprised to
learn that *he was married* last May to a lady at Shanghai.
Mrs. Kenrick was also taken with cholera, and died, by
a remarkable coincidence, *on the very same day.* I can
only suppose that his well-known views and principle
concerning matrimony made him unwilling to inform
either his family or his solicitors of his marriage at the

time, and have also been the cause of his otherwise unaccountable delay in making it known. As the marriage was so recent, I need hardly say that he has left no children. Most unfortunately, however, it appears that he died intestate. The last will he made is in our hands, under which the whole of his estate (wholly consisting of personalty) is bequeathed to yourself as sole legatee. But as you are doubtless aware, every will is revoked by the marriage of the testator ; and we are advised that he was about to make a new will, almost as largely in your favour, when he died. In effect, therefore, he died intestate ; and the practical result is that (Mrs. Kenrick being dead) you will be entitled to no more than your share of the estate after distribution. For your guidance, and pending proceedings, I may tell you that I expect the estate to realize about £90,000. This will give about £9,000 for each of Mr. George Kenrick's ten brothers and sisters who either survive him or have left surviving issue. The £9,000 which would have come to your father will be divided among his nine children, giving to yourself the share of about £1,000, which, deducting succession duty, will give you, in the result, not more than a clear balance of £970.

" I estimate that the amount coming to you may prove less, but cannot well amount to more.

" I shall be happy to see you and give further particulars any time you can give me a call."

I handed the letter to Mildred without a word. Why had I not put off telling her I was rich for one single half-hour more? Nine hundred and seventy pounds— not fifty pounds a year—for a man who had been carefully taught how *not* to earn his living, who at thirty years old had not even made a beginning, whose so-called profession had been but pastime, who had nothing else to turn to, who had been deliberately trained to exaggerated ignorance of business, and who had just married a wife whose means amounted to nothing! Who could quite have forgotten himself, and one far dearer than himself, in grief for the best uncle who ever lived in the world? I could see it all—how George Kenrick's dread and shyness of women had been only the instinctive self-defence of an exceptionally tender-hearted man; how one woman at last had, as a matter of course, caught his heart, and had proved too much even for the elaborate outworks with which he had guarded it round; how, after all his open and notorious boasts and scorns, he had felt the shame of a man who had proved himself a rank impostor, and had kept putting off the evil day of having to tell; how—always an easy-going procrastinating man—he had in like manner put off making a new will, which would record his inconsistency in black and white, and would, indeed, be very difficult to settle in such a way as to do justice both to his wife and her possible children, and to me. . .

"You have married a poor devil of a painter after all," said I, as Mildred laid the letter down; "and you might have been—"

"Hush!" said Mildred. "I might have been wicked and miserable and rich. I am just as happy now as I was when I only believed that we were poor; and that is, the happiest girl in the world! Surely *you* don't want money so much as to make you forget that he is dead who meant to be so good to you?"

And then I knew that, though I had married in haste, I should never have to repent at leisure. I think that in that moment I first became a man.

III.

But it was a terribly up-hill road that lay before me
now. Even when that nine hundred and seventy pounds
should come into my hands, it would not mean fifty
pounds a year, for I owed at least five hundred. If I
could get in the end so much as four hundred pounds out
of the ninety thousand I should be fortunate; and even
that I must still further diminish by anticipation, in
order to live for to-day. It is not good to belong to a
very large family when personalty has to be divided.

It was wonderful how uncles, aunts, and cousins
turned up their noses at my calling now that I had to
earn my daily bread with it instead of carrying it on as
Uncle George's whim. Even my brothers had to admit
that there was no room in their offices for an amateur
artist who had been fool enough to saddle himself with a
penniless wife, and to whom accounts were Hebrew and
Chaldee. They were right—except in calling Mildred's
husband a fool. I could not be of any use to them for
years to come, and then I should be too old for a junior
clerk or office-boy. I must paint—paint—paint, since
that was all I could do, and become an artist, if I could,
in fact as well as in name. I should very likely have
thrown away my brush if Mildred had not been beside
me. But she believed in me, and found heart and
courage for two till she made me share them.

Nor was she idle. While I went at my work with
patient effort, she threw herself into hers with joy. I
verily believe she was glad to find that poverty and
labour had not turned out to be dreams, after all. We
lived in three rooms—and lived like hermits, except when
we went out together on impromptu holidays to enjoy

ourselves nearly as much as we did at home. In time, what with lessons and with occasional sales in very bad markets, we earned something, and made believe that we were beginning to make our own fortunes with our own hands. She was always so bright and gay that I forgot to be as careful over her as I ought to have been, and had not the heart to measure the work for her, over which she found her life so well filled. Mine, I felt, was hard work; hers looked like play, though it took up nearly as many hours as it did of mine.

But I must add that, at accounts and economies, she was nearly as bad a hand as I. There were times when we lived neither she nor I knew how. But at last there came a time when we found ourselves consciously face to face with the wolf at the door; and Love, though he did not even dream of so much as the shadow of a glance towards the bolt of the window, did not reconcile us to the growl.

Unwillingly enough, I had to lay down my brush for a while, and to look about for work out of doors, since none seemed coming to me. Meanwhile, Mildred set to work on a real picture in the spirit of a real artist who can never be divorced from Hope, do what he will. Away from her easel she was the most modest-minded of women; but, when she worked, she seemed to be fired with some spirit that was strangely like ambition, though I am sure it was really nothing of the kind. It was a fine subject that she had thought over till it had become a part of herself; and, though her technical skill was still very imperfect, it already showed qualities that are beyond the reach of scores of far better painters.

I knew she was working at it hard, but how hard I never knew—till one afternoon I came back from giving some lessons at a school, and found her in a dead faint upon the floor. And then, and not till then, I learned how, as soon as my back was turned early in the morning, she had been toiling, hungry and alone, every minute of the day until I returned; how energy had burned into fever; how genius, without corresponding vital strength, is nothing better than a disease.

And I had thought that mine alone had been work, and that hers had been pleasure and play; and how could I, while away from her, have guessed how a delicate girl would have spent all her hours? I had not learned to know Mildred, even then—and was the knowledge only to come when it was too late, when— I could not finish the thought. I got her to bed, and then went for the nearest doctor as fast as I could go.

At three houses, with red lamps and brass plates, I knocked and rang before I found surgeon or physician at home at an hour when most were going their rounds. At last, by good fortune I found one at home where the plate bore the name of "Mr. E. Segrave, Surgeon and Accoucheur."

I waited for what seemed an age, though I doubt whether two minutes had passed on the clock dial. At last the door opened.

"Dr. Segrave?" I began eagerly.

"Not Dr. Segrave," said a tall, cool, shrewd-looking Scotchman who entered; "I'm Dr. Menzies, and I am attending to my friend's patients while he gets a little holiday."

"Never mind," I said, more hurriedly than politely, "it's all the same."

In five minutes more—for he seemed to have the art of doing things slowly faster than other people do them quickly—he was by Mildred's bedside, I waiting for him in terrible anxiety by the half-finished picture into which she had been putting her actual life day by day. At last he came back.

"Well?"

"From what you tell me, and from what I can see,

she's prostrate from hard work, and want of air and exercise, and star—well, from not taking time enough to her meals. She wants rest, and plenty of meat, and change of air; and let me tell you that you must look after her well, for I think she is one of those women that look after everybody but themselves."

"There's no danger, then?"

"There's no worse danger on earth than working too much and eating too little. But if you mean is there anything wrong with her that cannot be mended—not at all. Eating's the easiest thing in the world, and doing nothing's easier still. And that's all *she's* got to do if you can manage it."

A weight was lifted off my heart; but I guessed what he meant—and that his prescription might prove harder to carry out than he knew. "You will call again?"

"I'll see how your wife is getting on before I go; but I am going abroad in a week. I shall tell Mr. Segrave of the case, if you give me your name."

"Kenrick. And thank you for—"

"Kenrick! Indeed! I once had a patient of that name out in Shanghai. I'll write a prescription—"

"What! You knew my Uncle, Mr. Kenrick of Shanghai?"

"Yes. I was called in to attend him when he died in the cholera outbreak. Husband and wife both in one day. It was an awful time with us; people dying around in whole households; it was like a nightmare—"

"And strangely enough I *had* a nightmare on the very eve of my uncle's death, in which I seemed to feel it all, just as if I was there. Yes, *on the very night before he died.*"

"Nightmare's common and death's common; it would be strange if they didn't meet together now and then."

"I dreamed of the cholera cloud. I saw a Chinese city. I did not know my uncle was married; and yet I saw him and a woman turn together into corpse-candles, and die out together before my eyes. I seem to see it now. It was hideously grotesque ; but I did not recover from it for a whole day."

" Working too little and eating too much is as bad for the brain, you'll find, as working too much and eating too little. Anybody that knew George Kenrick would be sure to dream about a woman if they dreamed of him just because of the way he used to talk of them."

" Nevertheless, it was a strange dream, even in detail "—

" We can try that," said Dr. Menzies, getting interested. " You say they were turned into corpse-candles, burning one against the other. Did you know which was he and which was she ? "

" I knew them both to the end."

" Then you can tell which of them burned out first. If you're wrong, it will show that your dream was but a partial coincidence, just as I say. You would naturally dream of a near kinsman, and be safe to dream of a woman for the reason I gave. You knew he was in China, and might have seen in the newspapers—though you might have forgotten—that there was cholera in Shanghai. But you could scarcely know which died the first, unless I tell you ; for nobody was in the two rooms where they died but a Presbyterian minister and myself."

" Her candle went out first," said I. " I remember counting ten, and then his followed hers."

" That's right enough," said Dr. Menzies, a little surprised at last. " It *was* she who died the first, and—you counted *ten ?* It was just *ten minutes* by the watch before he followed her. Well, all I can say is that "—

" It's something more than strange ! "

" No, Mr. Kenrick. It seemed a little strange at first, but on second thoughts, no ! If you dreamed one went out before the other, it must have been one of the two, and it was no more than the chances of heads or tails which one it would be. If I throw up a penny and you guess heads, and it *is* heads, you were just as likely to be right as wrong. There's nothing about it that's either strange or not strange. That there are not more such coincidences than there are is almost a miracle. There's no such thing as waste in Nature, Mr. Kenrick. And if a dream like that was more than a common ordinary coincidence, it would be waste; for what would be the use of your dreaming that one of your candles went out before the other when the fact itself could be of no manner of use to you?"

Even so had Mildred herself argued; and I was perforce compelled to put up with a chain of reasoning in which her imaginative nature agreed with the prosaic system of Dr. Menzies. Certainly mine had been a useless dream, and must have been useless by its very nature. I had nothing more to say.

It was merely accident that had made me remember my nonsensical dream when Mildred lay ill, and it went fairly out of my mind again as soon as Dr. Menzies had gone. Mildred had fallen asleep; and I sat and watched by her bedside, thinking how I could contrive to put life straight for her. She had no friends to shelter her from the daily troubles of our life till she should be strong enough to face them again; and my marriage, even more than the loss of my fortune, had made my relations cease to be my friends. Perhaps I was wrong, but I could not bring myself to ask favours—that is to say, charities— from those who now regarded me as a ne'er-do-well, and Mildred as a blunder and a burden. I was a stranger in the land; no more a Kenrick, who had a right to the help and countenance of other Kenricks, than Mildred herself. My share in my uncle's estate had gone long ago; over five hundred in paying old debts, the rest in keeping us going while we had been working and waiting, now, as it seemed, in vain. Without Hope by my side in the person of Mildred, I felt that I must lay down my brush once for all, and find something or anything to do that would insure her health, however uncongenial it might be.

The idea of emigration came uppermost in my mind. I had not neglected my body, and could use my hands in better ways than in painting pictures that nobody would buy. But since Mildred must go out with me, and since she could not travel till she was well, and since I must, being no longer a bachelor, carry out with me some sort of means or capital, even emigration did not look particularly hopeful.

However, I managed next day to leave Mildred for an hour or two while I went out to make inquiries about colonial matters in such quarters as were open to me. I needed advice, and could think of none better worth having than that of Mr. Archer, a young lawyer, who had always been, in a way, one of my friends in old times. He was a shrewd man of business, with an essentially practical way of looking at everything, but with no intolerance for people of different natures. He would give me the best advice he could, I was sure.

"I beg your pardon for keeping you waiting," he said. "But I was very deeply engaged, and I'm afraid I can't give you much time now. So you think of giving up painting and going abroad? Well, it does not sound badly. Only, as a married man, you can hardly treat emigration as a simple adventure, and go out with nothing in your pockets but your hands. I must think it over. Sit down and have a chat—it's a long time since we met, you and I. Not since we've been married men. We've both had our romances, it seems. But I'm hanged if there's any romance in all your Bohemia that beats what we find every day in the law. Talk of fiction!

Why, if I wanted that sort of light reading, and had to choose between the novels and magazines on the one hand and the law reports on the other, give me the law reports any day. Do you know why lawyers are so notoriously fonder of reading novels than any other men ? It's because they get *blasés* with romance, and want to refresh themselves with solid, probable, heavy prose.   I was up to the eyes in a queer story when you came in, or rather in a wild sort of riddle that will take all the courts together years to solve. It beats *me*.   A, you see, makes a will.   Next to the law of marriage for conundrums give me the law of wills.   All A's estate is left to B, a married woman.   We'll call B's husband C.   Very well.   If B, the wife, dies and leaves children behind her, the estate goes to the children.   If B, the wife, dies and leaves no children, but C, the husband, survives her, the estate goes to *him*.   If B, the wife, dies and leaves neither children nor husband surviving, then the estate goes to a distant relation, D.   That, avoiding technical language, is the effect of the will.   And you'd never guess how such a plain-sailing every-day will as that could possibly become likely to puzzle the House of Lords."

"No," said I, already puzzled myself between A, B, C, and D, "I certainly do not see."

"It comes to this.   First of all, B, the wife dies. Afterwards A, the testator, dies.   To whom does the estate go?"

"To B's children ?"

"She had none."

"To B's husband, then?"

"He is dead too."

"To the distant relation, then?"

"D?   You're missing the point—that's the very question that's got to be answered.   If you'd been the least bit of a lawyer, you'd have asked me whether the wife survived the husband, or the husband the wife, you see. *Don't* you see? If the wife survived, the estate goes to the distant relation. If the husband survived, the estate goes to *him*."

"But if he is dead?"

"That isn't the question. The question is, whether the estate goes to the distant relation, D. And, therefore, D must maintain that B, the wife, survived her husband."

"And which did survive?"

"Now you're getting warmer! Heaven knows. They were found dead on the same day in two rooms of the same house, and so says the register. Get out of that if you can. It's an awful muddle. There's no rule of law. There are cases, of course—there always are. There's a great case where a man and a woman were washed off the same plank out at sea, and both drowned. On one side it has been argued that the man is likelier to survive because he's the stronger and the more selfish and the better able to swim. On the other side, that the woman is likelier to survive because women have more vitality than men, and because a man naturally takes more care of a woman than he does of himself, especially if he's a sailor; and so on, and so on, through leagues of nonsense unspeakable. But it all comes to this—that there's no rule, that every case must stand on its own bottom, and that the courts will have facts, and nothing to do with fancies. Now, Kenrick—why, that's the very name of the wife and the husband, B and C—that's queer! However, that has nothing to do with the question. The question is "—

"But it *is* queer!" said I. "*I* had an uncle and an aunt who died in the same house on the same day. Did I never speak to you of my Uncle George, of whom I was godson, eldest nephew, and almost son?"

"*By* George! It must be the very man. Not that I ever heard of your having any uncle in particular till now;

or, if I ever did, I don't profess to remember pedigrees that I'm not paid to keep in mind. This was a George Kenrick, who, with his wife, died of cholera on the same day in Shanghai."

"Yes, within ten minutes of one another. It is a terrible story—more than terrible to me."

"Ten minutes? How do *you* know that? What do you mean?"

"I was told so by the doctor who attended them both and was with them when they died."

"What! The doctor? Where is he? What's his name?"

"Dr. Menzies. I saw him yesterday"—

"Did he tell you *which* died, died first—he or "—

"She."

"*She!* . . . Can you lay hands on Dr. Menzies . . . in an hour? You can? Then . . . Don't you understand? Under the will of Miss Reynolds "—

"Miss Reynolds?"

"Under the will of Miss Jane Reynolds, those ten minutes have given you an estate in Lincolnshire worth at least four thousand a year! For she left everything to a niece who married your uncle, and he survived her by ten minutes; and it is all real estate which goes to your uncle's heir-at-law; and you, as the eldest son of his next brother, are he!"

I have been making a very long story very short indeed. My case was certainly as clear as daylight; but that, as Archer would say, is not the question, nor is it the question—though that, too, is a strange one—that Miss Reynolds, by disinheriting Mildred, had made the man in rags her sole heir. To me the strange thing is, and must remain, that all this could never have happened unless I had dreamed my dream. Had I not dreamed of the extinction of the candles in their proper order and of the number ten, I should never have mentioned the matter to Menzies, or learned the precise nature of the coincidence—if so it must still be called—from him. And, therefore, had it not been for my dream, I should have been without the one piece of evidence wanting to complete the chain and make good my legal title.

Nevertheless, I pass no definite opinion. I quite see that, being in an excited state of mind, I should be likely to dream ; that, if I dreamed at all, it should be of Uncle George ; that, dreaming of him, I should dream of a woman ; that, dreaming of two failing candles, one of them should go out without the other, and that it was a mere toss-up which went out the first of them. It is difficult to find even the elements of so common a thing as a striking coincidence in so simple a matter. My readers must decide as they please.

But was this all? In one way it may be yes ; but, in another, most surely no.

" Mildred," said I to her one day, not so very long ago,—" Mildred, I once had a very strange and a very wonderful dream. It was that I—I of all men—neither strong nor wise nor particularly brave, had been selected, by some mysterious piece of injustice, to be the husband of the best, truest, and bravest of all the women in the world. I dreamed it so vividly, that I went out among the hills, and married the first girl I met before I knew anything about her, except that I loved her. Was not that a strange dream for a fairly sane man? Well, I woke up—one always must wake up at last from the very best of dreams, and from the best the soonest— and I found that *what my dream told me* was "—

" What ? " asked Mildred, with at least a show of fear.

" *True !* " said I. And I say so still.

Truth, indeed, is always stranger than fiction. I add

a few words which may interest the reader who is struck
by the pivot of my narrative, and that narrow bridge of
time which in *ten minutes* led to such important results.

The genial skilful physician who stood by and saw the
two "life-candles" burn out, and whose testimony in the
case became so important, is at this moment a distinguished practitioner in "the Garden Isle," where his
knowledge of the healing art and of the world together
make him at once a most desirable "guide, philosopher,
and friend."

HALF A MINUTE LATE.

I.

*　　*　　*　　*　　*　　*

" PUNCTUALITY is the soul of business.

" I am aware that one of the Seven Wise Men, either of Greece or of Gotham, has preferred to read 'Punctuality is the thief of time.' And, on the whole, I am disposed to agree with the wise man. 'A proverb,' says another wise man, 'is the folly of many and the stupidity of one.'

" Punctuality is a bad habit. I say so distinctly. All habits are bad, because when they are not good they injure, and when they are good they are bad, because they deprive a good action of the merit of free-will and degrade it into mere slavery. But of all habits, punctuality stands first and foremost in point of utter badness. Defend me from a punctual man ! He is arrogant. He considers himself absolved from all other virtues, because he has one for which a clerk or journeyman is paid. He is worse than arrogant—he is an arrogant slave, so degraded as to brag of his slavery. He has no sympathy with free men. He is sordid and mean. To save a wretched minute he will miss a joy. He will put an end to the most interesting conversation to keep an appointment with a lawyer or a tailor—and he is a fool for his pains, because neither lawyers nor tailors

L

are punctual men, not even in sending in their bills. He is doubly a fool indeed, for he deliberately gives himself a bad character. He expects others to be punctual for his sake, which is selfish. If he is ill-tempered, as cultivators of the pettifogging virtues mostly are, he quarrels with them; he is incapable of imagining that human nature is not regulated by clock-work; in fact, and in short, and to sum up all, the punctual man is of necessity an arrogant, mean-minded, degraded, haggling fool ! "

*　　*　　*　　*　　*　　*

Harold Maynard was standing, in evening dress, with one hand upon the bell-pull, and holding in the other the evening paper, from which, during the interval between touching the bell-rope and pulling, he read this choice extract of wisdom—an extract from one of those bold dashes at paradox that newspaper readers are supposed to digest comfortably after one o'clock P.M. In the morning, telegrams ; in the evening, paradox, is the due order of the day's news.

There was no earthly reason why Harold Maynard should not have pulled so soon as his fingers had closed upon the cord. Though it was only in a lodging-house, the wire was in excellent order, and the cord unstrained. Indeed, the bell-hanger had put everything to rights only yesterday, and Harold was not one of those angry men who ring twenty times apiece for twenty things in a day. No, he might have rung instantly ; but his eye had fallen upon these few lines of print, which surely out-paradoxed paradox ; and he read them through, naturally enough, before he pulled.

Demons do not, as a rule, write in newspapers, nor was this special journal distinguished for demoniac energy. The passage would not have attracted him had it been of the usual style of that journal. But I think, if the passage was not written by a demon, some demon must have been at the elbow of the writer when it was penned.

Why did he write it? Probably he would have laughed at the question, and thought of pay-day. But how many people ever know why they do anything? For that matter, "Why am I born?" as a famous American lecturess on woman's rights commenced an eloquent peroration, with the sole effect of drawing from a little boy in the gallery the only possible answer, "I give it up, if you put it as a co-nundrum." Probably we do nothing for the purpose with which we do it. And the writer of the article, thinking of pay-day, and never having heard of this particular reader, was tricked by some jocular demon into writing what made Harold Maynard just half a minute late in pulling the bell.

For it was just half a minute, to a tick of the clock, between his touching the bell-rope and giving the pull.

It must have been for this purpose and no other that the article had been written : for the writer would have stared at learning that his paradox could have had any effect whatever upon man, woman, or child.

II.

Harold Maynard was a young man of about thirty, tall, broad-shouldered, and well made, a man of much muscle and with some brains. He had many excellent qualities, and not the least of them was that he thought less of his good points than others thought of them. He could ride a horse and pull an oar, and both without bragging or thinking that life was bestowed upon him for such things. He thought a great many of his friends very good fellows, and they returned the compliment.

He was proud only of two things: a character for being always up to time—neither too late nor, still worse, too soon—and of a very strong admiration for Letty Despard.

Of that he was very proud—as a man should be of loving a girl whom he thinks worthy the love of better men than he. He was proud of it, even though hope did not go hand in hand with pride. It was not that he thought it impossible for her to care for him. On the contrary, ever since that evening when he had asked a blossom of tube-rose from her after waltzing with her twice, and after she had refused it three times, and had ended by dropping it by accident when he was near enough to pick it up and secrete it, he had felt—in the subtle way one feels such things—that she was to be won. Won? Yes—but maintained? That was another thing.

Love has been defined as "an insane desire to support somebody else's daughter." And that was just what Harold Maynard could not do. It was as much as he could do to support himself alone, and he was not an extravagant man. He knew the value of time perfectly; and time is money, as all the world knows. Ah! if it only were, and if he could only pay into his banking account half the spare time he had on his hands! Though very much the reverse of the sort of man who looks at both sides of a sixpence, and lingeringly feels the edge before parting with it, he was a rigid economist; rather than lose a minute, of the value, say, of three halfpence, he would charter a special train from Edinburgh to London at seven shillings a mile. It may be that his very form of economy left him poor, and far richer in the wealth that is measured by minutes than that which is measured by pounds sterling.

At any rate, he was very much in love, and, in respect of fortune, like the gourmand and the goose—he found it too much for one, but by no means enough for two. And Letty Despard was very far from being a romance heroine, to be kept for nothing a year. She could eat and drink as a healthy girl should be able, and could dress—to perfection.

Many days, and many nights too, had Harold Maynard consumed in trying to find something to do. Many a man of his age and of twice his ability will know what that means who has neither the will of iron, nor the key of gold, nor the spoon of silver. Fortune is not a bird to come for whistling; she needs the salted tail. And how to salt her before catching her is a problem that puzzles others than children. I need not enumerate the plans that he laid out for life, how well they promised, how surely they came to nothing. It seemed to him as if Fortune were a ball rolled before him by an invisible imp, ever at his toes, never in his fingers. He did not despair, for love means hope; and he was not weary of the chase, for he was young and strong; but it did seem hard sometimes to feel time slipping away, and yet bringing him no nearer to the end. He felt himself the sport of an altogether peculiar destiny. All men's destinies feel peculiar—to themselves. And it was all the harder on a man who was always up to time, and never lost an instant—especially when he was expecting to meet Letty.

But it is a long lane that has no turning. Just as he was beginning the most keenly to feel that the world did not want another pair of strong shoulders when it already had so many—that is to say, at the most unexpected moment possible—he received a letter that made his heart beat faster than if it had been signed Letitia Despard, instead of being dashed off in bold male hieroglyphics that gave reading it the excitement of discovering a mystery.

"Dear Maynard,—O you blind burrage and honey running in the may of braid! Oil Despard by thunder hangs a filling jingo Hong-Kong—aged penny, cold congregation, strong in treacle—lungs, hurry in trances, plundering indefensible : so Yorick the merry man. Wing with me, wit, sing sharp to-day. Sting white, the irons not.

> " And believe me, evening shrine,
>
> " T. L. WINTER."

Tom Winter did not live in Hanwell; he simply had a heroic contempt for pot-hooks and hangers.

" Has he no respect for other people's time?" thought Maynard ; but the name of Despard was written legibly enough, and compelled attention to a letter that would otherwise have been turned into a spill. For that purpose, Maynard selected an unreceipted bill from his bootmaker, lighted his pipe, and sat down to see if that would help him. And, after a fair amount of study, he managed to make out as follows, omitting impossibilities :

> " Dear Maynard,—Do you mind turning an honest penny in the way of trade? Old Despard, my uncle, wants a fellow to go to Hong-Kong—good pay, good appointment . . . . business habits, punctuality indispensyble; so you're the very man. Dine with me at six sharp to-day. Strike while the iron's hot,
>
> " And believe me, ever thine,
>
> " T. L. WINTER."

And he made out the postscript over the page :

> " If you accept you will sail by the Ganges, from East India Dock, on Thursday. Mem.: Old Despard dines with me. He will take you, if you will go."

If he would accept! Why, here was an opening into the heart of dreamland. Old Despard was not only the uncle of Tom Winter, but the father of Letty, and a rich China merchant into the bargain. Into dreamland? Nay, into the land of certainty. Maynard was pretty safe to do himself credit with any employer, if he only had elbow-room. Whittington and the good apprentice are not the only men who have married their master's daughter. As a penniless failure he had no chance of becoming old Despard's son-in-law; as a trusted *employé*, working under old Despard's very eyes, if he had no chance he would be a fool. There was but one answer:

"Dear Tom,—Of course; and thank you. At six sharp—to the minute: you know what that means with me.

"Thine always,

"H. M."

Twenty minutes to dress—fiftcen minutes for a hansom to Tom Winter's. He measured it accurately. He was not more, not one second more, than half a minute late in pulling the bell.

"Fetch me a hansom!" he said to the girl.

III.

He was in ample, even superfluous, time for a dinner engagemant, as we blind mortals measure such things. Five minutes' grace is always allowed, to a most notoriously punctual man; nobody ever thought of half a minute. Maynard sat back in the cab with a good conscience on the score of his favourite virtue, and let no feeling of hurry interfere with his future as it lay panorama-wise before him. His start in life was assured; for he knew Tom Winter, who always understated everything, and whose letter meant that his appointment was secure. Old Despard liked him, he knew, as a man. And Letty, he knew liked him in the same capacity. It was only Monday as yet; before Thursday he would have ample time to turn his hope of Letty—so far as she was concerned—into certainty. He had never said the words "I love you" in plain speech, but in the plainer speech that lovers know the words had been said and answered. Looks and instincts only needed translating.

Suddenly the hansom stopped, as hansoms will so long as cabmen believe that narrow byways are shorter cuts than broad thoroughfares. A cart-horse had just fallen in front, and blocked the way. Maynard pushed up the trap over his head.

"Can't you go round another way? I'm in a hurry, and it looks like a long job here."

"Well, it ain't my fault. I didn't make the block. It would have been behind us instead of afore if we'd been half a minute sooner, that's all."

Nor had the half minute grown into more than a minute over, when the block was removed, and the cabman was touching his horse with the lash, to make believe he was making up for lost time. And a minute and a half is not worth minding—scarcely even in the matter of catching a train. It was full five minutes to six still, and he was not more than six minutes and a half at the outside from Tom Winter's. Had he been on his way to meet Letty anywhere the smallest delay would have put him out of temper. As it was, not even his principle of punctuality was offended. "That's the best of being in good time," he even said to himself, with self-gratulation. "One doesn't spoil one's digestion beforehand with hurries and worries. One can look after the hours, and leave the half minutes to take care of themselves."

The cabman had named the half minute, or it would never have occurred to him.

"Hulloh !"

I write it, not because it represents by any means what the cabman said, but because his real speech must be expurgated to be presentable; and "Hulloh," though not the whole truth, was really one word among many. The horse was pulled back hard against the splash-board, and Maynard thought he heard a cry, set in the cabman's volley of hard words like a lost heart in a storm.

It was just beginning to darken, and a street mist had been coming on that made the gas-lamps flare yellow and double the darkness. Maynard was out of the cab in an instant to see what mischief he had done. It was only too clear.

Among the hoofs of the horse lay a figure—whether woman, girl, or child, he could not tell at first. In the by-road and in the dark, a smaller crowd had sprung out of the pavement than usual, and he managed to raise, without much interference, her who had been so nearly run over, and with no more than some two minutes' delay. She was of small weight, and Maynard's muscles soon had her into the cab, leaning back into the farther corner.

"To the nearest hospital," he called out to the cabman, following her. "How far?"

"Not more than four minutes."

"Then look alive. Do it in three."

He was not thinking of himself as he urged extra speed, nor of Hong-Kong, nor even of Letty, nor of how, by compound interest, the first half minute had now become seven and a half; so that the five minutes' grace before meat had expired by the time he was near the hospital. He might have unwittingly caused the death of a fellow-creature for aught he knew. She was not dead yet, that he could make out —only stunned ; blood was running from under the hair over one of her temples, and she was ghastly pale. She was too close for him to see more in the alternate darkness and flare of the night: he could only support her with his arm, regardless of delay. He did not even say to himself, "What a bore!"

By the better light in the hall of the hospital, he and the house-surgeon together saw a young girl, not more than eighteen years old, still insensible and bleeding, still as pale as death, and dressed very plainly—poorly even, though not like the poor. Her features were small, good, and a lady's; but her set lips and closed eyes placed her for the present beyond criticism. She was long in coming to. But the surgeon brought her round at last. She opened her eyes, and said, in a very sweet voice,

" Mother, where am I ? "

The surgeon held her pulse as he said, " Don't be afraid. You've had a little accident in the street, that's all, and you've been brought to St. Martin's—the best place for you." He spoke with a little more tenderness and less quickness than are affected by men who have to deal with cases wholesale; and, now that she had opened her eyes and spoken, there was an indescribably pathetic air about her that made it impossible to speak to her merely as a case, or otherwise than tenderly. Maynard looked inquiringly at the surgeon. It is certainly more unpleasant to run down some people than others.

She suddenly put her hands to her head. " In a hospital! An accident! O, for God's sake let me go! " And she tried to rise.

" Not yet. Be a good girl. We'll see to-morrow. You can't go now. We will see to your friends."

A clock struck a quarter past six. The half minute had rolled itself on into fifteen. Harold Maynard had committed the unpardonable sin of a punctual man. He had been guilty of an act of charity, which means inevitable loss of time. Surely he might have sent her to St. Martin's in charge of a policeman. And now here was time flying without his hearing the flutter of a feather.

The girl fell back with a moan, and her eyes filled with despair. Harold felt conscience-stricken. What had he done? And, having brought new trouble into the world, what could he do? what should he not do? And it is only fair to say that, if the girl with the sweet face and the sweet voice had been some broken-down and utterly uninteresting old crossing-sweeper, he would have felt the same, and for a while have forgotten even Letty Despard.

"Is there anything I can do for you?" he said, gently and ashamed, touching her wrist slightly with his fingers.

"Only—help me to go home. I *must* go home."

Harold looked at the surgeon. The surgeon shook his head, and signified "Impossible just now."

"Can I see your friends?—can I let them know?"

"I have a mother, and she—is dying. And she has no friends but me; I—I have none but her. She is *dying*—alone. I went out for help, and "—

The girl's agony was beyond tears.

"Good God!" said Harold. "I will go—trust me, my poor girl. Tell me where she lives—her name. Will you trust me?"

The girl's eyes gave him a long look. Apparently they were satisfied; and they thanked him in that simplest and honestest of languages that has no tongue.

"20, Powys Place—the third floor. Mrs.—Despard."

The clock struck a quarter to seven. From the half minute had grown forty-five.

IV.

Nevertheless, more than unpleasant as was this interruption to the plans of a punctual man, whose career was dependent upon his being "up to time," and who had taken the special precaution of pledging himself thereto—nevertheless, the hospital was not so far from Powys Place, nor Powys Place from Tom Winter's lodgings, as to prevent Maynard's catching old Despard before he rose from table ; and though to prefer the affairs of a stranger to one's own is unbecoming in a business man, and speaks ill for him to would-be employers, it is like the police-magistrate's opinion of drunkenness—no excuse, but a paliation. For the moment the name of Despard did not strike him ; it was so constantly running in his mind in connection with Letty, that it came rather as an echo to his thoughts than as an interruption. He took another hansom, and threw away another double fare.

Powys Place was not so aristocratic as its name. It was nothing better, indeed, than a street of shabby, not to say doubtful, lodging-houses in the neighbourhood of a railway station, where respectable people might lodge, but most assuredly not of their own free will. It says much for the girl that Harold, who knew the world, did not take her character from that of her surroundings. Not that his instinct was singular, for pure eyes tell their own tale. He found No. 20, aud knocked at the door. It was opened by a red-faced man in shirt-sleeves, smoking a long churchwarden.

" Mrs. Despard ? " said Harold doubtfully.

" Third floor back," said the man gruffly, and disappeared into a darkness of dust and onions.

Harold groped his way to the third floor back, listened, heard no sound, and then entered, as noiselessly as he could, without knocking. For a while he could hardly see for the rushlight that darkened the little room with its glimmer. He hardly knew what to do. He had not till now realized what is meant by the word "alone." If the light showed him a dying woman, how should he approach the bed and speak to her, and what should he say? The house was as silent as if uninhabited, and he was not inclined to seek the help of the red-faced man who had opened the door. True, he might affect to be a doctor brought to the bedside by the girl, see what ought to be done, and account for the girl's absence in the best way possible. But whatever he might do, the situation was trying for any but a sister of mercy. For half a second he wished he had not come.

He listened in the half darkness, and fancied he heard the sound of breathing. The situation was ghastly altogether—alone in a light worse than darkness, in a poor room in a neighbourhood without an affectation of character, and by the bedside of a dying woman, when he should by rights have been dining himself into a career. Presently the wind began to howl, and a dog to howl in answer. The howl of a dog at night is bad for people with nerves, but, under such circumstances, bad even for those fortunate people who have none.

Harold approached the bed as softly as a perversely-creaking board would let him, and said quietly,

"The doctor, Mrs. Despard."

. There was no answer. He had heard breathing but an instant ago, and now the bed might be empty, for any sound he could hear. He listened again; he heard nothing but the howl of the dog and of the wind.

He took up the rushlight and brought it to the bedside, shading it with his hand. Then by degrees he lessened the shadow thus thrown over the bed until he could see

all that was to be seen. There was not much to see.
Only a dead woman—nothing more.

What was he to do now? To leave the corpse alone
with the wind and the other night-ghosts would be sheer
barbarity. He must provide a watcher somehow, if only
the man with the pipe and the red face—and then at the
risk of having to find a watcher for the watcher, lest any
little valuables the dead woman might by any chance
leave behind her should find an unintended legatee. No
doubt there must be a woman in the house—and yet if
there had been, Mrs. Despard would hardly have been
left to die alone. He closed the door behind him, turned
the key, and carried the rushlight downstairs. He met
nobody, and the rooms he passed were either dark or
empty. At last he found the head of the kitchen stairs.
These also he descended, and found himself in a labyrinth
of sculleries—so it seemed.

"Hoy, there!" growled a voice from somewhere that
smelled like beer. "Who are you?"

"And where are you? Mrs. Despard is dead."

"So's Queen Anne. I could have told you that an
hour ago."

"Why didn't you, then?"

"Because you didn't ask me. That's why."

"Is there any woman in the house to see to her?"

"There's the young woman, I suppose."

"Miss Despard? She has been hurt by a cab, and is
in the hospital."

"Well, then, she's all right. And the old lady's all
right. And I'm all right—they've paid to Saturday. I
don't mind a body in the house, not I. I'll see to it in
the morning."

"There's no other woman in the house? No neighbours you could send for?"

"You seem to think a mighty lot of a dead body,

young gentleman. Bless you, you wouldn't if you was me. You're a doctor, I suppose. Then look here—I'll make a bargain. Dead men don't tell no tales, nor dead women either, and there ain't a soul knows the old lady but her daughter, and she won't know but what she's buried when she gets out of hospital. You take the body for two sovereigns. Done? You'll get a whole woman to cut up, and I sha'n't be bothered."

"May I ask," said Harold, "who you are?" His tone was not amiable.

"Who I am? You're a green hand, I reckon, for a medical man, not to hear of Knaggs. I'm Knaggs. And I can get you an arm or a leg most days—and bones any time. But a whole body isn't an every-day thing."

It was useless to argue with a ghoul.

"Who is—was, Mrs. Despard?"

"A decayed gentlewoman, I suppose. That's what they call her sort. If she weren't a good bit decayed I wouldn't have had her for a lodger. But she scraped her rent together—or she wouldn't have had me for a landlord."

"It is not a common name—Despard."

"Nor's Knaggs."

"You can tell me nothing of her? Nor of the girl?"

"Bless us, I've told you enough, haven't I? I know no harm of the girl. She'd got a few pounds to keep out of the workhouse. I didn't ask how she came by 'em. I took 'em, as they came due."

Every natural instinct rose up in Harold. It was nothing to him, but he could not bear the thought of that sweet-faced, pure-eyed girl coming out of St. Martin's to find her mother dead—but not buried, and unable to find so much as a mound of turf to mourn over. Without another word to Mr. Knaggs he returned to the room he had left, and himself became a watcher of the dead—he himself could not have told, and indeed he never asked himself, why. He closed the eyes of the dead woman, and covered her face decently.

Then—it was a ghastly process—he set himself to rob the dead for the sake of the living. In that house of ghouls, with the wind howling round, he felt almost like a murderer as he searched the room for any articles of value to prevent their falling into dishonest hands. He did not find much—only the portrait of a handsome young man, brown haired and brown eyed : a miniature, well painted, and set in a black velvet case and frame. This he took; and then, with a sort of conscious sacrilege, drew from the dead fourth finger the woman's only ornament— a wedding-ring.

He sat down at the window, drew up the blind, and did not think it sacrilege to light a cigar.

"Only half a minute"—he remembered the words of his first cabman. And at that moment the clock from near St. Martin's struck one. Only half a minute late —only seven hours and a quarter. The snow-ball rolled and grew.

Harold Maynard was growing hungry. But he felt like a sentinel at his post, and it was too late even to dream of dinner now. So he dreamed of Letty and looked at the stars.

V.

It was a glorious relief when he woke from his dream, threw open the window, and let in the sun. He locked the door, carried away the key, gave it, with all needful information, to the sergeant on duty at the nearest police-station, breakfasted, and then went straight to the hospital.

"How is the girl?" he asked the surgeon. "I saw her mother—she is dead. Ought the girl to be told?"

"It would kill her—that's all. She is very weak and ill—and in my opinion she wants food as much as anything."

So there was nothing for it but to let her wait for the bad news. It was needless even to relieve her mind with kindly equivocation, for she was in a high fever before noon. And so, at last, Harold was left free to attend to his own affairs—and it was high time. He had missed his appointment: this was Tuesday, and on Thursday the Ganges was to sail.

Obviously the best thing he could do was to call at once on old Despard: and Tuesday was a good day, because he was always at home on Tuesday, and there was the chance of seeing Letty alone into the bargain. He must see her alone before sailing for Hong-Kong, and his heart told him that no loss of half a minute, or half a thousand minutes, could hurt him there. He had lost a dinner, but he had breakfasted, and there was an end. The sun shone, and the world was beautiful again—all but for the sad face of a girl whose mother had just died alone. And that, as he drew nearer to Letty, was smiled out by the sun.

It is a curious fact that when a man is in love the sun shines even when it rains—unless indeed it rains when the sun shines. But to-day the sun really shone.

And it was high time—for Hong-Kong or for anywhere. Harold had but one sovereign left in the world to call his own, and one that he had borrowed on Saturday from Tom Winter. But it was all right now. With Hong-Kong and Letty before him he could afford to be as poor as Job, or even as Midas, who was the poorest mortal ever known.

By good fortune, or rather by punctual management, he found old Despard at home. The China merchant was a tall, rather fine-looking man, with signs of port and portliness, handsome brown eyes and iron-grey hair —a commercial captain, every inch of him. People said he was difficult to deal with, and ill-tempered when the gout was upon him; but that is a not an uncommon failing, or rather was not when wine was wine, and men drank it without fear instead of taking it in timid nips all day. Old Despard's toes were often tender, but his stomach was sound.

He had a library, though he never read: and here he received Maynard.

"Take a seat, pray. Your business, if you please?"

"I was to have had the pleasure of meeting you at my friend Winter's."

"Indeed?"

"I was prevented—but it was to arrange about my going out for you to Hong-Kong."

"Ah, well. Is this your letter? H. M.—yes; Harold Maynard. Never sign initials, Mr. Maynard. I never do. I was informed you were a punctual man. In my business punctuality is indispensable."

"I pride myself on punctuality."

"An excellent pride. And you say in your letter you know what a minute means. Your letter is a written undertaking to be at a certain place at a certain time. I don't remember meeting you at my nephew's.

"Nothing could have vexed me more. But—well, I ran, or my cab ran, over a girl in the street, and I had to see her to a hospital"—

"That was not business, Mr. Maynard. There is a time for all things. You should not have done so."

"What else could I have done?"

"Kept your appointment. But too late is too late, if it's only by half a minute, Mr. Maynard. Not having met you I have this morning engaged another gentleman, who, I trust, will not waste my time in running over girls in the streets of Hong-Kong. Time presses, and the Ganges never delays an hour."

That wretched half minute! It seemed turning into a live thing. How could he have supposed that an errand of common charity would have cost him so much more than a dinner? And here, just because he had delayed in pulling a bell-rope for an inappreciable space of time he was as far from Hong-Kong as London, as far from Letty as from Hong-Kong; with only two sovereigns in the world, and one borrowed, and with no prospect of earning more.

The sun went out of the day. It was a cruel blow. But there was nothing to be done. After all, it was fair enough that old Despard should have supposed him indifferent, and have engaged another *employé* under the pressure of time. He could not even complain. He could only put a brave face over his heavy heart, and say, " I'm very sorry. Good-day."

But, as it happened, he had left his hat in the drawing-room. And on returning there to fetch it, found not only his hat, but Letty—so radiantly lovely that the sun came back again. He had never seen her so beautiful; and there was a shy joy in her face as she turned to him that contrasted bitterly with his own sad look of a beaten man.

But—was he beaten? Could he feel beaten when the girl whom he loved was there before him? Repulsed at one point, could he not do all things for her? Only he must have hope—he was no poet, to be willing to live for a dream. He must feel something to win. That she was more that half won he knew; but the word had never been said, and now, in his disappointment, he was longing and hungering for the word that would console him for all.

" Letty," he said, " I didn't mean to see you to-day, but—I'm glad. To see you, I mean. I'm not glad other

ways.　It's hard that a wretched cabman should have—
Well, it seems I must try again in England, after all."

"Well," she said sweetly, "I suppose you don't very
much mind?"

"Not mind?"

"I suppose if you'd minded—very much, you know—
you would have seen papa yesterday?　I heard all about
it, and—yes, I was very, very glad you were going to
Hong-Kong.　But, of course, if you can do better in
England I shall be gladder still."

"Letty!　What chance is there in England?"

"You know best, Harold."

"You know I don't know.　And you know why—why
I was so anxious to go to China."

"Indeed I don't know."

"Letty!　Don't you know what I live for?"

"If you had cared—so very much—I think you'd have
managed to dine with cousin Tom and papa."

"I couldn't, dear—Letty, I mean.　It was not my fault
—the devil seems to be in everything.　I miss my
appointment.　I lose my employment.　And now you
tell me that it was my fault, and that I don't care."

"If you had cared you would have done what you
cared," said Letty, with the sweetest obstinacy.

"But I had to look after a girl"—

"Yes?"

"My cab nearly killed her."

"Well?"

"Well!　what would you have done?"

"It depends on how much I cared for her, I suppose—
if I was a man."

"Letty!　I never saw her in all my life before."

"Then it was odd you cared about her so much as to
give up everything for her."

"Letty . . . . I love you . . . . Will you be my wife
. . . . some day?"

Letty had been charmingly composed. But the question was sudden, and it was at least a second before she recovered her composure. Well—she did like Harold Maynard very much indeed. He danced and flirted to perfection. He loved her. He was handsome and strong, and made love straight out, in the right way. She sighed. But—but—but—what was a girl to say to a man who not only had no money, and would only waste her youth in a long engagement, but was so obstinately unlucky as to throw away the one chance he had of winning her? " Yes " gave a little flutter in her heart; it almost spread its wings—but—

" O, I *am* so sorry, Harold ! " she said, with the most touching sweetness. And that meant No.

Could he have liberated the fluttering " Yes " even yet if he had refused to take her answer? Perhaps; but something prevented him.

It was now the gigantic ghost of that half minute—a half minute no more, no more even an hour, a day, a year—but a whole life, fortune, Letty, and all. The details might be absurd, but massed together they had swelled into a mountain, and the absurdities were the mocking grins of its gnomes. " Only half a minute ! " Only destiny.

But one effect of such combined assaults of Fate upon a weak man is to make him weaker ; upon a strong man to make him stronger. They are the tests of manhood and of will. The loss of Letty might be unbearable, but it had to be borne. The world must still go on, though for Harold all buying and no selling, all hunger and no food. Something *must* be done. He had said so a thousand times for Letty's sake : now he must say it once for all, and for his own. But even his pressing need did not keep him from calling at the hospital the next day with the girl's miniature and ring.

She could see him now. He sat down by her bedside and looked for a moment into the sweet, pure eyes, wondering what he should say to them. They were very different from Letty's eyes. He could not imagine them looking coldly upon a beaten lover—he could imagine them lighting up with sympathetic joy or softening into comfort. He longed to know by what name to call her. But, meanwhile, how should he tell her that she was alone in the world?

He looked at her gravely, and laid the ring before her.

"It is well with her now," he said. He took her hand that she might not feel all alone, and turned away his face that she might weep freely. The tears came, and then she sobbed bitterly; but her hand clung to his as if it had been a child's, and with a touch as innocent. The tears came into his own eyes.

"I will see you again," was all else he said to her. He felt he was giving her strength by being there; and soon she would have to face the world all alone. "What is her name?" he asked a nurse.

"Alice Despard."

"Will she get well?" he asked the surgeon.

"Who can tell?"   But he looked—"No."

Harold returned to his lodgings well-nigh heart-broken. The lost half minute had lost him fortune, love, hope almost, and had killed the sweetest face and voice he had ever seen or heard.

But when he reached home, his room was occupied— by a policeman, and a companion in plain clothes. The latter said, before he could ask their business,

"You are Harold Maynard. I am a constable. And I arrest you on the charge of wilful murder."

"What in Heaven's name do you mean?"

"The murder of Jane Despard. And you'd better come along quietly, as you must, and not say a word."

VI.

Harold Maynard—and wilful murder!

Think of yourself, you who read this, and couple your own name with two such words if you can. And then you will conceive the effect of such a charge upon such a man, who was as incapable of such a crime, even in imagination, as you.

And yet who shall say after this that the evidence of circumstance may not bear with crushing force against the most innocent of men?

The surgeon called in by the police had found that the woman in Knagg's house in Powys Place, Jane Despard by name, had been suffocated, not by nature, but by man, who does everything so much more artistically than she. Suspicion at first fell naturally upon the landlord. But he in the first place volunteered an ineffectual search of the premises, and, while still in custody, gave certain information that put a different complexion on affairs. A gentleman had come from St. Martin's Hospital while the poor lady lay dying. That gentleman was easily identified, by inquiries at the hospital, as Harold Maynard. Very slight inquiries were enough to make manifest that Harold Maynard was a very poor man, with the position of a gentleman to keep up, with many debts, no employment, and no means. He had been seen at the hospital in possession of a missing wedding-ring—that in itself was nothing. And at his lodgings was found a miniature, the property of the murdered woman. That was not much more. But—

The detective in plain clothes, who was sharp enough, had taken the trouble to dissect the miniature. And between the portrait and the back he found—Bank of England notes to the amount of two thousand pounds! Motive enough for murder and to spare, in the eyes of the law. *Cui bono ?*

And he who possessed the miniature, and had never delivered it out of his own hands, had been alone with the murdered woman during ample time for murder and robbery. If he had come with a charitable motive, with what motive had he carried away two thousand pounds? Temptation makes the thief, not the thief the temptation—as all the world knows.

It was a very triumph of detectivism. Why should a sane man rob a dead woman of a miniature that could be nothing to him if he did not know what lay behind? And the notes were old notes—a hoard well-nigh as old as the miniature must have been. There was no difficulty in finding them : no secret trick : the only thing was to have the idea. And even as the idea had at once struck the detective, so surely it must have struck Harold Maynard.

And so he was in the cell of the police-station, with a consciousness of innocence and a conviction that the proofs against him were overwhelming. He had a night's leisure to think over all things. Why was he charged with murder? Because, omitting minor steps, he had been alone with the dying Mrs. Despard. Why had he been there? Because he had run over a girl in the street mist. Why had he run over her? Because he had been driving over just that part of the road where she was crossing. Why so? Because he had been delayed by a block. And why delayed? Because he had not arrived at the spot just half a minute before. And why not? Because he had started half a minute late from his own door. Why? Because half a minute had passed between his touching his bedroom bell-rope and giving it a pull.

And finally, why? Because some unknown journalist had written a paradoxical article in an evening newspaper.

Messieurs et mesdames, such things are happening every day and all day long. Are there any little things in the world? Are there any great things?

> "Alas, how easily things go wrong!
> A sigh too much, or a kiss too long,
> There follows a mist and a weeping rain"—

But too often has that been quoted and misquoted. Half a minute late, indeed! Half a second, half the tick of a watch, and half that, and half that again. Life is made up of such things. Sighs and kisses are Brobdingnagian in comparison to the straws that do the undone work of Archimedes' lever and move the world. I would prove in the twinkling of an eye that the oak grows from the acorn, and the forest from a grain of mustard-seed. Not all our lost half minutes end in murder. But they may, ay, and do, end in worse—in blunders never to be redeemed, in life-long estrangements, in missed opportunities, in all the thousand ills that souls are heirs to. Half minutes have lost battles, and overthrown empires, and missed trains.

But these reflections, though philosophical enough in their way, and though he had leisure to make them, in no wise helped Harold Maynard. What was his defence to be?

He might feel sure enough in his own mind that Knaggs, the professional resurrectionist, was more likely to make sure of a body, during the absence of Alice, than he to make sure of a hundred thousand pounds. But nothing was found on Knaggs, while two thousand pounds were found upon him. The world is never tired of asking *Cui bono?* The world mostly mistranslates it, indeed, but that is the way of the world. And here it applied only too well.

In short, there was but one person in the whole world who believed in Harold Maynard—and that was she who of all people in the world had most reason to disbelieve in him, and to feel the need for revenge—upon the guilty, if possible, but in any case upon somebody. Stories of murders will find their way everywhere, even among people who never read : even into the wards of hospitals. Letty might forget that she had ever cared for a murderer in a deep flirtation with Tom Winter, who may have had his own reasons for so generously banishing a dangerous rival to Hong-Kong. Mr. Despard might set down murder as the natural and necessary outcome of being late for dinner—a less heinous offence, but far more fertile of general discomfort than murder. But Alice, on her sick-bed, with a glorious contempt for logic and the law of evidence, refused, with an obstinacy only equalled by Letty's, to understand how so kind a man could be a murderer—and of her own mother : it was too horribly impossible. She gave no reason for the faith that was in her : her instinct told her to believe, and she believed. And after all, is not that the only sort of belief worth having? Defend us from those who believe in us only when they have good cause : give us those who insist on believing in us because they love us, right or wrong. That sort of belief seldom errs.

Alice had burned with fever ; now she burned with anxiety. She had been mourning for the dead ; now fear for the living well-nigh swallowed up her mourning. She clutched at every feather of news. The new fever had a strange effect upon her health. I will not say that the surgeon who had given her over was disappointed to find his predictions falsified, but he must for ever after have had less faith in his own opinion. From the moment she heard of the charge against Harold Maynard her pulse

began to beat less quickly, her heart more strongly, and
a certain unsuspected elasticity of nature gave her a re-
bound from her illness.   Her cheeks were no longer pale,
but the colour of health began to glow into them.   And
so it went with her till she was discharged—cured, and
without a penny in the world.   And yet she did not
believe herself to be the rightful and defrauded heiress to
two thousand pounds.   If she had, she must have thought
her hero a thief, and if a thief, the murderer of her own
mother: and she refused to believe anything of the kind,
or rather was incapable of believing.

At last the day arrived when Harold Maynard—
gentleman, of no occupation: an ill-omened designation
—was to be brought up at Bow Street, before the magistrate, charged with the murder of one Jane Despard.

Despard is not a particularly common name, though,
oddly enough, it occurs twice in this history, as that of a
rich China merchant and of a poor lodger in Powys Place.
It would therefore have been natural enough for its
owner not to have been present on the bench during the
examination.   Men, as a rule, are not fond of having
their names aired under such conditions.   But pointing
morals is a favourite pastime, however unwilling modest
people may be to adorn tales.   He who first thought of
the idle apprentice and his virtuous contrast could have
found no better illustration of the virtue of punctuality.
Old Despard could see it all before him laid out like a
map from the beginning.   There was Tom Idle before
him in the dock, and beside him on the bench John
Goodchild in the person of Tom Winter.   Of course
Letty was not there: but that was in consequence of a
sacrifice of curiosity to the proprieties.   Perhaps she
might appear under a veil when the trial came, but she
could hardly take part with self-respect in the vulgarities
of a police-court: and besides her father would not allow
her.

All this happened but a short time ago, as a few fairly long memories for these hurried times will call to mind. But the passion for remands, for exhausting the funds of prisoners in preliminary investigations, and for turning a simple matter of business into a display of vanity and mutual admiration all round, had not come fully into fashion. It was quite possible that the examination of Harold Maynard might last no more than three weeks: some people said three days: a few thought even one day would be enough, as the prisoner was without counsel. But that remained to be seen. A clever prisoner, who wished to take full advantage of his situation, might give a good deal of trouble and delay, though without the advantage of legal training.

Harold Maynard felt his position there as an innocent man would—that is to say, he was overwhelmed with the shame popularly supposed to be one of the punishments peculiar to guilt by those who know nothing about the matter. Fear of death is a mere nothing to such shame, when the warm blood boils against the injustice of circumstances, not of man. He was alive to the actual peril in which he was standing, though not so much as to his name being bruited about as a murderer; to what Letty, the lost, would think of him; and last, but by no means least, how Alice would see her mother's murderer in the man who had been planning, even in the midst of his own difficulties, how he could in some way make up to her for the many cruelties of destiny. But, as he was waiting and watching, with no more than just one shadowy touch of a halter round his neck, the ticking of the clock grew louder and louder, till it seemed to become visible as well as audible. The half minutes could be seen. But they all seemed to obey and follow one arch half minute, that appeared to grin at him from the clock-face with a diabolical grin. He had raised that, and no other, and it had haunted him and was destroying him. He might have lost any other half minute in the universe with impunity—this alone had been fatally gifted, and this alone he had made his enemy. And it had grown and grown till it had filled up the whole measure of all life and death, and bade fair to open the gate of eternity.

The evidence, in spite of all that could be done, did not take long. Indeed the witnesses were few—the surgeon, the detective, and one or two others. Mr. Knaggs was not in court, but the prisoner's own statements as to admitting his presence in Powys Place at the time alleged made up for the want of that witness. It seemed likely that the examination of the prisoner would be concluded in a single day. And it was actually approaching conclusion and committal, when—

" May I say something?" said a sweet young voice from behind the dock.

" Certainly."

Harold Maynard looked at the new witness—and the fatal half minute descended from the clock-face, no longer a grinning imp, but tragically incarnate in Alice Despard. She was about to come forward as avenger—the harshest and sharpest scourge that Fate or time could ever find for him now.

And yet—as their eyes met—who shall explain electric sympathies? Though his reason told him this, he knew otherwise. There is a marvellous magic at times in that sudden flash from eye to eye. She had obviously come but lately from her bed in the hospital : her glow looked hardly natural, and as if the fever were still in her veins. Harold felt a strange pride in her thrill through him, as if he would rather meet his doom from her hands than from any that were meaner. If it were not love that ran through the air of the police-court from eyes to eyes, there can be no such thing: and love conscious, and visible. Love, thank Heaven, is not like Letty, and is blind to vulgarities, though clear sighted about other things.

"Who are you?"

"Alice Despard."

"The daughter of"—

"Yes, sir."

"And what have you to say?"

"The prisoner is not guilty."

Of course all the people laughed at the notion of a young girl, a mere witness, taking upon herself the function of a jury—as if every one of those who laughed had not been privately doing the same thing. The magistrate himself smiled for a moment.

"Tell me why you think so?"

"I don't think. I know it, sir."

That might be delightful nonsense to the court, but it was none to Harold Maynard. It was consolation in extremity.

"What are you?"

"I taught till—till she became ill: then I had to wait on her. I had a little money: it did not last for long. But long enough, sir—nearly. We had to live as—as we best could at the end."

"You mean, I suppose, that the money found on the prisoner could not be yours, your mother's, because she had none? Is that what you mean?"

"Yes, sir."

But it so happened that the force of her argument was considerably weakened by the fact that a pauper had lately died with two hundred pounds in notes hidden in an old stocking. The old lady might have been a miser, but still the point was something.

"Have you anything more to say?"

"Yes, sir—he is not guilty. The money was not ours, and he closed her eyes and watched her all night through. He came to see me at the hospital and brought me her wedding-ring, on my finger now. He"—

"Then"— began the magistrate.

But a new witness rose from near him on the bench.

"I have something to say before you think of committal."

It was old Despard.

" Well?"

" My name is John Despard, merchant, of London and Hong-Kong. I'm well known. And I say that neither the prisoner nor the—Mrs. Despard, nor anybody else could have known of the notes. Nobody ever touched them, and it was not the prisoner who secreted them."

" Who then?"

"It was I—thirty years ago. That portrait is of me. I placed the notes there with my own hands."

Let it be clearly understood, that not Harold Maynard, but old Despard is the hero of this history. Harold had done nothing heroic. He had only wasted half a minute, and looked after a girl whom he had nearly killed. For the rest he had been a hero in no more than the sense in which the heroes of Greek tragedies were heroes—in being the football of the three Fates whenever they were disposed for a game. But for old Despard to get up in open court, though but in Bow Street, and to tell his story, was a piece of genuine heroism for a martyr to gout, who hated everybody near his toes and cared nothing for a soul beyond them.

VII.

Not that he told all in court—for he was a man who kept to the point, and a great deal concerned him only.

When that picture of the brown-eyed, brown-faced young man was curiously handed along the bench for inspection under the eye of the police-sergeant, its guardian, what dim but never-to-be-forgotten springtides returned to the heart of the still brown-eyed but iron-haired man!—springtides when the sun was bright for him also, and when gout was unknown. Did he remember for whom that picture had been painted, and when? Did he remember his first love? Why, men will forget their last sooner—especially when the first and the last are one and the same. For Letty's mother had not been particularly lovable; and that perhaps accounted a little for Letty, apart from her beauty. But Jane Morris had been eminently lovable—and she accounted for Alice, the girl with the one virtue of standing up for the man she loved, without rhyme, reason, or power to help him, just because he was down. Of course old Despard, then young Despard—very young—had married Jane Morris, who of course had not a penny. And of course the old Despard of those days parted them; and the course of true love, not the less for being married love, ran rough, and the old story ran in the old groove; and the husband had to go out to China in a slow sailer, and the wife was to be cared for at home. It was then that young Despard sent his wife his picture stuffed with bank-notes —all he had—and worked his way out before the mast by way of compensation, and was reported dead—to his wife: and she disappeared in trying to live; and when the young man came back in those unletter-writing, slow-sailing days it was to find her dead as well as gone: so he was told.

And now it seemed that the very money had been thrown away. It was more than strange to find himself face to face, then and there, with his own old young self of thirty years ago. And there in the witness-box stood Jane's child; yes, as like Jane at her age as his own child could be, and—well, he forgot the gout, and was a man.

" The prisoner is discharged."

That woke old Despard from his reverie, and his waking left him very much ashamed. He had made a fool of himself in public—a thing he had never done in his life before, though in private no doubt as frequently as most men. He had raked up the ghosts of dead days, and set them up as targets for a Bow Street jeer. He had opened his heart; he would have opened his purse sooner.

" The carriage," he growled savagely to Tom Winter. " And bring me the girl. I can't speak to her here."

" You mean to adopt her—to acknowledge her ? "

" What's that to you ? "

VIII.

" No, sir, thank you."

It was Alice speaking to old Despard.

" You won't ? Don't you know you are my daughter —my first wife's daughter? Do you think I'll let you go out teaching again, or live differently from Letty ? "

" Am I your daughter ? "

" Whose else should you be? You're as like me in the nose as two peas ; but you've got Jane's grey eyes. And that fellow—that unpunctual fellow Maynard—I'm half sorry I got him off after spoiling a good dinner; that fellow closing Jane's eyes ! I wish with all my heart I'd let him be hanged."

" It was being with her, sir, that kept him"—

" As if I didn't know that ! As if that made me like him any the better ! As if I didn't know that I ought to have—no, it wouldn't have done ; he'd have been losing his confounded time in Hong-Kong. I'll get him something somewhere, and let him go to the devil his own way ; and you'll come with me."

" Sir "—

" And don't call me sir."

" I have promised—to go—with him."

Letty, had she been standing side by side with her sister before the glass, would not have been pleased with the comparison just then.

" With him ? Who's him ? "

" Mr. Maynard asked me to marry him, and I said yes."

" And when, pray, did Mr. Maynard ask you to marry him ? Why, you haven't seen him one minute since he was discharged."

Alice smiled. Was old Despard so obsolete a lover as to forget what one minute, nay, what half a minute can do ?

" I see. He thinks he is going to get one of old Despard's daughters, after all. Then all I can say is, if you go with him you don't get a penny from me. I'll give that very two thousand to a hospital—St. Martin's, if you like—but "—

Alice smiled once more. How could she tell that what her father hinted about her lover might not be true ? But she did tell—somehow.

" How do you mean to live ? " asked old Despard, who caught the smile, and was not soothed.

" I don't know."

" You don't know ? Then, by the Lord Harry, you *shall* know ! I'll—I'll—I'll—confound you, I'll send you both to Hong-Kong ! "

IX.

On the deck, not of the Ganges, but of the Euphrates, Harold Maynard and Alice his wife were standing arm in arm, watching the every-day wonders of the sea, and feeling the every-day wonders of love in one another. He was on his way to fortune, after all.

Suddenly there was a commotion near them. A wave had carried something under the stern, and a boat had been lowered.

It was only a glass bottle. But that means much five hundred miles from shore.

The captain of the Euphrates opened it, and read:

"Lat. —, long. —. Ganges of London, for Hong-Kong, sinking with all hands. Boats swamped. Forward to Preston & Co., Southampton."

That was all. Harold looked gravely at his wife. She knew all that was passing in his mind.

If he had *not* been HALF A MINUTE LATE he would have sailed in the Ganges, have never seen Alice, and been at this very moment at the bottom of the sea.

A COOL HAND.

I.

I AM an Irish Adventurer.

I am proud of my country, and I am proud of my calling. I should be proud of my country were I a Kalmuck or an Esquimaux—how much more reason for pride have I not in being a native of Dublin, which is admittedly the finest city in the finest country in the world! And as to my calling, it gives me brotherhood with every man who ever had a name worth naming in any country — strike the Adventurers out of your histories, and what's left won't be more than a day's reading. And as to being an Irish Adventurer—I've heard that name sneered at in my time, but never by anybody whose head wasn't too contemptible to be worth cracking.

My adventures have had a considerable range, and I could write my own life in twenty volumes as well as any man. For the present, however, and simply by way of preface to a short account of the strangest of them all, I'll content myself, and pique the curios.ty of the reader, by boiling them down into twenty lines. My name is Thomas Connor—an original O having been somehow lost in company with the rest of the family property, which had been regal in ancient times, but had been reduced to sevenpence-halfpenny on the day I came of age. It is true there were a few debts besides, but they could hardly be called possessions, seeing that I never knew precisely what they were. When my poor father died, nobody—not even himself—knew how much he owed : and it wasn't worth my while to go through the court for anybody's benefit, seeing that sevenpence-halfpenny wouldn't have paid for the mere whitewash, not to speak of a dividend. But, though I found myself on my twenty-first birthday better cleaned out than a hundred tubs of whitewash would have made me, I found no reason to complain of my friends. It's rubbish, and I know it, to talk of the badness of the world to a man when he's down. You'll be nearer the mark if you'll talk of the badness of a man who's down to the world. When a man complains of having been cut, or kicked, take my word for it, that somebody has for once got what he deserved. Why, I hadn't been one-and-twenty for four-and-twenty hours when I got a note from old Miles Cregan, whom my only sister, Kate, had lowered the Connors by marrying (for he was only an attorney), offering me a free passage to New York and five pounds over, without a word about being repaid, and with no conditions except that I wouldn't come back to Dublin until I'd made three hundred a year of my own—which of course it wasn't likely I'd want to do. I took it all the kinder of Miles, because he was so fond of money that he wouldn't even let poor Kate help me when I'd now and then wanted a pound or two to get out of a scrape, such as young men will tumble into without any particular fault of anybody's ; and once when I'd asked him myself for a loan, to be repaid punctually as soon as I'd be able, he said that he didn't invest in wild oats on principle — and when a man talks of his principle, you may be sure he means his pocket, and nothing less nor more. But as soon as I literally hadn't eightpence in the world, and nothing left but to enlist or else to live on my wits, this very man disproved for ever all the cant about the world's cold shoulder, and did for his wife's brother what I don't believe he'd have done for his own son.

So I thanked him, as warmly as he'd let me—for he was one of those men who under a cold outside hide their hearts.very much indeed—and then spent an hour alone with Kate, saying good-bye. I had no sweetheart just then, by some queer accident or other, so my sister was the last Irish girl I saw in Ireland. Poor girl! She cried when I told her how kind Miles had been, and tried to make me take all she'd got in her own purse, which was nine-and-fourpence — I remember it now; but I didn't like to take advantage, for I thought that, being as real a Connor as myself, it was likely enough that she too might have a debt or two that she wouldn't like to tell Miles. The next day, with three pounds in my pocket—for two of the five had gone off somehow in the night—I sailed for New York in the steerage of the Hudson, with no ties at home except Kate, and my word of honour not to see Dublin again without three hundred a year of my own.

It was lucky enough that I'd spent those two pounds before starting ; for the Hudson, as you may remember, went down not far from Newfoundland, and I lost the three that were left me. It was a bad start in life, but it might have been worse — and for that matter I've always noticed that nothing is ever quite as bad as it might be. I might have lost all the five pounds, and Kate's nine-and-fourpence into the bargain ; or I might have been drowned ; or I might have been five feet instead of six feet high, and twenty inches round the chest instead of forty, and so less fitted to take a porter's place in New York than I turned out to be. But I gave myself twenty lines for my self-introduction, and I have taken nearly one hundred ! I must omit therefore ten long years of adventurous ups and downs—my perils among miners and Indians in the Far West, my narrow escape from an Indian tiger, my second and third shipwreck (so that I began to stand in some fear of a rope for my end)—and come, at one bound, to where the arch adventure of my life began—namely, in South Africa. By the time I was thirty-one, I had not made three hundred a year; but I had got more than three-quarters round the world. And when I speak of the arch adventure of *my* life, I mean the most remarkable adventure that ever happened to any man.

I had been ostrich-farming up the country with a young Englishman named Paul Andrews—a fine fellow of about five-and-thirty. We got on famously together, though we were about as unlike as two men could be, and though we lived all alone. It's my experience that it's always easy enough to get on with any man. He was a gentleman all round (by which, however, I don't mean to say that he was as unlike a Connor as my words might be taken to imply), and I always used to think there was a sort of mystery about him : even out there, and in his rough dress, and in the middle of our rough ways, he always used to look as if he was a major in the Guards just dropped out of his club in a mistake, and yet, for all his cool and easy ways, he'd be liable to fits of silence that lasted for days, followed by the sort of spirits that make a man seem as if he wanted to forget something. But though we lived like brothers, he never told me much of his past life—nor, for that matter, did I tell him much of mine, except maybe about the tiger. No doubt I told him that, for I'll defy a man with a tiger story to keep it to himself altogether. I'd sometimes a sort of fancy that though his name might be Paul, it might turn out not to be Andrews—and when one suspects an *alias*, it's bad manners to ask questions. I have myself not always called myself Connor ; when one's proud of one's name,

one doesn't like it to be carried by everybody that one
may happen to be in the course of a voyage round the
globe. He was handsome, but it was in a different way
from myself—that is to say, while he was also a fine
figure of a man, he was dark, almost like an Italian, with
brown eyes that seemed to dream straight into the very
middle of you, and hair to match—he'd have stood, for
all he was an English gentleman, for a portrait of one of
Byron's Blackguards. He didn't drink much, and he
talked less—except when he was in one of his fever fits,
as I used to call them, and then he'd show, without making a show, that if he wasn't an earl himself, he'd been
hand and glove with them that are.

Somehow, however, though ostriches are undeniably
cheap beasts to feed, ours didn't do very well. Whether
feathers went out of demand, or whether there was a
glut of them, or whether it was the new fancy for cheap
funerals, or whatever it was, we didn't find them pay,
and we did find them die off in the most spiteful manner
you can conceive. So one day, said Paul,

" Tom, let's go for diamonds."

" We will," said I.

During six months we went for diamonds. I had my
regular luck ; that is to say, it was never quite the worst
possible. I wasn't robbed or murdered, either of which
would very likely have happened to me if I'd found anything worth robbing me of or murdering me for. Paul's
luck was worse than mine, for example. I did find a
few trifling stones, which we shared, being partners,
and so kept body and soul together ; but I don't
remember his finding any at all. I began to think
he was a downright unlucky man ; and, though a
Connor can't desert a man of his own accord, I wasn't
altogether displeased when he said to me one night,
when we were drinking whisky and water—that is to
say, I the whisky, and he the water,

" Tom, old man, this won't do. We don't get on as partners. We've tried feathers, and we've tried stones; and I don't know which is the worst speculation. Let's dissolve. You stay where we are, and I'll go a mile or two higher. There's a vacant bit there; and if that turns out no better than this has done I'll—I'll turn missionary, and see if that will pay."

In an adventurous life we get used to sudden and eternal partings from our closest friends, and take them easy. It's odd how little one minds other good-byes when there's one big " good-bye " sticking like a knife into one's heart; for ten years had made me want to see Dublin and poor Kate again, and I wasn't a bit nearer to them than when I left them. So I only said,

" Maybe you're right, Paul. Anyhow, there's no harm trying a change. But it isn't fair that I should have the chance of staying where we know there's *some* stones, and you should go where we know pretty well beforehand there's none at all. No, no. I've better luck than you, anyhow; I'll go and you'll stay. You're too generous by half, my boy."

" Nonsense," said he. " Perhaps I'm going because I don't want to stay. I sometimes think I'm the Wandering Jew. No, no. You make the best you can of the old ground, and let a wilful man go his own way. Whether you move or not, I sha'n't stay here."

Yes, there was clearly a mystery about this man, young, handsome, with an iron will, with no vices, who would have been an ornament to a crack regiment or a duchess's drawing-room, and yet hiding himself in poverty and Africa. I couldn't make it out at all. I didn't like to be outdone in generosity by an Englishman; but I felt it was a kind of destiny that was driving him, and that, as he said, his boots were beginning to boil. So the next morning we just shook hands, and

said, " Good luck to you, old fellow ! " and then he went
his way, and I mine, without more ado than if we expected to meet again at supper-time.

Will I ever forget that day ? I hadn't been at work
three hours before I knew myself to be master of a more
splendid diamond than I had ever dreamed of in my
wildest dreams. Yes, in our wretched little patch I had
lighted upon an African Koh-i-noor ! Don't turn up your
nose at Cape diamonds if you have never seen that one.
It was a queen ; and a tug at my heart told me what
our patch was going to be.

Our patch ? It was *mine ;* it was the sole property of
Thomas Connor. With a vengeance indeed had Luck
turned at the departure of Paul Andrews—poor devil !
It was a sin and a shame. He had lost his share by
three hours ; and all because he had been generous, and
had given up the old ground to me. My first thought
had been, Now for Kate and Dublin ! My second was
to get hold of a horse, and to gallop like mad after Paul
Andrews, to bring him back again into the firm ; for I
could no more have kept that luck to myself than I
could have picked a pocket. I knew which way he had
gone ; and one doesn't get far in that country in three or
four hours. But though I rode as much like mad as the
nature of the beast and of the ground would let me, I
couldn't come up with him. He wasn't at the new
place, nor anywhere else that I could hear or find. And
though I tried for days, and was more or less on the
look-out for months after, no news of Paul Andrews
could I hear. I almost felt like a thief ; but there was
no help for it. I could do nothing but put my back into
things, and work away.

II.

It was the height of the season when the South-Western Railway brought me from Southampton to London. It was with a sore heart that I made my first visit to the English instead of the Irish capital; but it couldn't be helped, seeing that I had not yet three hundred a year of my own; and Connor rhymes with Honour, as all the world knows. But I had what was worth it, if people were half as fond of diamonds as they are said to be. For that matter, I had, in the rough material, three hundred a year without counting the big stone, my first and finest find, which I had christened Kate Cregan, and meant to give to my sister in return for the nine-and-fourpence that she didn't give me, poor girl! And it would be a delicate way of repaying Miles; for, of course, one couldn't pay back a kindness in common dirty coin. I'd had it cut and set at Capetown; and I kept it about me till I could put it on Kate with my own hands.

But though I couldn't see her in Dublin just yet, I wrote to her—maybe Miles would let her run over to London, to have a bit of fun with a brother who hadn't turned up quite so much like a bad penny as had been expected of him. I hadn't written home since I'd been away, because, for one thing, I'm a bad correspondent, and, for another, I never knew from day to day where I'd tell her to send an answer. And I didn't write much of a letter even now, only a line or two just to say how glad I was to be back, and that I'd be free to come to Dublin in a week or two, and that I had turned up trumps in diamonds, and was her loving brother Tom. I didn't mention African Kate; that was to be for a surprise.

Then I went to work and settled my affairs as well as I could for the hurry I was in to be back in Dublin again ; and, for all my hurry, I did pretty well. Meanwhile, I'd been to a real tailor, and got him to make me look a little less like a ruffian than I'm afraid I did when I landed at Southampton, not forgetting a suit of dress-clothes ; for though I didn't know a soul in London in those days, an adventurer soon finds out the need of being ready for anything that may turn up at any time.

I was beginning to wonder, as the days went by, that I didn't get a line from Kate ; but I thought nothing wrong, as why should I ? I'd never been in London before ; and I had plenty to do in the way of sight-seeing. Even staring about the streets and the Park was enough just then for a man raw from Africa. The very day my dress-clothes came home, I had a fancy to put them on ; for I'd never felt myself dressed like a gentleman before, in all my adventures. So, having nowhere else to go, I took a stall at the Opera, and amused myself by thinking, " Well, Tom Connor, when you went down under the sea off Newfoundland, it's little you ever expected to be turning up here." And then, for the life of me, I couldn't help giving a thought to poor Paul Andrews, who ought to be where I was, if I was any judge of faces at all ; and who wasn't, just because he'd dissolved partnership an hour too soon. And I was beginning to feel lonesome too in London, where I didn't know the people nor the ways ; and the foreign music didn't seem up to Kate's old piano before she married Miles ; and the new clothes didn't feel to fit me somehow. I was wanting the old pipe and the old canvas jacket, and the grip of an old chum's hand.

With my eyes off the stage, I chanced to let them fall on the finger of a lady that sat beside me. I didn't think much of the finger, but I had diamonds in my head, and I noticed she wore one in a ring that wasn't to be named beside my own big one, only it was set in a way beyond anything they were up to in Capetown. It made me feel ashamed of the style of mine, or of Kate's rather : so I took a note of it in my mind, and settled to have it copied, or bettered if possible, by some first-rate jeweller. I don't know what the lady was like to this day, for I spent the rest of the time taking a photograph of the ring on my brain : and the next morning I took a hansom and drove to a man whom I'd been introduced to already in the way of trade. His name was Graves.

" I want a stone re-set," said I ; " and when you've seen it, I think you'll say it's worth the doing."

I put my hand into the breast-pocket, where I always kept it, in a little leather case, wherever I went, and — I'll never forget the cold shiver that ran down from the roots of my hair into the tips of my toes when I found it wasn't there! The jeweller waited patiently enough, while I felt in every pocket I'd got, thinking as hard as I could where the stone could have gone to. Surely there couldn't have been a hole ? And yet there might be, for I hadn't been to the tailor a day too soon. In another minute I stood before the jeweller with every pocket I'd got turned inside out, and hanging like bags all over me. But nothing fell out, and there wasn't a ghost of a hole.

I had never looked for such a thing as that, anyhow. It's enough to bother a man to miss a diamond that's not worth a penny less than eighteen hundred pounds : and what made it the worse was that I'd given it to Kate, so it wasn't mine to lose. But lost it was ; for I never had it out of my breast-pocket, so that if it wasn't there it couldn't be anywhere. I began to wonder if my diamonds hadn't been but fairy ones after all, like fairy gold, that, as soon as you think you've got it safe, turns to chips and straws.

" I expect you've been robbed, Mr. Connor," said

the jeweller. "London's a bad place for a man with stones like that, if he doesn't know the ways."

"As if," I said, "a man that's been in San Francisco, and New Orleans, and the Diamond Fields, ay, and Dublin, too, wants putting up to the ways of London or of anywhere!" And it isn't likely he would either. "As for being robbed, it's not possible. I've always kept it in this breast-pocket, under my right arm; and a tougher right arm you'll not find in a mouth or two;" and that was true too. "I'd like to see the London thief that would try to rob me."

The man had a trick of smiling, and he smiled then. "Of course you'll go to the police?" said he. "They sometimes find that a man has been robbed, even when it's impossible. Who knew of your having this diamond, Mr. Connor?"

"Not a soul. We learn to hold our tongues where I've been. You're the first man I've spoken to of it since I left Capetown."

I don't know why, but he smiled again; I suppose it was a manner he had with him. "If I were you," he said, "I should go straight to Scotland Yard—the head police-station, you know."

"Not a bit of it," said I. "I know the ways of the peelers, anyhow, and the lawyers. I'm looking for a letter every post that'll call me to Dublin by return of mail; and they'd be keeping me kicking my heels here while they were on the traces, as they call it, of some poor devil that had no more to do with the stone than you. Why, do you think I'd be robbed of a diamond like that under my very nose? I'd have to be made drunk or knocked down; and you may try me yourself, both ways, and see if that's easy. No; I'm sorry the stone's gone, but it's no more stolen than you are: and what's gone's, gone; and it's only fools that bother."

And it's true I was vexed more for Kate's sake than

my own; for it's sure enough that worrying over gone things is waste of time.

But the jeweller wouldn't rest so easily. I believe he thought me a simple stranger that wanted looking after, instead of a man who'd seen more of the world in ten years than he had in fifty. He made me describe the stone to him three times over, and wrote it down, setting and all, and said as my business in Ireland was so important he'd spare me the trouble of going to Scotland Yard if I pleased.

"That's as you like," I said, as if a diamond more or less wasn't of much account to a Connor—for it doesn't do to lower one's dignity before a tradesmen. "And of course I thank you for being so kind."

"You'll have to offer a reward," said he.

"I'll leave that to yourself," said I. "Anything in reason of course I'll pay, to get the stone back again. And I'll bet you ten pounds to one that it's not been stolen."

"I don't bet," he said, with another smile, I thanked him again, in an off-hand way, not to let him see how really vexed I was about it all, and went home.

But I was vexed, and the more I thought about it the more vexed I grew; for I'd just set my heart on giving Kate this diamond. "I wish I hadn't let that fellow go to the police," thought I. "He'll be sure to make some mess or another—I think I'll go myself, after all, and see that things are done properly. I'll drive to Scotland Yard, wherever it is, this very afternoon." Of course I'd hunted high and low for the stone, but it was no more in my lodgings than it was in my pocket; and I asked all the questions in the house that I could without hinting that it was a diamond I was looking for. I couldn't believe it was stolen, even now; but still there might be a chance if the police were put on the scent by a proper reward. But, all at once, just as I was thinking the least of poor Kate herself, and the most of her stone, a letter came in.

It wasn't from Dublin, though. It had only a London post-mark, and I didn't know the hand. I don't know, when I think of it now, whether it was fact or only an after-fancy, but the minute my fingers touched that common-looking letter I seemed to feel it was ill news. I opened it. Dated from London—signed Miles Cregan —what would it mean? What would Miles Cregan, the Dublin lawyer, be doing with No. 24, Melton Street, Mayfair?

And how is it that the very look of a letter, like a look of a face, will tell you, before you read, if the heart of things is changed?

"Dear Brother-in-Law,—Yours to hand. I am heartily glad you have prospered so well. Of course there is no objection now to your presence, or even to your residence, in Dublin. I am no longer there, which accounts for all delays in my receipt of your letter. I regret to have to inform you that your sister Catherine has enjoyed for five years the delights of another and better world, which makes it impossible for her to give you in person the welcome which you appear to have earned. For myself, I always believed you would eventually become a credit to your friends, though at the time I was disbelieved; but you have doubtless not forgotten the practical proof I gave of my confidence in you. I gather from your letter that the news has not yet reached you of my marriage, by means of which, and of Providence, I have transferred my office and practice from Dublin to London, where I have always had many clients, chiefly young military men of excellent family. As I am naturally anxious to be of service to my first wife's only brother, I may be able to invest your capital to better advantage than a

young man, without experienced and affectionate aid,
would be likely to do in this Den of Thieves where I
practise at this present. It would also give me much
pleasure to make you such advances as you may require
upon merely formal and nominal security. I am
occupied by business during the day, but it will give
Mrs. Cregan as well as myself the greatest pleasure if
you will come and see us next Wednesday evening.
A few friends may drop in, including some young
military men of excellent family; but we are very
quiet people, and I wish you to look upon this informal
invitation as of a purely domestic character.

" Believe me to be, my dear Thomas, affectionately
yours,

"MILES CREGAN."

My heart swelled for a moment as if it would burst,
and then sank down as if it had turned to frozen lead
in me. Poor Kate—the only girl I'd been coming home
for: the only soul there was to give me a kiss of
welcome after eleven years—and she was dead, and
I had never known. I sat for I don't know how long
holding Miles's letter in hands that were nigh as dead as
her own. . . . . "The hansom, sir," said the
servant, from the door. "Hansom! what hansom?"
"The one you wanted fetched to go to Scotland Yard."
"Then send it away!" What did it matter about
that diamond any more—Kate of Africa, when Kate of
Ireland had been buried five years; ay, and forgotten too
by her own husband, and by everybody but me? I
would not have had that diamond back now, no, not if it
were the Koh-i-noor.

I need not tell the story of that day and evening.
It seems odd that I should have done without my
sister for more than ten years, and without corresponding with her even, and yet that her death should have

struck me just like a blow. I'd never thought of the chance of her dying: and while she was alive, or while I thought her so, though I never saw her or heard of her, I hadn't felt quite alone in the world. But I did when I woke up next morning and lay half thinking, half dreaming about it all—terribly alone. I'd made money, but I hadn't a kinsman that cared twopence for me, and we don't make friends in my sort of life—we only make chums, who seem to come no-whence and to go no-whither. Paul Andrews had been most like a friend while he lasted, but he hadn't lasted. Of course I'd go and see Miles. His new offers of help were just doubling all his old kindness, and I somehow liked him for himself a little better now that he wasn't Kate's husband: I had never liked to think of him in that way. She seemed to have come back to the Connors now she was gone. And, anyhow, I hungered so much for the feel of somebody's hand that I'd have taken Cetewayo's even, if he asked me—and I must get him to tell me the last of Kate if he hadn't quite forgotten her. He was the nearest to me now, after all; and if the new Mrs. Cregan had got a child or two of poor Kate's, to whom she was perhaps acting as a good stepmother, and if they took to me, I might find something to do with my money now that it didn't feel of any more use to me. I didn't want to meet Miles's officers, but no doubt I'd be able to have a talk with him over a late pipe when the others were gone. So I just wrote him a word that evening to say I'd come, and set off for a twenty-miles walk, to get rid of the blue devils, and make myself feel like a man again. What's death after all? I've seen him face to face often enough, and I never could manage to think much of him. But poor Kate! It's easy preaching when one isn't one's own congregation. I doubt if she was ever quite happy with Miles, but I did wish she hadn't died quite so soon.

III.

It is not very far from Norfolk Street, where I was lodgiug, to Mayfair ; but somehow it took me a long time to get to Melton Street on Wednesday evening. It wasn't till the last minute that I made up my mind to dress ; and I only did at last because that was the only way I could go in decent mourning, though of course after five years nobody but myself would notice how I chose to go. And then I got hold of a cabman who didn't know the town, and as I didn't either, we lost a good deal of time on the journey. I was afraid to look at my watch when I got there at last, for Miles was an early man at both ends of the day. I was in too much of a hurry to notice much about the outside of the house as I went up to the door, though when I thought of it afterwards I called to mind one or two little things that might have surprised me; but when I was inside, " Faith," I thought to myself, " things have changed with Miles as much as they have with me—the new Mrs. Cregan must have had money anyhow." Indeed, at first I could hardly believe my own eyes. Miles had never been anything but rich, but even in the best Dublin days he'd been content to live in a little house and in the plainest way : the biggest thing in the shape of an entertainment was a potluck on Sunday to his priest and his doctor, and a tea-fight every now and then. But if I'd been in a duke's house I couldn't have been in a finer one than he lived in now ; and as for the few friends, there were hundreds of them all down the stairs—if he calls this a few, thought I, he must be hail-fellow-well-met with all London. And if Mrs. Cregan had mouey, she knows how to make it fly too : I don't see much here to remind me of Miles. And to think it was the merest chance I hadn't come in a light shooting coat—the thought of it made my hair begin to stand on end. Even now I don't know how or where to begin, I was so taken aback by the big hall, and the staircase that an elephant might have marched up, and the light, and the perfume, and the flunkies, and the guests, and everything I didn't expect to see : and down the stairs I heard music the like of which I'd never heard but once before, and that was at the Opera. I'd half a minute's mind to turn tail and run, though it had been my sister's house and was my own brother-in-law's now ; but before I knew where I was, I found myself drinking coffee in what seemed to me a bit of the National Gallery, where I'd been a week ago, mixed up with one of the hothouses at Kew. I'd never seen anything to beat it, not even in Dublin, though there are some fine houses there : and I felt proud to think that Miles was keeping up the credit of the old country, though it must have made him sore at heart to pay the bills. I wondered where he was, and, having finished my coffee, I went to the stairs, and by and by began to move up them. There were some pretty girls there, especially three or four that I'd ask Miles to introduce me to as soon as I could get hold of him.

But, by the time I'd got to the first landing, if one can call it so, for it was half a greenhouse and half a gallery looking down into the hall, I'd changed my mind about the three or four. The band was playing a waltz that made my toes tingle, and the flowers all round were breathing their sweetest, when I felt—Gone. There's nothing else to say. When a man's in love, he's in love —and if you can find another word to say about it you're a bigger poet than the world has known so far. Love isn't words. And it's not much good trying to say what she was like, there when I first set eyes on her, for ten to one you're in love with somebody else and won't agree with me that she was just the loveliest girl that ever was born. But she was, all the same : and that's the only point on which I'm not open to argue. She was just as fair as an angel, and precisely the height and size of one ; and she was about the age that angels are when they're eighteen, or maybe a little more. It's true that I'd just come from where angels, of that sort, are rare ; and before that evening I'd never mixed much with them anywhere ; so that falling in love at first sight might be a trifle more easy and natural to me than to landsmen in general. But that's neither here nor there. It wasn't so much the beauty that caught me, nor her look of a real lady, as something in her face which I'd never yet seen so plainly in any woman's. For all her beautiful fairness she had eyes which might have been the twins of Paul's for depth and darkness—only his never seemed to say anything, but only to go through yourself, while hers looked just like the very gates of Fairyland. And, just now, it seemed to be a sad story they were telling. All the people round were talking and laughing twenty-five to the dozen, or else whispering here and there ; but she was standing up all alone under some tall ferns, silent and lost in herself, and yet seeming to be looking out, all over the place, for somebody who didn't seem to be there. She wasn't looking at me, anyhow ; so I could watch her at my ease, and I did too, wondering if there was any way I could help her in, for she just looked like that ; as if she wanted a man's help in something, and as if, among all Miles's company, there wasn't one to hold her out a straw to cling to. Every now and then I could see her press her teeth into her lower lip, and move her foot in quicker time than the music went to ; and it was all out of impatience, for she looked too sad and anxious for anger. I didn't know her name, and I hadn't seen her five minutes, and yet I caught myself out in an uncomfortable wonder if the somebody who hadn't come was young, and a man—say one of Miles's military friends. No wonder he had lots of friends about him if this girl belonged to Mrs. Cregan. At last I got so full of the notion that I began to feel like a fool and half like a spy; and as I didn't like that sensation, I made my way to the door of a big drawing-room where I'd found out that Miles's wife was receiving the guests as they came in. I hadn't caught sight of Miles yet; but to look for a little man like him in such a crowd, all scattered about through a dozen rooms, was worse than looking for a needle in a bottle of hay.

Even with poor Kate fresh in my mind (so far as the girl on the stairs hadn't put her out again) I couldn't but own that Miles had gone more above himself in his second match than if he'd married another Connor. It was just amazing how such a lady could have taken up with a tailor-looking attorney like Miles; but it's always hard for men to make out what women see in other men, barring themselves. If you'll realize your ideal of what a princess ought to be, but isn't always, you'll have a better picture of Mrs. Cregau than I can give you; and as to her style and her manner, she might be a queen. It just took my breath away. She wasn't young, but she was as handsome a woman of forty as I'd ever seen, with eyes and the nose of an eagle, and the smile of a summer-day. However, I went up to her, and made a bow as if I'd been at court, and said, as well as the moving crowd round her would let me,

"I'm afraid I'm late, but 'tis never too late to find the way into Paradise. Do you happen to know where I'll find my brother-in-law?"

I had not meant my second sentence to be quite so sudden, but a dozen people were wanting to speak to her all at once, so I had to put my question and my self-introduction into one and the same quick word. I thought she looked half puzzled for just the tithe of a second, but she gave me a fresh smile all to myself, and put out her hand, which I took warmly, and said,

" I am very glad to see you indeed—late or early. No; I have not seen your brother-in-law for some little while. I hope "—

I don't know what else she was going to say, for just then somebody else came up, and then a second, and then a third, for there were later comers even than I ; so I was obliged to give up the chance of a chat just then, and maybe an introduction to the girl on the stairs, and move on to look for Miles, wondering more and more at the way he was living now. I half wished—my ancestors forgive me !—that I myself had been bred an attorney. I felt a sort of fascination drawing me back to the ferns on the stairs ; but I fought against it hard, and looked about honestly for Miles.

" Excuse me," said a gentleman in spectacles with whom I chanced to rub elbows, " I am very near-sighted. Can you tell me where our hostess happens to be just now ? "

" My sister-in-law ? " said I, feeling proud of Mrs. Cregan ; and so might any man. " She's there—just inside that door."

" Ah, you are her brother-in-law ? It's rather an informal way of opening an acquaintance, but I'm exceedingly glad to have made it. I daresay you have often heard her speak of her old friend, Lord Verner ? I am he. How is it we have never met before ? But ah, I remember—you have been abroad for a long while, haven't you ? "

" Yes," said I. " About ten years."

" That accounts for it, then, I did not know your brother before he married Lady Anne. You are in the army, aren't you ? "

Think of Miles Cregan being married to a Lady Anne ! Of course Miles wasn't my brother, but there was no occasion just then to bother a stranger with the exact relation of the Cregans to the Connors; and I wasn't proud enough of it, for that matter, to take the trouble. And moreover it wasn't becoming in me to lessen the grandeur of Miles and his house by saying that their kinsman had been an ostrich-farmer at the Cape, and a river-side porter in Brooklyn, and even queerer things than that now and then, when the devil drove specially hard. So I said,

" No, I'm not in the army. I've been in India," which was true. And maybe I'd have given him the tiger story if somebody else hadn't interrupted—for I noticed it was a queer fashion among Miles's friend's never to talk more than half a minute at a time to any one, which didn't seem sociable to my mind, and spoiled conversation. But I thought to myself, " If I get introduced to that girl among the ferns, it isn't only half a minute that I'll be!"

Only how was that to be done? Somehow, of course —for it isn't likely that a man who's fallen in love as I'd done won't find out some sort of a way. " I *must* find Miles," thought I, "and I will." But man proposes— the way in which I did get introduced to that girl is perhaps the most extraordinary occurrence in the whole history of fiction. I've even met with people who wouldn't believe it till I'd given them my word for its being true, and shown them the fact of it with their own eyes.

On my way after Miles, I went back to the stairs, half afraid for fear I'd see her eyes alight with talking to that other fellow who hadn't come. But she wasn't there any more—which made it the worse, if anything, because when you don't see a girl it is impossible to know what she's up to. Just as I was standing in the very spot where she'd stood, to keep it sacred from common heels, and was thinking how to steal the bit of fern that might have touched her neck or her arm—for I was just as gone as a man could be—a man in a livery came up to me, and gave me a twisted-up little note on a silver salver, without a bit of a direction on it anywhere.

"Is it for me?" asked I—for who was likely to send me a note to Miles Cregan's?

"Yes, sorr!" said the footman—and I was ready to shake hands with him for the sake of the brogue. So not even Miles, in all his grandeur, had forgotten that an Irishman ought to have Irishmen about him. Maybe the note was from Miles, to tell me where I'd find him.

It was a mere scrawl with a pencil—"I must speak to you instantly. Follow the Learer." And then came a worse scrawl for a signature, which after a bit of bother I made out to be "Grapes," or "Grace," or "Gravy," or "Graves." Graves?—Ah, of course, the jeweller; confound the man for meddling in other people's affairs! No doubt he'd been to Scotland Yard, and brought me some cock-and-bull story about the stone. But still it had been good-natured of the man; and if he'd come for my sake all the way to Melton Street, it wouldn't do to send him off without so much as a thank you or getting my sister-in-law to give him a glass of champagne for his pains.

"Is he downstairs?" asked I.

"Yes, sorr," said the footman.

"I'll come then," said I.

I followed him downstairs, and he got me my hat out of a heap of others, and then led me to the street-door. "We'd better manners," thought I, "in Dublin than not to ask even a tradesman to sit down in the hall while he's waiting." But I hadn't the time to think much when my fellow-countryman gave a whistle, and a carriage-door flew open, and after an "All right, your honour!" and a sudden shove from behind that forced me to put my foot forward to keep me from falling, I found myself half down the street, sitting in a close carriage, and with a girl's face against my chest, and both her arms round me as tight and as trembling as could be. Before I could make up my mind whether my head was straight on my shoulders, we passed a gas-lamp; and the flash showed me the face of the very girl I'd lost my heart to, under the fern !

"O Tom !" she began, in a voice full of tears, but as tender and as sweet as a dream of her own eyes. But I hadn't got her a hair's breadth closer to my heart when another gas-flash made her fly back as if I'd stabbed her, and she fell crouched into her corner of the carriage, and looked at me as if she was too terrified to scream. "Good God!" she moaned out at last, "What have I done?— what will become of me now? Who are *you ?* For pity's sake stop the carriage, whoever you are! Who are you, who have *dared* "—

Now I'll ask any man of the world what he's to say or do when the loveliest girl on earth first embraces him and calls him by his own short name, and then the next minute asks him how he dares run off with her—when it's she who is running off with him ? I don't think there's many a man who, when she told him to stop the carriage, would take her at her word. I'd never had much to do with young women, having been mostly out of the way of them ; but I'd not lived to two-and-thirty without learning some of the little ways that belong to the best of them. When a woman runs off with a man, it stands to nature that she'd take a little trouble to make things seem as if it was the other way round. And though, thank God, I've a pretty clear conscience about everything, still I wasn't christened Joseph, but Tom— and I'm not ashamed of that same.

So I didn't try to stop the carriage all at once ; but I said all I could to soothe her and comfort her, and to make it an understood thing that the elopement was all

my own doing, and not hers at all, and that my shoulders
were broad enough to bear any trouble that might come
to her. I can't repeat all I said, because one's talk in
such cases is apt to get broken, and because I can't
exactly recall all that I did say; but I felt an unknown
eloquence come into me as I assured her of my love
at first sight, and of the lifelong devotion I would give
her as the smallest return for the sacrifice she had made
for me. So much did I say, before I even put out
my hand to feel for hers, that she had no chance of
getting in a word; for the impulse carried me on, and I
didn't stop once to think what was the meaning of it all.
And faith, I wouldn't think much of a man who'd stop to
cross-examine the loveliest girl in the world, though he
doesn't know her name even, and though her behaviour
may not seem entirely the type of propriety. Maybe we
Connors would have been the richer for being unlike ourselves; but there are times when gentlemen must chance
things a little.

But even a man of the world may now and then be
wrong, and that just because he is a man of the world.

No sooner did I touch her hand than she dashed down
the window, and called to the driver to stop instantly.
What was I to think of it when the fellow heeded her no
more than if he'd been deaf, and when the more she
called "Stop!" the faster he made the horses go —for
there were two of them? He'd had his orders, I
supposed; and somebody must have given them to him,
and it hadn't been I. At last she sank back in despair.

"Sir," she said, in a slow, low voice that made
every tone thrill through me, "you are at least a man,
though you can be no gentleman. I don't know how or
why you have taken this cruel advantage of me. I
suppose you have bribed the coachman. But I tell you
this," she said, putting her arm through the window,
"that if you do not instantly leave me I will open

the door and throw myself out into the road. What can
you want with me, who never saw you in my life
before ?"

" On my honour," said I, "I have bribed nobody.
For Heaven's sake don't open the door ! Why should
you be afraid of a man who—who'd give his life to serve
you ? "

"I am not afraid," she said, with a sort of quiet scorn.

I don't know what else there was in the tone, but
it made me feel as if there'd been some horrible mistake
somewhere ; and it also made me feel that when she
talked of throwing herself out she was not making
believe.

" Madam," said I, " will you believe me when I tell
you that, as for taking advantage of a woman, it isn't in
me ; and that until I saw you this night I'd no more
thought of running away with a lady than I know now
how it's come to pass that I'm doing so ? I can't retract
what I've said about being in love with you, for it's true;
and sure any man may love any woman ? But beyond
wanting to be introduced to you, I'd no more plans than
a baby ; and I'd shoot myself sooner than make you
afraid. If you don't know who I am, my name's
Thomas Connor, brother of Miles Cregan's first wife ;
and I no more expected to meet you at his house
to-night than "—

I've always noticed that when a man's telling the
truth people mostly believe him — well nigh as often
as when he's telling them lies. Any way, some of the
scorn was out of her voice when she said, though as if
her thoughts were afar off,

" Who is Miles Cregan ? "

" Miles Cregan ? Why sure you know "—

" I never heard of him."

" And yet you've been at his house to-night "—

" Sir, I never heard the name ! Stop the carriage this

instant !" she said, as if she were a real empress, " and quit it yourself, and order the man to drive me back instantly to where you — you intruded upon me. Instantly, sir, if you please, if you are even so much as a man !"

" To where I—I found you? But that *is* Miles Cregan's," said I.

"You know as well as I do that it is the Earl of Hexham's," said she.

" Do you mean to tell me they've made Miles Cregan an earl? No, I can't believe that anyhow, though there's nothing else on earth you can tell me that I'll not believe—no, not even if you tell me I'm not dreaming."

"Will you stop the carriage, or will you not?"asked she.

I just looked at her face. There was no answering that, anyhow, but in one way.

"I will," said I; "and Heaven forgive me if I've given you one minute's distress; for Heaven only knows how it's been done." I stretched myself out of the window, and caught hold of the driver's near arm. "Stop, you thief," I halloaed, "if you don't want to be pitched over !"

"All right, sir, I know!" and he made the horses gallop again.

I was throwing the door on my own side open, in order to swing myself round to the box and seize the reins, when the girl laid her hand on my arm.

" Heaven help us all ! The man won't stop for you— no, nor for me !"

Won't he, though ! We'll see that, anyhow. I'll take the reins myself, and drive you back to the Earl of Cregan's faster than we came—on my honour I will. Can I do nothing to make you undoubt me? It's some awful mistake ; but how it began "—

" And—where are we now ?"

I looked out; we were racing past trees and hedge-rows. There was just light enough to see so much by. But for the rest, we might be at the sources of the Nile for aught I knew to the contrary. And I told her so.

"I must get on the box, and make this deaf fool of a coachman drive us back himself; for I'm lost in the bush myself," said I.

"It would be mad. The house would be closed. I—I am a governess there. We are on the road to Waltham-stow. Do me one favour, sir: leave the carriage your-self and let me drive on. Whatever the mistake is, who-ever you have taken me for, a night's walk will not harm you much, and I shall thank you to my dying day. But O!" she cried out, as all her calmness broke down into a storm of tears—"O Tom, my brother, what will *you* do—where are *you* ! Too late—always, always!"

My head wasn't of much use just then for want of knowledge; but my heart was just breaking to help her, if I could only guess how. She was right enough in one thing: it wouldn't do for anybody's governess, lord's or no lord's, to be caught or found out eloping with a young man. The world would hardly be so green as to believe that they didn't even know one another's name. The world's too clever by half; and that's why it's so often taken in. As for how Miles Cregan could have turned into an earl, that question didn't trouble my wits just then. If I could only help the governess, he might be a duke if he pleased, and I wouldn't bother my brains about the matter.

"I'll do just whatever you ask me," said I. "I'll even let you go on to your journey's end all alone, if that's the only way I can help you. I believe that confounded Irish flunkey mistook me for somebody else after all. I suppose your brother's in some sort of trouble, and for your sake I'd like to help him. Mayn't I even know your name?"

"Grace Brand. I mean "—

I remember her words that night a long way better
than I do my own; and I remember how quickly she told
me her name without thinking, and how hurt I was by
her trying to untell it again.

"It's safe with me," said I, keeping the widest space I
could between myself and her. "If I ever breathe a
letter of it I'll give your brother Tom the satisfaction of
a gentleman. Is there nothing I can do for you, but to
say Good-bye?"

"Nothing," said she, in the saddest voice I ever heard.
"You have done a cruel thing, but I think—I'm sure you
never meant it—and so—good-bye."

She held out her hand to me, and I just touched it, for
all my heart was gone after my wits, and that was out of
me, and was going to swing myself out into the road,
when all of a sudden the horses came to a dead stand as
if of their own accord.

But my foot was hardly on the road when I found out
why. We'd been pulled up by four constables—one was
on the box by the driver, one was at the horses, one was
turning a bull's eye on us all, and the fourth had a hand
on my shoulder. I looked for a minute at Grace: she sat
as quiet as death, and as dumb.

Well, they could do nothing to me. But there was
Grace—and whatever the matter was, there must never
be the shadow of a guess, if it could be helped by a
legion of lies, that a girl, whose character's her bread
and her life, had been caught at midnight running away
with a man. The stars be praised that she told me her
name! The way I'd get her out of the scrape I'd got
her into came on me like an inspiration.

"What is it?" said I, as coolly as if I'd been cool,
instead of being bewildered out of my seven senses.
"Can't a gentleman drive with his own sister to Walthamstow in the early morning without being stopped

by a parcel of constables, as if they were highway-
men?"

"Come, Mr. Brand, you know what we're after, and
of course we're as sorry as you can be. There's no need
to talk before the young lady; and there's no need to
detain *her*. If you hadn't tried to give us the slip by
getting out of the carriage you might have gone on quietly
to Walthamstow, and there'd have been this bother saved.
We've got a trap just behind, and the young lady "—he
touched his hat to Grace—" can go on."

"If I did know what you're after," said I, "perhaps I'd
agree with you."

"Which case? Why it's diamonds this time—Lady
Horchester's—and I'm afraid, sir, we must ask you to let
the young lady go on at once, and let us search you here.
Diamonds are things that can be made away with any
minute, you know."

"You may search and welcome," said I. "And if I've
got the ghost of a diamond about me, my name's not
Thomas Brand. There—I'll search myself if you please."

I'd got two reputations to take care of—the brother's
for the sister's sake, and the sister's for her own. In a
minute I turned out all my pockets before they could
interfere, just as I'd done at the jeweller's. Something
or other fell out of one; and the policeman with the bull's
eye made a dart at it as soon as it touched the road.

"That won't do, sir!" said he, giving it to the sergeant.
"And by the Lord Harry," he cried out, "if here isn't
the very identical stone that Graves of Cheapside was in
Scotland Yard about on Saturday afternoon—gold setting,
green leather case, and all! Fifty pounds reward! It's
not my fault, sir," he said to me. "Duty's duty, and "—
he said, measuring my six feet of height and forty
inches of chest with his eye—" you'll excuse me;" and I
was pretty soon in another sort of carriage, with handcuffs on my wrists, and in my mind, for a last memory

of Grace, an odd look that I hadn't the heart to think could be meant for a smile. But it looked bitterly like one all the same—after my trying to help her.

Of course I'd shifted the case into my new dress-coat when I went to the Opera, and of course, when I put on my shooting-coat next morning, I never thought of it's being anywhere but where it had been ever since I left Capetown. It had just gone where all the lost letters go.

But that didn't keep my situation from being an unpleasant one. The handcuffs weren't comfortable, and it was difficult to form any sort of a plan in the position where I found myself without knowing the bearings of anything. Only one thing was quite clear, as I hope every gentleman will admit, that I was bound to brazen things out, and, having done another man the honour of taking the responsibility of his behaviour on my own shoulders, to do as I'd be done by ; for if anybody, under press of circumstances, felt obliged to call himself Thomas Connor, I'd like him to do credit to the name. And as for Grace, the fact that a woman doesn't treat a man well doesn't make him the less bound to take care of her good name at any cost to his own; it makes him all the more bound, it seems to me. And as that was the one clear thing I had before me, I held my tongue, for fear of letting the constables get an inkling that they'd got hold of a wrong man again.

I slept the rest of that night in a cell at a police-station —for the first time since I'd been run in at Dublin for having been accidentally present at a row ; and I slept very well, for I was dead tired. Early the next morning I was told that there was a solicitor who wanted to see me.

"Is his name Cregan?" asked I ; if it had been I wouldn't have seen him, for then the murder would have been out that it wasn't her brother with whom Grace had been caught running away. But it wasn't Miles; it was quite a young man, dressed to the nines, of the name of Fry. As I'd never heard of the man, I had no objection to see him.

He shook hands with me in the most cordial manner; but I was on my guard against pumping, and put on a stand-off sort of way, waiting to get the pumping on my own side.

"My name's Albert Fry," said he. "I suppose you expected to see my father; but he's too old to attend to business much, and I'm just as much in his lordship's confidence as he used to be. I saw his lordship this morning. In fact I've just come from him."

"I'm much obliged to you for coming. And what does his lordship say?" asked I.

"Excuse me for saying so, Mr. Brand, but you *are* a cool hand!"

"Pretty well for that," said I; and so I was, if a fever's cool. "The hotter things are, Mr. Fry, the more one's bound to keep cool."

"It's a bad business this time—a very bad business indeed. I don't know what's to be done. You were asking me what his lordship said. It's no good mincing matters."

"Not a bit of it," said I.

"And so I'm bound to tell you that his lordship has determined, as he puts it, to wash his hands of you once for all. And so he has instructed me to say."

"Then tell his lordship that if he wants to wash his hands he had better go to Bath," said I; for such a message as that made me feel warm.

"Pardon me, Mr. Brand, but this is no joking matter. Such a family scandal as this would be fatal. He refuses to see you or to communicate with you; and under the circumstances, that is natural; indeed it is unavoidable. But, for the sake of the family, on my earnest representations, he has consented to make you a proposition. Or rather two propositions: for they are alternative."

"There's no harm in hearing what they are, anyhow," said I.

"The first is that you should obtain bail, to be repaid by his lordship for your flight," said he. "He is willing to pay as much as two thousand pounds for the family honour."

"And it's kind of him; and I'm glad to know the exact price of the family honour," said I, "in case I'm inclined to bid for it some day. And what's number two?"

"The second alternative is that you should plead guilty under an *alias*," said he, "so that the family name mayn't suffer; and when you've served out your time, his lordship will allow you three hundred a year, paid quarterly, so long as you're never heard of again; for if you are he'll let you go to the devil, were his lordship's very words."

"Guilty to what?" asked I.

"Come, Mr. Brand, I am your legal adviser as well as my lord's; you must have no secrets from me. But perhaps you mean to which of the cases? I don't mean Lady Horchester's jewels. There would be no fear of hostile prosecution in that quarter if that was the only matter. But it is this new business—that's where the trouble comes."

"But why not plead not guilty to everything?"

"Think of the evidence, Mr. Brand."

"I'd rather you'd tell me the evidence yourself, if you please."

"The police have been on the traces of Lady Horchester's jewels for a year. They have reason—

they're bound not to say how or why—to suspect
you. You leave the country suddenly : they trace you
to Africa. Can you prove that you did not leave the
country suddenly, and have not been in South Africa?"

"Faith, I can't do that," said I. " But"—

" Very well. With the help of the authorities at the
Cape, they find you at last farming ostriches up the
country, in company with a person named Connor. You
were on the point of being arrested, when, as if you had
some suspicion of the intentions of the police, you suddenly went away; and were lost until you were traced
to the diamond fields, still in partnership with Connor,
whom the police at first suspected of being your accom-
plice, but whom they now believe to have been your
tool—that is of course how they put it, not I. Once
more you disappeared when on the point of arrest"—

" For God's sake, don't tell me you're talking of Paul
Andrews!" I said, for he had been my friend, and I'd
believed in him.

" You see," said he quietly, " what would happen if
you plead not guilty. *I* hadn't mentioned the name you
went by, and you blurted it out in a way that would
make the jury find you guilty without turning round.
That was the name. And then they lost the track
altogether for a time, when they heard of you in London,
living as if the whole thing had blown over; but meanwhile they had got their whole case together, and were
going to take you into custody on your way home last
night from Lord Hexham's, when you almost gave them
the slip again. It is a thousand pities, Mr. Brand, that
you were taken in the act of trying to escape from the
carriage while it was going at full speed, and that you
tried to get rid of what you had in your pockets before
you were searched officially. You will have to be tried
for stealing, not Lady Horchester's jewels, but Mr.
Connor's. Your knowledge of his possession of it

is beyond legal question, for you were in his company
the very day when it was found. You and he were at
the Opera on the same evening. You have had financial
dealings with his brother-in-law, Cregan—who, between
ourselves, is the most outrageous old Shylock that ever
made a hundred pounds by lending ten. The diamond
was lost, strangely and mysteriously. Information of
the loss was at once given to the police by Mr. Graves,
the jeweller; and four days afterwards it was found
upon you. Believe me, Mr. Brand, you must have a
very strong story indeed to account for the lawful
possession of that stone—and then, how will Lord
Horchester himself be able to keep back the rest of
the scandal? Of what nature would your defence be?"

I was thinking of Grace, and of Paul, and I was
wondering.

"My defence? Pooh! I'll call Mr. Connor himself,"
said I. "He'll make it as clear as day to you. You'll
find him at once, if you'll go to his lodging in Norfolk
Street, Strand. And he'll tell you"—

What was I saying? I stopped short, flushing up to
my hair—the truth is, there was such a case against me
that I'd clean forgotten for the minute whether I was
myself or no.

"What will he tell me?" said the lawyer.

"I'm thinking that perhaps you won't find him in
Norfolk Street, after all," said I. "He was there, but
he had business in Ireland"—

"So he told Graves. You see how much better
informed you are about his lodging and his movements
than even the detectives supposed. But what would he
say, if he could be found?"

"On second thoughts, I'm thinking he'd say nothing,"
said I, beginning to feel I'd got into a real mess at last,
but not able to see my way out of it without harming
Grace anyhow.

" Then he must be kept out of the way, and you must plead guilty—if you can't get bail.   Can you get bail ? "

" Would you be one yourself? " asked I.

" That would not do at all.   It is essential that no name in the remotest way connected with the family should appear.   Cregan, rascal as he is, might do."

" Heaven forbid ! " said I, for he'd identify me ; and so for that matter would anybody.   So I said, " No ; I can't get bail—and I won't either."

" Then we must contrive an *alias* for you, and you must plead guilty," said he.   " After all, it will be the best way—there won't be a bit of scandal, and you'll get a ticket-of-leave in no time, and then you'll have a safe three hundred a year for the rest of your days.   May I take it as a settled thing ? "

Well, it did seem hard, that just because I'd put on a dress-coat to go to the Opera, I should have to plead guilty to a theft, and maybe get sent into penal servitude for five years or more.   But, once more, I put it to every Irish or English gentleman, what else could I do? Penal servitude isn't a thing to be jumped at, whether one deserves it or no ; but 'tis surely a joke to a man beside the loss to a girl of her good name.   And, try as I would, I couldn't manage to make myself the brute-beast and the mean cad that I'd have been if I'd run the least chance of having it thought that Grace had been caught running away at night with anybody but her own brother.   All the same, I won't pretend that I mightn't have found it easier to make a cad of myself if I hadn't just learned that my best friend was a black-guard, and if poor Kate hadn't been dead and left me all alone in the world—or if that last look of Grace had left me anything to look for.   I couldn't manage to care much about myself just then, and then there was nobody else for me to care for between the sky and the fields. I didn't even think when I answered him.

" Yes," said I, " that's settled, and the sooner the
better. So I'll wish you good-morning, Mr. Fry; and if
there's any trifling thing I want done, I daresay you'll
be good enough not to mind doing it for me." I held
out my hand and he took it, thief as I was; and I felt
more grateful to him than I had any need to be, for it's
a fact that I hadn't shaken a man's hand in kindness
since I'd left Africa.

" That's right," said he. " You've saved the family
honour : and as to the three hundred a year "—

" You shall not pay it to me !" said I, in a rage. " I
won't touch a penny of it—if his lordship thinks honour's
worth two thousand pounds, I don't think it's to be paid
for in diamonds !" said I. You see just at that minute
Paul's honour, blackguard as he'd been, was my own.

Mr. Fry stared : but he didn't say anything more that
was worth saying, and left me alone. But I'd been that
for a long time now, and was likely to be for a longer ;
so, as I'd had but a short night, I turned round on the
bench and went to sleep again. And what else was
there to do?

IV.

I don't know much about the laws of England, or how
long it's usual to keep a prisoner before taking him before
a magistrate, or whether there's any practical difference
about the rules when great people get mixed up in such
matters. Nor do I know how long I slept on that bench,
waiting for what was next to happen. I might seem to
be taking things easy ; but I wasn't at all. When I woke
up it seemed to be from a bad dream, in which I was
everybody in the world but one, and that was myself,

while myself was everybody in the world but me. I fancied the door was opened once, and if I didn't swear out loud I dreamed that I did, pretty forcibly- or somebody else did, in a way that was very much my own.

Any way, when I woke up I hadn't yet been to Bow Street, and, to judge from the light, I wasn't likely to be there that day. It was a bad, dark, ugly afternoon, which seemed to have been made expressly to fit me, and there was a fog in the cell though it was July. I was getting hungry, too ; and I wasn't sorry to hear the door open again.

" I wish it wasn't against the rules to light a pipe," I said. " I'll have time enough to learn to do without, in five years."

However, when I looked it wasn't a policeman I'd spoken to. It was one of the finest-looking fellows I'd ever set eyes on since I left Dublin- as tall as myself, and though perhaps not quite so broad as myself about the chest and shoulders, still bigger than most men are. I'd have been proud to try a fall with him, and I wouldn't have backed myself to win or lose. But it wasn't there his strength seemed to be. He looked about fifty years old, and every one of the fifty looked as if it had come like new strength to him ; it would have been easier for a weak man, I should say, to meet his arm than for a false man to meet his eyes. And he seemed to bear himself as you'd think a general would on a field of battle—quite easy, but not taking things less gravely than they need. I stood up as he came in, and we looked straight at one another.

" Who are you ? " asked he.

" My name is Thomas Brand," said I.

" The same who—who has lived in Africa under the name of Paul Andrews ? "

" The same."

In spite of his eyes, I looked into them as much like brass as if I wasn't telling a lie.

" And you say you are brother to the young lady with whom you were driving to Walthamstow? Are you aware that such an assertion is condemning you certainly to imprisonment for theft, probably to penal servitude ? "

He said the words hardly and sternly.

" I don't know what right you have to cross-examiue a prisoner in private," said I ; " hut I do say so, if it condemned me to be hanged," added I, for there was no going back now, and I wasn't going to be bullied by any man.

" Do you own this young Irish gentleman for a brother, Grace ? " asked he, half turning round.

My heart gave a great leap in me as I saw that Grace was there too; but I tried to keep myself calm, and made all the signs I could to her to own me and stand up for her own good name. For to have gone through all this for nothing would have been too hard, not to speak of the waste of it all. We Connors have wasted enough without wasting anything more.

" I thank you with all my heart, Mr. Connor," said she, looking at me as she'd never looked yet, and God bless her for every look she ever gave me ! " And how shall I thank you enough, or get you to forgive me for "—

I could hear the tears coming before they came; but they weren't like the last tears I'd seen in her—these were more content and quiet—and she tried to go on :

" For having left you last night to "—

But she couldn't go on, after all; and oh, if I could only have had her as near me as last night, I think I'd have known what to do.

" Mr. Connor," said the gentleman, striking in to save her from trying to speak while she was crying, " I

believe Grace ; and, without the least grain of offence, I
do not believe you.   What reason you can have had for
trying to serve a family of whom you know nothing is past
my guessing, as much as it is past my gratitude ; but,
since you have tried, you will be glad to hear that, thanks
to your throwing the constables off the traces, the unfor-
tunate young man whom you befriended has been able to
leave the country once more—never, I trust, to return.
No, Grace, never ; and it is best so, and you know it as
well as I."

Was it a trap that was being laid for me?

"Then I assure you," said I, "that you owe me no
gratitude in life, for I had not the least intention of
befriending anybody at all.   You say that my name's
Connor, and that I'm an Irishman, and you have no
more reason for saying either than for being grateful.   If
I like the name Braud better, I've a right to take it ;
and if I have a fancy for being in penal servitude, it's
nothing to anybody but me.   Perhaps you'll tell me first
of all why you take me for an Irishman, and why you
think my name isn't Brand?   It can't be the accent, for
I've got no accent at all of any sort, not even an English
one."

And that was true ; for though many people say that
I've never forgotten Dublin in my speech, who should know
better than a Dublin man that Dublin is the only place
in the world that has the distinction of having no accent
at all?

"I will tell you," said he very gravely, "why I knew
you not to be Thomas Brand.   *He* would not have
refused three hundred a year with scorn.   It was Mr.
Fry's telling me this that brought me here, for fear lest
some strange and terrible injustice should be done."

"I don't see why a man should want to sell his soul
for three hundred pounds," said I, and I didn't see it
then ; though since I've been older I've learned that

it isn't quite such an unheard-of thing. "Anyhow, perhaps you will let me know who it is I'm speaking to."

"I am the Marquis of Horchester."

"Thank you, my lord," I said, "for letting me understand that much anyhow. Not that it makes things much more plain."

"When this foolish child," said he, "heard that her brother was in danger of arrest, instead of trusting to me to see him safe from the worst, if only for his name's sake, she laid an absurd plan for carrying him off by night into hiding, with some yet sillier friends of hers at Walthamstow, as if we lived in the Middle Ages. Grace, it is only due to Mr. Connor that it should be explained. The coachman, whom she had to take into her confidence, served her so well that when he found the carriage pursued, he— But why should I tell you any more of this miserable story, miserable enough at its best, when you must now understand it as well as I? Grace has told me of your eagerness to redeem your mistake, when you found you had made one — of your honourable attempt to shield her, when nothing else was left for you to do. Can you forgive her for her silence, when she found that your chivalry was giving her brother time and misleading the officers? And what can I do for you in return?"

What would he have said, I wondered, if she had told him all the things I'd said to her before I'd found out I was making any mistake at all? I coloured up when I thought of them; and somehow, without looking, I knew that she was colouring too.

"She was quite right to hold her tongue," said I; "for that's all I wanted; and if her brother's clear off—and I'm glad of it, for he's a better fellow than you might take him for,"—I'm glad I said that, for the look it bought me,—"there's nothing more to be done. No, thank you, my lord. There's nothing you can do for me;

and I don't like selling things of that kind.   But there's
one thing I'll ask you to do ; and that is never to let that
night's ride harm the young lady.   There's been enough
of mistakes and false pretences ; and I don't want you to
think that I've been trying to get into penal servitude for
your name's sake, my lord ; for which it isn't likely I'd
care much, seeing I don't know it, or even for her
brother's, though, as it turns out now, he was once a
friend of my own.   So there's no call for talking of
being grateful.   If there's the least chance of her being
the worse off for last night's drive, I'd like her to remember
all I said to her at the first ; and that it's truer now than
it was then ; and that, now her brother's gone, she'll
never need to feel alone as long as I live," said I—for
she'd told me herself of her being a governess ; and I
didn't want her to feel even for a minute, in the very
middle of her troubles, that there wasn't somebody in
the world who was enough in love with her to go to the
gallows for her if need were.   It mayn't have been the
most convenient time or way of saying so ; but I'd already
told her I loved her the first minute I saw her among the
ferns ; and I felt that if it wasn't Now it might be
Never.

"Mr. Connor," said Lord Horchester, " Mr. Fry told
me that you are a cool hand—and I think you are.
When I asked you what I could do for you, I scarcely
thought that you would have made my offer include the
hand of my niece, Lady Grace Brand."

I *had* put my foot in it at last !   But I've always
observed that when one foot's in, the only way of getting
it out again is to put in the other.

" My lord," said I, " Lady Grace will tell you herself
that I thought her the governess ; and if her being anybody else stands in the way of my doing my best to win
her if she'll let me try, I'm sorry I thought wrong.   But
for the rest I'm afraid it wouldn't have made any differ-

ence to me if I *had* known ; for it isn't my fault that she's the bravest and loyallest as well as the most beautiful girl in the world—and as I'd say that of her behind her back, why, of course, I must say it to her face too. I'd say it of her if only for trying to help poor Paul in that very way—it wasn't a cold-hearted or half-hearted way, anyhow. And so I can't go back on my own words. I only ask for time, my lord. And as to myself, I make no doubt that the Brands are a fine old Saxon family; but I've yet to learn that a Connor, with the blood of kings in his veins "—

" Of course—of course," said he, naturally accepting an argument which indeed there was no answering. " But I think that it is I and Lady Grace herself who have need to ask for time, if you will kindly allow us a little. As soon as you are released call upon me, and we will consider what else there is I can do for you—whatever is to be, you have done for us more than we can ever quite repay."

I had not ; but I've never been able to convince them to the contrary. At that minute I was being repaid ten thousand times over.

" Thank you," said Grace, putting out her hand, " for the sake of my brother—your friend "—

" And not the least for your own ? " asked I.

But she didn't answer me just then.

She did afterwards, though. She is Lady Grace Connor now; and I won her fairly, though it took me some time. People may call me an Adventurer, who married for rank and money and all that; but I know better, and so does she. And that's why I'm proud of being an Adventurer : and good reason why.

I don't know that my love-story has much of a moral. But you may learn two things from it, both worth knowing. One is, always feel in your pockets when you change your clothes. The other is, when you give an evening

party be quite sure that you know who your guests are ;
and don't, like my wife's elder sister, Lady Hexham,
think you're bound to know a man because he seems to
know you. It's easy enough for an Adventurer in a
dress-coat to walk in anywhere ; and if he doesn't, like
me, steal your daughters or your sisters, he may steal
your spoons.

HOW I BECAME A MURDERER.

I.

"Thou shalt do no murder." I suppose that the response which sane men and women make in church to the sixth commandment is about the emptiest and most formal prayer of which they are ever guilty. Ask yourself, reader, if you have the faintest ghost of a fancy in you that, under any conceivable or imaginable combination of impossible circumstances, you could ever feel called upon to pray with meaning to be delivered from the temptation to murder, in cold blood, a fellow-man or fellow-woman? You have read history, and you read the newspapers, and you know that murders are not uncommon things. But, nevertheless, you think of them as belonging to an outside world, with which you—otherwise than as a just possible victim—cannot possibly have any sort of concern. You would as soon think of praying to be delivered from the sin of witchcraft as from the sin of murder. They are alike impossibilities to you. Of course I assume you to be of the type of the average reader—sane, but for a few harmless and probably wholesome crotchets; educated in the ideas and feelings of your time and country, and in sympathy with them; respectable and prudent in all weightier matters; and as comfortable, within and without, as the majority of your neighbours. If I were to tell you that you are a potential murderer, you would not even be angry with me—you would simply smile at such an absolutely preposterous notion. And so, in the face of such an accusation, should I have smiled—once upon a time.

Judge for yourself if I should not have had the right to smile. My name, by the way, is Alfred Lambourn ; and I consider my name as of some consequence to my argument, because I happen to be one of a family which can carry back its history for an exceptional number of generations, and without being able to name a single member of it who was not perfectly respectable and perfectly sane—not taking into account a certain hereditary tendency to let ourselves be imposed upon and our money to slip unaccountably through our fingers in the most contented manner. I should say that our family characteristics were steadiness, prudence, and plain common sense, combined with a somewhat inconsistent indifference to becoming higher or richer than we find ourselves at starting. But of course we have our distinguishing marks among ourselves. I am a solicitor ; and I cannot at this moment call to mind a case of a man's being murdered, at least in the flesh, by a solicitor. I live quietly, and in harmony with all my tastes and inclinations, in a little place close to the sea, and am, as I have always been, particularly strong and healthy, and fond of using my limbs without entirely neglecting my brains. I have a few cupboards in my house, but have never had the ghost of a skeleton in one of them. I have no turn for dissipation, and am quite as well off as I want to be. In spite of my profession I am, and have always been, absolutely without an enemy, which may be partly accounted for by the fact that I have exceedingly few neighbours and scarcely any clients, my practice consisting in a semi-legal, semi-agricultural stewardship to the best and dearest friend I ever had in the world— friends I should say ; for his wife is as dear to me as if she were my own sister, and his children as if they were my own.   Whom should *I* ever have been tempted to Murder, and why?   Put the same question *to* yourself *of* yourself—and answer it if you can.

My friend was Sir Reginald Gervase—of course you must allow just as much accuracy to my proper names as you please.   He had one of the largest estates in Foamshire, and lived mostly at St. Moor's, a splendid place near Spendrith, which is on the wildest and rockiest part of that grand and magnificent coast, as all the world knows.   My description of him is short—he was, literally, the best and finest fellow in the whole world.   Were Lady Gervase writing this story, I have no doubt she would say a great deal more of him ; mine must be a man's praise of a man.   He had not a single fault that I could ever discover, and yet was as far from being a prig as the South is from the North Pole.   He was nearly my match—which is saying something—in point of chest and biceps, and infinitely more than mine, or most men's, in brains ; and his heart was larger still. I sometimes used to think it his single misfortune that he was so rich and so happy and so full of a sense of all the duties that his b'rthright had thrown upon him. Had Fortune left him the struggling barrister that he was when I first met him in London, he would have made himself a great man, instead of merely growing into something much greater.   For he had by no means been born to a baronetcy and the ownership of St. Moor's. He unexpectedly inherited it from a cousin of about his own age, and apparently as strong and as healthy as himself, who had been struck down by death when hardly thirty years old.   It was a change to turn most men's brains, and to send half of them to the devil.   Sir Reginald took his wealth and his position with less elation than he had taken his first brief, went abroad for a while and then came back to settle down for good at St. Moor's.

The first thing he did—which was in an hour or two—
was to become first favourite of the whole country, and
that among his poorer, even more than among his richer,
neighbours. The next was to send for me, then managing
clerk to a London firm, to be his friend and counsellor.
The next was to marry, as wisely as man ever married in
this world. He had fallen over head and ears in love with
the best girl in all England, and she with him. Before
long they had a family of two boys and two girls, and
were fortunate in them all. The eldest was called
Reginald, of course, being a first-born Gervase. The
next was called Marion, after her mother. Then came
my own godson, Alfred; and then Nora. Their names
have nothing to do with the matter, but it is pleasant
for myself to write them. It is hardly more to the
purpose than to say that I too was on the eve of
marriage, after a long and weary waiting; but this, too,
I like to tell because this also was due to the position in
which Sir Reginald had placed me. What did I not owe
to him? Past, present, future: everything that I like
to remember, all my happiness now and to come. The
one trouble he ever gave me was the feeling that I could
do so little for one who had done so much for me. Anybody could have looked after his affairs as well as I.
I was never likely to be so much to him as the Mouse
was to the Lion.

In fact, the hardest work I ever did for him was
all pleasure and play; except that he made me feel
its interest and importance by throwing himself so
heartily into all that concerned the smallest cottager
or fishermen with whom he had to do. He looked upon
life as a trust not merely to be fulfilled but enjoyed, and
his wife agreed with him. I hardly know which we
learned to like best—our tasks or our pleasures. That
he liked the tasks best, I am sure. And I am sure, too,
that if Sir Reginald Gervase, even in this nineteenth

century, had taken it into his head to declare war against the Queen, there is not a man within ten miles of Spendrith who would not have turned rebel.

For two months every summer St. Moor's was left empty while the master and mistress were in town ; for they were by no means people who looked upon rusting and falling out of the great world's stream as one of the duties of those who have to do their best with the course of a comparatively small one. Though I missed them, I approved of their absence, for I could not get rid of my ambition for my friend ; it would be something if, as member for Foamshire, he could have the chance of doing for England some little of what he was doing for one of her remoter corners. One warm afternoon, while they were away in town, I was engaged alone in my office with some drainage plans, half at work upon them, and half thinking about what I could do, in the face of an approaching election, to get Sir Reginald Gervase to stand for Foamshire. It was too hot to work very desperately after an early dinner; and I am afraid I must confess that the rich blue of the sky without, the soft wind that scarcely took the trouble to carry the weight of its own scent through the window, the caw of the rooks on their way home, and the regular heave and rush of the sea against the wall of rocks close by, united to set me dreaming of anything but of drains. I was myself in love, remember, and Venus came from the sea on much such an afternoon.

I had a clerk in the outer office, who was also in love, and whom I strongly suspect of having been sleeping too. Our office was certainly not conducted on the ordinary principles of hurry and open eyes—a client from the outside world did not call once a quarter, and was not particularly welcome when he came. At any rate, Tom Brooks looked as if he were still dreaming when he stumbled into my own room and startled me with,

" A strange lady, sir ; and to see *you !* "

It is hard to wake up all at once. For a moment I almost took for granted that it could be nobody but my Lottie who had managed to fly through the window all the way from Newcastle-upon-Tyne, at the other end of the kingdom ; what other lady, a stranger to Tom Brooks, could want to see me ? But a moment more told me the absurdity of such a fancy ; so I stretched myself, rubbed my eyes, and said sharply, " Then wake up, and show her in."

She came in, with a silky rustle ; and I had certainly never seen her before. She Lottie, indeed ! I never can guess a woman's age, so I must content myself with saying that my visitor could not possibly have been more than thirty-six or less than twenty years old. She was of a moderate height and graceful figure, and was dressed much more fashionably than we were used to round Spendrith—in a brown silk with bows behind and down the sides, tight-fitting jacket and a sort of nondescript cross between a hat and a bonnet, from under which escaped a mass of fair brown hair—behind, in thick waves that flowed down to her waist, and, in front, in a fringe falling down to her eyebrows. Her face was a pretty one on the whole, clear complexioned, fair, and brightly coloured ; but her mouth was at the same time too small and too full, her nose too long, and her dark eyes a very great deal too large, as well as being too closely set together. Still the general effect was decidedly good, and had to be called pretty, whatever else it might be called, and however much it differed from my own two standards of beauty—Lottie Vane and Lady Gervase. My visitor looked grave and sad by nature, and as if she had a story, and that an interesting one. I showed her a seat, and she sat down.

" You are Mr. Lambourn : and you are a lawyer? "

she asked, in a voice that made her prettiness suddenly change into something more. It was a clear, liquid voice, with some sort of special accent in it, and a kind of singing quality about her first words.

" My name is Lambourn, and I am a solicitor. You call on business, I suppose? Whom have I the honour "—

She opened a mother-of-pearl case and handed me a card—" Adrienne Lavalle." " I come to ask your advice," said she. The name looked French ; and yet, though she did not speak quite like an Englishwoman, her accent was by no means distinctly that of a foreigner. Who could she be, that she came for legal advice to Spendrith? It is true that if anybody does happen to be suddenly in want of legal advice at Spendrith, he is bound to come to me.

I bowed and waited, and she went on.

" I am told that you are able and honest," she said, " and therefore I come to you. You asked my name, and I gave you my card. It is one of my names, the name by which I am known. I have one more. My birth-name is Ray—Juliet Ray. Did you ever hear the name before ? "

" Never in my life," said I.

" Then, before I tell you more, may I ask you if you are prepared to undertake, as a lawyer and as a gentleman, the cause of a woman against the most cruel wrong that ever was done by a man? A cause that will give you honour and glory throughout the land? "

" Never mind the honour and glory," said I. " The question is, whether I could find the time and spare the pains. Of course I shall be glad to help to get justice done, just for the sake of the thing, lawyer though I am. But I must hear the story first "—

" You shall hear it ; and you shall hear why I came to Spendrith for a lawyer. I did not suppose you would know the name of Juliet Ray. But I had my reason for asking, all the same. I was born in London. I had a mother, Mr. Lambourn, but no other relation in the world. My mother was on the stage. I cannot tell you all, for I do not know; but we were in Paris when my mother died, and when I was seventeen years old: without the means to live, but with the need to live, you understand. Perhaps you will find it hard to believe, but I was as innocent then as a young girl can be."

I let silence imply assent; but I was certainly beginning to wake up, and to call my professional wits together.

"It was in Paris that I met a young man—if I must call him so—who made love to me. I took him for a man of honour. He swore, Mr. Lambourn, a million times to make me his wife, in the sight of Heaven and in the sight of man. In the sight of Heaven he did make me his wife; and when we were soon after in London, he married me in church, as he should have done before. He is a scoundrel!"

"But if he married you at any time, he did his best to right you, it seems to me. Well?"

"I must not call him 'scoundrel'? Wait; see what *you* will call him, if you are a man! We went abroad again—to Paris, to Vienna, to twenty places—and then one day he left me, never to return."

"He deserted you? You did not hear from him again?"

"*From* him? No; never one word! *Of* him? No; not for years! He left me to live as best I could: without the means, but with all the need, once more. Perhaps you will not find it hard to believe that I was no more as innocent a fool as at seventeen."

Again I let assent be implied in silence; so much I did not find it hard to believe.

"But I hear of him at last, and he is married again!"

"You mean that you wish your husband to be prosecuted for bigamy?"

"No, Mr. Lambourn. I mean that I will have my rights, and that I will have my revenge! That is what I mean!"

And I could see, beyond any question, that it was what she did mean. If her story was true, she had certainly been ill-used; but, all the same, I wished she had not come to me. I felt that, from the beginning, I had not liked Miss, or Mrs., Lavalle.

"I don't care about taking criminal matters," I said rather coldly. "There are plenty of solicitors in the county. And if you want—since you speak of your rights—to make any sort of profitable compromise, must decline your case on any terms. However, as you came for present advice, I suppose you can prove your marriage?"

"I can prove it as surely as that I live!" said she. I have my lines. Will that do?"

"Certainly they will do. You will have to prove the second marriage too"—

"*He* won't deny that," said she, with a smile. "And he won't deny that I am I; and if he does, he can't deny that I was alive when his crime was committed; and if he does, there are scores and scores who will know. You ask me why I come to Spendrith? It is to make sure—to have him under my hand. I have not found him out and tracked him down to let him go again. And I come to you because your are here; because you can watch for me. When I have my rights, you will have yours too, never fear."

So she had set down my reluctance to undertake her case to a fear of not being sufficiently well paid? If I had not much liked her before, I liked her exceedingly little now. And who at Spendrith could possibly have been guilty of bigamy, and of deserting a wife abroad?

I knew every living creature in the place—there was not
one whom I could connect in the wildest fancy with
Mrs. Lavalle.

" Who is the man you say is your husband ! " asked I.

I suppose she thought that her last words had
refreshed my interest in her.

" The scoundrel who *is* my husband ? " said she.
" There ! "

A little theatrically she laid a document before me.
It was a perfectly good and authentic copy of a register of
a marriage solemnised at a London church between Juliet
Ray, spinster, and—Reginald Gervase !

My eyes seemed to darken and swim. What could it
mean? As she sat there, triumphant in her coming
vengeance or in her greed, I thought and thought ; and
the more I thought, the more clear the meaning grew.
Some months before the date of the marriage my friend
had been in Paris, I knew. Just before the same date
he had returned to town. And then there was his long
subsequent absence abroad for nearly a whole year.
But, still, was Reginald Gervase, who held duty to be
even above honour—if such a thing can be—a man who,
under any circumstances, would, when he found himself
suddenly rich and in a high position before the world,
rid himself of any woman—whether his wife or not, and
even if he had learned to hate and scorn—by leaving her
to starve ? No doubt she must have been false to him
first. But even so, the pride of my own life had gone :
every illusion I had darkened at such a shadow as this
must be. Perhaps he had thought her dead ? But, no,
that could not be, unless he had willed very hard
indeed to think her so.

" Leave me this paper," said I. " Call on me again
to-morrow at ten ; I will think over what you have told
me. Excuse me now."

" You will undertake the case, then ? "

" I will try to do whatever is for the best, Miss Lavalle."

" Who is Miss Lavalle ? " asked she, as she left me. " I am Lady Gervase."

II.

I locked the copy of the register in a safe, where I kept my own private, personal papers, shut up my office, and went out to walk myself cool. I had met with a skeleton from St. Moor's, indeed ! I could see the whole miserable history as if it had been written out for me. The young barrister had made a fool of himself, as many other wise men have done. He had been entrapped by this woman in Paris. Perhaps the pitifulness of her unprotected condition had imposed upon him quite as much as her bright cheeks and her great black eyes. She had stuck to him and drawn him into marriage ; no doubt his sense of honour had helped her, however much his reason must have opposed her. It was she, no doubt, who had swallowed up the whole of his little fortune and kept him under water. It was she who had been the cause of those long vacations in Paris, which he used to make even during term time. And then when fortune came to him, he had gone abroad to hide what had, no doubt, proved a disgraceful marriage. And then, no less beyond doubt, he had discovered unfaithfulness in her and had left her, half ashamed, half relieved, as such a man would have left such a woman, simply, utterly, and without a word of blame. And then true love had come into his heart. Perhaps he really believed his first wife dead. Perhaps the belief was too much due to the wish—who knows ?

It was not for me to judge Reginald Gervase. I knew the man as he was, whatever he had done, however weak he might have shown himself in one thing.

And what was I to do? Nothing?

Nothing? When I, and I only, realized the nature of the blow that was about to fall? On the one hand there was the true Reginald Gervase, my more than friend, brother, and father, who had plainly been able to free himself of the old shadow, trusted, honoured, loved by all the world, whose whole life was a growth in goodness and usefulness, and whose loss would be public as well as private, and felt none could guess how far round his home. There was the wife, who believed in him as a hero, and who loved him with her whole heart and soul. There were his young children—what need I say of them? On the other hand there were ruin, scandal, the dock, the prison cell, a wife's broken heart, and four children's lives blasted for all their days; and only because a worthless woman had not died. The thing looked too hideous to be possible; and I dreamed of such a word as —nothing! Well, thank God that he was not at St. Moor's. Every day delayed was a day gained, if only for thinking what could be done.

I was walking along the narrow coastguard path overhanging the sea, which was the shortest cut from Spendrith to the nearest market-town, when I was met by a lad who acted as rural postman and who stopped me with a letter. I took it with scarcely a word of good-evening, and opened it absently.

" Dear Lambourn,"—I read, without even taking heed of the handwriting,—" One line in haste to say that we shall all be home to-morrow evening, almost as soon as this reaches you. Everything's all right; but Jenny would rather be safe at home just now, and so would I. Look me up for a weed, there's a good fellow, about nine, and we'll have a good big talk about the drains. I feel like a schoolboy off for the holidays.

"R. G."

It was like destiny. He and his wife—yes, *I* would still call her so—were hurrying back full sail into the storm. I knew what their coming back sooner than usual meant : it was one of Gervase's crotchets that all his children should be of Foamshire, and of their home, bred and born. Well, that made matters worse a thousand times. He was coming where that woman—*I* could not call her his wife—was waiting to lay hands upon him and to destroy him more terribly than even she could dream. I was not to see her again till next day, and did not know where she was to be found. I suppose I had acted stupidly ; but it is hard to keep one's presence of mind where one's heart is concerned too deeply. How could I meet Gervase this very night with this terrible secret upon me ? I could not. And yet what right had I to leave him in his fool's paradise for a single avoidable hour ? I tried to ask myself what I should have done had I been simply his lawyer instead of his friend. And I could find no answer. It seemed strange that the thunder of the sea, as it rose higher and higher with the advancing tide against the cliffs, did not change its tone.

The letter-carrier could not have left me many minutes —long as they seemed—when he came running back breathlessly, shouting and pointing behind him with his arm.

" Mr. Lambourn ! " he panted out, " there be some un down yonder on the Carricks as lone as lone, and not half an hour o' tide ! "

I was startled out of such thoughts as even mine. I knew every inch of that coast as well as if I had been a smuggler of the old times, and nobody who knows the cliffs about Spendrith needs telling what being alone on the Carricks means within even an hour of high tide. The Carricks are a point of rather low rocks, projecting something like the blade of a scythe, or rather like the pointed ram of an ancient galley, from the base of the cliff, easily to be reached within about two hours of the highest tide ; but, after that, breaking the calmest sea into a rage and entirely cut off from reach either from above or below. At absolutely full tide the most shore-ward of these rock was a full couple of fathoms under high-water line. The cliff, itself a promontory, rose up sheer from the rocks for some distance, then bowed out over them, and then finished its course of some hundred and fifty feet to the overhanging path on which I was standing. All these meant, in a dozen words, that he who found himself alone on the Carricks half an hour before the tide turned would be a dead man in half an hour, for there was no point among the network of currents which the strongest swimmer could hope to gain.

" Who is it ? " I asked. " Could you tell ? "

"I couldn't see for sure ; but it looked to seem like Lucy Green that keeps company with Master Brooks "—

" A woman—good God !" In this peril, at least, something might possibly be done. As fast as I could cover the ground I was at the coastguard station, only to find a single old sailor on what was by courtesy called duty, a strong fellow enough, with any quantity of rope at hand ; but what could two men do ?

Nothing certainly, without trying. We could carry to the edge of the cliff rope enough to reach the Carricks twice over. But that was little. How could a woman, even if she had the courage, fasten herself safely to it, and keep herself from being dashed to pieces against the face of the cliff on her giddy upward journey ? And how could one man reach her, with but one pair of hands to hold the rope above him ?

Happily, the sea was tolerably calm ; otherwise, considering the shortness of the time at our disposal, nothing could have been done.   It was only too certain that somebody was there : the letter-carrier was positive that he had twice seen a woman on the rocks ; the second time, while I was on my way to the coastguard station, he had seen her trying to clamber farther out seaward, as if she had become fully aware of her danger, and was trying to place herself where she might have a chance of being seen from the shore.   I looked at my watch, and the sailor looked out to sea.   There was no boat that could be signalled, and not nearly time to obtain one for ourselves and to row round.

The question of the boat was settled in a single look from one to the other.   But the same look set the sailor's wits working.

"Run to the station," he said to the letter-carrier, "and get all the oars you can lay your hands on, and bring them here, and look alive."

He craned over the edge of the path, and so did I, though more cautiously ; but there were no means of seeing anything more in that way.   The sea had already risen in a surge of white foam and dark-green cascades over nearly the whole length of the rocks below, so that any prisoner upon them must have been driven for respite from death under the bulging part of the cliff, where she would be altogether out of sight of all but the sea-gulls.   Then the old sailor looked out westward, where a broken patch of white and grey cloud seemed to be rising from the sea into the sky in the shape of a spire.

"The wind won't be here till after the turn," said he "There won't be so much swing on as there might be.' He put his hands to his mouth and shouted downward, but no answer returned.   "Where's that young slug with the oars ?"

I could only hope he had some plan. I certainly could think of none. Perhaps, though as anxious as any human creature must be when a man or woman is drowning under his eyes, and when he can do nothing but wait above and listen for the dead heave of full tide against the cliff to tell him all was over, I may not have been so absorbed in the emergency as I should have been two or three hours ago. What was a moment's struggle with the sea compared with that worse than death against which I was trying to put out my hands no less in vain? I was not, I feel sure, at that moment consciously thinking of the greater peril in the immediate face of the less; but that it was the greater which had well-nigh paralysed me I know.

At last the lad hurried back with four long oars. The old sailor laid them all together, fagot-wise and bar-wise, over a cleft in the edge of the path, so that the bundle of oars might serve for one strong beam, and that the rope might run through the cleft for a groove before swinging from the projecting rim of the cleft out into the air. The beam of oars was kept from being pulled forward instead of downward by the form of the path, which rose up slightly towards the edge, and by the chance—on which the whole plan depended—that the natural gutter ran between two ears of crag just high enough to serve as posts for the beam behind them. He fastened one end of our longest line of rope, with practised skill, round the middle of the oars; he had already made the other end into a noose, as soon as his ready eyes had taken in at a glance the chances of the ground. He paid out the whole rope over the edge of the cliff: there was no time left for arguing about who should go down.

Indeed I felt as if forced by an impulse from outside myself to take that matter into my own hands. It is true I was a great deal younger and by so much the more active than the old tar, who was still as strong in the arms and shoulders as tugging at oars can make a man, but had certainly not been in the habit, as I had been, of spending his leisure in clambering among rocks instead of staring through a spy-glass at the offing; so that I was likely to feel a great deal more at home among the gulls and cormorants than he. There was every reason for placing him at the fast head of the rope, and me at the noose. But had it been otherwise I should have stood upon my rights, as representing the lord of the manor, to do as I pleased above the line of high water. Do something I must—something, anything which had the semblance of helping a living creature, however unconnected it might be with the storm that was gathering over the head of my friend. As I have said, there was no time left for a needless word; I took my way, and, resolutely thinking of nothing but of keeping my eyes fixed on the highest visible part of the cliff, was, before a word could be spoken, letting myself down the rope with my knees and hands. It was not that I had room left in my heart to care, save in the most general way, for the woman on the Carricks. I was in anything but a philanthropic mood, or in one that would excite me to risk a sprained wrist for any soul on earth but Reginald Gervase. It was all sheer impulse : neither foolhardiness on the one hand, nor courage on the other. I claim no credit for the climb ; rather blame. It could in nowise be of the smallest help to Gervase ; on the contrary, I was risking the only life that could in any way hope to aid him. Only I had no hope for him left in me, in the face of the proofs and of the woman in whose hands they were. It all came from just what I have said, the overwhelming hunger for action of any sort or form.

Of course our idea was to fasten whomever I might find below to the loose end of the rope, in the hope that the sailor, with whatever help the letter-carrier could give him, would he able to draw her up, and then let down the rope again so that I might follow.   With a view to the first part of the work, I carried down with me a second rope to fasten to the noose and to act as a guide from below, so that she might not swing against the face of the cliff on her upward journey.   As to my own return, I might manage a good deal by climbing, or I might at any rate be pulled up far enough to swing above the tide until further help should come.

At last I stood upon the last slab of slippery rock which the sea had not wholly covered.   There was just room enough upon it for two.   And I stood face to face with Adrienne Lavalle—nay, I must call her so—Lady Gervase.

Why had she been brought here, out of the reach of all aid but mine?   Why had the tidings of her peril been brought to me?   What was the true nature of that impulse which had brought me—me of all men—face to face with her thus, and here?

Think of the first sentence of this history!   We were absolutely, utterly alone, together, unseen even from the cliffs that rose up between us two and the whole world. Her secret was known to me alone; its proof was in my own hands.   If she had died there unaided, what would have signified the loss of a woman such as she?   Why had she not been left there to die?   And, if she was left to live— in one instant I saw the whole of that vision upon which my mind had been dwelling ever since she had left me—the ruined lives, the broken hearts, all the world's loss, all the shame, all the cruel punishment of an innocent mother and her children for the weakuess of a good man.   I had despaired of helping them all.   But what was that now?   Nothing, less than nothing, when I realized that all this storm would burst upon them, no longer from the hands of this woman because she lived, but from *my* hands because I did not let her die!

Would there not be something unspeakably mean and cowardly in preferring the perfect serenity of my own selfish conscience to the lives of those to whom I owed more than even a worse sin for their sake could repay? Surely the ways of justice are not the same as human law. For the sake of others we must punish what, for the sake of others, we must call crimes; but we do not call crimes necessarily sins, and what we condemn with our cold reason we may in our hearts and souls approve. At last I could do *all* things for Reginald Gervase. Was I to flinch, so that my weakness should let loose upon him all from which I could save him, and that in such a way that he would never even guess the peril in which he had been? I swear that I felt as if for this very purpose she had, as if by Providence, been delivered into my hands. If only that wretched lad had never caught sight of her! But was I to let such a miserable chance as that destroy Reginald Gervase? What was I there for but to counteract chance, and to do all things for him? Suppose I did *murder* her, what but good would have been done? I did not shrink from thinking of the thing by its name. I had completely cooled my blood by now.

What she read in my face, I know not. But something she must have read, for it was very far from the birth of a hope of rescue that I saw in hers. She seemed looking through my eyes into my heart, as if she feared it more than the sea. Neither of us spoke a word; but meanwhile the sea itself rose and rose, and the wind began to rise too.

I was absolutely making plans. I could leave her there—it would not be my fault if she had been found drowned. The body could be recovered at low water, and buried, and nobody would be the wiser. I must give up Lottie of course : it was one thing to commit a murder, but quite another to make her the wife of a murderer, even though of one who had right on his side. I could take it into my head to leave England, and should soon be forgotten.

"Can you save me?" she said at last. "What are you going to do with me?"

"I? with you?" I asked. "God knows. What are you doing with Reginald Gervase? Look, the tide will be waist-high soon. I am *his* friend. Are your rights, or is your life, the dearer to you? But I can't trust you."

I turned faint and sick at heart. How could I nerve myself, even for *his* sake, to be strong enough to let this weak woman die? Suddenly a heavy wave swept over the rock, brought her to her knees, and would have carried her into deep water at once had I not instinctively thrown the noose round her and held her so. It must be done, though ; it was some weaker self that had saved her for a minute more.

"You *can* save me, and you bid me sell my rights for my life?" she said, with real scorn, and with a courage that startled me. "Yes, you say truly; you *are* his friend. Like master, like man."

Should I have held her there till she was drowned? Should I have been able to face the unspeakable shame of returning to the cliff alone, or should I have waited there until the tide had covered me also? I say to myself, and I say to you, what I said to myself. God knows. I trust not; but I have never very confidently believed in the goodness of the good or in the badness of the bad, or the weakness of the weak or the strength of the strong, since that day.

"Ahoy, there! Hold on!" I heard a shout, and the grind of wood on the rocks, and the unshipping of oars.

I think we were both in the boat before we knew where we were. She was saved without my help, and I—I scarce know from what, if from anything, I had been saved.

Sir Reginald himself was at the helm. What could I do now? Absolutely nothing, at last, except give up everything to despair. I waited for the storm to burst even there and then.

It was simply to my amaze that no look or sign of recognition passed between the husband and the wife whom he—he, not I—had saved to destroy him. I waited in vain.

"Thank God I saw you from the yacht in time!" said he. "It was like you, old fellow, to try to break your neck for nothing, but I don't think both of you could have got up without damage. May I ask the name of the lady whom I have been lucky enough to—Allow me to introduce myself."

"I am Lady Gervase!" she said, with a scornful look at me. "I thank you, sir, for saving my life"—

"Lady Gervase!"

"You seem surprised? I am the wife of Sir Reginald Gervase, of St. Moor's. May I know whom I have to thank for "—

"I really must ask you to pardon me," said he, courteously bewildered. "But Lady Gervase happens to be on board that yacht yonder. *I* am Sir Reginald Gervase."

What could it all mean?

If you, reader, cannot guess, you must be as blind as I had been. You must have forgotten my telling you that my Sir Reginald had inherited St. Moor's from a cousin of his own age, and that Reginald was the family name. If that cousin had chosen to die suddenly before he had time to communicate with his wife or his friends, or to make a will, his wife was perfectly entitled to call herself

Lady Gervase if she pleased ; but it could not possibly affect his heir beyond compelling him to pay a certain part of the personal estate to the widow, which he was able enough to do. What a worse than fool I had been !

When I have heard people talk lightly of their temptations to do this or that, I have said, "The greatest and strongest temptation I ever felt was to murder, in cold blood. a woman who had never done me a shadow of wrong." People think me jesting ; but it is true.

THREE SHOTS WITH A REVOLVER.

I.

NATURALLY, considering the nature of my calling, I have been always particularly attracted by the scores of stories —not, I am inclined to think, always based upon actual occurrences—which tell of the ingenious plots coutrived by scoundrels to gain possession of other people's jewels, especially diamouds. In many cases such stories are, of course, but pure fiction. But as to those which profess to narrate facts, whether plain or coloured, I have only too much reason, from personal experience, to suspect that the real owners of jewels have, very often, more to do with their disappearance than easily-imagined brigands, swindlers, or thieves. Nevertheless, there is enough substratum of truth to make even purely-invented stories of this kind probable. Mine is not an invented story; but my reason for telling it is not so much its truth as its supremely extraordinary character. Its like, in any single detail, never happeued to anybody else in the world. Were it not for this, I would assuredly refrain from adding to the pile of jewel-stories in which some jeweller's agent plays the part of hero or victim. For I was myself agent to a very great firm of jewellers in London—I need not say to whom—when there happened to myself that terrible experience, terrible almost beyond the power of words to describe, which I am, for the first time in my life, about to try to tell in words.

I remember, as if it were yesterday, how one of our partners called me into his private room, and said to me,

"Morris, I must ask you to be good enough to start for Paris this very evening—that is to say, by the very first possible train. You know that parure of the Princess Mouranov that we had to put into new settings?"

"Of course I do."

"Well, you know the Princess as a customer, she is rather flighty; but she's too big a gun for us to disregard her whims. The parure is just out of hand, and was to have been delivered to her in Portland Place to-morrow morning; but—it's just like her—she's taken it into her head to set off on a voyage to America, and, an hour after she took the whim into her head, she was off, so I hear. It's just like her, anyhow. I believe she goes to Patagonia, where her diamonds—that is to say, her parure—she thinks, will be indispensable to her. I shouldn't have thought so myself, but I suppose she knows. Anyhow she's going to spend the whole of to-morrow in Paris, and her diamonds must be delivered to her there, and *paid* for—you understand. If we don't deliver the parure, she'll never forgive us; and if she doesn't pay before going off Heaven knows where, why, we shall never forgive ourselves. You'll have to be sharp, for it doesn't follow that she'll stay in Paris a whole day because she says she will; and you'd better avoid having to follow her, if you possibly can."

"Naturally! Where is Madame to be found?"

"At a place called Les Bosquets. It's outside Paris; but here's the address written down. I needn't tell you to be cautious—"

"Why?" asked I. "It all seems simple enough. I've only got to give the parure to the Princess—into her own hands, of course—receive the money, give and take a receipt, and come away. There will be no difficulty about the Princess's money, I suppose?"

"No. But, don't you see, I'm afraid you're still a trifle young, Morris. Those Mouranov diamonds are as well known to all the diamond-hunters in Europe—and they swarm abroad—as they are to me. Better than they are to you, by a long way. By some means or other, you may take your oath, one of those gentry will know you to have the charge of them. It's no good taking precautions against that; they'll know all the same, and precautions are only a way of putting people on the trail. Take care you go to the right house, my friend. Take care that you see the right lady. Don't eat and don't drink, however much you may be pressed, till you're safe back at your hotel. Don't shut your eyes till it's all over. If a strange woman speaks to you, cut her dead; if a strange man, knock him down. And—"

"Well, what else? But I'll take care of myself, never fear."

"You're an unusually handsome man, you know," said he, with a wink and a knowing smile, "and I suppose, like all handsome men, you're a bit of a lady-killer—without meaning it, you know. A nod's as good's a wink, you know; and *you're* not a blind horse, whatever you may be. Paris is a lively place, you know, for a man of your make, with diamonds next his heart worth thousands of pounds. It isn't the men I'm afraid of in your case; it's the women."

Every man likes that sort of chaff; and I was really weak enough in those days to take an especial pride in what I could not help knowing to be my personal advantages. So I was in the best temper as I answered modestly,

"Well, sir, nobody knows everything about all women ; but I do think I know enough about a few to guess a good deal about what the rest may be up to. I don't think I'm likely to be come over that way. And I should think this little fellow," I added, showing him a new revolver, "will be enough for common odds, not in petticoats."

"Don't put yourself in a position that'll oblige you to use it," said my employer. "And you won't, if you keep clear of the common odds—*in* petticoats, you know. I must be off now. Call at my house for the parure in an hour."

Full of confidence in my own resources, proud of the trust that had been placed in me, and altogether in a well-satisfied and fearless frame of mind, I started with the Mouranov parure by the very next train for Dover. The magnificent parure was safely packed by my employer himself before my own eyes, and I placed the packet securely in a case which I fastened round my neck and waist under my clothes with a couple of light but strong steel chains. In effect, the parure was absolutely safe from secret theft—effectually from any violence short of downright murder. I had bidden my mother and sisters a hurried good-bye, without telling even them of the invaluable charge I carried about me. And I arrived at one of the first hotels in Paris without the smallest adventure of any sort or kind. To imagine that any of the fraternity of diamond-hunters, male or female, had been watching my journey, or could even be aware of it, was simply absurd. To all with whom I came into any slight contact *en route* I must have been an ordinary Englishman, making au ordinary trip to Paris—nothing more. And, for that matter, except with booking-clerks and so forth, I don't think I had exchanged a word with a fellow-creature all the way. That I had never once closed my eyes, I know.

II.

I had just ordered some refreshment after my journey before proceeding to Les Bosquets, when,—

"Monsieur Alfred Morris from London?" asked one of the waiters.

"Yes," said I, though wondering how my name could be known to him, seeing that I had but just arrived, and had not even written my name in the list of persons staying in the hotel. Was my "Yes" a piece of imprudence? I hardly know to this hour.

"A young lady," he said, in English, "has been waiting for an hour to see monsieur."

A young lady, in Paris, waiting to see me! What could *that* mean? My employer's warning came instinctively to my mind. But I could not very well refuse to see her; indeed, it might prove important that I *should* see her. And certainly no possible harm could come of my seeing her in a large and crowded hotel.

"Mademoiselle waits in the *salon*," said the waiter. So to the *salon* I went, more curious than anxious about who the young lady might be who expected me in Paris, and who knew my name so well.

She was a stranger—a young Frenchwoman, rather pretty and exceedingly well dressed, and yet with something about her that showed she did not wholly belong to the *beau monde*, if that be the right term to use, for I don't pretend to be a French scholar.

"Monsieur Alfred Morris from London?" asked she, in precisely the same words as the waiter, but in a voice and accent which made the words sound very differently indeed, and made the girl herself look really instead of only passably pretty. Indeed, hers was one of the very sweetest voices I had ever heard.

"At your service, mademoiselle," said I, with a bow.

She smiled; and her smile was very sweet indeed. "I am truly fortunate," she said. "I was beginning to fear you would never come."

"And may I ask, mademoiselle, with whom"—

"Assuredly, monsieur. I am Mademoiselle Lenoir, principal *Demoiselle de Chambre* of Madame la Princesse de Mouranov"—

"Ah!" sighed I, a little disappointed. It was no adventure, then—only the affair of the parure, after all. Still—well, considering everything, that was perhaps all the better. Adventures, till the receipts were exchanged, would certainly be *mal à propos*.

"Yes; of Madame la Princesse de Mouranov," repeated she. "I am in all the confidence of madame's toilette—you comprehend." She was speaking in very good English, with an accent that improved my native language, it seemed to me. "Madame received a telegram from London, from your firm, saying you would be here to-day. It was a careful telegram, monsieur—and that was well. It is not prudent to let all the world know what you carry—without doubt nearest to your heart, monsieur! Have I not reason—I? But madame has changed her plans—that is the habitude of madame. I always know what madame will not do next, for it is always what she shall not say. She was for America last night: to-day, she is for Biarritz. But will want the pa—the affair monsieur knows of—all the same: all the more. Even so, she was going to Les Bosquets: in fine, she is not at Les Bosquets, but at the Villa Stefania, her own little house where she goes to be alone. Ah, madame will love to be alone at times—sometimes for one whole half-hour, monsieur! but she must have the parure on the instant, and in her own hands, so I come from madame myself to conduct you to Villa Stefania without delay."

All this was fully in accord with all that I had ever heard of the eccentric restlessness of the great Russian lady, nor had I the faintest reason, after hearing of the telegram from my employers, to doubt the simple good faith of so pretty and altogether attractive a young lady as Mademoiselle Lenoir. Still there was one obvious precaution that I ought to take, and I did take it; for I wish to make it absolutely clear that I acted in all respects as the most prudent of men could have done.

"Mademoiselle will permit me to ask," said I, "simply as a matter of business form, if she has the written authority"—

"Of Madame la Princesse? Assuredly," said she, with a bright smile. "It is good to treat with a monsieur of the prudence of monsieur!" She handed me at once a little sealed note, perfumed and gracefully written that ran as follows:

"Villa Stefania, January 12.

"Monsieur Alfred Morris, on the part of Messrs.———, will have the goodness to accompany the bearer, Mademoiselle Lenoir, to the Villa Stefania, without any delay, there to execute the commission with which he is charged.

"STEPHANIE DE MOURANOV."

I have that note still, to remind me of— But the end is not yet come. Suffice it that doubt, under the circumstances, never entered my mind; nor, I dare to swear, would it have entered the reader's, had he to judge before the event, as I had to do.

I found Mademoiselle Lenoir an exceedingly pleasant companion on the way to Villa Stefania, which fancifully-named residence we reached in about an hour and a half, partly by rail and partly *en voiture*. I supposed it some eccentricity on the part of the Princesse that she did

not, as she certainly might have done, send a carriage to
convey us the whole way. Perhaps she was one of those
people who take a pleasure in little mysteries and pointless conspiracies. Mademoiselle Lenoir talked the whole
time about all sorts of things and places, and I found her
sympathetic, intelligent, and singularly well informed, as
well as charming. I even began to flatter myself that I
had made a by no means unsatisfactory impression upon
Mademoiselle.

Villa Stefania, where we arrived after darkness had
fallen, I could not very distinctly see; but I made out
that it was a small house, probably not long built, standing alone and apart from all other dwellings in a sort of
shrubbery, and approached through a tiny court past the
lodge of the *concierge*. We were at once admitted, without any ringing or waiting. Mademoiselle conducted me
up a staircase and along a passage, both scarcely half
lighted, into a room so dark that I could scarcely see
where I was, or anything at all.

"Imbeciles!" cried Mademoiselle Lenoir. "Not a
light in the *salon*, not even a candle! That is how one is
served when one has twenty servants, monsieur, each
with his duties : we must have a twenty-first, to do
nothing but see that the sconces shall not be empty in
the *salon*—unless, perhaps, it shall be some fancy of
madame, for nobody to know you are here. I will see.
Monsieur is a brave man? He is not afraid of being left
alone in the dark till madame shall arrive? It will be in
one moment, monsieur. Madame is anxious, very
anxious, for the "—

I thought my being asked to wait in pitch darkness a
little odd, but I could only say,

"It is many years since I believed in Bogy, Mademoiselle."

"*Bien.* It shall not be long." And she was gone,
closing the door behind her, if my ears told truly.

Without believing in Bogy, it is not a pleasant thing to be left alone in a strange room in the dark, all the same —fancies will come into one's head, especially when the seconds grow into minutes without counting themselves on a visible watch-face, and when one has on one's person diamonds worth many thousands of pounds. Everything was all right, of course; and yet I could not help wishing that the Princess Mouranov had received me at Les Bosquets by the light of at least one candle, if not of day. And, though I was but a tradesman's *employé*, common French courtesy should not have kept me quite so long waiting for a light, even though a fine lady might not be ready to see me the very instant I arrived. I felt my way to a very comfortable sofa, on which I sat down, and waited on, waxing impatient, and feeling rather like a prisoner condemned to the dark cell. Manners forbade me to doze or whistle, and—

But impatience was soon to change into something more.

III.

Was that sound of voices in the room or no? If not in the room, close to the room it must have been; for I heard them plainly—sometimes darkness itself will strangely sharpen our ears, and there are certain words which, once heard, sharpen them yet more keenly.

I heard three voices. One was Mademoiselle Lenoir's. One was a strange woman's. The third was a man's.

"Neatly trapped enough," said the last, so slowly, in the German manner, that they brought their whole significance home to my dull British ears.

"But for the rest," said Mademoiselle Lenoir, "what ought one to do? If he goes back to England"—

"He must not go back to England," said the voice of the other woman—it was singularly cold, firm, and clear. "He must not leave France; he must not leave Paris 'till we are safely gone. Those diamonds"—

"If the worst comes to the worst," said the man, "what then? We are man to man. If he does not behave himself, he will have to reckon with me. These things are awkward, because of the police. But"—

"He will not resist," said Mademoiselle Lenoir. "And if he does"—

I thought I heard a sigh, so sharp had my ears grown. But from whom came the sigh? Whether from Mademoiselle Lenoir or that other woman I could not tell.

"If he does," said the man, "be it on his own head, whatever comes. You understand me, my friend. I do not like too much blood; but if there be resistance, there must be—what there must be. He must not trace the diamonds, nor you."

It had all passed through my ears to my sinking heart long ago. Fool that I had been to listen to a woman's story, however plausible it might seem! Some plot, invented and carried out with fiendish cunning, had brought me into a den of robbery and murder. I was to wait for death in that lonely house and that horrible dark chamber!

What, in the name of Heaven, in the name of desperate helplessness, was I to do? The voices grew confused, and then ceased altogether. I was alone. Nobody knew me in Paris; nobody would miss me there. If I did not return, my employers would set me down as having run off with the jewels; my mother and sisters themselves would believe me guilty, and break their hearts and starve. Could I escape from the house? Impossible—through unknown passages and a locked door!

Instinctively I felt for my revolver, useless as it must

be in a dark room. The murderer, or murderers, knowing the premises, could be upon me at any moment, and have me down before I could know of their approach; and one must have some faint light for an aim. I had known that all sorts of atrocities are even more common in Paris than in London; but how could I dream that such a doom as this, all for believing in the smooth tongue of a pretty serpent, would ever be mine? I say I felt for my revolver, though knowing all the while how vain a toy it would be now. A knife for close quarters would have been ten times its value; and that, too, would have been in vain. I don't think myself less brave than other men, yet I could not help a groan of despair at the thought that I was about to be murdered so helplessly, so hopelessly. How soon would it be?

I drew out my revolver, and, in doing so, a little fusce-box, with a few wax matches in it, fell on the floor. One moment's light would be something, though the last gleam I was ever to see. I groped for the box, found it at my feet, and struck one of the matches. Heaven! what met my eyes? The gleam of flame had indeed come not a moment too soon.

Straight in front of me, coming towards me through an open door, was as evil-looking a ruffian as I had ever seen; a murderous ruffian, if ever there was one, hideously livid, and with eyes that glared towards mine. Thank Heaven for that one gleam of light! It might be enough for a straight aim. . . . . No time must be lost. . . . . I am no fighting man, Heaven knows. . . . But . . . . . I fired.

For a moment the smoke clouded my eyes. But I heard a cry. The flame from my match had not wholly died. And by its light I saw— Great Heaven! I had not had one murderer to deal with. A whole gang of brigands were upon me and my diamonds. What was to be done?

Five more brigands at least were there. Well, I dared not pray for so hopeless a thing as life; but I would at least be true to my trust, and sell it dearly. My name, my honour, might be saved. First to right, then to left, I fired, and fired again—twice—three times—

And then the match went out, and left me to the mercy of the robbers and cutthroats into whose hands I had been drawn by a woman's words.

IV.

Suddenly a blaze of light filled the room, so bright, that my eyes, till now blinded by darkness, were more blinded still.

"What madman is here?" cried a woman's voice—that other woman's, not Mademoiselle Lenoir's. "O! O! O! My poor, dear, beautiful boudoir! Send for the gendarmes!"

Was I alive? I suppose so, since I could still hear and see. And how can I describe the scene that I beheld?

I was in an elegantly furnished room. On my left hand, with clasped hands, gazing at me with a face full of amazement, was Mademoiselle Lenoir. On my right, looking at me with wild looks of mingled anger, despair, and terror, was a handsome lady, who resembled a queen of tragedy.

"O Amélie!" cried the latter.

"O Madame la Princesse!" echoed Mademoiselle Lenoir.

"My favourite clock!" moaned the right-hand lady.

"And three whole mir—" Mademoiselle was beginning, when I felt my arms grasped tightly behind my back, and a man's slow stern, voice in my ear:

" Who are you? Are you madman or brigand? What does this mean? Who are you that made havoc with the boudoir of Madame la Princesse de Mouranov? Who, I say?"

I must confess it at last! I am a little near-sighted; and, by the dim light of the match, had mistaken the sixfold reflection of myself in the panels of an octagonal room lined with large mirrors for a band of murderers.

And that talk of death and diamonds behind the wall? Well, as I learned afterwards, the Princess Mouranov was, as it seemed half the world knew, busily occupied in flying from the pursuit of a husband from whom she was trying to keep not only herself, but her famous diamonds. Her eccentric movements had baffled him for long; but the temporary sojourn of her parure with our firm had nearly put him on the traces. Read the talk by the light of this and you will understand—even the big talk of Madame's last champion, a German Baron, who did meet the Prince in mortal fight with swords, and came off second best with a gash that went through his sword-arm. Who has got the diamonds now I neither know nor care.

But as for the revolver—well, if you must keep such awkward things at all, you can't spend three shots from one better than in obeying the precept,

> " Brise le miroir infidèle
> Qui vous cache la vérité."

Smash every lying looking-glass, whether it tells you you are a murderer, or whether—as is more common—it tells you, as my own, once upon a time, used to tell me, that I was a handsome as well as a near-sighted man. Alas, since that terrible night, no looking-glass dares to tell me that I am handsome any more. For I never saw an uglier ruffian in my life than my own double seen by the light of that fusee.

BURIED IN GOLD.

I.

At last !

What thousands of blessed and delightful things those words may mean ! The return home after mouths of wandering or years of exile ; the kiss of troth-plight after what has seemed a century of courtship ; the laurel wreath to one who has striven for it till it seemed too late to dream longer of a single leaf ; reconciliation after the estrangement of half a lifetime ; mastery of a long-pursued secret of nature—in short, any of the myriad cures of the heart sickness that comes of hope abandoned rather than deferred. But never meant those words to man or woman more than they meant to Lucas Constant one sunny moruing some two or three midwinters (or maybe more) ago. For they meant that he was, at last, free from the clutches of Dominic Van den Snees.

As the remarkable experience recorded in these pages is—barring, of course, certain precautions against too easy identification—as true as it is strange, such supreme felicity on the part of Lucas Constant as he marched, with free gait and head erect, across the quaint market-place of that little Flemish town, requires very special accounting for. The simple reason for both pride and felicity was just this—he was the first human being in all the social records of the place, who had ever contrived to escape out of the clutches of Dominic Van den Snees alive.

In a word, Dominic, though an excellent Christian, was just the hardest, keenest, greediest, gripingest, and most unscrupulously extortionate of the confraternity cf Shylock : while poor Lucas Constant had been condemned to play the *rôle* of Antonio, with that of Portia omitted. Had pounds of human flesh been marketable commodities nearer than the South Sea Islands, he would not have had half an ounce of flesh left upon his bones. Master of himself and of a fine estate at the age of nineteen, he had made the worst possible use of both, until everything he had once possessed was pledged or mortgaged to Dominic, who, in one way or another, had contrived to become the young prodigal's sole creditor. That had been the state of things when Lucas was one-and-thirty ; and in another year he would complete the term of twelve years popularly allowed for the full attainment of four cross roads or a madhouse by anybody who had sold himself to Mynheer Van den Snees.

Lucas was making a serious study of the former alternative when—but enough of him for the moment. For *Place aux Riches*, all over the world.

Dominic Van den Snees, then, banker, broker, anything that implied dealing with other people's money, had been gifted by nature with that order of beauty which pre-eminently requires lavish gilding. And Nature's gifts, both physical and mental, had been cultivated with the utmost diligence. I have said he was an excellent Christian : and as such he wasted no talent—especially if it belonged to another. This bright midwinter morning, his sixty-third birthday, found him developed to the highest degree of which he was presumably capable. He was a little, wizened old man, apparently made of parchment drawn tightly over an awkwardly-jointed wooden frame, without blood or muscle. The unappeasable hunger, as well as the characteristic features of the vulture were to be observed in his piercing, bead-like eyes ; his thin nose with its high bridge and depressed nostrils ; his barely visible mouth ; his unpleasant, unwholesome-looking baldness ; his long flexible neck ; his retreating chin. Nay, he carried his arms something in the manner of half-opening wings ; and there was more than a mere suggestion of claws in his long and crooked fingers. A commonplace conventional type of the theatrical usurer ? That may be ; and I think that the type must have been originally taken straight from nature, as represented by Dominic Van den Snees. For my part, I have observed that the usurer is mostly of the jovial and florid order, with delightfully genial ways, and that the jollier a dog is, the sharper is his bite and the harder his hold. Any such experience Dominic set at defiance. But then he was something more than a mere money-lender. He was that strangest of creatures, so strange that some have doubted its very existence outside fiction—a miser. So, at least, said rumour : and for once, rumour was not far wrong.

No guest had ever sat at this poor rich man's board. He kept no horse, no carriage, no servant even, save a single clerk whom he changed on an average once a quarter, and a woman of all work who came three times a week to cook and clean. He never took any amusement; he was never seen, except on pressing busi-ness, abroad. The name of Dominic Van den Snees was unknown to the poor who had no security to offer, and butcher, baker, tailor, and cobbler alike swore that the church mice were better customers to them all. He would go round the market during the last hour of the day, and forestall the town cats in the purchase of the refuse of the day's sales ; while as for his clothes—well, he had unquestionably bought one whole suit in eight years; or rather obtained one, for it was somebody else's misfit, and the tailor owed him rather more than its value.

I fear there is no question but that he was an exceedingly wicked old man; and therefore, it is to be hoped, a correspondingly miserable one . . . but as to the latter point I am not sure. We all plume ourselves on being men of business, the final outcome of centuries of progress; and it is not for a man of business to underrate either the delight or the dignity of feeling a continuous flow of gold out of other people's pockets into one's own, and not running out again. Rather, let me say, I should exceedingly like to try what it feels like—say for a year. Unless Dominic was a fool, the pleasure must be worth the sacrifice of all other things. And fool was about the only evil name he was never called.

"A great, *great*, GREAT Many Happy Returns of the Day !—There !"

Yes—it was a fact; Dominic the Usurer, Dominic the Miser, Dominic the tattered old fright, was being warmly embraced by the prettiest girl in all the town.

It is true she was little more than a child; but her promise in the way of being pretty was better than most girls' performance. I will not go so far as to say that the old villain smiled in an answer, but he gave a grin that may be called a smile by courtesy, and was not without a certain grotesque tenderness that would have made his clients stare.

"Thank you, Greta. There, that'll do. You'll rub the nap off my best coat with your elbows. . . . Ah ! We must begin to be careful now."

"Careful ?" asked Greta, puzzled, and looking round.

"Yes—careful. It's right and proper to make good resolutions on one's birthday; and we've been too extravagant—too extravagant a great deal. We must retrench, Greta. Why, only last week's housekeeping came to three florins—three whole florins, Greta. Now that we are about to become landed proprietors, we must range ourselves; we must give up all wasteful ways."

"Landed proprietors,—we?"

"Yes. That young fool Lucas Constant's bonds and hypothecations fall due at twelve o'clock to-day. If St. Ottilia strikes her twelfth stroke before he pays me down one hundred and thirty-seven thousand eight hundred and sixty-six florins in good notes or hard cash, I shall have twice the money's-worth in houses and land. . . . Yes, we must retrench; we must indeed."

"Lucas Constant!" exclaimed the girl. "Why, I thought he was the greatest and richest man in all the Province"—

"You're right. So he was, Greta. But *he* didn't retrench: and so "—

"Poor young man! Will he have nothing left him, after being so rich and so grand? You'll leave him a little, just a little, so that he mayn't be so very poor?"

"That's business, Greta. That isn't in your line. No; business is business, and principal's principal, and interest's interest, too; especially compound. We mustn't falsify the immutable laws of compound interest; that would never do. 'Twould be flying in the face of business—I mean Providence: and that's a sin. . . Holloa! if there isn't a whole inch and a quarter of twine lying under that chair. What waste! and to-morrow old Hannah will be here for cleaning; and she'll snap up that twine as sure as she's the miserliest old screw in all the town, bar none. Why, a man has lost a fortune before now for want of an inch of twine."

"Grandfather," said Greta, after a pause, very grave.

"Well?"

"I was wondering "—

"Well?"

"I've often wondered why you, who think always so much of—business "—

"I have to, Greta. 'Mind your own business;' that's the golden rule—next to the Rule of Three."

"I've often wondered why you should have burdened yourself with the cost of—of—me ?"

"Eh? Why—why, now that I come to think of it, it does seem queer. I wonder why! It never struck me in that light, to be sure. It *was* thoughtless, Greta. Yes— I remember it like yesterday: a baby not more than three years old at most, crying for a dead mother in the snow. I suppose I must have been drinking. I did take a glass of ale in those days, when I made an extra good bargain. Lord, to think if I hadn't I might have been, maybe, twenty florins richer this very hour! Yes, now I come to think of it, I must have been off my head to pick up a strange child out of the snow, and all for nothing. Well, well. Never mind, Greta ; I'll never do it again."

"And you've always been kind to *me*."

"There, there ; don't scold me. Let bygones be bygones. Don't let's think about it any more. It's the only time I ever did it : and "—

"Then, if you'll be *very* kind to me just once more," said the girl, with a half sad, half humorous smile, "I'll never ask you for another penny. Oh, it does go to my heart to think of that poor young man, that nobody finds any fault with, except not understanding money—of that poor young man being left to starve, or worse, while we— Grandfather, you are so rich, and you can be so kind : don't let us take away his all."

But as she spoke, Dominic's wizened face turned sour and hard.

"'To him that hath shall be given : from him that hath nothing shall be taken even that which he hath,'" said he. "I might have been a Lucas Constant ; he might have been a Dominic Van den Snees. He has chosen to enjoy his wealth in his youth ; I to enjoy mine in the evening of my days. No, Greta. Justice is justice, and business is business, all over the world. Sooner than do injustice I will carry all that he has spent into my grave."

" Ah ! there is no treasure of that sort there," she said, as if to herself, and scarcely half aloud.

" Master Dominic ! " bawled, putting his head in at the door, the banker's clerk, who, being very deaf, treated the rest of the world as if it were hard of hearing. " Here's Master Lucas Constant. Shall I show him in ? "

" Show him in, Claus, show him in ! " chuckled Dominic, rubbing his hands.

Greta rose with a sigh, and could not help letting fall a look of pity upon the young man who entered. He, for his part, started at such a sight in the heart of such a sordid cobweb. He would as soon have thought of finding a rosebud beginning to open from the stem of a nettle.

" Who in the world is that ? " he asked, as his eyes followed her through the door. " To think how often I've been here and never to have known you were a family man ! "

Dominic's face grew harder and sourer, while he scowled.

" ' Mind your own business,' Mr. Constant," said he, " is a golden rule. I should have thought you'd have had few eyes for any chit of a child to-day."

" True. But—well "— Greta's passing sigh must have been infectious, for he also sighed.

" Ah," exclaimed Dominic to himself, to whom a sigh could only betoken one thing. " This is my birthday; so I don't mean to be hard. I don't think it will be altogether a criminal act on my part to allow you an income of a hundred florins a year; and I'll charge you no more than five per cent. for the accommodation. No: on one's own birthday one can't be hard on an old friend."

Lucas stared for a moment; then burst into a laugh.

"Bravo, Dominic!" he cried. "Why, the skies must be tottering on their poles! I really couldn't think of taking such advantage"—

"Well, perhaps the offer was just a trifle strong. Say eighty florins, and ten per cent. interest; or seventy, at fifteen"—

"Or suppose we say nothing a year and no interest at all."

"Are you mad?" Dominic exclaimed.

"No, thank God. Congratulate me. You know I had just one little patch of mother earth left me unencumbered: a few acres in Brazil."

"I know. Not worth three florins an acre," said Dominic, "I won't touch it with a pair of tongs."

"That poor little patch has trumped the pack. I've sold it for a Diamond Mine to a company for one hundred and forty thousand florins: money paid. I thought I'd better tell you at once, as it's due in a couple of hours. Congratulate me— I can look the world in the face now —a free man. I'll be back with the cash sharp at a quarter before noon."

The church clock of St. Ottilia struck ten, or else he must surely have heard the angry groan that issued from the internal cavities of Dominic Van den Snees.

Having given notice to his creditor, and with plenty of things to occupy his mind, this suddenly appointed favourite of that most capricious of ladies, Dame Fortune, returned to his lodgings, where, in his unbusinesslike way, he had stowed his fortune, mostly in notes but partly in gold away in the cupboard where he kept a few books, a flageolet, a pair of boots, an ink-bottle, a canister of tobacco, a big sausage, and a bundle of *billets doux.* On the way, he stopped at a well-known cellar and breakfasted like a prince; and in the mirage conjured up by the glow of the Rudesheimer, the face of fortune grew singularly like that of the young girl whose contrast with her surroundings had taken him so much by surprise.

Despite the *billets doux* under the big sausage in the cupboard, Lucas Constant had kept singularly heart-whole; nor did he suspect the ghost of a danger of that sort from anybody connected with that horrible old spider, Dominic Van den Snees. So he could afford, with an easy mind first to speculate as to who she was; then to dream, then — but it struck eleven, and the payment was due within another hour.

And within that hour he might see her again; who knows?

So it was with a little more *empressement* than was to be wholly accounted for by a man who is only going to pay his debts that, having finished yet another flask of Rudesheimer, he loaded himself with his wealth and again betook himself to his creditor's abode.

A little to his surprise, the front door stood wide open; but as, after all, spiders do not usually close their doors against their clients, the flies, his surprise at such a detail was neither long-continued nor profound. He went quickly up the dusty staircase, meeting nobody by the way and hearing no sound save what rose from the street outside, until he reached the room door through which he had so often passed in shamefaced recklessness or in forlorn despair.

As he, in a very different mood from these, brought down his fist upon the panel, he fancied for a moment that he heard a sob. But no doubt it was only a fanciful translation of Dominic's wheezy " Come in."

So he went in, just as he had promised—sharp at a quarter before noon. The church bell was just chiming the third quarter, so he knew; and not being a man of business—notoriously the most unpunctual race on earth, be it in paying money, answering letters, or keeping appointments—he had the eminently unbusinesslike foible of being always up to time.

And there, sure enough, sat Dominic Van den Snees, who, being a really first-rate man of business, was invariably punctual when money had to be—received.

Lucas fancied the old gentleman looked a trifle pale; but otherwise he was just the same as ever.

"Here you are!" exclaimed Lucas, pleasantly. "One hundred and thirty-seven thousand eight hundred and sixty-six florins, all in notes and cash," said he, rattling down canvas bag after canvas bag on the table. "By Jove! One feels like Fortunatus, paying such a lot away all at one go. I should like to pay like that every day. There, old gentleman; count away—there's the last of them. And, when you're through, come round with me and bring Miss—I didn't quite catch the name—round to the Silver Apple Tree, and I'll stand you a dinner for an Emperor and a bottle of Rudesheimer fit for the Pope of Rome."

Dominic answered never a word nor sign; but his crooked talons reached out and raked up the gold. His lips moved in counting, but they uttered no sound.

"This is really jolly," said Lucas, who could never stand silence, lighting a cigar. "How some fellows can go on receiving money when it's so much less trouble to pay it I never could understand. Never fear, though— I've had my lesson; I'm not going to throw it away any more. I've done with cards; I've done with women; I've done with wine. And I'm hanged if there's any other way of throwing away one's cash, without getting anything for it, except on them. Do you know, I've actually got a notion that a man ought to marry? Did you ever marry, Dominic? No—she can't be your daughter. Grand-daughter, eh?"

But the lips went on counting silently.

"Yes," continued Lucas. "A man ought to marry. Not for fortune, but just for—for—for—whatever he ought to marry for. Were *you* ever in love, Dominic Van den Snees?"

Not a word; while the lips still counted on.

"No; of course you weren't. I wonder if you were ever young. I wonder if *I* was ever young—before to-day. Well —we'll begin together. You *will* bring—Miss— I really didn't catch the name—to the Silver Apple Tree? One doesn't pay a hundred and thirty odd thousand florins every day—

> " Gaudeamus igitur,
> Juvenes dum sumus,"

sang he.

Then, whether it was the effect of the Rudesheimer or of something more potent, I know not; but his thoughts rambled off into a pleasant dream. And when the dream passed, and he looked up, Dominic Van den Snees had left the room, without a word.

"And without so much as a 'Thank you'! Well, he always was a queer old—shark," said Lucas, who, however much disappointed, had perforce to drink any further Rudesheimer he might require alone.

At that precise moment the bell of St. Ottilia gave forth the last stroke of Twelve.

II.

It was a disappointment not to have caught another sight of the girl: and Lucas caught himself thinking of her a good deal—it seemed so very odd to have found anything of that sort in the establishment of Dominic Van den Snees. Indeed, as the days went on, he began

to be almost sorry that he had paid himself so clearly out
of the old miser's clutches, and even caught himself
meditating the negotiation of another loan, just for the
fun of the thing. . . . Why, he did not even know the
child's name.

Not that he was so far gone as to let his wits wander in
this wise in the town itself, where the fair unknown had
her home—if by such a name the miser's dwelling could
be called. For no sooner was he a free man than he took
a journey to the châtcau, five-and-twenty miles away, on
which he had not set eyes since his boyhood, and which
now belonged to him, free and unencumbered, once more.
Had he not been in a sentimental humour, such pilgrimage
was only due, now that, for the first time since it had
been his, he could look upon the home of his forefathers
without shame. He put up at a little cabaret in the
village, where he found himself clean forgotten. So he
assumed the *rôle* of a wandering painter—he could do
most things a little—and amused himself with strolling
about his own park, and imagining all sorts of things : a
kennel of boarhounds, for example; and a *châtelaine.*
And what was odd, or else not odd, the *châtelaine* was
always extravagantly young, and was always going out at
the door with a pitiful sigh, which ended in her coming
back with the gayest of smiles. No—if a man wants to
forget a woman's face, the very worst thing he can do is
to moon all alone about a park with a home memory
hanging from every bough, like toys on a Christmas-
tree.

But he had enough of this after awhile : or else the
example of the moths that fluttered of an evening into
his candle at the cabaret was of an infectious kind.
Besides, he really had reasonable affairs to look after.
So he set off for a final ramble round the château before
returning to the caudle—I mean the town.

It was an exceedingly pleasant ramble. The day was mild and open, though in midwinter ; and Lucas, as he caught from time to time the point of one of his own turrets through his own trees, was beginning to feel that he was at last growing into a real man, by whom these past twelve years of folly might still be redeemed. Château, park, village, the surrounding farms, were all his own, and he no longer had a debt in the world. What might he not, what ought he not, what *would* he not do with wealth and still early manhood at his command ? There is some moment in life when, if we are not blind, we realize what life means, and what we can make of it, if we only will realize it, when the meaning of ourselves and of our existence bursts on us like a sudden inspiration. And it was here and now that to him this moment came, sending a glow and a flash from heart to brain.

He was about, with this new resolution strong upon him, to leave the park, when, on emerging from a copse into the open, he came upon four men carrying chains and surveying instruments, which they presently proceeded to put in order for using. One had his eye to a spyglass, two others were unfolding a long chain.

Lucas's pride of ownership took fire. "What are you doing here ? " he abruptly asked the fourth, and apparently principal, trespasser, — a dapper, neatly dressed personage, with a finely-starched shirt frill and a bland smile. "Don't you know that this is private ground ? "

" Assuredly, my man. The *garde-chasse*, I suppose ? Perhaps you will be so good as to hold the other end of that chain."

" With pleasure, my man," said Lucas, seeing an opening for humour, "if you'll be so good as to tell me what for."

" ' My man,' indeed ! What boors these provincials

are! Perhaps you'll find your manners, young fellow, when I inform you that I am Maître Hopper, Notary Public of St. Bavon, and that that gentleman there is my friend Kropp,—so there!"

"Hopper? Kropp? Well, live and learn. And what are you doing here? and what is Kropp going to do with that piece of artillery there?"

"Artillery! That instrument, young man, is called a theodolite, and Kropp is going to survey."

"And what is he going to survey?"

"This estate, to be sure."

"That seems rather cool of Kropp."

"Cool?"

"Yes,—to survey an estate without the owner's leave."

"He would not do such a thing. He has the instructions of my clients, the proprietors of this estate, as you very properly call it, to make an exact survey thereof before its sale to the highest bidder. And I am here to see it done."

"The proprietor—a client of yours! Why, till this minute I never knew that there was a Hopper or a Kropp in the world. And a sale—a public sale—of this château! There's some mistake somewhere, Master Hopper. It must be some other place you've got to survey. This is the château of Lucas Constant, who "—

Master Hopper beamed. "Who was—*was*, Mr. Game-keeper!" said he. "Who *was* the owner, but who unquestionably isn't the owner now. A mistake! As if I could be mistaken about such a thing as that—I!"

"Who is the owner, then?"

"Why, my respected and estimable client, Peter Cornelius Boom."

"Hopper—Kropp—Boom! My good Hopper, you must be mad, or I. I never heard of any Boom, except, by the way, a little tailor in the market square, who once put a patch into one of my trousers ; and uncommonly badly, too."

" Hush !   That distinguished and honourable citizen is Peter Cornelius—that is the man."

" I beg your pardon.   I said either you or I must be mad.   I was wrong.   I retract.   It is not I.   It is un-hesitatingly you."

" Not a bit of it, young man.   I'll go as far as that in speaking of your manners ; but not a syllable more. Young Constant had to redeem his lands, everything he had, by noon last Monday, or lose it all.   Young Constant failed to make redemption.   Thus everything passed in due course of law to the representative of that most honourable citizen, Dominic Van den Snees."

" Failed to make redemption ? "

" Precisely so, young man.   And let his career be a warning to "—

" But he *did* make redemption : and nobody knows that better than I.   Come, no more of this nonsense, master Notary.   I am Lucas Constant.   So tell Kropp to pack up his traps and begone.   I don't know what the tailor has to do with it ; but you're trespassing as surely as I paid a hundred and thirty odd thousand florins to old Dominic with my own hands."

A bewildered look took the place of the notary's smile.

"You are Lucas Constant ? " asked he.   " And you tell me, Maître Hopper, Notary Public of St. Bavon, that you paid the redemption money to Dominic Van den Snees with your own hands last Monday before noon ? "

" That is certainly what I say."

" And you will produce the receipt ? "

" Receipt ?   By Jove, no," said Lucas colouring, as he realized for the first time that so regular a portion of the transaction had been forgotten both by creditor and debtor —and colouring also at the recollection of what had put

it out of his own head at the time. "But it doesn't matter.
Old Dominic himself will confirm every word I say, and
write out a receipt."

"I think not," said the notary, very grave.

"What!" cried Lucas, beginning to smell fraud.

"One question, Monsieur. At what hour on Monday
did you pay Dominic Van den Snees one hundred and
thirty odd thousand florins, if you please?"

"Just before St. Ottilia's struck noon."

"Sir," said the notary, sternly, "that is a lie!
Dominic Van den Snees died suddenly in his chair precisely when St. Ottilia's struck eleven! Intestate, sir,
and Peter Cornelius Boom is his heir-at-law. Don't tell
me, Lucas Constant, that you paid that money, without
even a receipt to show for it, to a dead man! . . . At
eleven o'clock on Monday, Dominic Van den Snees—
died."

Yes; there was no doubt about that. On his sixty-third
birthday Dominic Van den Snees had come to the only
thing which wealth and poverty have in common—an
end. He had been found by the clerk sitting where Lucas
had left him between ten and eleven, as dead as his own
gold. The groan he had given when he learned that his
scheme for getting hold of a great estate for half its
value had failed, was the last living utterance he had
made.

And, for all he had been so rich, he left nobody to
mourn him. His deaf clerk had bawled out notice to quit
his starved service some days before; his second cousin,
only known relation, and heir-at-law, Peter Cornelius
Boom, who had never had a nod or a penny from him in
his lifetime, did not even affect sorrow at being suddenly
transformed from a little tailor into a millionaire. No;
there was nobody—

Yes, though, there was one; just one. And, since
there was one to shed an honest tear over him,

therefore, not even Dominic Van den Snees, in spite of all his wealth, could be said to have lived entirely in vain.

No true miser ever makes a will. And yet Greta, though not a farthing came to her, shed a good many honest tears ; and she could not possibly have told why. She knew him, she could not help knowing, to be sordid, grasping, hard beyond belief ; and yet from the day on which some most uncharacteristic impulse had made him so false to himself as to pick up a forlorn little motherless child out of the snow, an odd sort of affection had grown up between the miser and the child. Perhaps it was because they were both so utterly alone : perhaps because so utterly different ; perhaps because of a thousand mysteries that will never be cleared up in this muddle-headed, but possibly not altogether muddle-hearted world. And now he was gone. . . . There was nobody to starve her any more.

As to what was to become of herself—the first consideration with most mourners—she had not as yet considered. Peter Cornelius Boom had not as yet made any movement to turn her out of the house. The heir could no doubt afford to be generous till after the funeral. At present, the only intrusion on Greta's solitude had been that of the undertaker's men, who had put the old gentleman's corpse into a ready-made shell within an hour of his demise : for the heir was in a hurry. So Greta had nothing to do but creep about and cry in the most contemptible way. For what could be more contemptible than for any girl of spirit to be sorry for such a good riddance as Dominic Van den Snees ?

If she had had her ears and her other wits about her, she would have heard the gossip of the town : and it was very serious gossip, indeed.

For it was nothing less than that Lucas Constant—that spendthrift scamp—had attempted to perpetrate a fraud, of which the shamelessness was only to be equalled by its folly. *He* pay such a sum as more than a hundred thousand florins ! That, in any case, was absurd. And to pay them without taking a receipt! More preposterous still. And when, though he described the notes in detail to the civic authorities, and put in evidence a list of them, not a note nor a florin (save the miser's own loose cash) could be found in the house, the outrageousness of his story was proved to the hilt— even without the gratuitous lie that he had paid the money to a man who had been laid dead in a shell an hour before.

There had even been whispers of murder. But of that, fortunately for Lucas, the surgeons who made a careful examination of the body, could find no confirmation. Beyond all doubt Dominic's ill-nourished heart had suddenly given way, he must have died in a moment, without a breathing space between living and dying. Besides, he must have died exactly at eleven : at which time Lucas was at the Silver Apple Tree and could therefore prove an *alibi.*

So not only was Lucas charged with fraud, and half-suspected of murder, but he had lost at one stroke both his ancestral lands and every penny he had received from the sale of his diamond mine. He was ruined, nay, beggared, for a second time ; and this time without a single fault of his own. For he was as convinced, as that he lived, that he had paid the money into Dominic's living claws before that fatal noon, despite such evidence as he would have held conclusive in the case of another man.

And just when the knowledge had been given him how a man's life was to be used ! . It was cruelly hard ; horribly strange.

Nor will any man, I think, venture to throw the first stone at Lucas Constant for giving way to an incomprehensible destiny, betaking himself to his garret and sitting down in sheer despair. He had become a man; but not more than a man.

III.

It was the day fixed for the funeral. St. Ottilia was tolling.   Peter Cornelius Boom and Master Hopper, dressed in superfine black, were breakfasting together before the burial, and breakfasting well.   Lucas Constant —but no matter about him.   Greta listened to the tolling : all the love that a cold and empty world had given her was about to be put underground. She had no place in the funeral ; but surely—

Yes ; she might, nay must, do that.   He had gathered just one blossom in his life: he must carry with him just one blossom to his grave.

In a few minutes more, the undertaker's men, who had already placed the shell within a coffin of which the cost would, little as it was, have made the corpse of the miser (could he have seen the bill) turn in the deepest grave, would come to nail all down.   So, for the first time since the old man's death, Greta crept out of the house and, in a corner of the market-place, bought a bunch of snowdrops—the fittest offering of the child who had been found in the snow.

She returned to the house, and went, no longer weeping, but grave and solemn, into the empty chamber where the dead man lay—as grim and ugly a corpse as ever was seen.

She leaned over *it* nevertheless ; and over *its* withered heart laid the bunch of flowers.

And, even as she did so, a sudden gleam from between

two of the vulture-like talons made her start. Too well
Greta knew the hideous sight of gold! How had that
come—*Here ?* Was the dead man trying to carry his
miserable hoards even beyond the grave ?

Yet even so it seemed! For how else could that shell
be freighted with treasure, in paper and gold? To Greta's
mind it could mean only one thing—that Dominic was
actually trying to convey his hoard into another world.
The very fancy filled her with horror : it was an unheard-
of blasphemy. One by one, with a pain as if she were
tearing out his heart-strings, she withdrew the symbols
of his life's curse : and, when the last was withdrawn,
the corpse was grim no more. With nothing but the
flowers upon his heart, the face of Dominic the Miser
became that of a little child.

And here I would fain close. For dull, indeed, must
be the reader who needs to be told that, when the money
found in the coffin was lodged with the Town Council, it
was found to correspond, not only in amount, but even in
the numbers of the notes, with the money which Lucas
Constant had asserted that he had paid.

I make no attempt to clear the mystery. It looks very
much as if the ruling passion was for once even stronger
than Death, and as if, rather than forego all those florins,
Dominic Van den Snees, in the dead flesh, or the living
ghost, or both, had really come back for five full minutes
to the life that he had left an hour before. Departed
spirits, we have all been told, will now and then come
back, drawn by the magnetic power of human love.
Why not, then, by the yet more mighty greed of gold ?

Or had, just on that day, the infallible clock of St.
Ottilia—after the universal habit of infallible clocks—
gone wrong ? Be that as it may, and whatever ways of
accounting for the still unsolved mystery may occur to
cleverer people than I, Peter Cornelius Boom was, very

wisely, contented to exchange landed estates for hard cash down, and—

Duller yet must be the reader who needs telling that the next time St. Ottilia chimed it was for the wedding of Greta with the man who had become a Man. . . . No : Dominic Van den Snees had not lived wholly in vain.

I.

You may talk of your fiddles, your bassoons, and all your squeaking and growling, but give me the Drum! There is something so solemn in its thud, so inspiring in its rattle. I have sat unmoved through the legerdemain performances of all the great fiddlers, from Paganini to Joachim, without feeling the ghost of emotion; when all of a sudden I have heard a roll from some far-off, dark corner of the hall that has brought the tears into my eyes. To my mind—and I boast of it with pride—the drum is the orchestral emperor; the most tuneful, the most pathetic, the most graceful, the most scientific, the most awe-inspiring, the most sentimental, the most eloquent, the most tender, the most—but hold: when I undertook to tell this story it was under a solemn pledge that I would keep a tight curb on my hobby, and not let it run away with me at starting. And here it is, taking the bit between its teeth, and bolting, even before I am fairly in the saddle. Well, there's some excuse when one's hobby is the honest Drum. 'Tis not as though it was a penny whistle, or a Jew's harp, or a tin trumpet, or that tooth-twinging impostor, the violin.

I am a drummer, I have always been a drummer, and a drummer (please Heaven) I shall die. Nay, I may say I was born a drummer; for my father, Anton Markwitz, served old Blucher, in the regiment of Pomerania, and was beating his drum while his general was beating the Frenchmen (fiddlers by nature) at Quatre-Bras; and in the precise middle of one of his rolls, as it was reckoned afterwards, I marched into the world. I never saw my poor father, for he never lived to finish that roll. But I took it up, so to speak, and went on with it; and when my sticks also are at rest, there's my boy Caspar to take up the beat at the end of the bar, and to keep true time like a good drummer—which, as all the world knows, is the same as to say, like a good man.

It was in the year 1840—for, since I am about to tell the most amazing and, in every way, the most intellect-baffling of experiences, I wish to be in every respect accurate and particular—that I was fulfilling an engagement in the city of Vienna. It was not a profitable one, from a financial point of view—but no drummer ever makes a fortune; he alone, of all men, follows art for art's sake, and not even for fame's. Kings and queens pay squalling *soprani* and squealing fiddlers with diamonds and titles, and the people with fortunes. But nobody ever gave a penny piece or an inch of red tape for a drum-beat, though as true to time as the sunrise, and—well, the short of it is, I was making enough to send a florin or two home, every now and then, to my mother in Pomerania, and meanwhile lived all alone with my drum, when we were not at work making people dance, as happy as a king—nay, happier, for no king ever played the drum. Our lodging was high, very high in the Stefan-Gasse. I'm afraid the old lane has gone the way of all the good old things, and I'm sorry, for I was very happy there once upon a time— until, having come home dog-tired one evening after drumming especially hard, I sat down to refresh myself with a little practice on my own account, and was just beginning, when I heard a prolonged and horrible wail just on the other side of the wall.

Only too well I knew it. It was the cry of a violin in pain. And how was I, a real musician, to make music with that abominable noise in my ears? In the impulsiveness of art and youth, I rushed down from my garret, seven steps at a time, and seized by both his shoulders the baker who kept the house and took the rent from the lodgers. I think he scarcely all at once comprehended the nature of my complaint; but he followed me upstairs readily, being a good-natured fellow, and having entered my room, stood, as if spell-bound, with his mouth open and his hands raised.

"Ah, it is indeed heavenly beautiful!" cried he. "I should have raised your rent, friend Markwitz, if I had known what you were going to have next door. Never mind—I will take it out in coming to sit with you, whenever he plays."

Never had the baker displayed the merest fragment of enthusiasm over my noble instrument, the drum. Not that this vexed me; for what does one expect from a baker but alum and weekly bills? But I could not help putting a good deal of vexation in my tone as I asked how he had dared to give me a next neighbour in the person of a street scraper.

"A street scraper! Gracious Heaven, it is an angel I have entertained unawares! The old man said he wanted a place where he could be in quiet, to practise the violin, and where no musician would be in the way to hear."

"No musician! Then—what am I?"

"Oh, a drummer! One does not count that music. But *that* is music—Listen! What is that old man doing in a garret? He ought to be leading in the opera—and what is more, he will be, before he dies."

"We'll soon see if a drum can't beat a fiddle at music," said I. "Thunder and battle against a pig with its throat cut—here goes." But, even as I raised my sticks to give the roll of Quatre-Bras, the violin sank into an unearthly sort of sigh, and was still. The baker burst into tears, and hurried from the room.

Alas! after that my peace was gone. Every evening, as soon as I was free from the dancing saloon, where I earned my bread and sausage, and had an hour or two left for the invention of new roulades, that accursed violin began again. You may think it would have been the easiest thing in the world to shift one's quarters. If you do, you are clearly no drummer. A drummer must settle where he can, not where he will—where he will not receive notice to quit within the first half-hour, or bring the fire-engines galloping up and down the street twenty times a day. Besides, I owed some rent, and the baker —being evidently no critic—was patient and good-natured. And finally, strange as it must appear, there was something about that fiddle that gradually fascinated me. It was not that I began to like it. On the contrary; I kept on hating it more and more. To most of what the world calls music I, being a true musician, am simply indifferent; this particular instrument inspired me with positive loathing. And loathing is as strong a magnet as loadstone —at least, so I found.

II.

Twenty times an evening I used to sit with my drumsticks poised in air, ready to thunder out a crash that would annihilate my invisible but only too audible foe. Possibly my inner self (my "subjective eye," as possibly my friend Fritz Nebelkopf would say) was satisfied with the sense of power. But, whatever the cause, twenty times an evening would my drumsticks fall upon the parchment with nothing louder than a muffled rumble, while the fiddle sang triumphantly on, as if inspired by the soul of a canary. And meanwhile I sat and cursed —and, when the song was ended, I cursed again that it was over and done. Can anybody account for such a mood of mind? Fritz Nebelkopf might, but assuredly not I. If I could have accounted for it, I should not have suffered from it, I suppose.

I positively began to lose my appetite for everything except beer. I had always been an exceptionally good sleeper, but now a poor ten hours out of the whole four-and-twenty was as much as I could do. On one occasion I counted forty-three and seven-eighths of a beat instead of forty-three and six-eighths, and, though nobody noticed it, it made me feel myself losing nerve—and a drummer without the nerve of a dozen rope-dancers may as well walk straight over the edge of the world. What was to be done?

And all this for a fiddle—a mere toy? It was absurd —and I the son of a man who had drummed and died at Quatre-Bras! Absurd? Nay—ignominious. It, or I, must come to an end. One evening—it was a Wednesday in December, when the whole city was wrapped in its featherbed of snow—I primed myself with a *schnapps*, and waited for the enemy to begin. Punctually to the hour began the nightly cry. And—as I had vowed— punctually to the very middle of the second phrase I thundered out with all my might what must have startled the very paving stones beneath the snow.

It was the roulade of Quatre-Bras!

With sleeves up to the shoulders, and with the perspiration, cold as the night was, streaming from my forehead, I thundered on, so that a whole army of violins must have been scattered like a swarm of Frenchmen before the uprising of Fatherland. In such an ecstasy of enjoyment and triumph was I, that I heard nothing but that glorious roulade, and saw nothing at all, until something like a snow-flake fell upon my bare arm, and a whisper pierced my ear—ay, a whisper, through all that din.

"Sir—sir! cease for Heaven's sake! Beyond that wall is—a dying man!"

I started to my feet, and my sticks fell to the ground. I did not burn much candle-light; but it was enough for me to see in the living, breathing flesh what I suppose any number of thousands of people have also seen—that is to say, the one loveliest woman in the world. What could I do but start? For I, at least, had never seen that apparently commonest of all sights before. Nor have I ever seen it since, save in that one form, common though the sight may be.

"Dying?" stammered I "And—and is none with him but you? As if I would not have thumped that Thing to pieces rather than disturb even a sick"— "Fiddler," I was going to add; but I had the presence of mind to substitute "Man." "Can I be of any service? Can I run for a doctor?"—

I was poor! and so, I judged from her appearance, was she. Her little figure, and the small face, redeemed from statuesqueness by the rich brown of the skin, the tenderly curled lips, the thick black hair, and the vivid brown eyes belonged to a foreign queen; but the dress was of my own humble class, and the entire absence of even the cheapest artificial ornament spoke of one even humbler. I could judge nothing by her voice, by reason of its sweetness. I not merely surmised, but knew she was poor, because of a look in those eyes that spoke of her being ready to take any help just because she was ready to give it—of a world where, there being no question of money, nothing is left to give or take but good-will, and help in kind.

I followed her into the next room; and the sight I saw, if I could have given any thought to the matter, would have made the nightly performances of the fiddle unaccountable indeed. In a garret like my own—which means empty enough—lay at full length upon a couch a strange, gaunt old man—one of those human creatures whom to see is to photograph upon one's brain once for all, though for far other reasons than the girl. He was well over six feet high, or rather long. The slope of his shoulders and the tapering delicacy of his white fingers were enough to show that he could never have been formed for strength, while his horrible skeleton-like emaciation showed that he was in the last extremity of weakness. The head was small; the yellow skin was drawn over the features as tight as the parchment of a drum. The features themselves were incongruous and *bizarre*—a large mouth, at once harsh and feeble; an aquiline and commanding nose, contradicting a weak and pointed chin. All the vitality about him was in the long and bushy grey hair, flowing down the sloping shoulders like a lion's mane, and such a pair of deep, dark eyes, that I can only liken them to smouldering volcanoes. He was breathing hard, and his hands seemed to be beating time. No sign of seeing me came into his face when I entered, and I was not sorry, for those eyes had made me afraid, though there was a strange look of the girl's in them, all the while.

I looked from one to the other, and then to the violin that lay, with its bow across it, on a rush-bottomed chair. She—I mean the girl—laid her fingers on her lips, and bade me be silent with her eyes. The old man still kept beating the air, as if an orchestra were in front of him.

How long this went on, I know not. But presently a stranger thing happened still. The girl took up the violin, put it to her shoulder, and began to play. But it was no melody known to me; nor, indeed, was it any recognizable

melody at all. If it was not wholly unfamiliar, it was
because I had been worried with it night after night—
cats' music I had called it then; but, seeing who was
making it, I called it so no more. It seemed to me she
was taking some violin part in an elaborate symphony,
wherein all the other parts had to be imagined, supposing
them to exist. She watched her father (if such he was)
as if he were conducting, and every now and then came
in, sometimes for a few bars, sometimes for a long passage;
but always, so it seemed, the rest of an orchestra was
needed to translate the music into coherency. Wood and
wind were wanting, and, of course, the drum. But genius
was, somehow, not wanting—so much I, though I am no
baker, could dimly tell. If this was a death-bed, it was
the queerest I had ever known.

"*Bravissimi tutti !*" cried the old skeleton, feebly
clapping his long white hands. "That will go, now ! The
first violins went best—my compliments to you, gentlemen ;
but all went well—very well. I thought at one time the
drums had gone stark mad ; but it was only a moment,
though it mustn't happen again. . . . This is the last
rehearsal ; next time—ah ! next time ! You shall share
my triumph at last, one and all ! Clara—come here."

I was too much interested in the scene to wonder
why I was there. I only saw the girl kneel down
anxiously by the couch, while the volcanic glow passed
out of the old musician's eyes, and a tender, rapt look
stole into them that would have told me they were
father and daughter even had I not known it before.

"Clara," said he, "in a very short while you will
know why I, with the genius of a Beethoven, have
chosen to live a life that a dog of the streets would
scorn. I suppose you are like all the rest of them—you
have thought that because I would flatter and cringe to
neither prince nor people, and would not coin into filthy
gold the gifts that God gave me—you have thought me a

madman, eh? You needn't answer; I know what Christian men and women think of people who don't sell their souls for silver and gold. Well—now you shall see! The great symphony is written at last, and I have put into it every scrap of blood, brain, and soul that was in me. For the first time a work has been done that contains the whole of a whole man! Here, under this very pillow, is the work that, in a few short weeks, will make your father's name the most glorious in the world, and will enable you to bathe in diamonds if you will. Everything is in it—my childhood, my youth, my manhood, my old age. I shall hear it, not with my inward spirit, but in all the light and colour of living sound: cities will fight for the glory of bringing it forth—the day I have lived for, Clara, has come!"

"What can I do?" whispered I.

"And who are you?" asked the old man sharply, turning his eyes full upon mine. "The doctor again? Oho—then I've cheated you this time! The symphony is finished—do you understand? So I was to die, was I? As if I could die before hearing my work and reaping its glory! Why, I'm bound to live till that's done; and then death may come when it will. See here—I'm as strong as a rock. I've not won the victory to lose the glory. Adieu, sir, and the day after the symphony is heard you shall have a hundred times your fee. For the present, leave me, and permit me to grow well."

He seemed to wander again into dreamland. "No," whispered Clara, reading my unspoken question, "I have never known him like this before. . . . He has been all his life at work upon a symphony, so that, with all his genius, he would, but for what little I can earn, have let himself starve—and I have picked up enough of the part for my own instrument, and even for others, to let him hear it in that way—poor father! But what he meant by all this, God knows—unless—unless—he is to hear it in another world—than here. You want to do something for a neighbour? Then go—go to,"—I forget the address, but it is no matter,—" and ask for Herr Emil Lenz; he will come at once, and will know what to do."

Had she bidden me go to Van Diemen's Land I would have gone.

At the door to which I had been directed, I came upon a young man just entering, with a big roll of what looked like music under his arm. I was too much agitated to observe his appearance particularly, but accosted him at once so as to lose no time.

"I am seeking Herr Emil Lenz," said I. "A friend of his is ill in Stefan-Gasse; I fear very ill indeed."

"Herr Lenz? Alas! then, Herr Lenz has left Vienna this hour, for Heaven knows where," said he, politely raising his hat, passing in, and closing the door.

That was the whole of my errand; which, despite its seeming slightness, I am bound to enter in its place for the sake of what happened after. Well, it was a pity; and yet I was not sorry, for Emil Lenz might have been young and good-looking, and it went against the grain to think of Clara turning at once for help to a friend with a masculine name. So I returned, thinking to myself, whatever Emil Lenz would have done, that will I do and more.

I re-entered the sick man's garret. He was once more rapturously beating time; Clara was again drawing strange music from the violin. And so it went on for a good hour. Then the old man suddenly cried, "*Bravissimi! Bravissimi tutti!* My day has come at last!"

And so it had; for with those exulting words he died; and the violin sang on, not knowing all at once what had befallen.

III.

In the year 1842 I was no longer living in the Stefan-Gasse; nay, nor in a garret at all. Things had gone well with me, for a drummer: and I was even putting money by, as well as sending it home.

And Clara—and her father? Well, they have disappeared as if they had never been. He was dead and buried; and she was gone without a sign; and no symphony, nor a note of music, had been discovered under the dead man's pillow or elsewhere, though before Clara vanished we hunted for it high and low. No doubt its existence had been a monomania, concealed during life, but called by the stroke of death into full play. Well, such oddities will happen; and I should not have cared a straw after a night's sleep had not my own heart been among the things that had been spirited away. Wherever Clara might be there also was my unlucky heart; and I no more knew where than I knew what name she went by besides Clara; and I soon found out that one might as well look for a particular Clara as for a particular John.

I did my best to find her. And one advantage of being a musician is that one can thump, or blow, or twang one's way all over Europe on a search—that one can roll, and yet gather moss all the time. I had been with orchestras in Stockholm, in Madrid, in Moscow, and in London, and I was just starting from my old quarters, Vienna, for New York, where I had heard that there were some dozens of Claras, when I happened to overhear a piece of the talk that chanced to be going on at the table where I also was taking beer.

" Are you going to hear that new symphony of Lenz?"

asked one—a critic, I judged, from the peculiar upward curl of his nose.

Lenz—the name caught my ear. It was associated with the first evening I had seen Clara.

"I suppose so," said the other carelessly. "Who is Lenz, by the way?"

"Oh, a young fellow—Emil Lenz. Not much in him, I fancy, but he was the only pupil of old Klaus. So, good or bad, the thing ought anyway to be queer."

"Old Klaus? Why, I thought he belonged to our great-grandfathers' times."

"So he did. Nevertheless he died but two years back; though it's true he might have been dead sixty years ago for all the good he'd done for forty. And yet he was a genius. Yes, a genius, if ever there was one. I knew him well before he took it into his head that great work could only be done by cutting oneself off from the world, and then good-bye. And what came of it? Just nothing at all. Why, when he died and was buried, he hadn't even begun the work he had made a martyr of himself for—nobody even knows what it was to have been."

"He was a madman, then?"

"No—a genius. But you're right, too. Madman—genius, 'tis much the same."

Emil Lenz. My heart flew back to my first pang of jealousy when I heard of Clara's friend, and now I learned that he was in Vienna, and young; and he would be as good-looking, of course, as the deuce—a hundred to one. Why had I never thought of searching after Clara Lenz? And yet, if that was the secret of her vanishing, what would be any more the good of my searching after her at all?

None. And, therefore—need I say it?—next evening found me in the hall where the new symphony by Emil Lenz was to be performed. It was a folly. For if Herr

Lenz knew anything of her, she was certain to be his wife; and if she was not, he would know nothing. One or the other it must be. That was my lover's logic, anyway. At any rate, folly or not, there was I, in good time and, therefore, in a good place, both for seeing and hearing: mark this, because of what I have to tell—for what I have to tell is true.

The orchestra and the company were in their places, and among these last was the critic whose chance word had brought me, and whose story of what happened, if he be applied to, will confirm my own—not that the word of a drummer is not enough for all things. A good-looking man, of perhaps, five-and-thirty years old, in faultless evening dress and gloves of straw colour, faced round from the conductor's seat, *báton* in hand, and bowed. My heart sank, and my eyes travelled round the hall when I saw that he was so fine and handsome a man, and so much like a prince not even in disguise. Somehow, I fancied that his bright and energetic face and his stalwart figure were not strange to me; and, of course, as a travelling musician, that was not impossible. Was it at London I had met him, or at Moscow? Well it did not matter; I saw him now.

And—never tell me there is nothing in coincidence, nothing in fatality!—as my eyes went from him round the hall—there, had not my heart foretold it?—there sat Clara; but no longer the grisette of the Stefan-Gasse. She was dressed in black silk and white lace, and sat with other princesses (to judge by the look of them), more lovely than ever. I had found her. And what was it to me? She was Clara Lenz—what else? And I—I would not go to New York. I would go to the devil.

However, easy as that journey is, I could not make it now. The first movement of the symphony began, and I was struck by it from the beginning, even before the drums came in. Moreover, I could feel, despite my despair, that the audience was struck by it also. Before the first movement was half through there fell upon the whole hall that mysterious atmosphere wherein all individual emotions lose themselves, and the hearts of hundreds beat as one. There is nothing can do this but music—nothing in the world. There is nothing else that can bring hundreds of strangers into sympathy closer than brotherhood—more complete than love's own.

It *is* something to live for ; to feel one's own self this magician, and, with one's own *báton*, one's wizard's wand, rather, to direct one's own spells to a magic circle from soul to soul. At least Clara and I were feeling this together—for once, for the first and the last time, we were one. I had no need to see her face to know what she was feeling. For not only she, nor only she and I, but all Vienna that had ears, were become the slaves of Emil Lenz, body and soul.

I need not name to all who have music in their souls (and who cares for others ?) the most glorious symphony that ever found its way into the world, Now its majesty, now its joy, now its infinite pathos, carried us away beneath the earth or above the stars. Emil Lenz would be a fool if he needed applause to tell him that he was hailed as henceforth music's emperor.

But, at the close, the applause was bound to come. We had fallen back upon common earth again, and had to do our best with mortal voice and mortal hands. You should have heard the thunderous cheer—seen the rain of flowers that fell from ladies' fingers round the throne, when Emil Lenz, this morning a nobody, to-night an emperor—

But hold !

It was no emperor, but some abject coward, who shrank pale and trembling into his seat, and who let the *báton* fall from his hands. It was not upon Emil Lenz

that the roses rained. It was upon a strange, gaunt
figure, well over six feet high, and looking like a skeleton
rather than a man—one could almost see the sharp bones
cutting through the yellow skin. The shoulders sloped
and stooped, and over them fell a leonine mane
of grizzled hair. But, wild and grotesque as was
the figure, one saw, one felt only the deep volcanic eyes,
glowing with the light of triumph unspeakable as he
placed his long dead-white fingers on his hollow chest,
and bowed, taking all the homage as his own.

"Great Heaven! Old Klaus!" cried the critics.
"Old Klaus out of the grave!"

It was the musician whom I had seen die—whose body
I had followed to the tomb. A nameless shudder ran
through the hall. And, as the figure slowly faded into
mist and then into nothing, bowing all the while, I heard
a woman scream, and saw Emil Lenz fall heavily from
the platform to the floor.

A Ghost—and seen by hundreds!

Ay: by hundreds. There is no escape from *this* ghost
story, whatever loophole may be found for others. But
what matters hundreds? Two are enough for one ghost:
and—it was *his* symphony that had been played: the life-
music of the genius who had died in a garret, and had
left nothing behind him but his score in the hands of a
death-bed thief, save so much as his daughter had
learned well enough to play him out of this bewildering
world. . . . He was right: not all the doctors in
Vienna, no, nor all the gravediggers, could keep him
back from his Hour of Fame. It had come at last: and
where could *he* be but There?

I am not sorry for Emil Lenz; though he never
recovered from that horrible swoon. He who would filch
a man's all from under the pillow whereon that man's
head lies dying, deserves worse than that; and assuredly

no pity. I leave all pity to Clara Markwitz, the drummer's wife : she has enough for all the world. Only when Fritz Nebelkopf comes with his stupid philosophy, to prove that all of us, being under the spell of the same music, were naturally made victims to the same fancies, I glance at my dear wife, and drown his nonsense with the roulade of Quatre-Bras.

It is when alone we speak solemnly, and feel that in truth love is stronger than death—whether it be love for man or woman, or only for fiddle or drum.

THE DEMON SIXPENCE.

I.

I HAD got to hate the very sight of it. And, in truth, there was something about that Sixpence which made it different from any other sixpence that I ever saw—and I have seen a few. I should know it, even now, among many. And yet, strange to say, I can hardly give any very distinct description of the manner in which it differed from every sixpence that happens to bear the same date, namely 1851. Features one can describe: but expression goes beyond the power of even a pen. It is true that it seemed to have been a sort of Pariah among sixpences—beyond most others it had been rubbed, and thinned, and scratched, and otherwise worried, tortured, and abused. The rim was entirely worn down to the extent of three-quarters of a circle, and the finger-nail, when drawn round it, was scarcely conscious that it had ever been milled. The oak and laurel branches on the reverse were hardly to be distinguished from mustard and cress: on the obverse of the coin, some seditious or profane idler had begun to drill a hole through the royal eye, but had stopped when half way through, either from sudden remorse or else because he thought it hardly worth while to wear so battered a coin for a luck-penny. But with crisp and defiant boldness the words " Six Pence " stood out under the crown, as if it would say, " I am worth six pennies : and the proudest piece of silver under a shilling, fresh from the Mint, can say no more." Yet all this does not touch the inward expression of the thing—its obstinate air, as if it had a character, nay, a will of its own.   Whenever I put my hand into the right-hand pocket of my trousers, that is to say, where I promiscuously thrust my loose change, I knew when I touched *that* sixpence, though it might be in company with a dozen more.

And an odd thing about it was that I could not manage to part with it, even if I tried.   I have no time to tell all the odd coincidences that raised a simple accident to the level of a superstition.   I don't even know how it first came to me : but it very soon assumed a kind of individuality, which I felt long before I became conscious of its having one.   I think I first became aware of its determination to stick to me through good and ill repute, by the observation of a waiter at the chop-house, to the effect of " No, sir—I don't go to say as it's a bad un, though there's such about—but I'd sooner you'd give me another one, all the same."   I did not find the prejudice, or prudence, of the waiter repeated in other quarters. But still the singular fact remained—that it remained in my pocket, in spite of chances and resolves, till I only wonder it did not burn a hole through the lining and get rid of itself that way.

Well—such experiences have been known, more or less, to most people, as well as to the miser in the Eastern story whose attempts to get rid of an old pair of boots ended in his nearly losing his head for murder.   Did you ever try to free yourself from the incumbrance of anything of any sort—from an old glove to a worn-out love affair ? Have you not found the awkward way it has of sticking to you as tight as slander, and of turning up in the most unexpected ways and at the most uncomfortable times ? The most curious thing about *my* form of the common experience was that sixpences are so much more easily disposed of than old loves and old clothes. A glass of wine—a cigar—the thing is done. But my sixpence obstinately refused to be either smoked or drunk, or even given away. By some strange instinct, there was always another in its company, and that other was the one to do its duty as a humble representative of the realm's current coin. When I was resolved to send it on its travels, it had an impish knack of hiding away in some inaccessible corner of my pocket, so as to make me fancy it was not there any longer, and then, when I turned out my money in the solitude of my chambers, of coming out with a smirk, as if to say, " Oho, master! here I am again!"

One thing I know. When it first came to me I was as lucky as most people in the opinion of my friends, and a great deal luckier than anybody on earth in my own. I had a good income without having to work for it—which is generally considered lucky—and I was engaged to be married to the best and prettiest girl that ever was born, bar none. But I could not, especially under the somewhat peculiar circumstances of our engagement spend my whole time in love-making ; and so, for pastime, I lived as I have noticed that young men with independent incomes and no immediate responsibilities, even when engaged to good and pretty girls, mostly do. I had a good many friends, in spite of my engagement to Bessie Lennox, and they were very good fellows, the very best of good fellows, one and all. They stuck to me like that sixpence—I can't say more. But—somehow— explain it who can—from the time that sixpence took to keeping company with me, there came a change. Mind, I *don't* say that it was the sixpence that made me back King of Spades for that confounded Queen's Plate when Rigoletto won against the judgment of everybody who had any. Nor do I say that when I had to curtail my visit to Homburg by five weeks it was because even at

Frankfort—where they take every sort of money they can get—my sixpence had refused to leave my hands. Only I do say that these, and all my other strokes of ill fortune, happened *after* my acquisition of that sixpence, and not before. It seemed—I say no more than seemed—as if that sixpence were somehow draining my gold away from me. What is a sixpence to ten thousand pounds? Just nothing at all—one in four hundred thousand. But, as the pounds grew less and less in number, the sixpence grew and grew in size till—well, I must out with it: it had become the fortieth part of my whole fortune. When one has just one sovereign left, a sixpence is large. Large? Nay, huge: it had fattened upon my fortune till it had devoured it all.

Yes—I left the chambers of Messrs. Heddes & Taylor, solicitors, and something besides, with one sovereign and one sixpence to begin the world with over again. Of course I knew that I had been a fool, in a general sort of way. But I could not admit that, in particulars, I had done otherwise than wisely. Only a fool would have backed the field against such a favourite as King of Spades. And who could have guessed or dreamed that black would have turned up running as often as —— well, never mind counting now. I looked at the sovereign and the sixpence, both of them, as I left the lawyers' door. That turning up was not hard to count, anyhow. The sovereign behaved himself as sovereigns usually do when they are looked at. But that infernal sixpence looked at *me*, with an "Oho! *I'm* faithful—you won't get rid of *me!* If your Bessie sticks to you half as tight, she'll be truer than—gold!"

Poor Bessie! Or poor me, rather—for I wasn't any longer a loss worth crying over. I must let her know the state of things without an hour's delay. I have said that the circumstances of our engagement were a little peculiar. She was one of a large number, no fewer than six, of orphan girls, of whom the youngest was eleven and the eldest twenty years old. Their father and mother had both perished in the Mutiny: they had been left penniless; and what would have become of Bessie and her sisters Heaven knows, if they had not found a friend in an old brother-in-arms of their father's, Captain Goodenough by name. The Captain was an elderly bachelor with ample means, and neither kith nor kin—it was not likely that any man who married one of the Miss Lennoxes would take her empty handed. He was the most aristocratic-looking man I ever saw: if I were a painter, and wanted a typical model for a duke, I would go to the Captain sooner than to any real duke I ever saw. His calmly, almost sternly handsome face, in which never a muscle was ever seen to relax or move, his erect, military figure, and his habits of reserve and silence, made up a whole of almost impossible dignity. Indeed, next to the immobility of his features, his silence was almost his most striking quality. If nobody ever heard Captain Goodenough say anything worth saying, that was obviously because nobody ever heard him say a word more than was absolutely needful. No doubt his adopted daughters were grateful to him for allowing them to make a home for the declining years of a lonely and elderly bachelor, but they, nevertheless, could not help largely diluting their gratitude with awe. He was certainly kind to them, but scarcely indulgent enough, considering what young girls they were. There was even something Puritanical about their bringing up under his hands. They had the best masters and mistresses; they went into the best society he could find for them, but he had such a mortal horror of the theatre that Bessie had never seen a play. He had even exacted a promise from me, as a condition of my engagement, that I would thenceforth and for ever refrain for the rest of my life from entering any place in the shape or nature of a theatre, from a music hall up to the opera. And, for Bessie's sake, I had given the promise, though I loved the drama in all its shapes above everything—except her.

For the rest, his life was as blameless and as regular as if it had been made and kept going by clock-work. Not even the possession of a lot of girls about him had made him break through certain fixed habits, which were no doubt those of a lifetime. He rose and breakfasted with Bessie and her sisters at the same invariable hour. He read the newspapers till lunch-time, and then took part with the girls in any of their plans for the afternoon. To my mind, his only eccentricity consisted in his keeping up the habit of dining out or at his club instead of at home nearly every evening except Sunday. But then I judged him by what my own feelings were with regard to Bessie; and I have even known husbands who, without being considered the least eccentric, do precisely the same thing. What his favourite club was I never knew. It was always, in his home circle, spoken of reverently as " *The* Club " — nothing more. But it must, to suit Captain Goodenough's tastes, have been of the most severely ducal order. He had never asked me to dine with him there.

This was the man whom I had to inform of my absolute ruin. I am neither shy nor timid by nature : but I own my heart failed me, as with twenty shillings and sixpence—*the* sixpence—in my right-hand trouser pocket I opened Captain Goodenough's study door. Under the circumstances, I have no doubt I entered rather abruptly. At any rate, I was not prepared, on entering that sacred den, into which not even Bessie dared intrude, for the sight that met my eyes.

I had expected to find the excellent Captain, whose tastes, though intensely aristocratic, were neither energetic nor intellectual, asleep over the *Times.* I found him standing bolt upright, with his face towards a large looking-glass over the chimney-piece, and his long, straight back towards me. It was from the looking-glass that I saw how he was amusing his solitude. The stately old soldier's stiff, not to say stony, face, was stiff and stony no more, but was writhed into the wildest and ghastliest of all imaginable grins. Never in my life had I dreamed of a facial contortion such as that into which Captain Goodenough's—Captain Goodenough's of all men's—eyes, lips, cheeks, brows, nay, even chin, nose, and tongue were combined. Could I describe it, I should be a literary Grimaldi. Reader—can *you* grin? Try —do your best—and Captain Goodenough will still have left you leagues behind. Anything more horribly fiendish in the way of a grin it is impossible to conceive.

I had read and heard of madmen who, conscious of their madness, have a terrible power of controlling themselves in public only to break out into a more terrible fit of self-indulgence in lunacy so soon as they are alone and unseen. I believe it to be a proved fact that reserved, quiet, steady men, without humours and eccentricities, are more prone to madness than those flighty people who let out their crazes comfortably every day without letting them run into arrear. I knew not what to say or do, in the presence of such a skeleton as I had discovered in the cupboard of Bessie's adoptive father. Of course I did the only really stupid thing I could—I tried to retreat and to close the door quietly: and of course it creaked sharply. Men must not look for good luck even in little things who carry such a sixpence as mine.

He faced round, with half the grin still upon him. And, for the first time, I saw this stern, unbending man in a rage.

"How the devil do you dare"— he began.

I had recovered my own presence of mind far enough

to make believe I had seen nothing. "I was told I should find you here," said I, in as indifferent a voice as I could manage. "May I speak to you—about myself? I have—something—of importance"—

Every trace of that wonderful grin had gone, and the handsome face had become restored to its natural calm so completely that I almost thought my eyes had been deceived. He still eyed me strangely, I thought, but it might have been consciousness of unwelcome intrusion that made me think so.

"Well?" said he.

"I have not seen Bessie. I must see you first—you know—you know that when I asked her to be my wife I believed that I should never have less—less money—than I had then."

"Well?" He was indeed a man of few words.

"Well, sir—I felt as certain that King of Spades would win the Queen's Plate as that I saw you—see you"—

"And what—what, sir, do you see in *me* ?"

"That I see you there. Anybody who knows anything about the horses would tell you the same. And it is against all reason that black should turn up twenty-five times running. Aud I never heard of people like Heddes & Taylor out of novels and plays. And the end of it is —except a sovereign to keep me till I can get another— there," I said, taking out my sixpence and laying it before him on the table, "there is the last sixpence I have in the whole world : all that's left of ten thousand pounds."

"Well?"

"That's all. And Bessie "—

"So that sixpence is your last," said Captain Goodenough. "And it is *not* a nice-looking sixpence to have for your last, I must say." My hopes of something —I hardly knew of what—rose, as the Captain, for him, indulged in such a number of words. He never used any that were needless, I knew. "But it is enough, and good enough, to buy a rope with, young man : and that, as you come to me, is what I advise you to do. I never approved of you as a husband for my Bessie as soon as I found out that you had been a haunter of the theatre—of the devil's church, young man. I know of what road that is the first milestone. The Theatre. The Music Hall. The Race Course. The Dice Box. The Usurer. The Halter. Bessie shall not marry a ruined gambler. Why, within a week of marriage you would be taking her to a play !"

" On my honour, Captain Goodenough, I "—

" The honour of a stage-struck gambler ! Be off with you ! No—you shall not see Bessie. She is well rid of you. Be off with you ! Go ! "

I had hardly reached the end of the street, in a state of shame for myself and of indignation with fortune that I cannot bear to look back upon—an indignation which certainly did not spare Captain Goodenough, who had turned me, in my poverty, like a dog from his doors— when, hatless and breathless, a boy in buttons ran up to me, with an envelope in his hand. I did not mean to give up Bessie, if trying to live a better life for her sake could help me keep her and win her ; and my heart felt stronger at the sight of what it told me was a message from her. Hurriedly, without heeding the direction, I opened it—the envelope contained my accursed sixpence, and nothing more !

" Demon of a coin ! " I cried, spinning it far away into the mud of the road, " it *is* you—you, who have robbed me of luck, and fortune, and love, and all that I have to live for ; you, who now come back to me to taunt me—begone for ever : curse whomsoever else you will."

A minute afterwards an empty hansom drove by. I hailed it, and sprang into it.

" Where to, sir ? " said the cabman.

" To the devil ! " cried I.

" All right, sir," said he ; and off he drove.

II.

It did not seem to me in the least singular that a stray London cabman should know the road as a matter of course, and without any further directions or inquiries. In truth, I never thought once about the matter. I was literally in a state of sheer despair. Not to speak of greater and deeper things, it had not been pleasant to be set down by a man like Captain Goodenough as a mere reprobate, for whom the best left was hanging. It horrified me to feel that—not to speak of Bessie—I had come to be regarded as unfit to enter the doors of a respectable man. Perhaps I had not been, myself, exactly what the better and colder half of the world calls respectable. But, nevertheless, I had the highest esteem, respect, I may almost say reverence, for Captain Goodenough and his grey hairs, in spite of a suspicion that the old gentleman's intellectual capacities were by no means of the highest quality—were not, for example, to be named in the same breath with my own. After all, though he was rich and could afford it, it was not everybody who would have troubled himself with the care and education of six growing girls who were of no manner of kin to him. No—I did not like to be treated as I had been by one who represented to me the sum total of the respectable world. Well, I thought to myself as I drove on and on without heeding where I was going, I will be revenged—before I am half a year older I will prove to him that I am not what he takes me for, and will win back Bessie and his good opinion together—I'm rid of that infernal sixpence now : and luck will turn again!

I suppose I was a little superstitious. But the certainty that I was rid of my sixpence at last, gave me more hope and courage than if I had suddenly found myself heir to another ten thousand pounds. Why had I never thought of spinning it away into the middle of the road before?

With new hope and courage, common sense also returned. I opened the trap above my head, and called out, " Stop! Where have you been driving me to?"

" You know that best, sir," said the cabman. " You told me where to drive, and I've been doing my best to get there."

" Well, I'll get out here, wherever I am." I jumped out. " I suppose I'm not very far from somewhere. What's your fare?"

Suddenly, it struck me that I was in a part of London where I had never been before: or at least that I did not recognize. It was a poor street, dark either with fog or twilight—with which, I could not tell, though it could scarcely have been with the latter, seeing that, when I left Captain Goodenough's it had been broad day. The darkness was accentuated and emphasized, so to speak, by a glare of gas jets over a doorway to what looked like some sort of a music hall. But I never like to seem ignorant of London, especially where a cabman is concerned, so I asked again, " What do you call your fare?"

" Well, sir, I hardly know what to say. Make it a even sovereign, and that won't be far off from about square."

" A sovereign! Do you take me for a Frenchman?"

" No, sir—but I do for a gentleman. And a gentleman don't go driving about for near seven mortal hours, with-

out so much as stopping for a glass of ale, all over the
town, and wearing out a horse all to his own self, and
then talk too fine about a pen'north of fare. I haven't
measured the ground and I haven't counted the time.
Maybe you have, sir. And I'll let you off for a sovereign:
and that's the cheapest drive you ever made."

Had I been driving about all London for seven hours?
Well, it seemed likely enough: and of course it was but
just that I should pay—under the circumstances—pretty
much what the cabman pleased. If he had taken advantage of my very general order, I had no right to complain.
Only that I should have thrown away my very last
sovereign—nay, my very last halfpenny—in so useless a
way, did seem absurdly hard, and I was getting hungry
too.

" Well," said I, " I can't say that you're wrong. But
seven hours—let me see—doesn't come to a sovereign,
even paying by time: and I can't suppose you've done all
that lot in miles. I don't make it more than nineteen
shillings for seven hours, as well as I can reckon in a
hurry." The shilling's worth of change would give me at
any rate some sort of a meal.

" Blest if I don't think you're one of the lot that
wouldn't part with a threepenny without feeling all round
the rim ! Twenty bob "—

" There, then," said I, " we'll split the difference—
Nineteen and sixpence. Here's a sovereign, and you
give me the change."

I thought the cabman smiled : whence I considered
that he was getting the best of the bargain after all.
" Here you are, sir," he said, as he handed me the
change. He pocketed my last coin, and drove away as
if his horse had *not* been already doing "seven mortal
hours."

My last coin ? No—I had the sixpence he had given
me out of the sovereign still left me. It would give me

bread, cheese, and ale. But what was this curious feeling at my finger ends as I held the coin, warm from the cabman? My heart sank within me. " Oho ! " I read in its face by the gaslight, " Oho, master ! Here I am again ! "

What was the use of good resolves when that Demon Sixpence came to scatter them to the winds in the very moment of their making? Why had the sharp eyes of just that very cabman seen just that very sixpence lying in the road? This was not chance — it was destiny.

" Very well," said I aloud. " In for a penny, in for a pound ; as well be hung for a sheep as a lamb. . . . Hang and confonnd that old humbug and imbecile of a captain. What right has *he* to make a slave of *me ?* I'll have her in spite of his teeth and his grey hairs —and it shall *not* be by becoming a respectable old tyrannical automaton like him. I won't spend this infernal sixpence in food, but in rebellion and revenge, as far as it will go. I'll toss for it with a shoeblack—I'll go into the gallery of a theatre—I'll have sixpennyworth of everything he wouldn't approve : and I'll be rid of that everlasting sixpence too. And then— By Jove ! And I'm at the very door of a music hall ! I'm not driven here for nothing ; that sixpence hasn't come back to me for nothing ; and—the deuce take Captain Goodenough— and in I go ! "

Call the thought boyish, if you will. But imagine yourself penniless, hopeless, hungry, disgraced, and haunted by a remorseless imp in the shape of that six- pence into the bargain, and say, on your honour, if you are certain of feeling very good tempered, and therefore not otherwise than wise. I was not fond of music halls, and I went in solely to spite the Captain, and because it was the most desperate thing, short of suicide, that I could afford to do. It seemed the most appropriate way of getting rid of my sixpence at once and for ever.

Wherever the street was, it was in a by no means aristocratic quarter. The young men and girls passing in and out were of an unmistakably Whitechapel cut : and I only wished Captain Goodenough could see me now. I no longer consciously thought about Bessie—she was gone, and a good riddance she had made. I paid just my sixpence to go into the best part of the house, which gave me full range of everywhere, from the gallery to the floor. Not that the privilege came to much, for a more crowded place of entertainment I had seldom seen—there was scarcely elbow room. I need only describe the place by saying that it was a large oblong hall, with a double gallery running round three sides, with a stage flanked by boxes occupying the fourth, and with a floor crowded with tables at which the bulk of the audience was drinking, smoking, and flirting after the manner of its kind. I stood up against a pillar and lighted a pipe—I did not sit down, lest I should oblige one of the potmen to ask for orders from a penniless man.

Having done the deed, and taken up my position, I looked round. The audience, though so large, was hushed—absorbed, apparently, by what was going on upon the stage. It was like an æsthetic audience during a selection of Future Music, so coughless was its rapt attention. And yet, oddly enough, the performance which caused such a profundity of enthusiasm was equally inaudible. I looked : and the cause of an effect which a *prima donna* might have envied stood revealed.

A tall man in faultless dress clothes, standing otherwise perfectly stiff and motionless, was giving a performance that was certainly unique in its way. Of what material Nature had made his face, I cannot guess : but I should say of some elastic material resembling india-rubber. In short, he was doing nothing more or less than making faces. And triumphs of art they were, in their way. Now, his tongue would touch his forehead with its tip, while his long nose bent sideways, nearly to his ear. He had absolute command over even those facial muscles which are generally considered, even by physiologists, uncontrollable. Now, he resembled an idiot; now, a lunatic; now, a murderer; now, a demon; now, a nondescript;—a sort of heraldic chimera.

" Who is he ? " asked I, of my nearest neighbour.

" Lord bless the toff ! " said he. " None o' your chaff —as if yer didn't know that's Seenor Crackjaw, the Champion Grinner o' the Vorld ! I'd give a fi'pun' note to grin like he. But he'll beat that before he've done."

Suddenly the suppressed applause burst forth : and, under its cover Signor Crackjaw turned his back to the company. But, in an instant he was round again, and grinning his acknowledgment of the storm by a grin that did indeed beat anything he had ever done before. Such a grin as I had never dreamed of in my life —but hold ! never since I had seen Captain Goodenough ; and, by Heaven, it *was* the very grin that I *had* seen !

I stared hard in sheer bewilderment to see that same impossible, preternatural grin on the faces of two such different men in one day. Then, as the fiendish face turned from right to left, slowly, and as if moved by clockwork, Signor Crackjaw's rolling and squinting eyes met mine. Never shall I forget the transformation that came over that grin. The eyes continued to meet my stare, as if mine had mesmerized them. But the features first relaxed, then changed, and finally fixed themselves into a petrified and ghastly likeness of — Captain Goodenough : of no other human being in the world. There was never any mistaking *that* man.

Had madness come upon me? But, if so, it was doubly reflected in the face on the stage that now wore no expression but one of terror and shame. Without

even the most hurried bow to the audience, this Signor
Crackjaw, or Captain Goodenough, or this illusion of
hunger and fever, turned and fled, as if suddenly taken
ill. But before he could reach the wings he stumbled
in his hurry, and fell prostrate on the stage, where he lay
seemingly unable to rise.

I—having special reason for my interest—hurried up
the stage steps to help him. And it *was* Captain Goodenough, who had been grinning in an East-end music
hall, as sure as I was I.

I never saw a poor fellow so overcome by shame as my
enemy the Captain when, in a little dressing-room behind
the scenes, he—unable any longer to throw stones—
faltered out his tale. " I couldn't help it—I couldn't
indeed," said he. " The only thing I could ever do well
was to Grin. I was famous for it at school—I was always
the bottom boy, but not even the top boy could come
near me at a grin! And I kept it up: for, you see, one
doesn't like to give up the only thing one *can* do. And
when poor Jack Lennox died—poor Jack, my old school-
mate, who got me the little place, they were glad to give
me a pension of two hundred a year to get me to resign
—No! I suppose I *am* an ass, but I couldn't let those
six poor children starve. But—I put it to you—I
couldn't bring Jack's children up to be ladies on two
hundred a year, and give them luxuries and education
and everything they'd been used to. I hadn't a trade or
a profession, and was too old to learn. So I bethought
me of the only thing I could do—and said I had plenty
for us all—and made myself into a wooden Captain by
day—and into Signor Crackjaw by night—and grinning
for a living: and, yes: I've grinned myself rich—but it's
all for the girls, sir, all for the girls. I've scorned and
loathed the life, for I've acted the respectable man—till
—till—well, this was to have been the last time—the

very last time : and I didn't think I'd have been found
out like this—but if you'd had six orphan babies, Jack's
babies, left on your hands, why, hang me, sir, why *you'd*
have Grinned too !"

Somehow, we found ourselves shaking hands. I had
only respected Captain Goodenough : I honoured Signor
Crackjaw. But he was so ashamed of having become a
mountebank that he was blind to every scrap of heroism
that lay behind—so humiliated by the lies he had been
acting that he looked upon my handshake as a thing to
be as grateful about as he had been to Jack Lennox
for—

"Are you the gent as guv me this here sixpence at the
door?" asked the money-taker, suddenly entering the
room before we had unclasped hands.

Great Heaven ! *That* sixpence again ! Was I never
to see the end ? But I could only answer, with a groan,
" I am that unhappy man. Why?"

"Cos vy, it's the very baddest ever I seed. I've broke
it in two—there's the halfs. And I'll trouble you for
another, if *you* please."

"This *gentleman*," said Captain Crackjaw, "is my
friend."

And so the Demon Sixpence—that miserable impostor
—was exorcised and broken to bits; and my adopted
father-in-law has remained my friend from that day till
now—I hope and trust with good cause.

AT THE TWELFTH HOUR.

I.

THE ground was as hard as iron, the sky blue as turquoise, the sunshine yellow as gold, and the air as still and as silent as only the hardest of frosts can be. Nobody, for weeks past had dared even so much as to dream of a fox —it was Reynard's holiday. Had things been as they ought to be, Rupert Grayshaw would not, late in the afternoon, have been found upon only two legs instead of four. Things being as they were, he was making the best, or the worst, of them by walking briskly along a winding lane that led from the village of Combe Bassett to nowhere in particular, at the rate of something over four miles an hour.

Rupert Grayshaw was going on for three-and-thirty years old, full of strength and life, handsome and something more. Few people noticed how fine a face he really had until they came to know him well, for those who saw him for the first, second, or third time were struck exclusively by all such signs and symbols of both mental and vital force as would have made plainness forgotten. He was a man who looked both eager and able to enjoy the whole of life all round, with body, brain, and soul. And assuredly, though the foxes were safe, it was a day on which life could be most amply and actively enjoyed. I need make no mystery about Rupert Grayshaw, for

there was none to be made ; and though, no doubt, he
had his secrets and his private affairs like other men, he
was known, on the whole, rather more openly than most
of one's friends. He was the only son of the younger son
of an old Yorkshire family ; he had taken high mathe-
matical honours at Cambridge ; he was a Fellow of St.
Kenneth's ; he was without near relations ; he had no
profession, but lived on his Fellowship, and, without
sacrificing any pleasures that were open to him, had,
with an enduring enthusiasm, adopted scientific investigation and discovery for a career. He held himself as
much above and beyond marriage as science is above the
brewing of small beer. He had come to Combe Bassett on
a visit to his father's old friend, Dick Derwent, for the
sake of the coverts ; and, so far as the coverts were concerned, had come in vain. And that is his whole history
as completely told as any man's can be—from the
outside.

The lane presently led through a thick but now brown
and leafless wood. Rupert vaulted over a stile to the
left, and his feet were soon enjoying the never-palling
delight of trampling and crunching over fallen and frozen
leaves. He was glowing with health and exercise, and,
it might be, with some still more peculiar joy. The wood
was a maze of paths, but he either knew their clue by
heart or else gave himself up to chance more decisively
than most men go towards a known goal. And so, either
by accident or design, he reached at last a solitary cottage
standing in a small garden and nearly hidden among the
trees. It was a humble place enough—a little, but not
much, better than the common run of labourers' dwellings
in that part of the country—low, rough-cast, and straw-
thatched, with small latticed windows and immensely
deep eaves. The long strip of garden was given over to
vegetables, except a patch in front of the porch, where it
was not hard, though in midwinter, to conjure up, in fancy,

a little wilderness of full scents and strong colours. Some style was given to the place, even now, by the creeper with evergreen leaves and scarlet berries that covered the porch, and the thick ivy that darkened the lower windows. As if he knew its inmates and all their ways, Rupert went to a window at the side of the cottage and tapped thereon three times. Then he leaned against a pear-tree and waited patiently.

Or perhaps impatiently. For presently the lattice opened, and like a live portrait set in a frame of ivy leaves appeared a face that seemed to say, " Ah! he has a secret in his life, after all—and I am she!"

Yes: when a man comes to look for foxes and finds frosts, he must find something wherewith to fill up his idle days—something or somebody. Of course it is unlucky when it happens to be somebody instead of something—when he has both publicly and privately forsworn marriage, and when, if he forswear himself, he must give up the means of study and take to bread-winning instead of working for science and glory. Perhaps it is rash for men to take long holidays until they are at least seventy years old. For if ever there was a face made to come between a student and his books, between a sportsman and his sport, between a sworn bachelor and his vow, it was the face that Rupert had called from out the ivy as if his three taps had been spells. It was a very young girl's; she could not possibly have been more than seventeen. But her number of years was to be gathered from the indefinable expression of girlhood rather than from any palpable signs. She was neither child nor woman, but blent in one face the charms of the two. The delicate glory of perfect health breathed from her; the biting air did her no wrong, but merely deepened the glow on her cheek that proved no frost to lie within. She could be called neither dark nor fair, but simply harmonious; and so quick were the changes of light and shade that

Rupert seemed to hear her looks with some subtle inner sense as if they were the melody of a song. And whatever else the words of that song might be, they were at least gentle and pure. Why need I describe her feature by feature, line by line? Enough, that passing and heedless eyes would have called her lovely, while Rupert's as clearly found her a great deal more.

She was no cottager's daughter, though she was found in this out-of-the-way, almost hidden cottage. She suggested one of those lost princesses whom travellers find by chance among woodcutters and charcoal-burners in the forests of Fairyland. All things favoured the fancy —the brown, dark, windless wood; the blue sky, the silence, and the loneliness everywhere. She herself had not spoken, except with a smile; and, after a moment of such greeting, shut the window again. But Rupert, having had his answer, went to the door, raised the latch, and entered. And then he seemed to turn over another page of a fairy tale. He passed through an ordinary kitchen, with an open chimney and a brick floor, with nothing out of the common about it except that it was empty on so hard a day, when labour had nothing to do but sit and rest by its own fireside. But the room into which he passed out of it was very different indeed; in such a place it was even startling to find such a room. It might have been a boudoir of any great lady in the land, if it had not been so obviously an enchanted maiden's bower. In that country of Once upon a Time, soft carpets, fine hangings, luxurious upholstery, books, and pictures cost nothing more than a few waves of a wand, or else their presence here would have seemed something more than strange. And here she, whose face we have for a moment seen, ran forward to meet Rupert quickfully and joyfully, and let him take her in his arms.

"I have good news, Bertha!" said he. "And you will never guess it. The post, this very morning, brought

me the news that I am rich enough for all things—for
You, and Work, and Gladness, and all life means to me:
for You and Love, above all!   Yes, my darling, it's true.
I shall be able to give you a better bower even than the
mysterious enchanter who keeps you here in his power."

"Oh, Rupert!   What *has* happened?   What is going
to happen?   What do you mean?"

"Everything has happened, Bertha!   A far-off cousin
of my mother's, whom I never saw in my life, is dead,
and has left me a fortune—an immense fortune for me
and you, but not too large to be a burden—only on condition that I will change my name"—

"What!—you are not to be Rupert, *my* Rupert, any
more?"

"Oh, I shall keep that name—*that* is yours!   But I
shall give up my Fellowship with more pleasure than I
had in getting it; for I hate the least thing that has
kept me from you; and there is nothing left but a form
or two to keep me from my wife for another hour!   When
will you come to me?   In two weeks?—In one?—
In"—

"Rupert!   *Is* it true?"

"All true—every word!   When will you come?"

"And may I tell my father"—

"Your father!   Bertha, my darling, now that I can
claim you I think this mystery ought to be at an end.
Just think what our story has been—a story that nobody
could believe.   I come down to Combe Bassett with a
heart as empty as life without *you*.   I wander into a
wood—I find, by chance, in a common cottage, a fairy
queen.   I win her heart, and her trothplight, and at the
end of weeks I know no more of her than that her name
is Bertha—Queen Bertha— and that she has no surname,
but only a mysterious, nameless father, who comes to see
her, like an enchanter, from far away—flying, I suppose,
on a magic carpet, or a brazen horse through the air.

She is attended by invisible hands—for none but her own have I seen. I am sworn to ask nothing more than if she loves me. She forbids me to enter her bower without a signal, and unless it is answered. And yet I know that she is as innocent as the lilies, and as pure as the snow. Sooner than lose you, Bertha, I would consent to know nothing but that you are lovely, and good, and true, and that you love me: but is it in man not to wish to know more? And is it not time?"

" As if I would not tell you every thought I have in me! But, O Rupert, how can I tell you a name I never heard? As *you* say, I must have another name than Bertha, I suppose it is true. As *you* say, my father must have some dwelling-place of his own, I suppose that is true too. And "—

" And you really do not know who you are?"

" Surely—that I am Bertha, and yours. . . . But if it is time "—

" It *is* time."

" Then—my father comes to-morrow, at five o'clock in the afternoon. I *have* told you why you must not come to me without a signal: because *he* does not wish to be seen, and because I do not always know when he is coming. But I do happen to know to-day when his next visit will be—for he never fails to see me on the first day of the New Year "—

" Yes—to-morrow *is* New-Year's Day. Well?"

" Come, Rupert, and come openly, and tell him "—

" And if he says No?"

" Why should he say No? And—if he does—do I not love you? He cannot forbid that, Rupert "—

" My darling! I *will* come, enchanter though he be."

Rupert left the cottage just in time to reach the Hall (as his host's place was popularly called) before dinner. He met nobody on the way but an old woman in a blue

cloak, of whom he took no special heed—for what were
all outward things to a man who loved, and was loved,
and before whom the future was opening out in rainbow
colours? Even the mystery of his love-story gave it
an additional charm to him, whose imagination, chroni-
cally kept in the grooves of hard study, needed now and
then to take a flight into the free and open air.

There were not many guests at the Hall. Dick Derwent
was a bachelor of five-and-forty, who did not care to fill
his house for the sake of having it full. The few who
were there were men who were waiting for the frost
to break, and with whom Rupert—engaged as he was
with his own affairs—had but little sympathy. He liked
Dick, who was the best of good fellows, and had shown
him much kindness ; but he cared little for Dick's friends.
And even to Dick, good fellow as he was, he had
never breathed a word of his love-story. There were
many reasons for silence, of which each was all-sufficient
for him. In the first place—until to-day—marriage had,
from his point of view, been simply impossible. He had
been merely drifting, and had hardly cared to open
his own eyes as to the course he had been taking.
In the second place, to profane the mystery of his
romance by speech would be sure to reduce it from poetry
to prose. Again, how could he bear to tell such a story
to open-hearted and free-tongued Dick, who had never
kept a secret in his life, and would be sure to make
Bertha and Rupert's love for her a matter of rough chaff,
even if they did not some day, for want of better sport,
ride out and draw the cottage with " Yoicks " and
" Tally-ho ? " And who was Bertha's father, and what
secret might he not have that ought not, in honour, to be
betrayed ? Had Bertha's existence been known of at the
Hall, he would himself have been the first to hear.

Dinner and billiards had lasted the evening through,
when the stroke of a church bell sounded full and close

through the thin air. Dick Derwent rose and filled his tumbler to the brim.

"Let all who love me, follow!" cried he, in his bluff, ringing voice. "At the first stroke of twelve, I throw open the front door with my own hands, to let the Old Year out and the New Year in!"

Dick Derwent was a fine, stout, hearty country gentleman, with all manner of jovial ways. He was the very pink of generosity and honour. He had been Rupert's father's staunchest friend, and had, at old Mr. Grayshaw's death, transferred his affection from the father to the son. Indeed, it was more than common affection that he showed towards Rupert on every possible occasion. Though so much the elder, he had a strong belief in the prudence and worldly wisdom of the younger man, which cannot be supposed to have been altogether ill-founded—at any rate, Dick Derwent was not the man to have let a hundred Fellowships stand in the way of marriage had he been that way inclined. But, then, it is true, he was not a man of science, but only a jolly middle-aged gentleman who kept up old customs and followed the hounds well.

The half-dozen young and middle-aged men, without a woman or a child among them, gave way to their host's whim, though not without smiles and shrugs of the shoulder at taking part in such a piece of obsolete folly.

"What does it all mean?" asked West—a young man who was wiser in his own eyes even than Rupert Grayshaw was in Dick Derwent's. "Why should we trouble ourselves to let out a good time—thanks to you, Dick—and let in what nobody knows, may be death, may be marriage."

"Marriage, eh?" said Dick, turning upon him suddenly. "Perhaps I know more about that than you. But that's neither here nor there—marriage won't come inside this door for many a long day.   That isn't what it means.   It means that the master of this house has, with his own hands, let in two hundred New Years, and that I'm not going to be the first inhospitable fellow that has been surnamed Derwent and christened Richard. Now, then—Welcome, whatever you are!" he said, loudly, as he threw open the front door and let the first cold blast of the New Year rush into the Hall. "God speed the Old, and God bless the New!"

"I know it's a common custom," said Rupert, "for the master of the house to open his door at the first stroke of the last midnight of the year.   But I could never find out what it means, and yet every superstition must have a meaning somewhere.   I wonder what people think would happen if the New Year came to a house and found the door closed?"

"Happen?" said West.   "Why, that fewer people would begin the year with a sneeze.   What else do you suppose?"

"I dare say," said Dick—"I dare say they knew once upon a time.   Well, it's done now, and after all it would never have done to have the frost break everywhere else, and not round the Hall."

But the first day of the New Year did not bring a thaw, either round the Hall or elsewhere.   To-day was yesterday's twin brother.   Nor was Rupert sorry for it, for, had it thawed, he would have found it exceedingly difficult to invent an excuse for staying at home while the other men were all a-field.   Of course, while the ground was hard it was natural enough for a philosopher to take solitary walks in company with problems.   But problems when the scent lay—even a broken leg would hardly serve as an excuse for him then, after three long weeks of iron.   Happily, the weather allowed him, with no more difficulty than usual, to be at the cottage by five in the afternoon.   If he had believed in omens, he would have felt that *his* luck at least had not changed with the change of year.

He was neither shy nor timid by nature, and was eager rather than anxious for his first interview with the mysterious personage who kept his daughter so strangely confined in such an unaccountable prison. Beyond all question, Bertha was nearly as ignorant as he of her own history. She scarcely knew of any other life, except after the vague and untrustworthy manner of dreams. She was fairly well educated, for she had been thrown upon her own mental resources all her life, and had been put by this same unguessable father into the right road for using them. Oddly enough she was most familiar with the very books and branches of knowledge that Rupert himself would have chosen for her had her education been given into his hands. She had lived in this way—so he learned from her—all her life, seeing none but her father and an elderly nurse who attended to her admirably, but told her nothing. She was under a strict discipline which she had never thought of breaking through, never going out for exercise except in the early morning in the woods, or being allowed to have a friend. Short of making inquiries, Rupert had invented a thousand theories to account for the mystery, but had rejected them all. But about one thing there was no mystery at all. No wonder that a young girl, with such infinite capacity for the life that had been withheld from her for seventeen years, had snatched at life, love, and liberty as soon as they found her out in her solitude. She was the sleeping princess who woke when the prince had forced his way to her through the thorns.

But now, at last, the whole secret was to be disclosed. Of the result, Rupert had absolutely no fear. He was rich enough to satisfy any earthly father, and in love enough to satisfy any father, man, or demon, who loved his child. His high spirits of yesterday were nothing compared with to-day's. He hardly felt the ground as he walked, but seemed to tread on air.

He reached the cottage well before five. But—

The door stood wide open, and the front garden was littered with bits of broken wood, ends of cord, and straw. The kitchen was without a fire. With a strange feeling of fear in his heart he went at once into Bertha's bower—it had turned into nothing but a shrunken square cupboard, with four bare walls and an empty floor. The lattice was open, and the air seemed deadly cold.

Had it all been but a fairy dream? But it was no dream that he loved her with his whole heart—and she was gone.

II.

One : Two : Three :—Ten : Eleven : TWELVE !

He whom bettered fortunes and a testator's fancy had transmuted from Rupert Grayshaw into Rupert Hildreth did not rise from his chair, or throw open so much as an inch of window at the sound. He laid down his pen— but that was all. The twelve strokes came to his ears muffled through double windows and close doors.

" I am not such a fool as that," thought he. " The Old Year's a good deal too good to lose, and *I* don't want a better. I've done for six years past with wanting more than I have, since—since—No : I've done with dreams. Perhaps *they* might come back if I opened the door to a change. Let those open their doors who are sick, or sorry, or sinful, or poor : not I, who am rich, and content, and sound in heart and limb and brain . . . and who knows what happened once, when I let out the one sweet dream of my whole life, and when that better waking came in through the open door ! Never again.

I might let in sickness, or discontent, or worse—who knows? I'll be as I am, with one long, faithful Old Year all to myself, that I've tried and proved. Yes, it has answered. Fevers have come with the New Years, and have emptied other houses, but they have passed by *my* doors, that had kept out the evils of the unknown like those of a wise man. Fortunes have broken : but mine stand. Others, in the New Years, have married and died; I, with the Old Year under my roof, am as alive and free as I was six years ago. I have seen others grow grey and wrinkled : I am near middle age—and young. Life palls on others, unless they renew it in their children : I have only myself and my books—but they are as fresh as of old. . . . Why, if there be a grain of truth in old wives' tales, to bar the New Year out and to bolt the Old Year in means to stand still at one's best all one's days, to be for always as one is, and to fear no chance or change that comes to the rest of the world. . . . So knock on, New Year, as hard and as long as you like— you'll find one door bolted and barred against you and yours."

He took up his pen again, and worked on. It was true that, ever since that midnight of six years ago, he had practised the new superstition of keeping his front door close shut, so that no New Year could find a chink whereby to creep in. For on that night of long ago he had lain down with joy and hope which the New Year had, with its first touch, taken away. Perhaps—so he felt in fancy—if he had kept the New Year out, Bertha and the Old Year would have staid with him : nor was the fancy quite so unreasonable in a man of science as it may seem, for what had Bertha herself ever been to him but a fancy and a dream? And it was true that, while the New Years had brought troubles enough on others, they had left Rupert Hildreth, the scholar and chemist, un- disturbed in his life and labour. With him the same Old

Year seemed for ever to abide, until it had earned by custom an undisputed right and title to a place by his hearthstone. He and his life never knew a change, from year to year, from day to day. He lived, for quiet study's sake, in the outskirts of the town of Rainham. One year a plague of cholera swept through the place, and broke up households—that would have been safe had they never let the Old Year go. But he never troubled himself about the matter, and just lived and worked on. Some thought he kept himself too much aloof in a time of trouble: and no doubt that same sad New Year, while it brought death to bodies, brought good to souls. But what has he to do with the things of New Years that have never come to him? Another New Year had brought among its gifts a great financial crash that had been felt in most homes, but had not given Rupert Hildreth, though a rich man, a moment's doubt or fear. He had never loved a new face, or made a new enemy. From January to December every year had been one and the same.

There were some who thought him hard, cold, and selfish. Others—women mostly—could not help believing that, early in life, his heart had been broken by some great sorrow with which a woman had had to do, and that this made his days so changeless and his life so lonely and self-contained. He would have denied such a theory, had it ever come to his ears, with scorn. His treatment of New Years and its effects might be but a superstitious fancy ; but he lived as if he thought it based on truth and reason. Never, since that New Year's Eve, had he seen, or even, despite of all his searching, heard of Bertha again or of anybody who had ever heard of her. And now he had shut out the threats of another New Year.

He worked late, and rose late, without taking note that a New Year had begun for all the rest of the world. Why should he, indeed, when it was still the Old Year, of years ago, for him?

It was certainly nothing particularly new, though a little unusual, that he should receive a visit from a stranger in the course of the afternoon. The card by which the visitor introduced himself was that of Mr. J. Dimond.

"Mr. Hildreth?" asked Mr. Dimond, a stiff, middle-aged man, with a professional look about him. "Then, in the first place, I have to wish you a happy New Year."

"Ah—what? I beg your pardon," said Rupert, absently. "You are on business, I suppose?"

"It is odd you should expect that—very odd indeed, considering the day. It is a rare holiday that has brought me to Rainham, where I happen to have friends. But it is business, all the same; and I have taken the opportunity of doing it without wasting a day. Time has a way of flying, you see"—

"Or of standing still."

"Not with me, Mr. Hildred; not with me. Years—landmarks—and so on. I believe you were acquainted with Mr. Richard Derwent, of Combe Bassett. I have been his legal adviser for some years. Perhaps you are not aware"—

"I knew Derwent well; but I have seen nothing of him for some years—some time, I should say. I hope he is well?"

"He is dead, Mr. Hildreth. He died last November, in town. And his little girl"—

"Dick Derwent dead! Well. . . . But a little girl? Well, he was just the man to get married before he died."

"She has no mother. She died, you know, when the child was born. Well, Mr. Hildreth, to make a long story short, Mr. Derwent had two ideas—perhaps more, but certainly two. One was an unbounded trust and confidence in your prudence and honour, as his will testifies. The other was an overwhelming dread lest his little girl should grow up a prey to fortune-hunters, or be contaminated by the companionship of other girls. He believed that every girl ought to grow up alone, with no knowledge of, or communication with, the world. He had had experiences of the other sort of thing, you see, when he was a young man. So, Mr. Hildreth, knowing your prudence, your honour, your friendship for him, and your hermit-like mode of living, he leaves you a legacy of ten thousand pounds on condition that you will, as joint guardian with myself, undertake the sole and entire charge and education of the child (she living here with you) until she attains the age of twenty-four, at which age Mr. Derwent believed that a girl, properly brought up according to his views, ought to be able to run alone. She is now in charge of an aunt, Mrs. Joy. You accept the charge of course "—

"What, I? No. No, Mr. Dimond. Without hesitation, and most decidedly, No. New Years bring, and shall bring, no new things to me. What should I, a student who live alone with my books, do with a girl—a child "—

" The orphan of your friend "—

" Whom I do not need, and who does not need me. No. I closed my doors last night, and I close it still. I will have nothing new in my life "—

" Not- ten thousand pounds "—

"No. No, once for all." He bowed Mr. Dimond out, and went back to his work, without giving another thought of the New Year's cunning but vain attempt to creep within his doors in the shape of a child.

It was all very well for the lawyer of fifty to speak of a grown girl of three-and-twenty as if she were no more

than a child in arms. Equally reasonable was it for
Rupert to argue that, since Dick Derwent was unmarried
some six years ago, his orphan daughter could hardly be
five years old. But there is nobody so good at keeping
a secret, when he likes, as your bluff, frank, hearty,
talkative, open-mannered man. Mr. Dimond knew, and
thought his client's intimate friends knew also, that the
Squire of Combe Bassett had married once upon a time,
and had been left a father and a widower within a year:
nor only so, but that, surrounded as he was by society of
which he was as unwilling to deprive himself as he was
anxious that his daughter should not share it, he had
taken extraordinary precautions against the discovery of
her existence till she was fully grown. His friends were
mostly good fellows with no money to spend, who would
swoop down on an heiress after the genial manner of
their kind.

One bright, cold morning, when, in midwinter, her
own heart was overflowing with spring and joy, the old
nurse who served and guarded her was suddenly
dismissed; she was carried, by road and rail, many
miles away from her old home, and presently her father
came and took her to travel with him abroad. She
could not speak to him of the dream which he had
doubtlessly discovered, and had thus answered. It is to
be hoped he was satisfied. She was docile and gentle,
and her father was always kind—kind now, even in
keeping her to himself; for she had seen all the human
beings she needed to see in seeing one whom she saw no
more. He need not have feared the adventurers and
fortune-hunters whom he now, as if ruled by a craze,
spent his whole time in avoiding. He need not even
have made that will when he died, so that his hand,
though dead, might still guard her from lovelessness in
marriage and all lesser harm. Mr. Dimond must have
been terribly right when suggesting what the Squire's

own experiences of the world must have been before he settled down in Combe Bassett with the soul of a girl on his hands.

She mourned, honestly, when he died. Perhaps not the less because he had made her life so dull and empty. But presently she had to mourn for her living self, even more. She was an heiress—she had learned to hate the very sound of the word. And she was left in charge of another guardian: a hard, stern man, named Hildreth so she heard; a recluse, who had been chosen by her father for the office because of his being the only man in the world who could be trusted to carry out, consistently and thoroughly, her father's views. Hitherto, her life had been slavery, but love therewith. Henceforth it must be double slavery, and therewith what must needs become hate, at least on her side.

And yet it was with a strange feeling, very far indeed from pleasure or relief, that she heard from Mr. Dimond of Mr. Hildreth's decisive, almost scornful and angry, refusal of the charge that had been left to him. She had somehow expected that he would have received her for money's sake, and then, for duty's, have made her life hardly to be borne. But here was clearly a man who would neither do a kindness nor accept a duty, if they were inconvenient to him, even for ten thousand pounds. If there were to be refusals and rebellions, they ought to have come from her.

"It seems to me you have had a lucky escape, Miss Derwent," said the lawyer, when his holiday was over and he came in person to bring her news. "There is something about that fellow Hildreth that I neither like nor understand; he's not like other people at all. He refused a legacy of ten thousand pounds. That is being far too imprudent to have the charge of a young girl."

"At any rate, *he* is no fortune-hunter," said she.

"Perhaps my poor father knew that, and that was why—. And what am I to do now?"

"That's just the point, you see. The terms of the will are perfectly clear. In the event of Mr. Hildreth's refusal to undertake the charge of you—why, then, as you say, he will have proved himself very much of a fool. But, as he will also have proved that he doesn't care about money, I am—I am sorry to say—instructed to make him the offer of your hand."

"Of my hand? Of *me?*"

"Even so. And it must be done. For, if I do not, I shall lose my own legacy; and it is too much to lose. If he refuses *that—* But he can't be such a fool as to refuse the heiress of Combe Bassett, you may be sure. Your honoured father did know men."

"But there is something else to be said, it seems to me! How if *I* refuse?"

"Then he is to have Combe Bassett *without* you. You are to have enough to live in comfort while you remain single; but under no circumstances will you have anything more if you marry anybody but him. It is a cruel will, Miss Derwent; but it is a clever one for its purpose, I must say. Whatever happens, the man who marries you must marry you for love and not for fortune, you see; and "—

She heard no more. No wonder, thought she, that her father had done his utmost, alive and dead, to keep her from a world where men, as a matter of course, assumed only the meanest and most sordid motives in one another —judging, no doubt, from their own experience of their own. *She* marry! Why, if her heart and soul had not been married and widowed long ago, she would return with joy to her old prison in the wood rather than give herself to any man as an uncomfortable condition attaching to her lands and her gold. Let him who had refused to be paid for the care of her ask her for herself

with her lands a hundred times—she would refuse him a
hundred and one. Let him take Combe Bassett and
welcome, so long as he left her free.

And then the pittance that was to be hers in case she
refused—even that, according to what she had been
taught of the world, would be all too much ; even
that might be enough to attract some man who was
poorer still. Was she to be a slave to the world's
meanness all her days? Her heart went back to him
who had loved her wholly for herself, if there was
any truth in all those magical signs of love that cannot
lie. What had become of him? Where was he now?
Had he forgotten her in all these years? Had he
sold himself to some other woman, for gold? Like
enough, being a man ; and men being what she had been
taught they were. But, had they never been parted, he
would have loved her well enough, she knew.

Since love had been lost, better now, even than love,
was liberty, for that had become her all. Passionately
she felt, " He shall have everything but me ; I will
not keep for myself one smallest coin that may make my
No less full and whole." After all, there was under the
skies another world, where men made no wills, hunted
no heiresses, laid no plots or counterplots, never talked of
love when they meant money, and, above all, were free.
It is the world where we live without love, without
Gold, and alone. It was the world wherein she herself
had lived for her first sixteen years, where men were
not, and where she had been tended as are the lilies
of the field. It was where she had had the dream of her
life, and where she might—she fancied in her heart—go
back, and live alone with her dream, and be free.
Never, since she left her hermitage, had she been happy
for an hour. She had been, as it were, a wild flower
transplanted into a garden, where it can only feel itself a
weed, and dread the scents and hues around that others

find beautiful. She had once longed for the world, as the wild flowers may for the gardens while they are unknown and far away; and now—well, if she could not find her field again, any place would be better than the garden of the world; even the wayside.

She could not think or feel as those can who have grown up in the garden all their days. So little, or so much, had she learned that, when she heard such an everyday thing merely named and spoken as the sale, by a woman, of her hand and heart for the sake of keeping her land, she was as struck with unspeakable horror as if she had turned over the soil of a bed of roses and laid open the entrance of a charnel, black and foul. We, with our sensible bringing up, our well-regulated minds, and still better regulated hearts, may think her view of such everyday trifles a little overstrained. But then we have seen such things with our eyes; she had never so much as heard of one of them till now. Such a world was not to be lived in; there was nothing to be done but spread one's wings, and fly from it with all speed.

III.

It was the 12th of January, and Rupert Hildreth had not yet heard another word worth mentioning concerning his friend's orphan and her affairs. It is true he had received a letter from Mr. Dimond containing some rubbish or other about something that was to happen if he married the child when she became of age; but, as that could not happen for nearly twenty years, and as it could not possibly concern him in any way, he had naturally thrown the letter, half read, into his waste-basket, and, being deep in an all-absorbing investigation, had forgotten to send a word of answer. He worked on, without giving a real thought to such impertinent non-sense ; and if another girl's form would sometimes come between him and his labour, or between his paper and his pen, he had become used to that ghost, and would even have missed it if it ever ceased wholly to come.

So far, therefore, he had made himself secure for another course of an Old Year which had so consistently proved good to him, bringing him no evil, and, on the other hand, increasing satisfaction with himself and indifference to all the rest of mankind. Every day he had risen at the same hour and worked on till his brain was heartily tired. Every night he insured himself a long sleep, too deep for dreams. The man, day by day, was turning into a machine ; and so he willed.

On this night of the 12th he was working, as usual, and was even more than usually absorbed. It was a lonely old house in which he lived, near the town, but yet with no close neighbours. Those dark winter nights were as long and as noiseless as the heart of student could desire, even though, now and then, he might hear the rush and scream of the night mail that passed Rain-ham without stopping, and, every hour the chiming of the church tower. It was more to keep out these than the rush of the train that Rupert Hildreth had double windows to all his rooms, and kept them close even in summer time :—one of his principal eccentricities was a morbid antipathy to the sound of church clocks, especially when they struck twelve.

He made his servants go to bed punctually at ten, for he liked, during his night work, to feel absolutely alone. And never, since he had settled at Rainham, had he been disturbed after that hour. At first, therefore, he could hardly believe his own ears when, late in the evening, and long after his servants were out of the way, he heard a bell ring through the house—no sound of a church clock, but within the house itself, as if such an impossible thing were happening as that somebody was pulling the bell of *his* front door.

It could only be fancy—such things often happen to minds so absorbed in thought that outward things often become confused and obscured, and when the senses, cut off from real sights and sounds, are compelled to find their own food. He had almost forgotten the matter, when the bell rang once more.

It must be real, then, thought Rupert, angrily. If it happened again it would wake the servants, throw the house into a tumult, and rob him of a whole night's work—and that must never be. If only to say No to somebody, he must go down himself and stop the ringing, otherwise nothing would have moved him from his desk had all Rainham been on fire.

He opened the door just in time to save himself from another ring. By the bright light of the moon then at her full, he saw a young girl well wrapped in a cloak with her hand upon the bell.

" What does this mean?" asked Rupert, sternly. " Who are you? What do you want here?"

" I—I'm afraid," said the girl, looking round her doubtfully, " I'm afraid I've lost my way—I saw a light here, and no other house near—I came by the train—is it very far?"

" No. It is straight along the road," said Rupert, rather roughly. It was something more than annoying to be disturbed in full work, and to be rung up at such an hour for such a trifle as a lost way.

" But—is it very far?"

There were limits to even his cultivated likeness to a machine. There seemed something strange about the girl, he thought, as she spoke thus doubtfully and wearily. She did not look like one to be rambling about alone at midnight; and though nothing concerning a stranger could possibly mean anything to him, he had not as yet wholly ceased to be a man. "I suppose," he said, "you have friends at Rainham and are on your way to them? It is not very far, but I am afraid it is both very far and very late—for you."

"No; I have no friends. I suppose there is an inn?"

"You have business, then? Nobody ever comes to Rainham without business or friends." He thought again; for it began to seem to him that there was something about her not wholly strange. "Yes," he said, "of course there is an inn; but"—

"I have to see a Mr. Hildreth to-morrow, who lives here. That is all."

"You have to see Mr. Hildreth? And what possible reason— You have to see *me ?*"

"*You* are Mr. Hildreth?"

"That is my name. And yours?" All his sternness had returned. Had his well-trained Old Year gone crazed?

"You will know who *I* am," said she, sadly and proudly, "when I tell you why I am here. It is to tell you with my own lips, before I leave such a world as this, where men buy love, and let hearts starve, that Combe Bassett is yours, every blade of grass, every stick and stone, without your having to be put to the shame of asking for the hand of one whom you refused even to look at when she could be nothing more to you than the orphan of your friend. That is all. . . ."

He looked, almost in amaze, certainly bewildered, from her into the dark entrance through which the night wind had followed her, as little welcome as she. "Pardon me," said he, "but this is a matter with which I have nothing absolutely to do. Do you mean to tell me, whoever *you* are, that you are in league with those who seek to bring into my house and life the child whom I am bidden make my wife in my old age?"

" What child ?"

" What else ? Are you playing me some trick ? " He turned aside to light the lamp : partly to think, partly to see. " I remember—only eleven days ago some lawyer fellow wanted me to let in the New Year in the shape of a child. I refused him at the right time : it's too late now ! What have I to do with Dick Derwent's child ? There is an early train to-morrow : take it, and go back again. And tell those who sent you here that if wealth, and power, and glory, and wisdom, and love, came knocking altogether at my door, I would say, as I say to you—I want none of you ; Go ! "

" I tell you that I, Bertha Derwent, refuse "—

The lamp was lighted. ONE ! struck Rainham clock. And never since Rupert had lived there had he heard so loud a stroke. For it made no muffled thud through double windows, but a full, heavy boom through the open door, which Rupert had thrown open at the second ring and had neglected to close—on *Old* New Year's Eve !

The lamplight was on both their faces : in the ears of both boomed the bell. No chimes heralded the birth of this New Year of theirs, though that twelfth day of January is as surely New Year's Eve for those who will as Twelfth-Day is Old Christmas Day. For those who will ? well, maybe any day in the year will do as well. Only it did so happen that, when Rupert left the door ajar for a young girl to enter, he had forgotten that, where evil is to be let out, and good let in, Time is good enough to give us at least Two New Year's Days—an Old as well as a New ; or rather a New as well as an Old.

" Rupert ! "

" Bertha ! "

" And *I* refused *you ?* "

"And *I* barred out *you* when I barred out the New Years—but how could I tell? And what else have I barred out? Harm, yes—but what else? Heaven knows. One blessing—how many more?"

" Do you bar me out still?"

He looked at her—then far away, as if round the world. " Neither you, nor whatever Time may bring," said he. " This is New Year's Eve for me. Good and ill—ill and good, let all come : they all come from the same place by the same road. Let them all come together, so they come, at last, with you. . . . God will bless the New, and God speed the Old !"

Rainham clock took a long time to strike : all this, and more had been told, when it boomed—TWELVE !

THE END.